He didn't want to open up his heart to God again.

He was still so mad at God, it hurt to even try to form a prayer in his head, let alone voice that prayer.

But tonight he somehow found the courage to do just that. For Brittney.

"Lord, help me. Help me to be a good father again."

Because today Nate had realized something so terrible, so tragic that he felt sick.

He'd been ignoring his children, simply because they reminded him of their mother. He'd been a shell of a father, moving through each day with slow-motion efforts that sometimes took all his strength.

Until today.

Today an autumn-hued angel had appeared on his doorstep and offered him a chance to find a little salvation. A no-nonsense, full-steam-ahead angel who'd somehow managed to be gentle and understanding with his forlorn, misunderstood children, in spite of her all-business exterior.

Which meant Leandra Flanagan wasn't always all business…

With over seventy books published and millions in print, **Lenora Worth** writes award-winning romance and romantic suspense. Three of her books finaled in the ACFW Carol Awards, and her Love Inspired Suspense novel *Body of Evidence* became a *New York Times* bestseller. Her novella in *Mistletoe Kisses* made her a *USA TODAY* bestselling author. Lenora goes on adventures with her retired husband, Don, and enjoys reading, baking and shopping…especially shoe shopping.

Mia Ross loves great stories. She enjoys reading about fascinating people, long-ago times and exotic places. But only for a little while, because her reality is pretty sweet. Married to her college sweetheart, she's the proud mom of two amazing kids, whose schedules keep her hopping. Busy as she is, she can't imagine trading her life for anyone else's—and she has a pretty good imagination.

One Golden Christmas

New York Times Bestselling Author

Lenora Worth

&

Sugar Plum Season

Mia Ross

LOVE INSPIRED
INSPIRATIONAL ROMANCE

LOVE INSPIRED®

INSPIRATIONAL ROMANCE

ISBN-13: 978-1-335-28491-4

One Golden Christmas & Sugar Plum Season

Copyright © 2020 by Harlequin Books S.A.

One Golden Christmas
First published in 2000. This edition published in 2020.
Copyright © 2000 by Lenora H. Nazworth

Sugar Plum Season
First published in 2014. This edition published in 2020.
Copyright © 2014 by Andrea Chermak

This edition published by arrangement with Harlequin Books S.A.

For questions and comments about the quality of this book,
please contact us at CustomerService@Harlequin.com.

Love Inspired
22 Adelaide St. West, 40th Floor
Toronto, Ontario M5H 4E3, Canada
www.Harlequin.com

Printed in U.S.A.

Recycling programs
for this product may
not exist in your area.

CONTENTS

ONE GOLDEN CHRISTMAS

Lenora Worth

To my nieces—
Layla Baker and Brittney Smith
With Love Always

A man's heart plans his way,
but the Lord directs his steps.
—*Proverbs* 16:9

Chapter One

Leandra Flanagan didn't know how her life could have changed so completely in just a few days. One day, she'd been a top advertising executive at a major Houston firm, making more money than she'd ever dreamed possible, and the next day, she was back in her hometown of Marshall, Texas, applying for the job of Christmas Pageant Coordinator for the city of Marshall.

She'd come full circle.

And she wasn't too happy about it.

"Ah, now, honey, don't look so glum," her mother, Colleen, told her, a hand on her arm.

That gentle hand was dusted with flour and cinnamon from the batch of Thanksgiving cookies Colleen was making for the church. That gentle hand brought some measure of comfort to Leandra, in spite of her own misgivings.

"Sorry, I was just thinking about the strange turn of events in my life," Leandra said, pivoting away from the kitchen window to help her mother with the leaf and turkey shaped cookies. "I'm just worried, Mama. I never thought I'd wind up back here in Marshall. I still can't believe I let you talk me into coming home."

"'The Lord will give grace and glory,'" Colleen quoted, her smile giving enough grace and glory to make any gloomy soul feel better.

"Mama, I appreciate that, but what I need along with any grace or glory is a good job. I had a good job and I guess I messed up, big time."

Colleen huffed a breath, causing her gray-tinged bob of hair to flutter around her face. "Sounds like you made the right decision to me, a decision based on your own values and not what your boss at that fancy advertising firm expected you to do."

In spite of the pride shining in her mother's eyes, Leandra didn't feel as if she'd made the right choice. But in the end, it had been the only choice she could make. She'd quit a week ago, and at her mother's insistence, had come home for an extended holiday, hoping to work through her turmoil before going back to Houston after the new year.

And now, her mother had gone and gotten the idea that Leandra could "fill in" down at city hall, just for a few short weeks.

"Well, no sense in worrying about it now," she said, spinning away from the long counter where her mother had baked so many batches of cookies over the years. "I guess I'll just go and see what this pageant job is all about, at least earn some money through the holidays and keep myself busy."

"That's my girl," Colleen said, a bright smile centered on her round, rosy face. "Then come on back for lunch. Your brothers will be here and they're all anxious to see you."

"I suppose they are, at that," Leandra replied, grabbing her wool coat and her purse. "They probably can't wait to rub it in—about how I had to come home with my head down—"

"I'll hear none of that kind of talk," Colleen retorted, her words gentle as always, but firm all the same. "Your brothers are proud of you, and glad to have you home, where you belong."

"Oh, all right," Leandra said. "I'll try to pretend that I planned it this way."

Colleen beamed another motherly smile at her. "Maybe you *didn't,* but maybe God *did.*"

As she drove the few blocks to city hall, Leandra had to wonder what her mother had meant by that remark. Why would God in all of His wisdom bring her back to the small-town life she'd always wanted to get away from? Why would God want Leandra Flanagan to wind up back in Marshall?

Her mother would tell her to wait for the answer, that it would come soon enough.

But Leandra was impatient. She didn't want to wait.

"I can't wait for you to get started on this," Chet Reynolds told her an hour later as he shoved a stack of folders in her arms and directed her to a small, cluttered office in the corner of the building. "And first thing, ride out to Nathan Welby's place—it's the big Victorian-style house just out on Highway 80—and hire him on to build the set. He's the best carpenter in town—a single father of three. He works full-time in construction, but he's off for Thanksgiving this week, and he needs the extra cash. Only he's kinda stubborn and prideful, hard to pin down. Can you get right on that for me, Leandra?"

"Am I hired?" Leandra asked, still in a daze. They'd barely conducted a proper interview, mainly because Chet Reynolds had never been one to talk in complete sentences. He just rambled on and on, merging everything together.

"Why, sure." Chet, a tall man who wore sneakers and a Tabasco sauce embossed polo shirt, in spite of the cool temperatures, bobbed his balding head over a skinny neck. "Known your mama and daddy all my life, watched you grow up into a fine, upstanding young woman—that's all the credentials I need. That, and the fact that my last coordinator had her baby three weeks early—won't be able to come back to work until well after Christmas—if she comes back at all. I'm trusting you to do a good job on this, Leandra."

So, just like that, Leandra had a new job. A temporary job, but a job all the same, based solely on her parents' good name and a little baby's early birth. The hiring process had sure been different from all the interviews and questionnaires she'd had to endure to land her position back in Houston. And the salary—well, that was almost nonexistent, compared to what she'd been making in the big city.

Good thing she had a substantial savings account and some stocks and bonds to fall back on. Listening to her father's advice, she'd built herself quite a little nest egg. And a good life as a *happily* single city woman who'd enjoyed pouring all of herself into her work. That is, until she'd gotten involved with the wrong man.

But that life is over now, she told herself as she squeezed behind the battered oak desk in the pint-size office.

"Must have been a closet in another life," she mumbled to herself. Dropping the folders on the dusty desk, she sank down in the mismatched squeaky wooden swivel chair. She hadn't seen furniture such as this since—

Since she'd left Marshall five years ago.

Putting the size and spaciousness of her plush, modern office in a high-rise building in downtown Houston out of her mind, Leandra spent the next two hours organizing the haphazard plans for the pageant. It was going to be a combination of songs and stories that would tell the miracle of Christ's birth, complete with a live manger scene—which meant that someone had to start building the elaborate set right away.

She couldn't put together a Christmas pageant without a proper set, and the entire production was already weeks behind schedule, and now with just a short month until Christmas, too. Well, first things first. She called her mother to say she'd have to miss lunch after all.

She was back at work and she aimed to get the job done. Her parents had taught her that no matter your job, you did the work with enthusiasm and integrity, and she needed this distraction right now to take her mind off her own worries. She would put on the best Christmas pageant this city had ever seen.

With that thought in mind, she hopped up to go find Nathan Welby.

It was the biggest, most run-down house she'd ever seen. And Nathan Welby was one of the tallest, most intriguing men she'd ever seen.

The house must have been lovely at one time, a real Victorian treasure. But now, it looked more like a gingerbread house that had been half-eaten by hungry children, a total wreck of broken shingles and torn shutters and peeling paint. An adorable wreck that begged to be restored to its former beauty.

And the man—was this the best carpenter in town? Someone who lived in such a sad place as this? He was sure enough a big man, a giant who right now was wielding a very big ax and using it to slice thick chunks of wood into kindling.

"Chet, you've sent me to find Paul Bunyan," Leandra muttered to herself. "Hello," she called for the third time.

The big man chopping wood in the backyard had to have heard her. But he did have his back—a broad, muscled back—turned away from her. And there was lots of noise coming from inside the dilapidated house.

Leandra had shuddered at all that noise. It sounded too familiar. Being the baby and only girl of a large family had taught her that she didn't want a repeat in her own adult life. She had no desire to have a large family and she certainly had no desire to stay at home and bake cookies and cart kids around to various events the way her mother had.

That was why her relationship with William Myers had seemed so perfect. No commitments beyond companionship, no demands about marriage and a family. William hadn't wanted any of those things, either. But he'd certainly asked for a lot more than she'd been willing to give in the end.

But she refused to dwell on *that* mistake now.

No, Leandra thought as she waited impatiently for the man to turn around and acknowledge her. She only wanted to get back to her own plans, back to her civil, peaceful, *working* life in the big city, minus William's domineering influence.

And yet, here she stood, out in the middle of nowhere, about to hire a man she'd never met as carpenter for a one-month project.

Why had she ever let her mother talk her into taking this job?

She'd knocked on the heavy double doors at the front of the house several times before working her way around back. Music, giggles, screams, dogs barking, cats screeching—had she only imagined this house of horrors, or was it real?

Was he a real man?

He turned then, as if just now realizing someone was calling to him, and Leandra saw that he was very real, indeed.

Real from his golden blond wavy hair to the blue-and-red-plaid flannel shirt he wore, to the faded, torn jeans covering his athletic legs to the muddy hiking boots on his feet.

Real from the intense, wary look centered in his hazel, catlike eyes, eyes that spoke a lot more than any of the other noises coming from this carnival fun-house.

"Hello," she said again on a much more level voice, now that she was standing about ten feet away from him. "I'm Leandra Flanagan, from city hall—"

"I paid the light bill, lady," he said in a distinct East Texas drawl that sounded almost lazy. Dismissing her with a frown, he turned to center the ax over a wide log.

Leandra watched as he lifted his arms in an arc over his head, the ax aimed with calculated precision at its target, and in a flash of muscle and steel, went about his work.

The log split in two like a paper box folding up on itself. A clean split, with hardly any splinters falling from either side.

There was nothing lazy about this man, except that enticing accent.

Leandra swallowed back the shocked awe and justified fear rolling into a lump that felt as dry as that split log in her throat. "No, I'm not here about the light bill," she said, stepping over an old tractor part to get closer. "I'm here because—"

"I paid the gas bill, too." He turned away again, his head down, then reached to heave another log up on the big stump.

Off in the fenced pasture behind him, a beautiful palomino gelding neighed and whinnied, tossing its almond-colored mane and pawing at the dirt, its big eyes following Leandra.

Well, at least the horse had acknowledged her presence.

In spite of her frustration at being ignored, Leandra had to marvel at the sheer strength of the man. And the sheer brawny force surrounding him like an aura. He practically glowed with it, standing there in the fall leaves with the sunshine falling like glistening gold across his face. He was real, all right. A real woodsman, yet he was like someone who'd just stepped out of a fairy tale.

If only she believed in fairy tales.

He's only a man, she reminded herself. But so different from all the men she'd had to deal with in Houston. Refusing to dwell on *that,* she also reminded herself why she was here.

"Mr. Welby? I'm not here for any bill collecting." She waited, extended her hand, saw that he wasn't going to shake it, then dropped it by her side.

From inside the house, a crash sounded, followed by shouting and more dog barking. This caused the horse to prance closer to the fence, obviously hoping to get in on the action.

"'Scuse me," the man said as he dropped the ax and

moved to brush past her. Then in his haste, he politely shifted her up out of the way as if she were a twig or a hanging branch.

He stomped up on the porch, opened the paint-chipped back door and bellowed like a lion. "Hush up in there. We've got company out here. Mind your manners, or you'll all three be washing supper dishes well into next week."

Miraculously, the music—a melancholy country tune—stopped in midwhine, the dog stopped barking and the screams tapered off to a few last whimpers of "leave me alone."

Even the big horse stopped his pawing and stood staring, almost as if he were posing for a perfect autumn picture, complete with a weathered gray barn in the background.

Then silence.

Silence over the golden, leaf-scattered woods surrounding the house. Silence as the November sunshine sent a warming ray down on Leandra's already hot cheeks. Silence as Nathan Welby turned around and stared down at her, his eyes still that wary shade of brown-green, his mouth—such an interesting mouth—twisted in a wry, questioning tightness that almost passed for a smile.

Silence.

"You were saying?"

Leandra realized she'd been staring. "Oh, I'm sorry," she began, then because she was at a disadvantage, having to look up at him, she took a step up onto the long, wraparound porch.

Only to fall through a rotted floorboard.

Only to be caught up by two strong hands, brought up by two strong arms, like a rag doll being lifted by a giant.

Only to find herself face-to-face—when she lifted her head about three inches—with those incredible ever-changing eyes again.

He settled her onto a rickety old wicker chair on the porch beside him, then kneeled down in front of her, his expression etched with a sweet concern, his long straight nose and wide full mouth giving him a princely quality. "I've been meaning to fix that. Are you hurt?"

Leandra brushed at her dark tights and pencil straight wool skirt. "No, I'm fine. Just a scratch, maybe."

His eyes followed the length of her leg, then he leaned over for a closer look. "Did it snag your hose?"

Clearly flustered, Leandra rubbed the burning spot on her calf muscle again. "No, really. I'm fine. Old. I mean the tights are old. It doesn't matter."

"Okay," he said, his gaze still on her leg. Then his glance shifted to her face and the lazy, easy-moving accent was back, along with the wry smile. "Now, what can I do for you?"

She at least now had his full attention. It was very disconcerting, the way he stared straight into her eyes, like a great cat about to pounce on its prey.

She brushed her suddenly sweaty palms across the tail of her tailored suit jacket, pushed at her chin-length curly brown tresses. "Well, I've just been hired as the Christmas pageant coordinator—for the city, you know—to coincide with the Marshall Christmas Festival. The pageant will be held at the civic center right across from the First Church—the big one downtown. The church sponsors the event."

Nathan Welby stood up then, crossed his arms over his broad chest and rocked back on the heels of his worn boots as he stared down at her. "Okay, and what's that got to do with me?"

She was at a disadvantage again, having to look up at him. And with the rich autumn sunshine streaming behind him like that—

She squinted, swallowed again. "I want—that is— the city wants *you* to build a new set. I've been told you're the best carpenter around here. I mean, I know you're busy, but if you could find the time, we'd pay you."

He kept rocking, his eyes never leaving her face, his whole countenance still and watchful, as if he were on full alert.

At first, Leandra thought maybe he didn't understand. She was about to explain all over again when a little girl with blond hair falling in ripples down to her waist came rushing out onto the porch, her eyes bright, her hands held together as if in prayer as she gazed up at Leandra.

"Are you gonna be my new mommy?"

Completely confused, Leandra could only form a

smile and stare down at the beautiful, chocolate-milk-stained child. "I—"

"Brittney," Nathan said, taking the child up in his arms to wipe her face with his flannel sleeve, "this nice lady is Miss Flanagan from city hall, and she came to offer me a job. I don't think she's in the market for any mommying."

He gave Leandra an apologetic, embarrassed look, a kind of sadness coloring his eyes to deep bronze. As he held his daughter with one strong arm, he tugged at the gathered skirts of her blue denim jumper with his free hand.

The child, as if sensing that sadness, kissed her father on the cheek then laid her head against the curve of his neck, causing something inside Leandra's heart to shift and melt.

Then the little girl's next words, whispered with such an innocent hope, made that shift grow into a big hole of longing in Leandra's soul.

"But, I've been praying each and every night since Mamma went away and only just now, Daddy, I asked God to please send me a new mommy, so you wouldn't be sad and grumpy anymore, and so Matt and Layla would quit picking on me so much."

She turned to Leandra then, her big blue eyes, so different from her father's, so open and honest, so sweet and beseeching. "And now, here *you* are. And you're so pretty, too. Isn't she, Daddy?"

Leandra watched as this lumberjack of a man swallowed back the obvious pain she'd seen in his eyes.

Giving her a shaky smile, he said in a husky voice, "As pretty as a little lamb, pumpkin."

Leandra's utter confusion and nervous energy turned as golden and warm as the sun at her back. If that statement had come from any other man, she'd have laughed at the hokey, down-home line. But coming from Nathan Welby, said in that lazy drawl and said with such sweet natural sincerity, the remark became something entirely different, and took on an intimate meaning.

A meaning that Leandra did not want to misinterpret.

It was a compliment, said in daddy fashion to appease his daughter. Nothing more.

Apparently pleased with that answer, however, Brittney placed her plump little hands on her father's cheeks and touched her forehead to his, a wide grin on her rounded face. "Isn't she perfect for the job, Daddy?"

Chapter Two

Nathan looked down at his daughter's big blue eyes, so like her mother's, and wished he could feel good about all the hope centered there. Alicia's eyes had always reminded him of the sky over Texas, big and vast and deeply blue. Now, both his Brittney and her older sister, Layla, looked so much like Alicia it hurt him each time he came face-to-face with either of them. And he hated turning away from his own children, but that's exactly what he did sometimes—to hide his pain.

His gaze moved from his daughter to the woman standing in front of him. Leandra Flanagan's bewildered look caused her features to scatter and change like leaves floating through a forest. Yes, that was it. This woman reminded him of autumn—all golden and cool—whereas his Alicia had always reminded him of springtime—refreshing, colorful, blossoming.

Stop it, Nate, he told himself as he shifted his tiny daughter in his arms. Why did he always have to compare every woman who came along to his deceased wife?

Yet, there was something about this particular woman that made her stand out from the crowd. Only, Nate hadn't quite figured out just what it was, exactly.

"I'm sorry," he said now to Leandra. Placing Brittney down on the porch, he rubbed a hand across her wheat-colored curls. "Sugar, go on in the house now and let Daddy talk to the nice lady. I'll be in in a little while to help you with those leaf place mats you're making for next week's Thanksgiving dinner."

"Okay, Daddy, but don't forget what I said." Brittney gave Leandra another pleasant, gap-toothed smile. "You wanna stay for supper?"

The woman's expression went from baffled to downright panic-stricken. Nate watched as her big pecan-colored eyes widened. He could see by the way she was squirming and shifting, she felt uncomfortable with this whole situation. She'd come out here to offer him some much needed extra work, and instead had been asked on the spot to become a mommy to his children.

Something she obviously hadn't expected, or wanted, and probably something she didn't run into every time she conducted business.

Well, he couldn't blame her for being a bit put off. Leandra Flanagan was clearly *all* business, from her spiffy wool tailored suit, to her dark tights to the expensive loafers covering her tiny feet.

But in spite of that aloof, sophisticated air, he liked her hair. It was a curly, chin-length golden-brown that changed color and direction each time she ran a hand through it.

And he kinda liked her lips, too. They were a pure pink and rounded. They fit her square, angular face perfectly.

Too bad she wasn't mommy material. Not that he was looking, anyway.

Wanting, needing to explain, he waited, his heart hurting for his child, for Leandra to answer his daughter's question. To her credit, she handled the embarrassing moment with savvy.

"That's awfully nice of you to ask," she told Brittney. "But I've already missed lunch with my four brothers. I think I'd better go on home for supper."

"You got four brothers?" Brittney held up her hand, showing four fingers. "That's this many."

Leandra laughed then, a genuine laugh that filled the afternoon with a lilting melody. "Yes, that's this many." She raised her own four fingers. "And I'm the baby of the bunch."

"I'm a baby, too," Brittney admitted. "Not a real baby. Just the baby of my family. And I get tired of it, sometimes."

Leandra bent down, her dark hair falling forward in a perfectly even wedge of curls as she came face-to-face with Brittney. "I get tired of it, too. My brothers love to pick on me."

Brittney rolled her big eyes and bobbed her head. "That's 'xactly why I need a new mommy. I get picked on, 'cause I'm the youngest and all. You could...pro-teck me."

"It's pro*tect*," Nathan corrected, "and I don't think

we need to discuss this with Miss Flanagan any more today. Now, scoot. I'll be in in a little while, okay?"

"Oh, okay," Brittney said on an exaggerated breath. "Bye, Miss Flan-again."

Nathan saw the amused expression on Leandra's face, and relaxed a little himself.

"Well, Miss *Flan-again,* bet you weren't expecting all this when you made the drive out here today."

"No, not really," Leandra said, rising to face him, that curtain of hair covering one eye. "Your daughter is precious, Mr. Welby. And I'm flattered that she thinks I'm a good candidate…but—"

"But you aren't the one needing extra work, right? And call me Nate."

She laughed again. "Call me Leandra, and yes, as a matter of fact, I took this job because I did need work."

Her smile was self-deprecating. She looked uncomfortable again, standing there shifting her tiny weight on those fancy leather shoes.

Nathan noticed her lips, her smile all over again. While he enjoyed the attraction, the feeling also brought him a measure of guilt. He hadn't really noticed another woman this much, in this way, since Alicia had died. He couldn't do that to her memory.

Deciding to end this interesting diversion, he indicated the steps. "Care to sit a spell?"

"Sure." She joined him there, her hands pulling at her tight skirt for modesty's sake.

It didn't stop Nathan from admiring her shapely legs, though.

"Leandra, I appreciate the offer, but I'm afraid I'm going to have to turn you down on this job."

"Why?"

Her gaze locked with his, and again, he felt as if he were lost in a November forest full of sunshine and leaves and cool waters.

Before he could answer, three blond-haired children and a reddish-blond-coated, shaggy dog came crashing out of the door to fall all around them on the old, rickety steps.

"'Cause Daddy swore he'd never set foot in a church again after Mama died."

"Matt, that's enough."

Leandra heard the pain and anger in Nathan Welby's words, but she also heard the gentleness in the reprimand to his son, too.

Watching as the beautiful Irish setter roamed the backyard and barked with joy at falling leaves, she wondered what she had walked in on.

This family had obviously suffered a great loss. His wife. Their mother. No wonder a sense of gloominess shadowed this old house.

"I'm sorry...about your wife," she said, hoping she wouldn't add to their discomfort.

Nathan glanced at the children. "You three go finish raking those leaves by the big oak, all right?"

"But Daddy—"

"Go on, Matt. And don't throw leaves at your sisters."

Reluctantly, the three overly-interested children trudged down the steps.

Nathan turned back to Leandra, his voice low. "Thank you." He looked away then. "She died three years ago, in a plane crash." His shrug said it all. "I guess I've got some reckoning to do. I haven't quite gotten over it."

Leandra's heart slammed against her chest and the gasp was out of her mouth before she could stop it. "How awful."

Then, the silence again.

But not for long. The three little ones were back in a flash, chasing the big dog right back up onto the porch, their eyes and ears set on listening.

Nathan didn't fuss at them this time. He seemed lost somewhere else, completely unaware his children had stopped their chores.

Not knowing what to say, Leandra got up to leave. "Well, I guess I'd better be going. I'm so sorry I bothered you—"

"Wait," Nathan said, his big hand on her arm. "I'd like to clarify that statement, if you don't mind." Sending a fatherly glare to his three children, he added, "And if certain among us could remain quiet and use their manners and quit eavesdropping, I'd highly appreciate it."

"But we want you to take the job, Daddy," the older girl told him, her arms wrapped across her chest in classic teenage rebellion mode. "You need to get involved again."

"Yeah," Brittney added, hopping up to twirl around. "And we figured we could help out, too, so you won't be so scared about going back to church."

"How's that?" Nathan asked, a certain fear centered in his golden eyes.

Leandra knew his fear wasn't that of a coward, but of a father who was afraid to hear what his children might have decided behind his back, a man afraid of his own emotions, his own sense of unspeakable loss.

"I want to be the angel," Brittney said, flapping her arms. "Don't you think I'd make the bestest angel, Miz Flan-again?"

Her mind clicking, Leandra saw the opportunity presenting itself to her. If she hired on the children, the father was sure to follow, regardless of his aversion to churches.

And a child shall lead them.

"You know, we do happen to have an opening for an angel," she said. "But have you had any experience?"

Brittney scrunched up her pert nose. "Once, when it snowed, I made angels in the snow with my hands and legs. Does that count—'cause it hardly ever snows here—and I don't get much chance to do that."

Leandra made a point of placing a finger to her jaw, as if she were deep in thought, although there was no earthly way she could have turned down this little girl. "I do believe that counts. If you've made snow angels, then you know all about the importance of this job. When can you start practice?"

"You mean I'm hired?"

"You're hired," Leandra said, extending a hand to seal the agreement.

"I'll be there whenever you say," Brittney replied, her big eyes shining, her small, slightly sticky hand pumping Leandra's. "I'm going inside to practice angel stuff right now."

"Wait a minute—" Nate said, holding up a hand.

"But, Daddy, you can't say no," the older girl told him. "And I want to sing." She looked at Leandra with the same big blue eyes as Brittney's, although hers held that tad of attitude that just naturally came with being an adolescent. "I've sung some in the youth choir at church anyway, and they said they were looking for people for the Christmas pageant. I could help out there." She shrugged, just to show it was no big deal to her either way.

"Another experienced applicant," Leandra said, slapping a hand to her side. "We do need all the voices we can get for all those wonderful traditional Christmas songs. I'll let you know when we start rehearsal. And… I didn't get your name."

"Layla," the girl said, her eyes wary in spite of the tiny smile on her freckled face, her standoffish attitude breaking down a little.

"It's nice to meet you, Layla," Leandra said. "And I appreciate your offer to help."

"What about me?" Matt said.

He had white-blond hair and even bigger blue eyes than his sisters. And an impish quality that made Leandra think of her own brothers. He was probably walking trouble, but how could she refuse those big, questioning eyes and those cute dimples?

"What about *you?*" she asked, squinting as she leaned over to study him closely. "What do you think you're qualified to do?"

"I guess I could be a shepherd," he offered, his hands jutting out from his hips in a businesslike shift. "I helped Daddy round up some cows once that had strayed over onto our property from Mr. Tuttle's land. And I was only around seven at the time."

"How old are you now?" Leandra asked, caught up in wanting these children to be a part of her pageant.

"Ten. Is that old enough?" He asked it with such sweet conviction that Leandra knew she'd just lost her heart forever.

"As a matter of fact, I need a ten-year-old shepherd," she told him. Then she shook his hand, too. "You'll have an important job, you understand—watching your flock by night and all of that."

"I know," he replied. Then he rubbed the fingers of one hand with his other hand in a nervous gesture. "But I might need help with my costume. Our mom always made that kind of stuff."

Leandra swallowed back the sorrow she felt for this lovely family. "We'll find someone to help with that, I'm sure."

Having settled their immediate futures, Layla and Matt turned to go back in the house with Brittney. At the door, Layla whirled to her father, her long straight hair flying out behind her.

"Will you help, too, Daddy? Please?"

Nathan let loose a long sigh. "I need to talk to Miss Flanagan now, honey." When his daughter just stood there, her eyes sending him a beseeching look, he hastily added, "Oh, all right. I'll think about it."

That seemed to satisfy the teenager. She smiled and went inside the house. Then Leandra and Nathan heard a loud "Yes," followed by laughter and clapping.

"I didn't get to interview the dog," Leandra said by way of cutting through the tension centered on the porch.

Nathan shot her a wry smile, then lifted his head toward the Irish setter pacing the yard again. "Oh, and I guess you just happen to have a spot for that big mutt, too. Maybe dress that setter up as a camel or a cow? Might as well throw in the horse—he'd fit right in in a stable."

"You're not pleased with this, are you?"

He dropped his hands down on his faded jeans. "Now what gave you that impression?"

"Oh, I guess the glare in your eyes and the dark, brooding frown creasing your forehead."

"Well, no man likes to be ambushed and sideswiped all at the same time."

"I didn't ambush you. I simply asked your children to be a part of the Christmas pageant."

He scoffed, held his hands to his hips, and looked out over the cluttered yard. "More like, they told you exactly what they wanted and you fell for it, right off the bat."

"Sounds like you've had experience in that area yourself."

He grinned then, and took her breath to a new level. She liked the way the skin around his eyes crinkled up when he smiled. He had a beautiful smile.

"I've had lots of experience being railroaded by those three, that's for sure." Then he turned serious. "It's just hard, saying no to them since—"

"Since their mother died. Nate, I'm so sorry. It must have—must still be—so hard for all of you."

"We have our good days and our bad days," he said. Then he motioned for her to follow him out into the yard.

"She loved this place. We'd just bought it, been here about three months, when she died."

"That's terrible."

"Yeah, terrible. Just like this place. I've been meaning to go ahead and fix it up, but my heart's just not in it."

"It's a lovely old house," Leandra said, her gaze shifting over the peeling paint and fancy fretwork. "It could be turned into a showplace."

"Maybe."

"Nate, if you don't mind me asking—how did it happen?"

"The plane crash, you mean?"

She nodded.

The silence stretched between them again in a slow-moving arc much like the sun stretching over the sky to the west. The air felt chilly after the wind picked up.

He looked out over the pasture, his gaze following the prancing horse as the animal chased along the fence beside the Irish setter. "She was going to visit her folks back in Kentucky. She hadn't been home since…since we got married."

Leandra sensed a deep regret in him, and a need to have this burden lifted from his shoulders. But she wouldn't force him to talk about something so personal.

And yet, he did just that.

"They didn't want her to marry me. I was dirt-poor and from Texas, after all. She came from a rich family—money, horses, all that bluegrass class. That's how we met—she came here with her father to buy a horse from this rancher I was working for and—"

"You fell in love with her."

"Yeah, from the beginning. But I was beneath her and I knew it. So did her folks. They gave her an ultimatum—them or me." He stopped, sighed, ran a hand through his golden locks. "She chose me."

He said those words with awe, a catch in his throat that only brought a painful roughness to Leandra's own throat.

"She hadn't planned on ever going back there, but her mother got real sick. They kinda patched things up and she was so happy. Couldn't wait to get home and tell me all about how her parents finally wanted to meet their grandchildren."

Leandra wanted him to stop now. She didn't think she could bear to hear the rest of this tragic story.

But then, Nathan needed to tell it.

"They sent her home on their private plane—can you believe that—and it crashed in a bad rainstorm just before landing at the Longview Airport. Killed her and the pilot. We waited and waited at that airport, me and the kids, but she never came home."

And he was still waiting, Leandra told herself as she clutched her arms to her chest to stop her own tears from forming.

"I am so sorry, Nate." She placed a hand on his arm. "I didn't mean to dredge up all this. I'm sure you have your reasons for not wanting to be involved in church, but I'd love to have you working on this project with me."

When he didn't answer, she turned to go. To leave him to his grief and his memories. She wished she'd never come here. But then, the children needed to be involved, needed to have the support and love of a church family.

Maybe that was why God had sent her. Not for Nate. But for the children.

"Hey, Leandra?"

She liked the way he said her name in that long, tall, Texas drawl.

She turned at the corner of the house. "Yes?"

"When do you want me to start?"

"You mean, you'll do it? You'll build the set for me?"

He nodded. "Yes, for you…and for my children."

She stood there, her heart breaking for him. He didn't want to do this, but he loved his children enough to try.

"What was your wife's name?"

"Alicia," he said, again with that reverence.

"Alicia would be proud of you."

He nodded again, then dropped his head.

That beautiful golden silence moved between them, bonding them like a cord of silky threads.

"And what's the dog's name?"

"Mutt," he replied with a shrug and a lopsided grin.

She chuckled then. "I think I have a spot for Mutt, too."

"The horse is named Honeyboy," he told her. "I bought it for her."

She didn't have to ask to know he was referring to his wife.

"About this job—" he began.

Afraid he'd already changed his mind, she said, "You can start first thing in the morning, if that's okay."

"I'll be there."

And she knew he would.

Chapter Three

"I met the most incredible family today," Leandra announced at supper that night.

It was good to be sitting here, safe and warm in her parents' rambling home nestled in the heart of one of Marshall's oldest neighborhoods. This big oak dining table had been the center of many such family meals, and now with two of her brothers married and fathers themselves, more chairs had been added to the long table.

The noise level had increased through the years, too.

"What did you say, suga'?" Her father, Howard, asked, cupping a hand to his ear, the twinkle in his brown eyes belying the seriousness of his expression.

Leandra threw up her hands. How could anyone carry on a civilized conversation in such utter chaos? It had been this way all her life, that is until she had escaped to the quiet sanctuary of her own tiny apartment far away in the big city.

Looking around now, however, she realized she had

actually missed the big family gatherings. She'd missed her brothers, in spite of their opinionated observations, and she'd especially missed her parents.

Her oldest brother, Jack, was busy cleaning up the spilled peas his two-year-old son, Corey, had just dumped on her mother's prized braided dining room rug. His wife, Margaret, was soothing their five-year-old Philip's hurt feelings at losing out on one of the drumsticks from the big batch of fried chicken her mother had prepared for the clan.

Michael, Leandra's next-to-the-oldest brother, was holding his six-month-old daughter Carissa, trying to burp her and eat his own meal at the same time, while his wife, Kim, passed food to their four-year-old, Cameron, and worked on crowd control so Colleen could rest for a few precious minutes.

Mark, the brooding professor who taught at Panola College and broke hearts on a regular basis, was actually reading a book and eating a chicken leg at the same time. No wonder the man was still single!

And Richard, only two years older than Leandra, was smiling over at her, his brown eyes assessing the entire situation much in the same way he watched over his customers at the old-fashioned general store he ran just outside of town.

Everyone seemed to be talking at once, except Richard.

"Tell us about this interesting family, Sis," he said now, his hand perched on a big, flaky biscuit.

Surprised that anyone had heard her, Leandra thankfully turned to her handsome brother. Richard had always looked out for her. "The Welby family," she said by way of an explanation. "I was out there today, and I hired Nathan Welby to build the set for the Christmas pageant."

"Oh, really," Colleen said, her gaze centered on one of Jack's noisy little sprites. Shoveling mashed potatoes onto little Philip's cartoon-character plastic plate, Leandra's mother didn't seem to be aware of anyone around her.

But Leandra knew her mother better than that. Colleen never missed a beat. She was almost superhuman in her maternal instincts and her ability to keep everything organized and together, in spite of the chaos surrounding her large brood. Leandra could never understand how her mother did it, nor why Colleen seemed so content to be a homemaker.

"Yes," Leandra replied in a loud voice, so her mother, at least, could hear her. "Mr. Welby—Nate—agreed to build a whole new set, and I signed all three children up for parts in the actual program."

"You sure had a productive day," Howard said, his gentle gaze moving down the table toward his only daughter. "Nate is a good man. He's had some bad times, but he's a hard worker. I talk to him in the bank every time he comes in."

"Which is every time he needs to borrow more money," Jack, who was also a banker like his father, stated in his businesslike way. "I don't see how the man keeps up, what with the mortgage on that dilapidated house, those three kids, and with that huge animal to feed."

"Are you talking about the dog or the horse?" Leandra said, irritated at her brother's high-handed attitude.

Because he'd come from a good, comfortably blessed family, Jack had always held the notion that he was somebody special. And he looked down on those who didn't meet his own high standards.

"Both," he said, smug in his little corner of the dining table, his pert, pretty dark-haired wife smiling beside him. "The man needs to find a better-paying job and he needs to learn to control those three brats of his. Are you sure you should have invited them to be a part of the program, Lea? They can be very disruptive at times."

"Yes," Margaret, who always, always agreed with her husband, added, her nose lifted in the air. "I taught that middle one—Matt—in Sunday school last year— that is when he showed up. He was loud and unruly, not well-behaved at all. That man needs a firm hand with that little boy or there will be trouble down the road."

Leandra's guard went up. Bristling, she said in a level voice, "Matt seemed perfectly polite to me, considering the sad circumstances. I just think the Welby children need some positive attention. The little one, Brittney, is going to be an angel. Layla will be singing in the choir, and Matt will be a shepherd."

"You'll regret that choice, I'm sure," Margaret said through a sniff. "He'll knock down the entire set."

"I don't think I'll regret anything," Leandra snapped back. "I think I can control a ten-year-old." When Margaret gave her a look of doubt, she sweetly added, "I did grow up with these four, after all."

"But you aren't married, and you can't possibly know how to deal with children," Margaret stated, her smile of maternal wisdom extending across the table to her own precocious five-year-old who'd insisted he wanted to sit by his nana.

The cutting remark hurt Leandra, but only for a minute. She'd long ago learned to ignore her sister-in-law's pointed remarks regarding her own often-voiced choice to remain single and motherless for as long as possible.

"You're right there, Margaret," Leandra replied in a calm, firm tone. "But I've watched Jack and you with your own children and I think I can safely say I've learned so much from your…uh…parenting skills."

As if to help his aunt make her point, little Philip picked up his spoon and hurled it over the table like a boomerang. It landed, soggy mashed potatoes and all, right in his mother's lap.

Margaret instantly hopped up, an enraged expression causing her porcelain skin to turn a mottled pink. "Young man, that was totally uncalled for. Philip, that is unacceptable behavior. Do you hear me?"

Philip smiled, stuck out his tongue, then looked up at his grandmother with such an angelic expression that Colleen had to turn away to hide her own amused smile.

"Tell Mama you're sorry, sugarpie," Colleen coaxed in a grandmother voice. Then in a stern, firm tone, she added, "Philip, we don't throw spoons in Nana's house, okay?"

The boy looked sheepish, then bobbed his curly head. "'Kay, Nana. Sowee."

His sincerity was sorely questioned as he proceeded to mash his peas into a green, slimy blob with his balled-up fist.

Margaret turned to Jack. "Would you please talk to your son?"

Jack tried, really he did. "Philip, behave and eat your food, or I'll have to move you over here between your mother and me for a time-out."

That brought a pout and a gut-wrenching sob to Philip's upturned face.

"Now look," Margaret huffed. "You've made him cry."

Colleen soothed her grandson's feelings, and brought him under control, too. "Philip, we don't want a time-out, do we?"

"Nope."

"Then please finish your meal, so we can all have some apple pie."

The little sandy-haired boy turned demure as his grandmother smiled over at him.

"As you were saying," Mark called to Leandra, his book still open by his plate, his quiet, intelligent gaze falling across his sister's face.

Mark was so good at that, listening quietly, observing, taking everything in, even with his nose buried in a book.

"Oh, just that the Welby family is very interesting," Leandra continued, hoping Jack and Margaret would just stay quiet and let her enjoy what was left of her dinner. "And it's just so sad—about his wife, I mean."

Mark nodded, then pushed his tiny glasses up on his nose. "Alicia was a beautiful woman. And well-educated, too. We often talked about literature when I'd see her at church functions. She loved poetry."

Leandra let that tidbit of information settle in. So Nathan had married a beautiful—Leandra couldn't imagine her any other way—wealthy, educated woman who liked to read sonnets. Alicia was beginning to take saint status in Leandra's mind.

"How'd she ever hook up with the likes of Nate Welby, then?" Michael, who'd been quiet, finally asked.

"She loved him," Kim, his wife, said, poking him in the ribs. "It was a fairy-tale romance, from everything I've heard. She was lovely and he's sure a handsome man. They were a striking couple."

Yep, that's exactly the way I see it, Leandra thought. Only now, Nathan was suffering too much to see his own potential, or that of his children. He'd let everything come to a standstill. His faith was in ruins, just like his house. Leandra wondered how someone could ever get through that kind of grief.

"Well, it sure had a tragic ending," Jack said in his superior way. "They were ill-suited from the beginning. I knew that the day they moved to town."

Ignoring him and the hurt in her own heart, Leandra asked, "When exactly did they move here? I never knew them before and I don't recall running into any of them on visits home."

She certainly would have remembered Nate, at least.

Colleen pushed her plate away and leaned back in her chair. "They came here a little over three years ago, I guess. Apparently, from what I've heard at church, Alicia Welby took one look at that old house and had to have it."

"And Nate tried to move heaven and earth to get it for her," Howard added. "They came from Paris."

"Paris, France?" Margaret asked, her eyes brightening at the prospect. Margaret loved sophisticated people, and fancied herself one, from what Leandra could tell.

"No, silly," her husband retorted, rolling his eyes. "Paris, Texas."

"Oh." Margaret looked properly chastised, then shrugged. "Well, I didn't know."

"An honest mistake," Colleen said, amusement coloring her merry eyes. "Nate worked on a big ranch near Paris, dear. But he took a construction job here, hoping to make more money. That's when they bought the house."

"A few weeks after he started his job, though, Alicia was killed in a plane crash," Howard explained. "And then, to top things off, her mother died—whether from bad health or heartbreak over the loss of her daughter—who knows. But I hear Alicia's father doesn't have anything to do with Nate or the children." Howard shook his head, then glanced at Leandra. "Such a tragedy, but Nate put his nose to the grindstone and now he's made a name for himself around here. People respect

Nathan Welby. They know they can count on him to get the job done."

"He told me about his wife's death," Leandra said in a quiet voice. "But he didn't mention Alicia's mother, or her death. I guess he and the grandfather don't get along, since he didn't say much about that either." She paused, then looked down at her plate. "I think he works so much to take his mind off his wife's death, maybe."

The whole room quieted after that. It was certainly a sad situation. Even Jack looked solemn for a minute.

"I'm glad you hired him, Lea," her father said as he got up from the table. "Nate is a proud man, he's just lost his way, can't shake his grief. Maybe having something spiritual to occupy him will help." Then Howard turned to Colleen, "Good dinner, honey. How 'bout me and these boys do the dishes?"

"Oh, how thoughtful," Colleen replied, her gaze locking with her husband's. "You don't mind, do you, boys?"

Amid groans and whines, came the reply, "No, Mama."

Leandra had to smile. The love her parents shared was so obvious and abiding, it practically glowed. She loved how with a sweet smile and a calm, level voice they got their children to do things. And she loved the way they still called their grown sons boys. It was an endearing trait that somehow brought tears to her eyes.

She had to wonder what was going on right now at the Welby household. Was little Brittney vying for her father's attention? Was beautiful Layla pouting in her room? Was Matt getting into trouble? Was Mutt curled up underneath the dining table?

Would they have someone to say their prayers with them, to hug them good-night and tuck them in to bed?

Leandra hoped so, and then promptly told herself to quit worrying about the Welbys.

Looking around, she realized in spite of the noise and disorganization of a Flanagan family dinner, she loved her family and enjoyed being home with them, even if it was for just a short time. After the holidays, she'd have to head back to Houston, hopefully with another high-paying job lined up, thanks to her contacts there who had supported her decision to leave Myers Advertising.

After Christmas.

After she'd organized this grand production.

After she'd spent well over a month working side by side with Nathan Welby and his three lovely, slightly manipulative children.

Well, at least her time here wouldn't be dull or boring. She'd been worried that it would be hard to get over what had happened with William, hard to settle into small-town life again. But today had been filled with excitement from the get-go. Now, she didn't think she'd have time to dwell on the mistakes of her recent past.

Being anywhere near Nate Welby would cure that particular malady, she was sure. The man caused her heart to jump and her palms to become sweaty, for some strange reason. And she had to admit, William had never done that for her. He'd been a comfortable convenience, at the most.

Nate was anything but comfortable or convenient.

Probably because he was just so very different from any man she'd ever encountered. And probably because she was feeling such a sweet sympathy for his plight.

Just thinking about him, however, made her kind of tingly inside. Even now, hours after she'd left him standing by the fence watching his beautiful horse, his big hand centered on Mutt's shaggy back, Leandra felt a soft, golden bond with Nathan Welby. The feeling wasn't unpleasant, not at all.

Leandra looked up then to find her mother regarding her with a calculated little smile.

And silently hoped that her all-knowing mother hadn't read anything into this new development, or the dreamy expression that Leandra was sure had been plastered across her face.

He wouldn't get his hopes up.

Nate sat in the overstuffed recliner in the darkened parlor of the rambling old house, Mutt sleeping peacefully at his feet, and wondered if his luck was about to change.

He had lots to do between now and Christmas, at least. An extra job would mean even more time away from the children, but then they were used to his long hours. But he liked to keep busy, he reminded himself. He had calls every week for carpentry work all over East Texas, and he was next in line to be promoted to construction foreman at work. He liked to work until he was too tired to think, so he'd hired on with a construction crew that sent him all over, sometimes here, sometimes over across the line in Louisiana. But he didn't like to leave the children for too long, so he didn't take anything farther than driving distance.

But there was never enough distance between him and the emptiness he felt as he sat here each night, remembering.

Yet, he didn't take any jobs that would cause him to have to move away from this house.

Because he felt so close to Alicia here.

And because his children loved their home.

Since Alicia's death, they'd settled into a routine of just getting through each day, making ends meet, making sure they took care of each other. Now, Nate knew that grief-dulled routine needed to change.

Layla helped him out with the younger ones, but she was at that age where a girl really needed a mother.

And Matt, bless his heart.

Matt still missed his mother, still cried out for her in his sleep, even though he tried so hard to be a little man.

And little Brittney always seemed lost in a child's world of make-believe, happy and chattering and content, too young to understand or notice her father's pain, or express her own.

Now, Brittney had announced that she'd been praying for God to send her a new mommy. And she'd decided Leandra Flanagan was the one for the job.

Why hadn't he noticed that his children were hurting just as much as he was?

Maybe because he'd made it a point to always find

something to occupy his time. Maybe because he buried his own sorrows in his woodworking hobby out in the barn. Maybe because he just couldn't bring himself to think about it.

Nate felt the tears pricking at his tired eyes, and swiped a hand across the day-old beard stubble edging his face. He didn't know whether to laugh or cry.

Lord, he'd cried so many nights, sitting here in front of an empty fireplace, waiting, watching, silently screaming his wrath at God.

He was tired of the burden, the weight of his grief.

And yet, he couldn't let it go just yet. He was selfish that way. He wanted to blame God a little bit longer. It helped to ease his own guilt.

Thinking back over the day, he remembered Leandra. She was a pretty woman. Petite and tiny-framed, delicate, but so precise.

So different from Alicia.

Why did Brittney think a businesswoman, who obviously didn't have time for children, would possibly want to be her mommy?

Was the child just so lonely, so afraid, that she'd picked the first woman to come down the pike to be her mother? Were his children that desperate?

Or, had Leandra Flanagan come along for a reason?

Had God answered his baby daughter's prayers?

Nate sat there in the dark, wondering.

He didn't want to open up his heart to God again. He was still so mad at God, it hurt to even try to form a prayer in his head, let alone voice that prayer.

But, tonight, he somehow found the courage to do just that. For Brittney.

"Lord, help me. Help me to be a good father again."

Because today Nate had realized something so terrible, so tragic, that he felt sick to his stomach with knowing it.

He'd been ignoring his children, simply because they reminded him of their mother so much. He'd been a shell of a father, moving through each day with slow-motion efforts that sometimes took all his strength.

Until today.

Today, an autumn-hued angel had appeared on his doorstep and offered him a chance to find a little salvation. A no-nonsense, full-steam-ahead angel who'd somehow managed to be gentle and understanding with his forlorn, misunderstood children, in spite of her all-business exterior.

Which meant Leandra Flanagan wasn't always all business. The woman had a heart underneath all those layers of sophistication.

No one, since Alicia had died, had ever actually taken the time to just talk to his children. Not even their father.

But Leandra Flanagan had done just that, and had pulled them into something good and noble, simply by asking them to be a part of her show.

Nate wouldn't forget that kind gesture, ever.

"You don't have to hit me on the head, Lord," he said into the darkness. "I hear You loud and clear."

Leandra Flanagan might not be the answer to his

prayers nor Brittney's, either, but the woman had sure made him see himself in a different light.

"I'm going to build the set for this pageant, Lord," he said. "And I'm going to do a good job, but I can't make any promises past that."

Nate didn't want God to win him back over. He still had a grudge to nurse, after all. He had to do this, though. He had to go back to church. To pay back Leandra for her kindness.

To make his children proud of him again.

And maybe, to bring a little Christmas spirit to his own grieving heart.

Chapter Four

"Okay, everybody, we need to show some real Christmas spirit here."

Leandra looked around at the group of people gathered in the civic hall to begin rehearsal for *One Golden Christmas*. While the event was being put on by the church, it would be held in the town civic hall to accommodate what they hoped would be a sold-out performance on Christmas Eve.

Smiling, she continued to explain how things would go. "I'm just here to oversee everything from rehearsals to ticket sales. You have a fabulous director. Mr. Crawford has the script all ready and you each have your assignments. If there are any concerns, please see me later. Now, I'm going to sit back and listen to Mr. Crawford's instructions right along with the rest of you."

Leandra took a seat, then turned toward the doors at the back of the large building. Where was Nathan Welby?

Glancing at her watch again, she wondered if he'd

changed his mind about building the set after all. If he didn't show up, she'd be in serious trouble. The set should have been built months ago, but it seemed as if everyone involved in spearheading this project had procrastinated until the last possible minute. She might wind up having to talk her brothers into helping out.

Well, at least Nathan's children had made it into town. All three were here, along with all the other children who were out of school for the week of Thanksgiving.

The Welby children had apparently hitched a ride with their neighbor, Mr. Tuttle, who was playing Santa Claus. And he looked the spitting image of Father Christmas with his white beard and rounded belly.

Right now, the children were being assigned to an adult coordinator who would oversee their costumes and rehearsal schedules.

Leandra groaned silently when she saw her sister-in-law Margaret taking the Welby children and several others over to one side of the center. Apparently, Margaret had volunteered to help out, since little Philip had a brief appearance in one of the production numbers. Well, she'd better be nice.

After making sure Mr. Crawford didn't need her, Leandra got up to go outside. Maybe Nathan was already here somewhere. Had she remembered to tell him where to meet her? Since the church was practically across the street from the civic center, she didn't think he'd have a problem finding them.

It was a crisp, fall day. Cars moved down the street at

a slow pace, contrasting sharply with the traffic snarls Leandra had sat through on a daily basis back in Houston.

The air smelled fresh and clear. Leandra inhaled deeply, more to calm herself than to enjoy the weather. She was afraid she'd made a terrible mistake in hiring Nathan Welby.

But he'd said he'd be here.

That's when she heard the sound.

It couldn't be possible, of course. But it sure sounded like the clippity-clop of a horse's hooves moving up the street. The sound echoed loudly off the historic old courthouse down the way, then grew louder.

Leandra strained her neck, looking around to see what was making all the noise.

Then she spotted him.

Nathan Welby, riding Honeyboy, coming up the street as if he rode a horse into town every day. Looking just like a cowboy, coming straight in off the range. Looking mighty fine in his battered brown suede cowboy hat and flannel shirt. Of course, he had on jeans and cowboy boots, too.

And there it was again, that golden aura that seemed to permeate everything about the man. Or was it just that each time she saw him, she saw him in streams of brilliant light?

Leandra had to swallow. For a minute, she wondered what it might be like to be swept up on that horse and carried away by Nathan Welby.

Since he was headed right for her, the feeling grew. To

defend the sudden overwhelming daydreams whirling like flying leaves around her mind, Leandra wrapped her arms across her midsection and waited with what she hoped was a professional look of disapproval on her face.

Nathan rode right up to the steps, slid off the horse with a natural grace, then tethered Honeyboy to a nearby iron bench before tipping his hat to Leandra.

"Morning."

"Good morning," Leandra replied, amazement fluttering through her heart as she watched him remove his hat and shake out his golden locks. "Do you often ride your horse to work, Mr. Welby?"

"It's Nate, remember," he told her as he stepped forward, one long leg on the step just below her, his hat in his hand. "Sorry I'm late. My truck wouldn't crank. I called old man Tuttle to bring the kids while I tried to get the thing to work."

Leandra nodded, then smiled over at Honeyboy. "Obviously, the truck didn't cooperate."

Nate gave her a slow, lazy grin. "Obviously."

They stood there, silent, for what felt like a long time to Leandra. Since Nate didn't seem in any hurry to converse, she tried to get things rolling. "Well, let me just go in and tell someone where I'll be, and then I'll take you over to the city hall work area, so we can go over the plans for the set."

He nodded, leaned back on his boots, kept the lazy grin. Then he said, "I'm gonna walk on over to the church and ask Reverend Powell if I can let Honeyboy graze on the back lot. Want to meet me there?"

"Sure." She whirled to go up the steps, very much aware of his gaze following her. Telling herself to slow down before she tripped over her own feet, Leandra burst through the doors only to find Margaret standing there, waiting for her.

"This will never do, Lea," Margaret said, her hands on her hips. "We have to talk."

"What's wrong?" Leandra glanced down the aisle where Mr. Crawford was talking to the group, going over the script and songs. "Is there a problem already?"

"Yes," Margaret replied, taking Leandra by the arm to guide her out into the hallway off to the side. "It's about those Welby children. They're already proving to be quite a handful."

"Why? What happened?"

"Well, that little one—Brittney—she insists that you promised she could be an angel, and I've tried to explain to the child that my Philip wants to be an angel. Whatever you told her, you have to change it. Give her another part or something."

"I will not," Leandra countered, her tone firm. "I told you at dinner the other night that Brittney was going to be an angel. You didn't object then."

Margaret shrugged. "I didn't want to bring it up in front of everyone."

Meaning she knew better than to bring it up, Leandra figured. Colleen would have set her straight right away, and Margaret knew it. Well, Leandra was Colleen's only daughter, and just as assertive. But not nearly as sweet and patient.

"Margaret, listen to me. I promised that child she could be an angel in this pageant and that's exactly what she'd going to be. I won't break my promise."

Margaret gave her an indignant stare. "Not even for your own nephew. Philip will be heartbroken if he doesn't get to be an angel."

Leandra lifted her gaze heavenward to ask for patience. "I don't want to disappoint Philip, either." Trying to figure out what to do, she threw up her hands. "We can certainly have more than one little angel. We'll have a whole chorus of angels, with Philip and Brittney being the smallest ones. How's that?"

Margaret didn't seem too pleased. "Well, I wanted him to be the *only* little angel. I just thought he'd be so cute, you know?"

Leandra had to smile. "He is cute, Margaret, and I'm sure he'll be a wonderful asset to the pageant. But I promised Brittney. Remember, Philip has a large, loving family to support him. Brittney deserves that chance, too. We can be her church family, and support her efforts as well."

"Oh, all right." Margaret waved a hand as she pranced away. "But I'm warning you, I won't put up with any foolishness from those three country bumpkins."

Leandra had to check herself or she would have grabbed her sister-in-law to give the woman a good shake.

"Lord, grant me patience and understanding," she whispered as she pivoted to leave again. Then she remembered she was supposed to let someone know where she'd be, just in case any problems came up.

And with Margaret's attitude regarding the Welby children, Leandra knew there would surely be more to come.

Already, this little project was turning out to be more complicated than she'd ever imagined.

One of the main complications was waiting for her in the churchyard. Nathan stood talking quietly with Reverend Powell while Honeyboy enjoyed munching on the dry grass surrounding the prayer garden.

Why did her breath seem to leave her body every time she was near Nate? Why did he look so natural standing there, that enticing grin on his handsome face, his trusty steed nearby? Why did it seem as if she'd been waiting for just such a man all her life?

Ridiculous, she told herself as she made her way down the meandering pathway leading to the tranquil gardens and church grounds. Towering oaks swayed in the morning breeze, loosening yet more fall leaves. They made a swishing sound as Leandra trudged through them.

At least she'd had the good sense to dress casually today. Her lace-up boots, jeans and long sweater fit right in with Nate's standard attire. And Reverend Powell never bothered to dress up, except for Sundays. He, too, was wearing a flannel shirt along with khaki pants.

I could get used to this casual atmosphere, Leandra thought as the two men glanced up and waved to her. When she'd first gone to the big city, all she'd wanted was to be sophisticated and elegant. She'd abandoned jeans and flannel and anything else that might appear casual and country.

But, it didn't seem half-bad now. It felt right, here in this beautiful old town.

And casual took on a whole new look on Nate Welby. He could easily pose for one of her ad campaigns.

That thought reminded her that she was no longer in advertising. She no longer had the sophistication and elegance of being in the big city. But she would go back soon, she promised herself. And this time, she'd be a little wiser and a whole lot smarter. And successful once again.

After everything that had happened, she didn't feel so successful right now, however.

"Why the frown?" Reverend Powell asked her as he held out his arms to greet Leandra with a bear hug. "It's too pretty a day for that stoic face, Leandra."

"Hello, Reverend," she said, smiling in spite of her worries. "I'm just working through some concerns, but it's so good to see you again."

"Good to have you back home with us," the Reverend replied. "And in charge of the big pageant, too. You always did like to stay busy. But don't forget to enjoy this time with your family, too."

"She's probably frowning because of me," Nate interjected, a puzzled look settling on his face. "I was late to work on my first day. And I don't think our Miss Leandra here fancies people who show up late."

"You had a good reason," Leandra said, hoping to convey her understanding. "But I do hope you can get that truck fixed."

"It's just the fan belt. I'll pick one up at the auto parts store," Nate countered. Then he shrugged. "Don't worry, Honeyboy needed the exercise, and Mr. Tuttle hauled my tools in his truck."

Leandra nodded, then lifted a brow. "Remind me to thank Mr. Tuttle later."

Reverend Powell gave them an astute grin. "Well, I sure am glad to see Nate back at church for a change—horse and all."

Nate acknowledged that comment with a slight nod. Then he gave Leandra his full attention, smiling sweetly at her. "Ready to get started?"

"Yes." She turned back to the Reverend. "I told Mr. Crawford I'd be over at city hall if anyone needed me. I have my cell phone, but in case I miss a call, or you hear—"

"Don't worry. I'll take a message," the Reverend said, turning to head back to his office. "You two kids have fun."

Fun was the farthest thing from Leandra's mind. She felt Nate's presence as surely as the wind and the sun.

Business, she told herself. This is business. And she'd learned not to ever again mix business with pleasure.

* * *

"So, here are the plans. I'm not sure who designed the original set but the props are old and need repairing and repainting, and some of them need to be done over from scratch. We're way behind, so feel free to change things to suit your own interpretation—that is as long as it fits in with the script."

Nathan leaned back against the long conference table, crossing his arms over his chest as he watched Leandra. She moved around like a little bird, flittering and fluttering, fussing and fixing.

"Hey, calm down. It'll get done."

"Will it?" she asked through a laugh that sounded more like a choking spell. "I'm beginning to have my doubts. I don't know why they waited until the last minute to get going on this, but—"

"But it will get done," he repeated, looking down at her. "That is, if you relax long enough for me to ask you a few questions."

She stopped then, bringing a hand up to push that irresistible hair away from her flushed face, her dark eyes dancing to a standstill. "Oh, I'm sorry. What questions do you have?"

"Are you married?"

She skidded like a cat caught in a paper box. "Mr. Welby, you know I'm not married. I mean, your daughter asked me to be her mommy the other day and I would have certainly mentioned it if I were already attached to someone." She stopped, looked down at her boots, pushed her hair back again. "Well...you under-stand what I mean, I'm sure."

"I'm sure," he repeated, grinning. "Didn't mean to upset you. It's just that you seem so...single."

Leandra looked up then, giving him a chance to see the little flash of fire in her eyes. "Single? I seem *single*." She tossed her hair off her face. "And what's that supposed to mean?"

Nate turned to stare down at the plans spread out on the table. The nativity scene, the Christmas trees, the stars, the doves and angels—all meant to be cut out of plywood—lay there in a flat uncluttered pattern against the table, waiting to be created, to be shaped into some-thing special, something with meaning.

"You're all business," he said, still looking over the patterns and shapes. "All energy and fire. All stressed-out and high-strung. Most people I know who act like that are workaholics, and usually they're single since they don't have time for any type of personal relation-ships." He wanted to tell her he knew firsthand about working all the time, but instead he stopped, pulled a hand down his jawline. "And it just seems this project needs a calming touch. It is all about peace and tran-quillity, after all. Are you sure you're up to this?"

She was mad now. He could see it in the little pink spots underneath the bridge of freckles moving across her pert nose. He could see it in the tapping of her booted foot and in the way she let her hands slide down to her hips in a defiant stance.

"I think I can handle things, thank you," she said, her

gaze moving over him then back to the plans. "Back in Houston, I was in charge of several very large advertising accounts, Mr. Welby. National accounts."

She stressed the *national* part. "It's Nate," he told her. "Call me Nate. And I didn't mean to offend you. But, lady, you're not in Houston anymore, and you need to take a deep breath and learn to enjoy yourself."

She huffed a deep breath. "*You're* telling me to enjoy myself. *You,* of all people? Don't you work a lot of long hours, too? Don't you have obligations, things that have to get done?"

"Yeah, I guess I do," he said, dropping his gaze back to the patterns. Well, she'd surely nailed him there. And he didn't have a quick comeback. Except to say, "But I don't get all flustered over every little thing. Mostly, I just go about my business, and I do take a minute here and there to enjoy life." Even as he said it, though, he knew that wasn't really the truth. And he knew he was picking on her to ease his own nagging guilt.

"That does it," Leandra told him, pointing a finger at the table. "I *am* enjoying myself, and my status, married or single, is none of your concern, and *if* I seem a little nervous, it's because I like having things in order and on time. And while we're standing here chewing the fat, things are not happening, Mr. Welby—"

"Nate."

"Nate. Nate! I need you to concentrate on making some sense out of this mess. Can you possibly do that for me? Can you actually get started on this—today?"

Nate lifted his hands, palms out, to ward off another

tirade. "Sure. Sure. Just trying to help. Just wanted you to take it slow." He shrugged then. "I guess I just wanted you to know that it'll be all right. I'm here and I'll get my part done on time. And if you need help with any of the rest, just let me know. I thought after our talk yesterday, that we were friends, kinda."

She actually looked sheepish, then her skin blushed like a fresh pink rose. "Well, all right. Thank you… Nate. And I'm sorry if I seemed a bit snappish. We are friends, of course, and I do appreciate your willingness to help." Then she whirled like a little tornado. "I think I'd better go check on the children."

"Good idea. I'll round up the plywood and my tools and get these patterns cut, at least. Check back with me in a few hours and we'll see where things stand."

But he already knew exactly where things stood between his new boss and him. At an impasse, obviously.

She nodded, already heading for the exit.

Nate watched her stomping away, then moved a hand over the pattern of a dove lifting out toward the heavens. "Well, *Mr. Welby,* you sure have a fine way with the ladies. Scared that one right out the door."

Which was just fine with him, Nate told himself.

He surely didn't need someone as complicated and high-strung as Leandra Flanagan messing with his head.

And yet, the scent of her perfume lingering in the air did just that.

Three hours later Leandra returned to the work space that had been set up for Nate behind city hall. With worktables and extra, needed tools provided by Reverend Powell and the city, Nate had gone to work on cutting out the patterns for the backdrop of the pageant.

But Leandra didn't find him working.

Instead, he was in the churchyard, apparently giving all the children a ride on Honeyboy.

And little Philip was up on the big horse right now, laughing merrily as Nate guided the gentle gelding around in a wide circle.

Frustrated beyond measure, Leandra felt her blood pressure rising. Everyone said Nate was such a hard worker. But did the man ever do any work!

Before she could scream her wrath, she stopped to watch Nate with the children. He smiled that lazy smile and cooed softly to Honeyboy, all the while assuring little Philip that he was safe up on the big animal. Even Margaret seemed to be grudgingly captivated as she watched her son's beaming smile.

"Hey, Mommy," Philip shouted, waving as he went round and round on the horse, Nate taking him through a slow canter.

"Hello, darlin'," Margaret called back. "I want to get a picture of you up there." She pulled a camera out of her big purse and snapped a couple of shots. Turning to Leandra, she said, "Isn't that just adorable?"

"Sure is," Leandra replied, her gaze scanning the crowd. "But Mr. Welby—Nate—is supposed to be working on the cutouts."

Margaret took another picture, then waved a hand. "Oh, he did. Look over there."

Leandra turned in the direction of the prayer garden, then let out a gasp. "Oh, my."

They were all there. The Santa kneeling over the baby Jesus, the angels, the doves, the Christmas trees, the squares that would become gift boxes. They had yet to be painted and decorated, but the patterns that had been flat and lifeless a couple of hours ago where now all cut out and ready to be finished. And Nate had them all lined up, as if waiting for her inspection.

"So the man can move fast when he has to."

Margaret lifted her brows. "What?"

"Oh, nothing," Leandra said, her gaze shifting back to Nate. "Just mumbling to myself."

Margaret watched Leandra as she watched Nate. "He's handsome, don't you think?"

"I didn't notice," Leandra replied with a shrug.

"Well, maybe you should," Margaret countered, an impish smile spreading across her porcelain complexion.

Before Leandra could find a retort, Philip called to her. "Aunt Lea, come ride with me."

"Oh, that's okay, baby," Leandra said, waving him on as she walked up closer. "You go ahead."

Nate turned then, his gaze sending her a definite challenge. "Oh, come on, Aunt Lea. You're not scared of horses, now are you?"

"Of course not," Leandra replied, acutely aware that all the children were watching her. And just to prove to the man that she could relax and actually enjoy herself, she strutted across the yard to pet Honeyboy. "I just don't feel like riding today, that's all."

"Nonsense," Nate said. Turning to Philip, he added, "Hold on now."

And before Leandra knew what was happening, Nate lifted her up in his arms and forced her up onto the horse, behind little Philip. She had no choice but to gracefully settle back in the saddle, the imprint of his big hands lifting her, and his face so close to her own clicking through her mind like one of Margaret's pictures.

While she glared down at him in shock, Nate leaned close, grinning up at her. "As pretty as a lamb and as light as a feather."

Leandra's mouth fell open, only to snap back shut. Oh, this would never do. How could she work with this man over the next few weeks? He was a major distraction.

And she did not like distractions.

But as she held on to Philip and let Nate guide them around, with all the children and their parents clapping and laughing, and Margaret snapping pictures, she had to smile.

And Nate smiled right back up at her.

Well, at least she'd managed to accomplish one of her goals today. She'd told Nate she was enjoying herself, working on this project. At the time, however, she'd been too keyed up over being around him for that to be a true statement.

But he'd done his work, kept his part of the bargain

and all in all, things had gone pretty smoothly with the rest of the rehearsals and the million other things that had needed her attention. It had been a productive day.

So right now, she had to admit in spite of how the man made her palms sweaty and her heart shaky, she *was* enjoying herself. Way too much.

Chapter Five

The Wednesday before Thanksgiving dawned dark and cloudy with the promise of rain, which didn't help the mood of Leandra's little band of actors, directors, stage hands and general all-around volunteers.

The production was going well, over all, however. They'd gotten through the first few rough rehearsals enough to iron out the kinks and get everyone accustomed to their parts. Since it was mostly singing and a few one-liners, Leandra felt good about things so far.

When she *could* concentrate on *things*.

Never one to daydream, for the last three days she found herself constantly wondering what Nate had been doing. Had he finished painting all the Christmas trees? She'd better go check, just to make sure he'd capped them off with the glistening gold-tipped snow like she'd suggested. Or maybe he hadn't understood her instructions about the huge gift boxes. Maybe he wouldn't remember that she wanted one gold-and-white striped and another red-and-green edged.

Any excuse to just be near the man.

"I've really got to stop this," she told herself as she headed around the corner to just get a peek at Nate's work area—just in case he needed her—just to see what he was doing today.

What he was doing was sitting on a bench, just sitting there staring at his finished products.

Leandra had to give the man credit. He'd worked hard, and in just three days, he'd finished most of his assignment. She knew he'd taken some of the pieces home with him to work on at night. Layla had told Leandra this in a huffy voice, claiming her daddy had stayed out in the barn until well past midnight all week, painting "those big Christmas things." And just when he'd finally taken a week off from work, too.

Those big Christmas things now represented a beautiful backdrop to the pageant. In Nate's talented hands, the shapes and figures had taken on a new life. He'd taken the basic patterns and turned them into art—his colors were brighter than Leandra had imagined them in her mind, his angels more holy, his doves more alive with bright white-and-gold flight, his trees almost touchable, close to smelling like real cedar.

Everything was perfect.

Except the expression on Nate's face.

"What's wrong?" Leandra asked as she came to sit down beside him on the stone bench.

"I'm finished," he said simply, his tone quick and resolved. "Nothing left for me to do here."

"And that's a bad thing?"

He didn't look at her. Made it a point not to look at her. "I like to keep busy."

"Now who's the workaholic?" she asked, nudging him with her elbow, a teasing edge in her voice.

When he looked up, however, any further teasing remarks vanished. Leandra had never seen such a tragic, sad look in a man's eyes. It frightened her, touched her.

"Nate?"

"I'll be okay," he said at last, his hands clutched together almost as if in prayer, his head bowed. "I get like this when I'm done with a project." He sat silently for a minute, then said, "Sometimes, when I'm working on a construction job and we're finished—say it's a new house, I stay after everyone else is gone, just to get the full image of that house in my mind. But I don't see the wood and beams, the new windows and fresh brick."

He looked up at her then, his amber-colored eyes reflecting the storm clouds rising above them. "I see children running in the grass. I see a woman planting flowers by the front door. I see a husband coming home to his family from a good day's work. Safe, warm, happy, together. That's what I see with each house. That's what I want for each house."

Leandra swallowed, but for the life of her, she couldn't tear her gaze from him. He'd just spoken of such beautiful things—the things most common people wanted in their lives—with such a great pain in his eyes, that it hurt physically to look at the man. And yet, she couldn't look away. And she didn't know what to say.

So she just sat there, her gaze locked with his. Then

something passed between them on that stone bench, with all of Christmas spread out before them in golden bright colors.

Before she knew what was happening, she took his hand in hers. "Nate, I was wrong about you. I didn't think you'd get this done, but…it's absolutely beautiful. Everything is beautiful."

"And now I'm through," he said again, a trace of panic threading through his words. "Time on my hands."

And then she understood.

Most people who worked too much were working toward the future and success. But Nathan Welby was working against the past, and what he deemed his failure. Other people worked to brag, to validate what they'd accomplished, while Nate only worked to hide, and to forget what he'd lost.

And yet, out of that work, he created beauty. Only he couldn't see that. Or maybe he did; maybe it hurt him to see such beauty and know he'd lost part of his soul.

She had misjudged him. His slow and easy ways were an ingrained part of his nature, but he fought against that nature by staying busy with steady work that kept him from having any quiet time to remember.

Leandra longed to convince him that he had a future, a future bright with the promise and hope of his children, but she didn't know if she had that right, since she'd always put her career ahead of marrying and settling down. And she certainly wasn't the person to preach platitudes to him, since she'd made such a mess of her own life.

But she could pray for him, ask God to help this gentle giant, this sensitive, easygoing man, to find his way home again, for the sake of his children.

And she could quit looking at him as a distraction, and start looking toward him as a friend in need.

"Nate, I—"

Children, gold-hued children, laughing and shoving to reach their father, interrupted her next words. Layla, Brittney and Matt all scrambled around them like an explosion of bright burning sparklers.

"Daddy, I tried on my wings this morning," Brittney told him, hopping on his lap to give him a kiss. "They fit perfect-ity."

"They fit *perfectly*," Layla corrected, the old eye-roll exaggerating her words.

Matt clamored for his own bragging rights. "And my shepherd robe fit real good. Miss Leandra's mom made it for me. She's nice."

"That was nice of her," Nate said, a smile chasing the gloom away from his features. "And, Britt, I can't wait to see you as an angel, sugar."

"Can we go home now?" Layla asked, pushing long blond strands of hair out of her eyes. "You promised you'd cook a turkey on the grill for tomorrow, remember?"

"I do remember," Nate said, his gaze locking with Leandra's. "We like smoked turkey sandwiches."

"On Thanksgiving?" Leandra couldn't hide the

shock in her voice. "What about dressing and gravy, pumpkin pie and cranberry sauce, all the trimmings?"

"We don't got trimmings," Brittney said, twisting to hug her father close. "We only got bread and turkey, and a bag of cookies."

"I'm not much of a cook," Nate said on a sheepish note. "Except with a barbecue grill, of course."

Leandra didn't know how the next words came out of her mouth, but somehow they popped out before she could think it through. "Then you can all come to my house for Thanksgiving. We'll surely have more than bread and turkey. And I know my parents would love to have you."

Amid the cheers and high fives of his children, Nate gave her a look caught somewhere between panic and pleasure.

"Are you sure about this?"

"I'm not so sure about this," Leandra told her mother early the next morning. "I should have asked you first, Mom."

"Don't be silly, honey." Colleen moved around her big kitchen with the efficiency of years of putting on big spreads for her family. "We have plenty of food, more than enough, and you couldn't very well let that adorable family have sandwiches on Thanksgiving, now could you?"

"I didn't want that," Leandra said, shaking her head. "I guess I forgot how lucky we are, to be such a close-knit clan. Even when we fight, we've still got each other. The Welbys don't have anybody, really."

"Well, now they have us, thanks to your kindness," Colleen replied as she handed Leandra a dozen boiled eggs. "Make the deviled eggs for me, honey. You should be safe with that project."

Leandra made a face. "I guess I need to learn to cook."

"Might come in handy one day," her mother teased.

Leandra watched as Colleen mixed the ingredients for her famous corn bread dressing. She loved watching her mother in the kitchen. Colleen always had a peaceful smile centered on her face when she was cooking.

Leandra longed for that kind of serenity, wished she could be more like her mother, but it just wasn't in her nature to be…serene. She'd always been scattered, anxious, in a hurry. And for what?

What was she searching for?

"How are the eggs coming?" Colleen asked with a mother's knowing grin. "Now, don't worry about your brothers, Lea. This is my house and if I say we're having company for Thanksgiving dinner, then that's the final word on the subject."

"If you say so," Leandra replied, cracking and peeling eggs in a hurry. "But we both know they'll resent this—they do like to be clannish at times."

"Well, they can get glad in the same boots they got mad," Colleen said. "I'll have no fighting and squabbling on Thanksgiving."

"Who's squabbling?" Jack came in from the den, carrying a baking dish. "Here's the macaroni and cheese. Now what's up? You two fighting over deviled eggs?"

"No, we were just discussing dinner," Colleen told him as Margaret came through the arched doorway. "We're having guests."

"Oh?" Margaret gave her mother-in-law a questioning look. "Anyone we know?"

"I believe you do know them," Colleen replied, an impish spark in her eyes. "The Welby family."

Margaret's smile turned as sour as the pickle relish Leandra was dumping into the deviled egg mix. "What? Surely you're joking?"

"I don't joke about dinner," Colleen replied, her smile intact. "Leandra invited the Welby family here for Thanksgiving dinner, so Margaret, be a dear and set four extra plates—one at the main table and three at the children's table, please."

"You're putting those three heathens with my little Philip and Corey, and Michael's Cameron? They'll ruin the boys' dinner."

"How so?" Colleen said, her dark brows lifting.

"Well, I don't know. They'll probably throw food and...they might not have the best of manners. They are just so...rowdy."

"Then we'll just have ourselves a rowdy Thanksgiving this year," Colleen said. "Set the table, Margaret. Time is ticking away."

"Well, I never." Margaret slammed the dinner rolls she'd baked from scratch down on the counter. "Leandra, I don't know what's gotten into you. First, giving that little girl the best angel part, now this. What's next—you going out to their house to hang Christmas decorations?"

"Now there's a thought," Leandra replied dryly, amused at her sister-in-law's antics. "Margaret, they were all alone and planning on having sandwiches. How would you feel if that were your situation?"

Margaret held the plates she'd grabbed from the cabinet to her chest. "Well, I'd be sad and lonely, of course. Oh, all right, I guess what's done is done. We can't un-invite them, after all. But I'm going to keep my eye on those three."

"That's the giving spirit," Colleen said, all the while stirring the big pot of dressing mix. "Now, troops, let's get this together."

With that, she started issuing orders to everyone who happened to walk in the door. "Howard, honey, could you make sure there's enough wood for a fire? And Michael, make sure we have enough chairs—get some of those foldable chairs from the garage, dear. Kim, you can mix the tea and make sure we have enough juice for the children. Jack, don't sit down just yet. We need you to check on the turkeys—they've been in the cooker since dawn—just about time to pull them off to cool down. Richard—now where is Richard?—he needs to put the ice in the coolers and get the drinking glasses lined up. Oh, and everyone, we're having four more for dinner. The Welbys are joining us, and I'll hear no protests, whines, moans, nor will I tolerate any rude, unneighborly behavior. Is that clear?"

Amid the nods, surprised looks, and "Yes, ma'ams" Colleen called out, "Oh, and whose turn is it to carve?"

"Mine, I believe," Mark said as he entered the kitchen and let out a long sigh. "Ah, the smells of home and hearth. Mom, you've done it again."

"What's that, son?"

"Made me glad to be a Flanagan," Mark said as he managed to sidestep several fast-moving bodies to give his mother a peck on the cheek. "Happy Thanksgiving, Mom."

Leandra stood back, in awe of the organized chaos surrounding her. At one time, she'd hated this—hated the house full of people, talking and walking all at the same time, hated being shoved here and there by too many brothers and too much commotion, hated not having a private moment to herself. But today, today, she was so very glad to be right in the middle of the Flanagan clan. Safe at home. Loved. Centered.

How had she walked away from all of this? And why?

She watched as her father held little Carissa and made the baby bubble over with laughter. Watched as Cameron and Philip ran through the den, little Corey right behind them, chasing a remote control car that threatened to uproot anyone who got in its path. Watched as Margaret and Jack chuckled and whispered husband-and-wife nothings to each other as they set the table together. Watched as Michael leaned over to kiss Kim, a special quietness in the look meant only for his wife. Watched as Mark recited horrible on-the-spot poetry out loud—"Ode to Giblets"—while he polished the carving knives.

Her family was quirky, unpredictable, clannish—and so special to her. And yet, she still felt set apart, detached almost, from the close-knit group. Where was the missing link?

Then she looked up to find Nathan Welby and his three children, huddled in the middle of the big den with confused, afraid looks on their faces.

"Nate," she said as she rushed toward them, so glad to see them here.

He looked directly at Leandra, then smiled that lazy smile. "We knocked," he said, "but I guess no one heard us. Can we come in?"

"Of course," Leandra said, smiling as she took the platter of turkey Nate had brought.

"Since we had it anyway…" he explained, shrugging as he handed her the heavy foil-wrapped plate.

"It smells wonderful," she told him. "C'mon in."

Layla and Matt hung back, shy, while Brittney rushed forth to get involved with the remote control car race. Philip immediately grinned at her and sent the car crashing against her white tights.

"Wanna pway?" he asked while he rammed the revving vehicle against her black Mary Jane shoes.

"Can I?" Brittney asked, her little hands on her hips. "Can I have a turn steering?"

"Guess so." Philip shrugged, then handed her the controls.

Nate smiled as they took off together. "Your nephew's a cuteypie."

"And walking trouble," Leandra said in a low whisper, a grin covering her face. "But I think Brittney can
handle him."

"She can hold her own, that's for sure," Nate replied.

Wanting to make them feel comfortable, Leandra
urged Matt and Layla into the kitchen. "Mom, look
who's here."

"Well, hello there," Colleen said, wiping her hands
on her Kiss the Cook apron as she came around the
long counter. "Nathan, it's good to see you again. It's
been a while."

"Yes, ma'am." Nate extended his hand to Colleen's.

"And Layla, how are you, darling?"

"Fine," Layla replied, a shy smile turning her face
from pouty to pretty. At Nate's pointed look, she added,
"Do you need some help, Mrs. Flanagan?"

"How nice of you to offer." Colleen glanced around.
"You can fold the napkins and help Margaret put them
around the tables."

Layla nodded, then took the white paper napkins
Colleen offered.

"And Mr. Matt? What would you like to do?"

Matt shrugged, then tucked his hands in the pockets
of his baggy jeans. "I don't know."

Just then Richard came in, carrying pies and soft
drinks. "Hello, everyone." If he was surprised to find
Nathan Welby and his children standing in his moth-

er's kitchen, he didn't let on. "Hey, Matt, Nate. How's it going?"

"Fine." Nate shook Richard's hand. "Need help there?"

"I sure do," Richard said, handing Nate a box. "I bake these pies at my grocery store and so I brought two to help Mom out. We need to pop them in the refrigerator." He turned to Matt then. "And buddy, I think you can set these colas on the counter then help me check on the turkey and ham—see if they need to come off the grill?"

"Sure," Matt said. "I love ham."

Much later, after all the greetings and small talk, Howard said grace, then the dinner progressed with lots of conversation and eating, one small food fight between Brittney and Philip, and then a whole lot of groaning from overstuffed tummies. When they were finished eating, Colleen gathered the older children up and took them for a nature walk in the big backyard, while Margaret and Kim got the little ones settled down for their afternoon naps. As everyone else gathered around the big television in the den to watch football, Leandra found herself alone with Nate in the kitchen.

"I'm glad you came," she said, then laughed. "Did I already say that?"

"It's nice to hear it again," he replied. "It's good to be around a big family. I—I never had that."

"Really?" Wanting to know more, she handed him a slice of pecan pie and a fresh cup of coffee, then led him to a quiet corner of the breakfast nook where a small built-in storage seat was nestled underneath the bay window. "Where is your family, anyway?"

"I never really had one," he told her as he gazed into the leaping flames of the big kitchen fireplace, the music of a half-time show on the nearby television blaring in the background. "I—I lived in a children's home most of my life."

Not understanding at first, Leandra stared over at him. "You—"

"I was an orphan. The Children's Home took care of me until I was old enough to get out on my own."

Leandra felt that little warm spot in her heart growing to a fiery heat inside her very soul. "I can't imagine," she said, wishing there was something better to say.

"No, I don't suppose you can," Nate replied, looking back into the den where her relatives sat around in complacent camaraderie. "You're lucky to have such a big, loving family."

"I was thinking the same thing earlier today, but I didn't always think that," she admitted, mortified that she'd often wished to be an only child. "But I'm learning to appreciate them."

"That's good." He glanced back at the fire. "I used to dream of a family like this. Loud, noisy, pushy, fun. I guess that's why I don't always discipline the children the way I should. I like having them in the house, like the noise and shouting. And I like knowing they will always have a home. At least, I'm trying to give them one."

"You're doing a pretty good job," Leandra said, proud of his quiet strength. "Underneath all their bluster, they really are sweet children."

"All things considered, I reckon so," he replied. Then he said, "Hey, don't go feeling sorry for me. I'm okay. The people at the home were good to me until it was time for me to move on. I had some rough years as a teenager, but then I grew up and tried to be responsible, and for a while, I knew what it meant to have a real home."

"You mean Alicia?"

"Yes. She was my heart, my home."

He grew quiet then.

"Well, you still have your children," Leandra said. "They are so beautiful, Nate. And they are a part of you and Alicia."

Just then a loud crash from the front hallway, followed by a wail of childlike pain, brought them both to their feet.

"I have a bad feeling about this," Nate said as he urged Leandra toward the noise. "I think one of my beautiful little angels just destroyed something."

Chapter Six

"Well, we almost made it through the day without any catastrophes," Nate told Leandra an hour later as he headed his family toward his waiting truck. "And I mean it, Leandra. I'm going to replace your mother's vase."

She waved a hand in the air. "I told you, it was old."

He glanced up at the well-maintained white two-storied house. "Yeah, and probably priceless."

Leandra didn't miss Nate's wistful look or the resignation in his words. Based on what he'd told her earlier, he'd never had a home of his own until now. With a little fixing up, his home could be every bit as lovely and traditional as her parents' one-hundred-year-old rambling house, but Nate probably still wouldn't feel the kind of security her family had always taken for granted. That chance had been snatched from him when Alicia had died. It would be hard to make him see that most of her family wouldn't judge him as harshly as he seemed to be judging himself.

Trying to reassure him, she said, "No, it held more of

a sentimental value. She got it from the local discount mart years ago."

Leandra didn't have the heart to tell him that she'd given the white ceramic vase to her mother for Christmas when Leandra was around twelve years old, or that it had been bought and paid for with ten dollars of hard-earned allowance money. That didn't really matter right now.

But it mattered to Nate.

He lowered his head, then kicked a cowboy boot in the dirt. "I don't know if I can find one exactly like it, but I'll come up with something."

"That's not necessary."

"I insist."

Leandra knew he'd make good on his promise, too. Nate had been embarrassed to find Brittney standing in the front hallway, holding the pieces of what had once been a white vase full of silk mums and fall leaves.

Before Brittney could stop crying and explain, Margaret had rushed into the foyer to grab little Philip, who lay kicking and screaming on the floor as he held a hand to the goose egg on his forehead.

After they'd all calmed down, Brittney had explained between hiccuping sobs that they'd finished their walk and decided to play hide-and-seek, and she'd accidentally bumped into Philip as he'd rounded the corner by the stairs. Philip had somehow been propelled into the round walnut pedestal table centered in the big hallway, and in an effort to stop himself, he'd grabbed at air. Instead, his hand had hit the tall vase, causing it to topple over and fall to the tiled floor.

Colleen had come up on the whole scene, explaining that Philip had run ahead of them, hoping to hide. But when he'd come around the corner, he hadn't known they'd be just opening the front door.

"You really don't have to leave," Leandra told Nate now, wishing Margaret hadn't made such a scene about the tiny bump on Philip's head. "Philip is all right. He's had worse scrapes."

Nate turned, a smirk on his handsome face. "Yeah, but your sister-in-law doesn't think too highly of me and my brood right now, so I think it's best we head on back home. It's getting late and I've got some work to finish up anyway."

"You said you weren't going to work today," Layla told him before stomping toward the truck.

Before Nate could reply, Brittney tugged at his jeans. "I'm sorry, Daddy. I didn't mean to bump into him. It was an…accee-dent."

Layla opened the passenger side door. "Yeah, and you're an *accident* waiting to happen. Get in, Brittney."

Brittney's blue eyes teared up yet again. "I said I was sorry."

"Brittney, honey, it wasn't your fault," Leandra said, rushing around the truck to take the little girl in her arms. "Philip said you were both running and that you just bumped together. You can't help it if he hit the table with his head."

"And knocked the vase over with his hand," Matt

reminded them, clearly glad he wasn't the one in trouble this time.

Leandra remembered after the walk, Matt had stayed out in the backyard, talking to Howard. The two had hit it off immediately, since they both had a passion for fishing.

"I fell down, too," Brittney replied, her big eyes solemn. "But then I got up to pick up the vase parts."

"Are you okay?" Leandra asked, her eyes scanning the child for any signs of bleeding or bruises.

"Just hurt my bottom," Brittney admitted, her cherubic lips turned down. "I don't want to go home, though."

"We have to leave, sunshine. It's late and everyone's a little tired," Nate told her. "Now let Miss Leandra buckle you in tight. And tell her you had a very good time."

"I had a very good time," Brittney echoed. "And I still don't want to go home."

"Will you come and see me again?" Leandra asked, giving the child a peck on the cheek.

Brittney smiled, then giggled. "Can I?"

"Why sure you can."

"Nate?"

Both Nate and Leandra turned to find Colleen and Howard coming down the steps.

"Wait. I have some leftovers for you," Colleen told him.

Nate herded Matt into the truck, then turned to Leandra's parents. "That's mighty nice, Mrs. Flanagan. But I don't think I could eat another bite."

He rubbed his completely flat stomach, causing Leandra to wonder how the man could pack away so much food and still look fit as a fiddle.

"Then save it for tomorrow," Colleen said, handing him a grocery bag filled with plastic containers of food. "We sure did enjoy having you and the children over."

Nate nodded, shifted his feet, then said, "We had a nice time, too. And I do apologize for the broken vase."

"It can be replaced," Colleen said. She glanced at Leandra with her own apologetic smile. The vase had been one of her mother's favorite things, but Leandra knew that her mother put people and their feelings ahead of material things. "Besides, my grandson is just as responsible for breaking it, even though his mother might not see it that way. But I was there and one child was coming from one way and the other from another way and they collided. It was an accident, plain and simple."

Nate shifted his feet again, then nodded. "Well, I still feel bad about the vase. But I appreciate the dinner and the leftovers."

"Y'all come back any time," Howard said, shaking Nate's hand. "And don't worry about the vase or Philip. His head is as hard as a fence post."

"Is his mama calmer now?" Nate said, a hesitant grin splitting his face.

"Margaret's a bit high-strung, but she'll be okay. She's rocking Philip to sleep in one of the bedrooms. Too much excitement." Howard winked then. "And I think my grandson has a crush on your Brittney."

"She's a heartbreaker," Nate admitted, smiling over at his youngest daughter.

And so is her father, Leandra thought. Every time Nate smiled, the whole world seemed to turn golden and sunny. He should smile more often. *And I should quit acting like a silly schoolgirl.*

Howard laughed, then leaned into the truck. "Matt, son, I meant what I said. Just give me a call and we'll go down to the pond and do a little fishing."

"Okay," Matt said, a shy smile cresting his face. "Thank you for showing me your boat and fishing reels."

After a wave goodbye, Leandra's parents went back inside. And Nate was still smiling that lazy, knowing smile. It was a mixture of embarrassed pride and sincere gratitude.

The late-afternoon air was crisp on Leandra's flushed cheeks as she gazed up at Nate. "They really are glad you came."

"Oh, they're just being polite. You have a very nice family."

"And we're working on Margaret," Leandra teased, poking at his arm. "Guess I'll see you Monday."

"After work," he reminded her. "It might be seven before I can get there."

"No problem. We'll be rehearsing every night between now and the week before Christmas. So you can finish up the set and work around us, if you don't mind."

"I don't mind at all."

"And I'll have your check waiting for you tomorrow night," Leandra told him. "We appreciate you helping us out on your week off, Nate."

They stood silent for a minute, until Layla moaned and groaned inside the truck. "Can we just go home now?"

"She's pouting," Nate said underneath his breath. "Her siblings always embarrass her one way or another."

"She's at that age," Leandra reminded him. "My brothers used to embarrass me in the worst kinds of ways, too."

"They teased you a bit today, if I recall."

Leandra recalled, too. Somehow, her four brothers had managed to get in digs about her single status, her inability to cook, and the fact that she was very cranky in the morning. She'd be surprised if Nate ever talked to her again.

"Hey, I didn't believe a word they said," he told her now, his smile so sparkling and sure that she had to grin right back.

"Well, they were telling the truth—to a point. I like being single and I don't like to cook, but they exaggerated my shortcomings just a tad. I'm not too cranky after I have a cup of coffee."

"But you are a real city girl, aren't you?"

The question seemed so serious, she wasn't sure how to answer it. Maybe because right now, she didn't know the answer. She wasn't so sure about what she wanted from life anymore.

So she nodded. "Or so I thought."

He gave her a long stare, his bemused expression belying the serious gaze centered in his topaz eyes. "Right now, you look like you belong right here."

Leandra felt the heat rising to her skin, in spite of the cold November afternoon. "Do you think so?"

Nate leaned around the open truck door, close enough for her ears only. "Yep. You're all fresh-faced and dewy, like you've been on a long winter walk. You look like you're just waiting for someone to snuggle with on that window seat in your mama's kitchen."

Leandra became frozen to the spot, acutely aware of his eyes on her, of his gentle smile, of his lips, his hand stretched across the door handle.

To break the magnetic pull that seemed to be bringing him ever closer to her, she laughed and tossed a curl off her face. "It *is* chilly out here. The fire will feel good when I go back in."

"Then don't let me keep you," he replied, standing back as if he'd just now realized he'd been flirting shamelessly with her. "Go on inside and get warm."

Leandra *was* warm, too warm. But she shivered anyway and wrapped her arms across her midsection. "Well, goodbye then. See you later."

"Later." Nate gave her a reluctant look, then slid into the truck with his children.

Leandra watched as they took off up the highway, headed toward home and what looked to be a glittering winter sunset.

And she knew she'd never look at the window seat in her mother's kitchen in quite the same way.

Nate looked at the birdhouse one more time. He'd finished it late last night, and he had to admit, it had turned out better than he'd imagined. But would it be good enough for Leandra?

He wanted it to be pretty—for Leandra and her mother. It was a gift to thank them for their kindness last week at Thanksgiving, and to replace the broken vase.

And a good excuse to see Leandra again.

Who was he kidding, anyway? Nate tossed down the paintbrush he'd used to put the finishing touches on the birdhouse. He wasn't in the same league with Leandra Flanagan and her family, not by a long shot. Being around her and her prominent, well-mannered family only reminded Nate of all of his miseries and shortcomings. Reminded him too much of Alicia's family and their disdain for their son-in-law. That disdain now separated his children from their own grandfather, Davis Montgomery.

He'd never been good enough for Alicia's father, especially since her death. Then after Mrs. Montgomery had died, too…well, the old man hadn't made much effort to keep in touch. Which just proved Nate surely wasn't good enough to become involved with Leandra, either.

And yet…

The door to the old barn creaked open then. Layla stomped in, slamming the door shut behind her. "I figured you'd be out here."

"Hello, sunshine," Nate said, feeling a little more than guilty for daydreaming about a woman he couldn't have. He placed the birdhouse back amid the clutter of his worktable. "What's up?"

"Matt needs help with his math and Brittney's been coughing and sneezing. I think she's getting a cold, not that *you'd* care."

"Hey, wait a minute there." Nate turned to face his hostile daughter. "Layla, want to tell me what's eating at you? You've had a burr in your bonnet for weeks now."

Layla's sigh shuddered all the way down her slender body. "Daddy, why do you stay cooped up out here all the time?"

Nate glanced around, then back to his daughter. "I work out here, honey. You know that."

"You work at your regular job, during the day," she retorted. "Then you head out here as soon as we're finished with supper."

"I—I like working with my hands," Nate said, hating himself for the weak excuse.

Layla moaned, then turned to leave. "Well, it sure would be nice if you'd come in the house every now and then to check on your younger children. I get tired of having to be their keeper."

Nate halted her with a shout. "Stop right there. Young lady, you are not going to talk to me in that tone."

Layla looked down at the dirt floor. "I'm sorry, Daddy, but…it's the only way to get your attention sometimes. I'll go check on Britt, give her some cough syrup."

Nate stared at her for a minute, hoping to decipher all the hostility he saw on her frowning face.

"Thanks, honey," he finally said on a softer voice.

"I'll be in soon, I promise." He looked up at her then. "And Layla, I'm sorry, too."

She closed the door and left him standing there amid wood shavings and power saws. But he knew she was right. He needed to learn how to just sit still and listen to the sounds of his children. He'd tried so hard to do just that, but somehow he always wound up out here, or worse—taking on extra projects that kept him busy at least two or three nights a week.

He'd been depending on Layla too much lately. Making her watch her younger brother and sister, making her do housework, probably making her life miserable in the bargain.

Now that he stopped to think about it, she really didn't get out much and do the things most teenage girls did, such as go to the movies or the mall, or have sleepovers. No wonder she was sullen and pouting all the time.

"I'll make it better, Lord," he promised. "Somehow."

Maybe Leandra could help him there. She knew about girls. He'd ask her about taking Layla on a shopping trip, let Layla pick out a special Christmas present for herself.

But ultimately, Nate knew the task of seeing about his oldest daughter fell to him. If he started depending on Leandra and then she up and went back to Houston, that would only make matters worse for Layla.

Which only reinforced everything he'd been thinking about earlier. He had no business pursuing a relationship with Leandra right now. Maybe ever.

Especially since he'd made a big fool of himself on Thanksgiving by coming very close to kissing Leandra Flanagan right there by the truck. But she'd sure looked tempting, standing there in her baggy sweater and jeans, her wind-tossed hair falling across her freckled face.

He had to get over this need, this temptation to take things further with her. The woman had made it clear from the time she'd set foot on his property that she wasn't interested.

Yet…he sensed something there. It was in her eyes when she looked at him, in her smile when he walked into a room, in her every action. Was she fighting against this as much as he was?

And what was she really fighting? Leandra hadn't told him much about her big-city life or why she'd suddenly left it all to come home. Whatever had happened had apparently left a bitter taste in her mouth and given her cold feet about any new relationships.

He had to know. Wanted to know.

Maybe he'd just up and ask her.

Or maybe he'd just mind his own business and try to be a better father.

He looked down at the wooden birdhouse, thinking it wasn't good enough. Nothing he'd ever done had been good enough.

But right now, it was all he had to give.

"Can you stop by my truck?" Nate asked Leandra the next night after rehearsal. "I have something for you."

Leandra swallowed back the surprise she felt. He'd

been avoiding her since Thanksgiving. And now he had something to give her.

"What is it?" she asked, wondering why Nate had seemed so distant over the past few days.

They'd worked together, getting the set ready for dress rehearsals. The props looked great and Nate had just about finished designing the entire set. After Nate was done with his official chores each night, he'd sit and watch the production, or sometimes he'd wander off into the night. Several times, she'd found him outside, gazing at the stars. Sometimes she'd find him talking quietly to Reverend Powell.

That, of course, was a good sign and might explain his distance and quiet aloofness. Maybe Nate was wrestling with his faith; maybe he was quietly coming to a change in his life. And maybe that meant he didn't want any distractions from her.

"Nate," she said now, "what do you have for me? Another prop? Another complaint from Margaret? Or did you ride your horse to work again?"

"Nope, I didn't bring Honeyboy this time." His smile broke the tension lining his face. "I've finished most of the props and thankfully, Margaret hasn't had one complaint tonight, but hey, the night's young, right?"

Leandra laughed. His sense of humor might be dry and unexpected, but Nate got in his own zingers when he wanted to. And he was obviously beginning to understand that her high-strung, well-meaning sister-in-law would probably never be satisfied with anything in life.

"Margaret would complain if the moon shifted," Leandra said in a whisper, "but some people are happy even when they whine their way through life."

Nate nodded. "I know. And she was as cute as a button when she stomped that little foot the other night and demanded to know who stole Philip's angel wings."

"We had to break it to her gently that the angel himself left his wings in the little boys' room." Leandra grinned, then shook her head. "Even angels have to go to the bathroom sometimes."

Changing the subject, she poked at Nate's arm. "Okay, so what's this big surprise in your truck?"

"C'mon and I'll show you," he told her as he took her by the hand. "And hurry before my kids come charging out the door."

Realizing they'd be alone near the moonlit prayer garden, Leandra had to take a deep, calming breath. She'd never been alone in the dark with Nate, but she sure had thought about being alone with him. A lot.

"They're having cookies and hot chocolate," she managed to pant out. "They should be out in a few minutes."

"This won't take long," he said as they reached the truck. "I made you and your mama a little something, just to replace the vase."

Leandra watched as he hauled a bag out of the back of the pickup. "Nate, I told you—"

Whatever protest she'd been about to mount ended when she saw the object he offered over to her.

It was the most beautiful birdhouse she'd ever seen.

Chapter Seven

Leandra took the delicate wooden birdhouse in her hands, holding it up to the nearby streetlight so she could see the intricate design better.

"Nate, this is so pretty. Where did you get it?"

When he looked down, then shifted his booted feet, she suddenly realized he hadn't bought it.

"You made this?"

He nodded, still looking at the ground. "It's not a vase, but I thought it might be pretty sitting on your mama's hall table during Christmas."

"Absolutely," she replied, silly tears springing to her eyes. "She's going to love this."

"It's no big deal," he said, looking up at her at last. "I just wanted to do something to thank you both for your kindness."

Leandra turned the birdhouse around in her hands so she could again hold it up to the streetlight just over their heads, careful not to drop it on the concrete. It was about a foot wide at the top and just as tall, made of what looked like pinewood. The roof slanted down in an inverted V-shape to cover the square base. The whole thing had been varnished and lacquered until it shined, but what really caught her attention was the detailing.

The slanted roof was shingled with dainty little wood cutouts tipped in white paint that sparkled like freshly fallen snow. The door and two side windows held intricately designed wooden shutters also touched with brilliant white icicles. There was even a smaller window just below the roof, right above the little open door, which had a small window box complete with flowing ivy. And all around the roof, the snow-tipped eaves had been painted with tiny red poinsettias and holly berries, set against little green magnolia leaves.

It was exquisite.

"It reminds me of a cuckoo clock," she said.

"Without the cuckoo," Nate replied, smiling sheepishly. "I'm glad you like it."

"I love it," Leandra said, a catch in her voice. "How did you make all the little curlicues and swirls around the openings and roof? And the snow and flowers—they look so real."

"I have all kinds of jigsaws and sometimes I carve pieces by hand. I paint the designs on."

"Amazing. Sounds as if this isn't your first effort."

"I've made a few," he admitted. "It's just a hobby. Something to pass the time. I'm working on a version for each season of the year."

Leandra carefully placed the delicate house back in the bag. "This is much prettier than that old vase. My mother will be thrilled. I'll go put it in my car right now."

Nate took the bag from her. "Here, let's put it back in the truck for now." He placed the bag inside on the driver's seat. "Want to go for a walk?"

Caught completely off guard, Leandra didn't have time to come up with all the excuses she needed to refuse. "Sure."

He took her to the prayer garden in the churchyard just opposite the civic center.

But then, she'd known that's where he was going to take her, at least had hoped he'd do so.

"It's a pretty night," Nate said as he pulled her to a wooden bench with a tall, spindled back. "I like the quiet…sometimes."

"Me, too," she said, wondering what the "sometimes" meant. "These rehearsals sure do get noisy and disorganized. It's nice to find a moment to just sit."

"You're doing a good job, bringing all these folks together."

"I've had a lot of help," she told him. Sensing his need to talk, she prattled on herself. "You know, this production started as a small play in the church fellowship hall. But it became so popular, with so many people coming, they had to add extra performances and move it to the civic center."

"Well, the Wonderland of Lights sure brings in a lot of tourists."

Leandra looked down the street where millions of tiny white lights blinked and twinkled on the old courthouse centered in the middle of town. The Wonderland of Lights brought in thousands of people each year from Thanksgiving until New Year's Eve, and this year had been no exception. Already, Leandra had seen the buses and cars full of people coming each night to see the awesome Christmas decorations.

Not only was the courthouse strung with over 250 thousand lights, but just about every other building in Marshall, both commercial and residential, was also decorated. The civic center was decked in bright colorful lighted cutouts, and the church held a breathtaking lighted cross. There was also a lighted star over a nativity scene made completely from white wire figurines covered with the same tiny white lights that were hanging all over town. It was a Marshall tradition that had made the city famous throughout the world. Even the trees glistened with starlike white lights.

"It's impressive," Leandra said, remembering how she'd always enjoyed the lighted city during the Christmas season each year. "Have you and the children taken the official sightseeing tour yet?"

"No. I've been so busy—" He stopped, looked at the lights. "Guess I'll have to make time."

Leandra shivered as a cold night wind whipped around the corner. "The temperature's dropping."

Nate took off his lightweight denim barn jacket and wrapped it around her. "How's that?"

"Better," she said as she looked up at him. Even better than better, she thought to herself. The jacket still held his body warmth and the clean, woodsy scent of whatever soap he had used that day. She'd like to buy a gallon of the stuff, whatever it was.

Nate glanced over at her, his catlike eyes appraising her with that lazy, I'm-taking-my-own-sweet-time way. "You're almost lost in there."

"You're a lot taller than me," she said by way of explanation. "Thanks, though."

"You're welcome—though."

His eyes held hers, shimmering as brightly as any Christmas lights she'd seen. Mercy, when Nate Welby set his mind on flirting, it made her insides curl into ribbons of fire. She was very glad she was sitting down.

Then he tilted his head, his eyes centered on her face.

"You didn't thank me properly for the birdhouse," he said, his voice as gravelly as the pebbles beneath their feet.

"I didn't say thank you?" she asked, acutely aware of how he'd managed to wrap a long arm around her neck.

"You might have, but I was kinda hoping for a hug or maybe a peck on the cheek."

"Really?"

"Really."

"Is that why you brought me to this secluded bench?"

"Maybe." He shrugged, turning serious. "Or maybe I just wanted some peace and quiet."

"It's up to you," Leandra said, meaning it.

If Nate Welby wanted to kiss her, she wouldn't stop him, couldn't if her heart depended on it. But she wouldn't push him into something he might regret either. Because her heart also depended on that not happening. She couldn't bear his regrets.

"I reckon you're right there," he said. "Maybe I won't find any peace until I have kissed you."

Then he pulled her head around, his fingers gentle on her cheekbone, and touched his lips to hers, tentatively at first. After lifting his head to gauge her reaction, he kissed her again. This one took a little longer.

"You're welcome," he said as he let her go, his eyes holding hers in the glittering moonlight.

Leandra felt as if she'd been in a snowstorm and was now melting in a puddle of heat like Frosty the Snowman. Nate's kiss had dissolved her completely, making her a pile of helpless mush.

But apparently it hadn't brought him that peace he was seeking.

"I shouldn't have done that," he said as he stood up and pulled her with him. "I told myself not to do that, and look at me. I went and did it anyway."

Confused and hurt, Leandra asked, "Was kissing me that painful?"

He turned then, taking her back in his arms. "No, Leandra, it was that good. Too good."

"You're afraid of me, aren't you?" she asked, her tone full of disappointment.

"Yes, I guess I am," he admitted, his hand coming up to cup her chin. "But more than that, I'm afraid of myself. I don't want to mislead you, and I sure don't want to hurt you."

"Because you're not over Alicia?"

"Because I never did right by Alicia, and I don't know if I could do right by you."

Leandra's frustration brought her back to reality.

"That's ridiculous. You have to stop blaming yourself, Nate. If you don't, you'll never find any peace, any happiness."

"Maybe that's my punishment."

"Only if you let it be."

Then he turned the tables on her. "Yeah, well, what's your excuse? You left Houston for some reason. Want to tell me about that?"

"No, I don't," she said, thinking he sure would go to any lengths to take the attention away from his own problems.

Then he surprised her yet again. "I'd really like to know."

The soft edge in his husky voice almost did her in. But she wasn't ready to tell him the whole sordid story. "Let's just say that I had no choice."

Leandra could see the determination in his eyes, even in the muted moonlight. Nate wasn't going to let this go so easily.

"You left a high-paying job to come back home. That right there shows it must have been pretty bad. What with you being such a gung ho city girl and all."

Now he was becoming downright sarcastic. "Nate, I didn't just leave a job," she blurted out. "I left a bad relationship with an older man who happened to be my boss."

He didn't say a word. He just stared down at her.

Mortified, Leandra hung her head, refusing to look at him. "Satisfied?" she asked in a quiet whisper.

"Not nearly enough," he replied just as quietly.

With that, he let her go, then turned to head back to the truck. Leandra followed, emerging from the shadowy garden just as the Welby children came running toward their father. She quickly shoved Nate's jacket into his hands, thinking he'd never want to kiss her again. He'd looked both shocked and appalled by her revelation.

"What were you doing in the garden?" Layla asked, suspicion in every word.

"Were you kissing?" Matt chimed in, grinning from ear to ear.

"Does this mean Miss Leandra might be my new mommy?" Brittney shouted as she hopped from foot to foot. "I knew it, I just knew it."

"Hey, hey," Nate said, embarrassment making his voice shaky, "you three need to mind your own business and quit trying to rule my private life. To question number one, we were just talking. To question number two, Miss Leandra was thanking me for the birdhouse, and to question number three—Britt, Miss Leandra can't be your mother. We've talked about this, honey."

Brittney stopped hopping and glared up at the two adults standing stiffly in front of her. "But you said you liked her."

Nate sighed, then ran a hand across his chin. "I do like her." He turned to Leandra then. "A lot."

Leandra quickly quelled the relief flooding through

her system. Maybe Nate wouldn't judge her as harshly
as she tended to judge herself—something she realized
they had in common at least—but that didn't mean he'd
try kissing her again, either. She'd have to settle for
being liked. A lot.

"Then what's the holdup?" Brittney asked.

Layla moaned and turned to stare at her sister. "The
holdup, dummy, is that our daddy still loves our mama
and that Miss Leandra doesn't want to be stuck with
the three of us and that old, falling-down house we live
in. Now, can we please go home? I've got to study for
a spelling test."

"Layla, I think you owe Miss Leandra an apology,"
Nate said as he stomped after his retreating daughter.

"For what?" Layla asked in defiance. "It's the truth,
isn't it?" She looked from her father to Leandra, hope
warring with despair in her blue eyes.

Nate lifted his head toward the stars, as if asking
for God's wisdom and guidance. "I will always love
your mother, no matter what happens, sunshine," he
said. "And Miss Leandra will be going back to Houston after Christmas."

"So it is the truth?" Matt glanced at Leandra, his
gaze accusing. "I thought you liked us, too."

Leandra didn't know how to deal with this, especially after the exchange Nate and she had just had.
Bending down, she said, "Matt, I do care about all of
you, but, honey, being an adult is complicated. Your father is a wonderful man, but he still misses your mother.

And I don't know what I'm going to do after Christmas. But we both want what's best for all of you."

"You being my mama would be the bestest," Brittney said with a pout as she twisted a thick blond curl around her chubby finger. "Can't you please just think about it, Miss Lea?"

"It's Miss Leandra," Nate said, correcting her.

"Lea is fine," Leandra replied, turning to scoop Brittney up in her arms. "All of my friends call me Lea."

"And we are her friends," Nate told his children. "Let's just leave it at that for now, okay?"

Layla hurried to get inside the truck, slamming the door behind her. Matt gave Leandra another inquisitive look, then followed his sister. But Brittney held on to Leandra's neck and hugged her long and hard.

"I'm gonna talk to God one more time."

Leandra returned the hug, wishing with all her heart she could make this sweet child understand that she was asking too much—of both her father and Leandra.

"We can all talk to God, Brittney," she said. "Maybe He'll provide us with the answers we need."

Nate took the child from her, his eyes meeting Leandra's over Brittney's head. "Don't forget your birdhouse."

Leandra followed him to the truck, then took the bag from him, lowering her head to avoid his gaze. "Thank you. It really is beautiful."

Nate tugged at her chin so she had to look him in the eyes, his expression full of remorse and pain. "I hope it makes up for...for everything."

"It does," she said. The birdhouse made up for everything except the great pain centered in her heart. "Thank you again, Nate. Good night."

Then she turned and walked back to her own car, the memory of his kiss still as fresh as the cold wind blowing across her face.

And just as elusive.

"It's one of the most beautiful things I've ever seen," Colleen told Leandra later as they stood in the kitchen admiring the birdhouse. "And Nate made this?"

"Yes," Leandra said, her hands wrapped around the mug of hot chocolate her mother had offered her the minute she walked in the door. "Amazing, isn't it?"

"Very," Colleen said, her attention turning from the birdhouse sitting on the counter to her daughter. "What's wrong, sweetheart? Hard rehearsal tonight?"

Leandra took a long sip of the creamy liquid, marveling at her mother's ability to make it just right every time. The taste of rich chocolate milk laced with vanilla and cinnamon only made Leandra want to cry for some strange reason.

"No, rehearsal went well, actually. Everyone is getting settled into their parts and, for once, Margaret didn't make any demands. She was quite pleasant tonight for some reason."

Colleen laughed, then patted Leandra's hand. "I think Margaret's in good spirits these days because she has wonderful news to share with the rest of us."

Leandra glanced up to see the maternal pride on her mother's face. "Another baby?"

"Exactly," Colleen replied. Then she placed a finger to her lips. "But keep it quiet. She wants to announce it at Sunday dinner. You know how she likes to make a big production." Colleen smiled again, then tugged at Leandra's hand. "Now tell me, what's bothering *you?*"

But Leandra's melancholy mood had just gone two shades darker. "First Kim has another baby and now Margaret again. Those two sure are fertile."

"They're married women," her mother pointed out, her eyebrows lifting. "And most married women like to have children."

"Not like me, I suppose," Leandra couldn't help but spout back. "Single and without a maternal bone in my body, right?"

A frown skittered across her mother's face. "I didn't mean to imply—"

"Oh, Mama, I'm sorry," Leandra said, pulling her mother's hands into hers. "It's just been a long day and I guess I'm worried about the future. Christmas will be here in less than three weeks, and then my work here will be over. I don't know what to do with my life after that."

Colleen pulled up a bar stool and indicated to Leandra to do the same. "Are you having second thoughts about returning to Houston?"

"Yes, I think I am," Leandra had to admit. "At first, I told myself I had to go back—you know, to face the music, to get back on that ol' horse. But now…" She shrugged, tried to smile, then looked toward the window seat across the kitchen. "I just don't know."

Colleen looked at her daughter, her face once again as serene as always. "God has a plan for you, Lea. You know that, right?"

"Yes, I believe that with all my heart, Mama. It's just hard to sit back and wait for Him to reveal that plan. Why does He have to be so slow sometimes?"

Colleen laughed again. "Oh, you always were the impatient one. You couldn't wait to get out of Marshall and get on with your life."

Leandra nodded. "I thought my plan had been formed already. But I guess even the best laid plans change, right?"

"They sure do. And we can't blame God for that, or cast doubt about it. We just have to come up with a new plan, with His guidance."

"I'm trying," Leandra said. Then she looked down at the birdhouse. "It was so sweet of Nate to build this for us, don't you think?"

Colleen touched a hand to one of the tiny open windows on the little house. "Yes, very considerate. But then, Nathan Welby is a considerate man." Mimicking Leandra, she added, "Don't you think?"

Leandra saw the inquisitive look centered on her mother's face. "Yes, Mama. I think he's considerate, interesting, and…off-limits."

"Oh, really?"

"Really. Nate has made it very clear he's not ready for anything beyond friendship."

"Oh, and what about you?"

Leandra shook her head. "I'm not ready either. I have to get my life back on track before I can even consider having a relationship with someone again. William's betrayal left a distinct fear in my heart."

"William Myers wasn't worth your time or effort, darling. And I'm glad you got rid of him."

"More like, he got rid of me."

Colleen leaned forward. "Did you love William?"

Leandra thought about that long and hard, fighting the image of Nate's disgust when she'd told him about her past. That led to a comparison of her feelings for William with how she now felt about Nate.

But there was no comparison. The little bit of something she felt for Nate right now, this very minute, far surpassed anything she'd believed she'd felt for William.

"No, I don't think I loved him at all. I was enamored of his image, of what I thought he could do. I thought I was happy with William, and I was content to keep things on an even level, without any further commitment. I felt safe with William. There were no hassles or demands."

But all of that had changed, she remembered, the thoughts of their last days together turning her hot chocolate to a bitter taste in her mouth.

"William was exciting, dashing, wealthy, powerful. All the things I had always dreamed about in a man. But, you know, those were the very things that turned me against him in the end."

Colleen let out a long sigh. "Well, good. Because

what that man expected from you could only have led to heartache and regret." Colleen got up to come around the counter. Putting a hand on each of Leandra's shoulders, she said, "You did the right thing, walking away. You stuck to your morals and the upbringing your father and I tried to instill in you. And that makes me so proud."

"Thanks, Mom," Leandra said, hugging her mother close. If only *she* could find some pride in herself again.

They both heard footsteps on the tiled floor, then parted to find Howard standing there with a questioning smile on his face. "Everything okay in here, ladies?"

"Everything is more than okay," Colleen said. "Since you both worked late tonight, I held dinner—red beans and rice."

"That sure sounds good," Howard said as he came to stand by Leandra. "I'm a starving man."

"We can't have that, now can we?" Colleen said as she took his hand across the counter.

Howard's gaze moved from his wife's face to the birdhouse. "What's this? It looks like a little Christmas cottage."

"It's a birdhouse," Colleen explained, turning it to admire it all over again. "Nathan Welby made it for Leandra and me."

"Well, how about that." Howard whistled low, then stood back to admire the ornamental little house. Then he put a finger to his chin. "Seems to me I remember Nate and Alicia coming in to the bank a few years back to talk about this very subject."

"Birdhouses?" Leandra asked, surprised. "I got the impression this was a hobby Nate had just taken up."

"No, I'm pretty sure they wanted to talk about a possible loan—to start some sort of craft business. Alicia went on and on about how Nate could create anything from wood."

Leandra looked down at the lovely house. So, Alicia had been in on this dream, this design, too. Somehow, that rubbed salt in her already wounded heart. She'd believed Nate had created this just for her.

Turning back to her father, she asked, "What happened? Why didn't they start the business?"

"She died a little while after that, honey. Guess Nate didn't have the heart after that." He went to the refrigerator to take out the tea pitcher. "I was prepared to give them the loan, too. It would have been risky, but they seemed so excited and happy.... Of course, you are not to repeat that, understand?"

Leandra nodded absently, then sat still as her father's voice trailed off. So Nate had had a dream of creating these beautiful houses, of turning it into a business. And yet, that dream had crashed right along with his wife's plane.

Dead. Put aside in a cloud of grief.

Until now.

Suddenly, her heart soared with renewed hope. Regardless of Alicia's influence, Nate had designed this house for her, for her family.

For Leandra.

Maybe he was beginning to work through his grief.

Maybe he did feel something besides friendship for her, after all.

And maybe there was a way she could show him that she supported him and believed in him.

A lot.

Chapter Eight

"Daddy's not home yet," Layla told Leandra two days later.

Leandra stood on the porch of the big house with Mutt sniffing at her long trouser skirt. She wondered why she'd acted on impulse and decided to ride out to the Welby place. She had tons of extra work to do—Chet thought she'd make a great marketing director for the city—and apparently in his mind, had already hired her for the job.

Standing here now, she thought burying herself in work would be the perfect solution to keeping her mind off Nate Welby and his children. And yet, here she was at their front door.

"Well, can I come in anyway?" Leandra asked, hoping she could at least have a talk with Layla while she was here. The girl was obviously in need of some feminine attention, but all that attitude got in the way.

"I don't know—"

Before Layla could finish the sentence, Brittney

came bouncing down the stairs. "Miss Lea! I'm so glad you're here. We need help with the Christmas decorations."

Layla gave her young sister a warning look. "Dad said we have to wait until he gets home, remember."

Brittney shook her head, causing her two long pigtails to swing from side to side over her shoulders. "Uh-uh. He said we needed adult superfision."

"Adult super*vision,* squirt," Layla corrected. "And you need a speech therapist."

"Do not.

"Do, too."

"Girls, girls," Leandra said, still waiting on the porch, still petting the overly friendly dog, "please don't fight. I'd be glad to help, as long as Layla thinks it's okay for me to come inside."

Layla looked back at Leandra, her expression changing from concerned to resigned. "Well, you aren't a stranger and you are an adult. Yeah, sure. I guess Daddy won't mind. He's working late *as usual.*"

She backed up to open the big door wide. Mutt took that as his cue to come in. He pranced ahead of Leandra and headed up the wide wooden staircase, barking, his shaggy tail wagging. She heard Matt calling out to the dog upstairs.

Leandra stepped into the foyer, her eyes scanning the large, spacious rooms. "Wow, this place is incredible. It's so big and airy."

"And drafty," Layla said, pulling her zippered fleece jacket tighter around her midsection as she looked longingly at the empty fireplace. "We aren't allowed to start a fire when Daddy's not here. He's worked on the furnace, but sometimes it still goes out. We're supposed to get a new one after Christmas."

Brittney nodded, then took Leandra by the hand. "Yeah, cause Daddy's getting a big bonus check from his boss. That's how he's gonna fix the furnace. And we get presents, too."

"That's good," Leandra replied as she allowed the child to guide her into what looked like the den off to the right. On the left, a matching room held a huge battered antique dining table and eight matching chairs.

"Twin parlors," Leandra said, marveling at the potential of the house. "That dining table is beautiful."

"My mama bought it at a garage sale," Layla said. "She'd planned on redoing it, but..."

Her voice trailed off, causing Leandra to glance over at her. "Your mother sounds like a wonderful person."

"That's her picture," Brittney said, pointing to a brass-framed print over the fireplace mantel.

Leandra didn't have to see a picture of Alicia Welby to know the woman was perfect in every way. Long blond hair, big blue eyes, a smile that would light up any summer meadow. She could just imagine Nate and Alicia, running through a field of wildflowers together, falling down in the grass, laughing, loving.

Shaking away the image, Leandra decided she'd made a big mistake, coming out here. She wanted to see the rest of Nate's designs, talk to him about producing them for the public. But now, she wasn't so sure Nate would be ready for that.

But she'd already talked to Richard about the possibility of Nate displaying some of his birdhouses in Richard's store out on the highway. Flanagan's Food and General Merchandise would be the perfect place to showcase Nate's work, since the store was designed like an old-fashioned general store and carried art and crafts by several local artisans.

Once Richard had seen the house Nate had made, he agreed Nate had talent and could probably sell lots of the dainty little birdhouses. Especially during Christmas. It made perfect sense to Leandra.

But would it make sense to Nate?

Well, all she could do was ask. If he said no, then that would be that.

In the meantime, she could at least spend some time with his children and help them get this lovely old house ready for the Christmas season. That would save Nate some time and maybe improve his own spirits.

And she'd start by building a fire in the fireplace.

He couldn't make any sense of the way he'd been feeling lately.

Nate turned the pickup off the interstate, taking the highway that would lead him home. Just ahead, the sun was setting over the western sky, and with it that old sense of dread settled around Nate's shoulders like a welcome yoke.

He always dreaded going home. He loved his children, but pulling the truck up that long gravel driveway every night was one of the hardest things he had to do.

Until now.

Lately, Nate hadn't been dreading it as much as he used to. And that had him confused and wondering, and even more determined than ever to hang on to his dread.

If he let go of the dread, of the pain, then he would be dishonoring his wife's memory, wouldn't he?

If he thought about kissing Leandra Flanagan again, as he'd done just about every waking hour over the past couple of days, then he'd be unfaithful to Alicia, wouldn't he?

"Tell me, Lord," he said out loud, beating a hand against the steering wheel. "Tell me how to let go—of both of them."

He longed to be free of the guilt and grief that had colored his world for so long, longed to let go and give his children the love and attention he knew they craved. But if he gave in to this need to be free, that would mean having to finally let go of Alicia, too.

And he wasn't ready to do that.

And yet, Leandra's kiss kept beckoning him.

Her lips had been so soft, so sweet against his. That sweetness had jolted him all the way to his toes.

Which was why nothing made any sense anymore. How could he have feelings for two completely different women—one dead, one very much alive?

His dread was being replaced with a new feeling, one that he really wasn't ready to acknowledge.

And yet it was there, staring him in the face, coloring

his melancholy with vivid shades of autumn fire. Liquid brown eyes, flashing. Fiery brunette hair, shining
in the sun. A bright smile that seemed to change even
the worst winter day to something bright and brilliant.
And a big heart, so big it seemed to be trying to burst
out of her petite little body.

Leandra.

He didn't want to hope. Couldn't bring himself to put
a name to his feelings. He wanted to cling like a desperate, drowning man to his only lifeline.

His dead wife.

One more mile and he'd be home.

Then a voice echoed through the rumbling truck, a
voice so clear, so distinct, that Nate thought he'd left
the radio on.

But it wasn't the radio.

*Alicia's not coming back, Nate. She's gone and she's
at peace now. She'd want you to find your own peace.
She'd want you to love again.*

"No," Nate said, fighting against what he already
knew in his heart. "No, I'm not ready yet."

And then he turned the truck off the road, toward
his home. And slammed on the brakes so hard, gravel
spewed up to hit the driver's side door.

Dusk surrounded the old white house. Dusk, and
a thousand twinkling white lights strung around the
porch posts, and across the front of the gabled roof.
White icicle lights that moved and glittered like golden-
white stars.

And on the door, a big evergreen wreath with a red and gold shiny ribbon trailing down from its top.

Somebody had decorated his house for the holidays.

Somebody had dared to disrupt Alicia's memory, her domain, *his* sacred, sad sanctuary.

And he had a pretty good idea just who that somebody was.

The little whisper of hope was gone now. And the dread was back, a welcome ally as Nate prepared to do battle.

"She might be gone," he told the voice he'd heard earlier, "but that doesn't mean I'm ready to have someone come in and take over completely."

It was time he got his head back on straight, then set Leandra Flanagan straight about a few things.

Nate entered the house, ready to roar his outrage. But he stopped just inside the door, his roar turning to a whimper of protest that he couldn't begin to voice.

There was a fire in the fireplace.

The mantel had been decorated with red, glowing candles and magnolia leaves. The den had been cleaned up, the pillows fluffed, the throw rugs straightened and swept. Two bright, fresh poinsettias sat on either side of the huge hearth.

He had to shut his eyes to the sheer beauty of it.

Hearing laughter in the kitchen, he opened his eyes and turned to the big dining room that they never used. It was set for dinner, with the old, chipped china they'd bought secondhand years ago. Another poinsettia graced the center of the table, and on the mismatched buffet, white candles burned in the silver candelabras Alicia had found at a flea market.

Everything looked homey and cozy, like a scene from a spread in a magazine. Everything seemed perfect.

Except for the horrible smell coming from the kitchen.

Determined to nip this intrusion in the bud, Nate stomped down the hallway to the rear of the house, intent on giving Miss Leandra Flanagan a dressing down she would never forget.

Instead, he came upon a scene he would always remember.

His three children were centered around the butcher block counter he'd build years ago, flour on their hands and all over their faces, their backs to him as they watched Leandra and noisily offered encouraging instructions. Mutt lay by the back door, a dubious expression coloring his dark eyes. When the dog saw Nate, he lifted his head, rolled his doggy eyes, as if to say, "Don't ask," then whimpered and flopped his head down on his paws to stare up at his master.

But the woman standing by the stove really caught Nate's attention. Leandra had more flour all over her than any of the kids. It was in her hair, on her hands, all over her black cashmere sweater, and all the way down her checked trouser skirt. She even had flour dusted across her black loafers.

"What's going on around here?"

At the sound of his voice, the room went silent. Nate's children and Leandra all whirled around at the same time.

"Daddy, you're home!" Brittney said, rushing to fling herself in his arms. "Did you see? Did you see the lights? We did it ourselves. Miss Leandra wouldn't let me get up on the ladder, though. I got to do the short parts."

"I saw, pumpkin," Nate said, giving the child a kiss before he set her down and wiped a dab of flour from his own face. He glanced toward Leandra then. "I've seen all of it. You've been very busy."

Matt pointed at the stove. "And we're making you chicken and dumplings for supper."

Layla shrugged, then wiped her hands down the front of her jeans. "Except, we sorta burned the first batch."

"That explains the smell, at least," Nate replied, his gaze still locked with Leandra's. "I thought I told you kids, no cooking or fires while I'm not here."

"But Miss Leandra's an adult," Brittney pointed out.

"Are you sure about that?" Nate said, then instantly regretted it when he saw the hurt look in her dark eyes.

"I'm sorry," she said at last. "I can't cook. But I wanted—"

"She wanted to make you dinner," Brittney interjected, "and surprise you with the decorations. And tomorrow, we're going to get a tree, right, Miss Leandra?"

"If your father doesn't object," Leandra said, her hurt expression hidden by a slight smile. "Now, I'd better watch this new batch of dumplings. Maybe this time, I'll get it right."

Matt glanced over into the bubbling pot of white mush. "Yeah, cause Mutt wouldn't even eat the last batch and that dog eats anything."

Upon hearing his name, Mutt lifted his head, sniffed, then got up and ran from the room, his tail wagging a hasty farewell.

Leandra's smile turned into a frown. "I *can't* cook. I don't know why I tried. I shouldn't have done this."

Layla shot Nate a warning look, then hurried to the stove. "But these dumplings look okay, Miss Leandra. Really. And they smell good, too."

"Better than the last ones," Matt said, grinning.

Brittney pulled Nate close, tugging at his hand. "See, Daddy, don't them look right?"

"It's those," Layla corrected.

"Okay, okay," Brittney said, moaning. Then she made a dramatic effort to correct herself. "*Those* dumplings look just right."

Some of Nate's initial anger drained away, to be replaced with a teasing tone. "Well, how many poor chickens had to die for this dinner?"

"Only one," Layla told him. "We used canned broth with the chicken broth to make the dumplings, but we got most of the chicken out before the dumplings got scorched. We had more canned broth, so we started another pot with that."

"I'm going to drop the chicken meat in once I see if this batch is edible," Leandra told him. "Honestly, I don't know what went wrong. This is my mother's recipe and I followed her instructions."

Nate stared over at her, enjoying the skittish way she tried to explain, her hands lifting in the air with each word. Which only made little flour dust balls float out all around her. Then he reminded himself that he was supposed to be angry with her.

"We just forgot to turn the heat down," Matt explained, wiping even more flour across his smudged face.

Leandra checked the burner button, then went to the sink to wash her hands. "Hopefully, this will be ready in about ten minutes." Then she turned to the children. "Let's get this cleaned up, and we'll get the salad and tea out of the refrigerator. I'll drop the chicken back in to heat it up, and Matt, you can pour the milk."

The three children went to work wiping down the flour-dusted counter while Leandra tried to dust herself off with a dish towel.

After the children had gone into the dining room, carrying drinks and condiments for the salad, Nate walked over to Leandra. "Why'd you do all of this?"

She looked up then, into his eyes. With a little shrug, she said, "I'm wondering that same thing myself." Lowering her head, she added, "You're mad."

Nate couldn't deny that. "I *was* good and mad, yeah. When I pulled up and saw all those lights—"

"The children asked me to help, Nate." She gazed up at him then, a pleading look centered in her eyes. "I came by to see you, but you weren't home yet. They wanted to decorate, so I agreed to help. Then we had so much fun, and you were late, and it was dinnertime and they told me you like dumplings—" She stopped, turned back to the sink. "I'm sorry."

Nate tried to find the words he needed to say. He wanted to tell her that this wasn't her house, that she had no right to just come barreling in here and take over, changing things around, trying to make this house something it could never be.

But when she looked up at him, with flour smudged across her cheek, with her heart in her eyes, all he could do was reach out and touch her face. "You've got a glob of flour right there," he said, his fingers brushing away the white specks. Then he smiled. "Actually, you've got flour on just about every part of you."

Leandra let out a little rush of breath. "I think I've got more on me and the kitchen floor than in the dumplings," she said. "We should have just ordered pizza."

"They don't deliver way out here," he replied, his fingers still touching on her face. "And I do like dumplings, even scorched ones."

She reached up to take his hand away. "But you're angry with me. I—I overstepped the bounds, didn't I?"

"Yes, you did," he admitted. "We normally don't go all out for Christmas."

"But why not?"

"It just makes…it makes it harder."

"But the children—"

"My children are just fine. They've been just fine."

"So you *are* angry, and you think I should mind my own business?"

"Something like that."

She pushed past him then. Taking the plate of chopped chicken off the counter, she dumped it into the dumpling pot, stirred it, then turned off the burner. "Well, here's your dinner. And I'll be leaving now."

"Hey, wait just a minute," Nate said, reaching out to catch her by the hand. "Since you cooked it, you have to eat it. Or are you afraid you'll get food poisoning?"

"Don't try to make me feel better, Nate. I messed up and now I don't know how to fix it."

"More flour and a new pot," he replied, his hand in hers. "Don't leave."

"But, I'm so stupid. I thought—"

"You wanted to help my children," he reminded her. "Look, Leandra, I know how persuasive those three can be, especially when they gang up on a person. And they know that you're too nice to turn them down."

She looked down at the floor. "It was hard to say no, but I enjoyed helping them decorate. They said you hadn't done it in a long time."

"No, and I did promise them," he said, guilt in each word. "It's just hard sometimes."

She glanced back up then, her eyes wide. "But it can get easier, Nate. With time and prayer. That's what my mother always tells me when I'm struggling with a big problem."

"Time and prayer," he repeated. "Seems like I'm all out of both."

"You only have to ask."

He let go of her hand then. "Ask what—that God

give me my wife back, that He show me how to give my children the life they deserve? What should I ask for, Leandra?"

"You're mad again."

"I've been mad for the last three years," he retorted, pushing a hand through his hair in frustration.

"Then you need to ask for relief, Nate. You need to find some peace, some closure." She reached a hand to his face, her fingers treading like an angel's wings over his skin. "You need to let go of the past and look toward the future."

The need he felt for her then caused him to back away. He couldn't, wouldn't pull her into his arms and ask God for salvation or peace. He would fight against this, with his every breath. Because he liked being miserable too much.

"I'm not ready to let go," he told her.

"I know," Leandra replied. "And that's why I should just leave right now."

But she didn't get to leave, after all. Brittney bounced into the room, pushing between them. "Can we eat? I'm starving."

Nate picked up his daughter, then tickled her tummy, his smile belying the darkness in his eyes. "I'm hungry myself. And I sure don't want to miss out on those dumplings." Looking at Leandra over Brittney's head, he said, "C'mon, Leandra. You cooked. You get to serve. And then, I'll wash the dishes and clear up everything else."

"Not everything, Nate," Leandra told him as she

whirled past him. "There's a lot that needs to be cleared up between us, but I don't think you're ready to admit that just yet."

Chapter Nine

Nate had cleaned the kitchen, all right. After they'd eaten dinner, with the children laughing and talking over the loud silence between the two adults, he'd promptly done his part, then stomped off to the barn to "check on Honeyboy and do some work." That left Leandra with the children. Since tomorrow was Saturday, she'd told them to settle into their pajamas so they could watch a late movie.

Earlier, in the midst of a fit of impulsiveness, she'd promised them hot chocolate and cookies by the fire, to cap off what she had hoped would be a lovely evening. But that had backfired the minute their father had arrived, with a pop every bit as loud as the dry wood now crackling in the fireplace.

Nate did not appreciate any of her efforts.

And to think she'd started out with the best of intentions.

Since they'd had the night off from rehearsals, she'd decided it would be a good time to talk to Nate about mass marketing his birdhouses. Then, suddenly, she'd been up on a ladder stringing Christmas lights—lights that she'd had her brother Richard deliver from his store, along with the poinsettias and candles, and supplies for making dumplings.

"You're turning into a domestic dynamo," Richard had teased on the phone. "What else did you need? A chicken and three cans of chicken broth? Leandra, I'm worried about you—if you're cooking for this man, that means it's serious, and that also means his health is in serious danger."

Although her brother had been joking, his words now rang true. She'd not only ruined dinner, but also any chances of furthering things with Nate.

And since when had she decided to further things, anyway? Since that kiss, dummy, she told herself as she poured hot chocolate into mugs on a big tray next to the cookies. She then carried it into the den where the kids sat already watching the movie.

Seeing the three Welby children all curled up with pillows and blankets by the roaring fire only added to Leandra's misery. She wanted Nate there, too. She wanted to curl up with him by that fire.

But Nate had retreated into his memories and his guilt.

"Does your father work in the barn every night?" she asked Layla now, concern for the girl motivating her question.

"Just about," Layla replied as she took a mug from

Leandra. "He's always taking on extra work, even though he's been promoted at his regular job."

"But surely he spends time with you, right?"

"Only when he's forced to," Layla said, her words low so the younger children wouldn't hear. Then she added, "He's a good daddy, Miss Lea. He just misses our mama, and I guess you figured out I look just like her."

Leandra nodded. "You're just as pretty."

"That's why he hates me," Layla blurted out. Then, clearly mortified, she said, "Don't tell him I said that."

Leandra put her cocoa down on a nearby table. "Honey, you're wrong. Your father loves you. Surely you know that."

"He loves me because he has to—that's his duty as a father. But..." Her voice trailed off, and Leandra watched her swallow back the tears. "I remind him of her and because of that, he hates being around me. That's why he goes out to that old barn every night."

"Oh, baby." Leandra pulled the girl into her arms, rocking her back and forth while silent tears slipped down Layla's face. "Shh. Don't cry now."

"What's the matter?" Brittney asked, ever curious even if she was sleepy-eyed.

"The movie," Leandra said, grabbing the first excuse she could find. "This is the sad part and Layla doesn't want to watch. Better hurry, or you'll miss the ending."

With that, Brittney snuggled back down inside her old quilt. "Don't be sad, sister. It's just a movie."

Leandra wished life could be that way—just like a

movie or a book with a happy ending. But life didn't always play out the way people dreamed it would.

"Have you talked to your father about this?" she asked Layla a while later, after the girl had settled down and both Brittney and Matt were snoozing on the floor by the fire.

Pushing Leandra away, Layla fought for the attitude that had kept her true emotions hidden so well. "He's not the talking kind, or haven't you noticed?"

"Yes, I've noticed," Leandra admitted. "But if you went to him, told him how this makes you feel—"

"No," Layla said, jumping up off the couch. "I couldn't do that. He'd just get even more mad at me. He doesn't like to talk about Mama at all. And Brittney is always asking questions—she was too young to even remember Mama. It would just make things worse if he knew I'd said something to you." Grabbing her blanket, she said, "You can't say anything, Miss Lea, please. You can't tell him."

"I won't, I promise," Leandra told the jittery teen. "But he needs to know, honey."

"He knows," Layla said, the wisdom of the two words warring with her youthful expression.

Suddenly, Leandra understood the girl's predicament. Layla and Nate were tiptoeing around each other, each trying hard not to disturb Alicia's memories. And neither of them had even come close to dealing with her death.

That had been obvious tonight.

Nate had been so angry! She'd seen it, felt it, the

minute he'd entered the kitchen. And just because his children had wanted the house decorated. But he didn't want anything changed or rearranged. He wanted to keep this house intact, even though it was in obvious need of some tender loving care. He wanted to freeze time, to keep things the way they were when Alicia had lived in this house.

"Well, she wouldn't want this," Leandra told herself a few minutes later as she rinsed their cups and put away the cookies. "She would want her children to be happy and healthy. She'd want them to celebrate life, not preserve it in a time warp. And she'd want you to be happy, too, Nate."

But would she want you to be with someone like me?

Leandra finally got the children off to bed, then turned to go out to the barn. "I'm going to tell him I'm leaving now," she said to Mutt. "And while I'm at it, I just might give the man a piece of my mind, too."

Mutt whimpered his response to that suggestion, then wagged his tail in anticipation.

Nate moved the tiny piece of wood back and forth through his fingers, trying to decide if he wanted to carve it into a leaf or a flower.

Then again, maybe he'd just leave it the way it was. Why couldn't people leave well enough alone, anyway?

He thought of Leandra, standing in the middle of his kitchen, standing in the very spot where Alicia had stood so many nights. He could still hear Leandra's laughter as he'd entered the front door tonight.

But he couldn't remember Alicia's laugh.

And that hurt so much.

Throwing the wood down, Nate stood there staring at his workbench. He couldn't even hide behind his work tonight. Couldn't even think beyond Leandra trying to make dumplings.

Dumplings!

He'd eaten them, scorched parts and all, just to please his children, just to be polite to her, and actually, the food hadn't been half bad. And all the while, he'd noticed her hair, shining softly in the candlelight, her laughter echoing across the table at him, calling out to him, her eyes, beseeching and encouraging, glancing his way as she chattered away with his children.

Her lips.

"How can I feel this way, Lord? How can I want to be with another woman? A completely different woman?"

Different in so many ways.

Yet, so like his Alicia in other ways.

Leandra had once again been kind to his children. She'd once again taken over where no one else had bothered to even lend a hand. She'd put their needs, their requests, above her own comfort. She'd made them happy, laughing and carefree again.

And that, he had to admit, had been her saving grace.

Suddenly, all the anger drained out of Nate, leaving him with a fatigue so great, he swayed against the sturdy workbench. "I need some help here, God."

"You sure do," Leandra said from the open doorway.

Nate whirled to find her standing there, staring at

him, her hands in the big pockets of her wool overcoat. He didn't miss the pain etched across her face. He could see it clearly from the dim overhead light.

"Go ahead," she said as she walked closer. "Tell Him your troubles. Don't let me interfere."

Nate shuffled his feet, looked down at the saw-dust covered floor. "Can't a man have a private moment to pray around here, at least?"

"I'm sorry," Leandra said, backing out of the barn. "I just wanted you to know the children are in bed and I'm going home."

"Wait," he said, turning around. "We need to talk about a few things. You said we needed to clear the air."

Leandra stopped just outside the door. "I came out here to do that very thing, but now I think the air is completely clear, and so are your feelings toward me and my...intrusion. Again, I am so sorry."

Nate let out an irritated sigh, then in two long strides had her by the arm, pulling her back inside the barn. "Would you just quit apologizing? You haven't done anything wrong."

She scoffed, glanced away. "Oh, except decorate a house you didn't want to decorate in the first place, no matter what you promised your children. Except cook a meal that turned out to be a fiasco even on the second try, and make myself a general all-around nuisance. I'd say that's a lot to be sorry about."

Nate stared down at her, hoping to make her understand everything that was troubling his tired heart.

"It's not you," he told her, his hands on her arms. "It's

me, Leandra. It's my bad attitude, my problems, me and my pain and guilt, and my lack of faith."

"Oh, I understand," she told him, her eyes glistening in a pool of unshed tears. "And that's why I came to say good-night. I won't push myself off on you again, Nate. It was foolish, considering that I've already been through one bad relationship. I should have learned from that, but no, I had to come home, take on this job just to tell myself I'm still worthy of some kind of work, then just like that, I saw you standing by that pasture, with your dog and your horse and your three adorable children, and I got this funny notion all the way down to my toes."

"Leandra—"

"No," she said, pushing him away as she turned her back to him. "I guess I was on the rebound, you know. Same old tired reasoning. I took all the signals the wrong way, wanted more from you than you were willing to give. But, I can see it all so plainly now. You don't want my help, don't need me in your life. You've got it all planned out, exactly the way you want it."

She whirled then. "Except that your children are suffering because you are so lost in the past, you can't even begin to see that they need their father."

"I'm a good father," he said, anger clouding his better judgment.

"Yes, you are," she replied. "You are a good, dutiful father. You do all the things that are expected of you. But what about the unexpected, Nate? What about that?"

The anger was back, refreshing and nurturing, and so welcome he almost cried out with relief. "You have no right to come into my home like this and tell me how to raise my children. You don't know the first thing about children, and from everything I've seen, you don't even want to have any of your own."

She stood there in the moonlight, her hands shoved in the pockets of her coat, shivering. Silent. But her eyes, oh, he'd never forget the pain in her eyes. That pain shouted a message, a warning, to him.

He wanted to take back what he'd just said, but the words were still echoing out over the night. Never to be taken back.

"Leandra," he said, reaching for her.

"No," she said again, her voice strained and husky. "You're absolutely right, Nate. I don't know anything about raising children. I never thought I'd want children. I thought I had my life all mapped out and then everything changed. Everything turned ugly and I came home, a complete and utter failure."

She shrugged, her laughter brittle with a bitterness that tore through his hard heart and made his anger feel like a brick pressing against his windpipe. "I guess you and the children were just a distraction, a way to prove to myself that I had a heart, and some maternal qualities, after all. But, hey, I even failed at that, too, didn't I?"

He tried to reach out to her again, and again, she pushed him away, her hand flying out in defense.

"No, it's all right. I understand what you're trying

to say to me. We weren't meant for each other, and it's silly and a waste of time for us to pretend. So…let's just keep this as business. You're just about finished with the set and the props and I've got your check all ready down at city hall. Two more weeks and I'll be on my way back to Houston." She whirled and started toward her car. "And then, I guess I'll see what else I can do to make my life a total mess."

Nathan stood there, stunned, as she got in her car and backed it around. And then she was gone, leaving him to stare off into the night.

Mutt came running up, whimpering for attention. But Nate couldn't give the dog the attention he craved.

Maybe Leandra was right, he thought as he locked up the barn and made his way to the house. Maybe he was making all the right moves, but would he ever be able to really love anyone again?

Would he ever be able to give his children the one thing they needed the most—his heart?

That heart hurt tonight, hurt from the cold wind on his back, from the cruel words he'd flung out at Leandra, and mostly, it hurt from her response, her own self-condemning speech.

He'd caused her pain, the one thing he'd hoped to avoid. He'd turned things around, blamed her for his own inconsistencies, his own failures.

"I shouldn't have let things go this far," he reasoned as Mutt hit the porch ahead of him. "I shouldn't have flirted with her, teased her. And I surely shouldn't have kissed her there in the prayer garden."

But you did, Nate. Now what are you gonna do about it?

"Mutt, did you learn how to speak?" Nate asked, glancing around.

But Nate knew that what he'd just heard had come somewhere from deep inside himself. His conscience was arguing with him.

His conscience was telling him to go after Leandra and ask her for another chance.

"I'm not going to listen, not tonight," he said out loud. "I've already hurt her enough."

Mutt groaned, then barked to be let inside where it was warm, where his bed waited just inside the pantry doorway.

"I hear you, boy," Nate told the dog. "It's gonna be a long, cold night, that's for sure."

Especially with the scent of Leandra's perfume, and a faint whiff of scorched dumplings, still lingering in his mind.

Chapter Ten

The next Monday night was hard for Leandra. They would rehearse early in the afternoon and on some nights this week, to accommodate everyone's work schedules. Now that the children were out of school for the holidays, everyone was more able to go through a full-scale dress rehearsal. Soon though, it would be the real thing in front of a sold-out audience each night.

Next week, the pageant would have a four-day run with the last performance ending on Christmas Eve, just before the annual candlelight service at the church across the street. The service was every bit as popular and anticipated as the pageant. Leandra expected a big crowd there, too.

Now that the pageant was becoming a reality, it seemed almost anticlimactic. She should be excited. The rehearsals were going well. The stage decorations and props were incredible, and everything was moving along right on schedule. She'd worked so hard, such long hours, not only on the pageant but on several other projects Chet had dropped in her lap, and becoming involved with Nate and his children had only added to both the stress and the joy of this whole production. What would she do once this was all over?

Things were already over, she told herself. At least as far as Nate was concerned.

All weekend, she'd dreaded tonight, dreaded seeing Nate's face, the memory of his words forever etched in her being as a reminder of her utter failure.

"You don't know the first thing about raising children. You don't even want children."

He had been so right. And so wrong.

Because she'd changed over the past few weeks.

Now, Leandra's heart was playing tricks on her. Now, each time she thought about being in that drafty old house with the three Welby children, drinking hot chocolate and eating cookies by the fire, she only longed to have that chance again. Over and over again.

All day Saturday, she'd moped around until her mother had put her to work wrapping Christmas gifts. Sunday, she'd gone to church, hoping to find some solace in Reverend Powell's powerful words. But even the scriptures leading up to the birth of Jesus couldn't bring her any joy.

Sunday afternoon, she'd gone for a long walk in the cold, praying, listening, hoping to find some answers in her silent meditations.

But now, as she sat here watching people file in for the rehearsal, she knew there was only one answer.

She couldn't fall in love with Nathan Welby.

She wouldn't fall in love with Nathan Welby.

She'd certainly never set out to do that.

Quickly, she made a mental inventory of why she'd been thrown into this situation in the first place.

I quit my job. I came home. Wanted to stay busy, so took job as pageant coordinator. Had to hire a carpenter. Children wanted me to be their mommy. Couldn't do that, so decided to be a good friend, even though I'm terribly attracted to their daddy.

It should have ended there, except that she'd rushed headlong into asking Nate and the children to Thanksgiving dinner.

That dinner, at least, had been nice. Wonderful, except that her mother's vase had been broken.

Nate gave me a birdhouse. *For my mother.*

Nate kissed me.

I got this crazy notion to help him sell birdhouses. So I went out to house. Got talked into building a fire, decorating for Christmas, and cooking dinner. Ruined dinner. Ruined our friendship. Ruined everything.

Fools rush in where angels fear to tread.

And now I am utterly confused and miserable.

End of list. End of story.

Now, she had to muster up the courage to face him. She didn't have any choice. She had to get through this week, then the performances next week, and then it would be over.

"I can do that," she said out loud. "I have to finish what I started."

"You're talking to yourself," Margaret told her as she

sat down in the seat beside Leandra. Then she took one look at Leandra's face and groaned.

"My, what's wrong with you? Are you coming down with the flu? I don't want the baby exposed—"

Leandra took Margaret's hand away from her stomach. "I don't have the flu, so stop worrying. I'm just in a mood. Tired, I guess."

Margaret grinned knowingly then poked Leandra on the arm with a slim finger, her diamond solitaire shining in the muted auditorium light. "Richard told Jack and me about your dinner with the Welbys. No wonder you're exhausted. Cooking for those three children and that man—"

"I'd rather not talk about that," Leandra said, her tone dismissive. "And Richard shouldn't have told you, either."

Margaret twisted around to stare at her. "Oh, he just thought it was so sweet. Face it, Leandra, you've never gone to this much trouble for a man before. We're all dying to hear the details."

Leandra got up, her clipboard and papers clutched to her chest. "Look, there are no details." Then glaring down at the dubious expression on Margaret's face, she added, "And just for the record, I *did* cook for William every now and then."

"But mostly, according to what little you've told me about the time you spent with William, you ate just about every meal out," Margaret interjected. "You told me that. Told me he took you to fancy restaurants all over Houston."

"Well, that's over and so is any more attempts to cook for the Welbys," Leandra said, her patience snapping.

Margaret got up, too, then placed a hand on Leandra's arm, the teasing lilt in her voice gone. "Are you okay?"

Leandra saw the concern in her sister-in-law's eyes, and instantly regretted her outburst. "I'm fine, Margaret. Just stressed about this production. I'm sorry I took it out on you."

Margaret patted her arm. "You know you can tell me anything, and I won't blab like Richard did. Not if you really don't want me to—just say so."

"Thanks," Leandra told her, appreciative of Margaret's rare show of discretion. She felt sure she *could* trust Margaret if she really needed to confide in her, but Leandra wasn't ready for that. "It's nothing, honestly. I just overstepped my place with Nathan and now I feel awful about it. I shouldn't have cooked dinner at all. And I intend to keep my distance from now on." Then she glanced around and whispered low, "He's not over Alicia."

Understanding colored Margaret's big eyes. "Oh, I see. You know, Lea, it's hard to lose someone we love. Friends and family try to bring us comfort, but it takes a long time to accept. Death is so final, and the answers aren't easy. Maybe Nate's just not ready to take that next step." She shrugged then shook her head. "And... I'd sure be hesitant about stepping in to fill Alicia's shoes. How she put up with those children—"

Leandra held out a hand to quiet her, almost glad Margaret had stopped philosophizing and was now back to her old snobbish self. "I know. But believe me, the children aren't the problem. I've figured it all out in my head. I was on the rebound from breaking up with William. I needed to feel needed, and the children pulled me into this relationship. Nate is a kind, wonderful man, but I'm pulling myself out. As of now."

"Oh, really?" Margaret sounded doubtful. "Well, I hope for your sake, that's true." She placed her hands on Leandra's shoulder, then leaned close. "'Cause Nate and the children just walked through the back door."

He tried not to look for her. But Nate couldn't help himself. His gaze automatically searched the crowd gathered in the auditorium, looking for Leandra.

Then he saw her, standing on the other side near the stage with her back to him, talking to Margaret.

This was going to be hard.

All weekend, he'd cursed himself for a fool. He shouldn't have treated her so callously after she'd been so nice and helpful to his children.

His children, he reminded himself now. Leandra had tried to tell him how to take care of his own children. That wasn't right.

But she'd been right about him. And so very wrong, too.

He loved his children. Yet he knew he'd been avoiding them, letting them drift along on the coattails of that love. He'd only been mad because Leandra had pointed out the obvious. Yet, he wasn't ready to let someone else in on his misery. He wasn't ready to relinquish paternal rights to another woman besides their mother.

He'd just have to do better at being their father. Having thought about this all weekend, he'd made good on his promise by taking the children to a movie, then Christmas shopping. He'd even toyed with the idea of taking them to church on Sunday, but a million excuses clouded that promise right out of the way. He had stayed away from the barn, at least. They'd put up a Christmas tree on Sunday afternoon.

And he could still remember Brittney's words.

"I thought Miss Lea was going to help us decorate the tree, Daddy."

"She couldn't make it, honeypie. But we'll get the job done."

And he would get the job done. Alone. He didn't need some city woman telling him how to raise his children, how to decorate his house, how to…smile again, laugh again, feel again.

He didn't need Leandra Flanagan.

So here he stood, trying hard to be a good father, trying hard to live up to the pressure, the pain, hoping he could make it through this next week of staying here in the same room with her to watch his children rehearse. He'd promised them he wouldn't leave. He was going to keep that promise, no matter how much he wanted to go to Leandra and beg her to come back and make more dumplings.

* * *

"We have a major problem," Chet Reynolds told Leandra a few minutes later.

Everyone was settled into the seats directly below the stage to go over last minute business items. Leandra intended to make a few suggestions when Chet came rushing in the back door, his hands waving, his big feet flapping against the concrete floor.

"What's the matter, Chet?" she asked, concerned for the man's health. His face was red and he was breathing heavy from rushing up the aisle.

"It's the lion," Chet began, then took a long calming breath, his Adam's apple bobbing. "And the lamb."

Leandra glanced around. "Where is Mr. Emory anyway? He's our lion and he gets to try on his costume tonight."

"Was our lion," Chet said, waving his hands again. "He had a heart attack about two hours ago. He's in the hospital."

"Oh, my." Leandra hated hearing bad news such as this. Mr. Emory was a sweet old man and he loved being a part of the theater since he'd done some acting in his younger days. He wouldn't want to miss out on being the lion in this production. "I hope he's going to be all right," she said above the murmur of concern moving through the crowd.

"He's fine," Chet told her, his sentences choppy and breathless. "Lucky it was mild. Rest and therapy. But he can't be in the pageant. Doctor's orders."

"I understand," Leandra said. "And I sure hope Mr.

Emory recovers soon. Luckily, we still have time to find another lion. Someone tall and willing to roar a bit now and then."

"My Daddy'd be perfect for that," Matt shouted, grinning from ear to ear. "He roars at us all the time."

Leandra's gaze instantly connected with Nate's. He was sitting at the back of the crowd, slightly away from the main players. After hearing Matt's rather loud suggestion, Nate slouched down in his seat and ran a hand over his chin in agitation.

Before Leandra could say anything, Chet spoke up. "Nate, you would make a good lion. You got the right coloring and everything."

Nate stood up, then shook his head. "Nah. I'm only here to help with the set. I work behind the scenes."

"But Daddy, we need you," Layla said, twisting in her seat to stare at her father. "We don't have much time and all you have to do is march out when we're singing the animal song."

"And he gets to roar really loud," Matt reminded her.

After the laughter had settled down, Nate stood there with his hands in the pockets of his jeans, a distressed look covering his face. "Oh, all right," he said at last, defeat in every word. "I guess I can do that much, at least." Then he looked directly at Leandra. "It'll give me a chance to spend some time with my children."

"Yea! My daddy's the lion," Brittney said, rushing headlong into Nate's arms. "Now you get to rehearse with us every day."

"I sure do," Nate said, his eyes still on Leandra.

She could read that expression well enough to know he was only doing this to show her he could be a good father. Well, she was glad for that, at least.

Chet tugged at her sleeve, bringing her back to reality. "And what about the lamb?"

"What about the lamb?" she asked, wondering what else could go wrong.

"Thelma Nesmith," Chet said, his eyebrows shooting up like bird's wings.

"Yes, Thelma is our lamb. Don't tell me she dropped out of the production, too?"

"Got a cruise for Christmas from her rich son over in Dallas. She'll be leaving in two days. Saw her at the post office today. Said she was gonna call you tomorrow. Might as well tell you tonight, though. We need a new lamb."

Leandra smiled, took a long breath, then nodded. "I'll go through the directory and find someone tomorrow, Chet. No problem."

"You could be the lamb," Brittney said, smiling at Leandra. "My daddy said you're as pretty as a lamb, 'member?"

Leandra groaned silently while the flush of embarrassment went up her neck and face. "Uh—"

Margaret raised her hand then. "You would make a lovely lamb, Leandra. That has a nice ring—Leandra the lovely lamb. And you have to be nice to the lion."

Making a mental note to seriously strangle her sister-in-law later, Leandra shook her head. "I have enough to do without wearing a lamb's costume."

"But Miss Lea, we need someone tonight to practice," Matt said. "C'mon. You're the same height as Miss Thelma anyway. We won't even have to make another costume."

"I..." Leandra stopped to find too many hopeful gazes all staring directly at her. She'd asked all of them to give of their time and talent, so how could she refuse at this late date? "I guess I could fill in," she said at last, "since we don't have much time and I won't have to learn too many lines."

Chet beamed. "Shucks, all you have to do is sit with the lion and let there be peace on earth, goodwill to men."

"Is that all?" Leandra said, her chuckle just as shaky as her heart felt right now. "A piece of cake."

"This production just got a whole lot more interesting," Margaret said, grinning from ear to ear.

"I'll deal with you later," Leandra told her under her breath as everyone headed to find their costumes for the first dress rehearsal. Then, pulling Margaret to the side, she added, "I thought you wanted me to stay away from Nate Welby and his children."

Margaret glanced around to make sure no one could hear them, turned back to Leandra, smiling. "That was before I realized you're in love with the man."

"I am not."

"Oh, Leandra, you'd better practice in front of the mirror before you become that little lamb. 'Cause that big, bad lion has a thing for you, and I think you feel the same way about him—and it's not my place to interfere with that, what with peace on earth riding on this entire relationship."

"I'm glad you find this so funny, Margaret."

"It's just good to see you in love at last, even if it is with that cowboy and his brood—better you than me," Margaret told her before she scooted away, her grin still intact.

What does she know? Leandra silently asked herself. Margaret was so shallow and snobbish, she was probably just enjoying Leandra's discomfort. Yet, in her heart, Leandra knew even Margaret wasn't that rotten. Margaret had good qualities, and she had been concerned earlier. It must be the hormones from the new pregnancy making her act and sound crazy.

I am not in love with Nate Welby, Leandra told herself.

Then she looked up and saw Nate standing there, watching her, his eyes that golden, hazel shade of wonder, his hair curling around his face like a lion's mane, his lips twisted in a wry, resigned expression. The man didn't have to roar; she could read him loud and clear.

"I certainly feel like a lamb," she said as she headed to find her own costume. "A lamb about to go to the slaughter."

Mr. Tuttle came up to her then, already dressed as Santa Claus. "The lion and the lamb—Nate and you," he said, his chuckle moving down his big belly. "Now that's worth the price of a ticket."

When Leandra gave him a mock-mean glare, he only

winked and smiled, as if he knew exactly what she wanted for Christmas.

Suddenly, this production had taken a new twist.

But Leandra couldn't be sure it would be for the better since she knew in her heart there would be no peace between her and Nate Welby, at Christmas or any time soon.

Chapter Eleven

"And so, right there in front of everyone, Leandra and Nathan both agreed to being the lamb and the lion in the production. It was so funny." Margaret gave a dainty little shrug and giggled behind her hand. "Especially the look on Leandra's face."

Everyone around the dinner table was now looking at Leandra in hopes of a repeat of her shocked expression, no doubt. Well, she wasn't going to give them one. "Margaret, I can't understand why you're so fascinated with all of this. To hear you talk, you'd rather eat nails than be seen in the same room with the Welbys."

Margaret stopped giggling to glance over at Jack for support. "Well, I wouldn't exactly put it that way, Lea. I just had some legitimate concerns about the man and those ragamuffin children, but I have to admit since I've been working with them on this production, I've kinda gotten used to them."

Colleen smiled, then passed the barbecue sauce to Howard. "Thanks for bringing dinner, Richard. I was afraid with all the last-minute work on the pageant, I'd have to serve grilled cheese sandwiches for dinner."

The pageant rehearsal had been early today, so they were having a casual midweek family dinner consisting of barbecue and all the trimmings from Richard's store. He cooked and smoked his own meat on a huge grill out back. His barbecue, baked beans and potato salad were all famous for miles around. As were his homemade pies.

Taking the hint to change the subject, Richard grinned and saluted his mother. "My pleasure. But I think next week we ought to let Leandra whip up some of her famous dumplings. From what I hear, they keep you full for days to come."

Leandra threw down her napkin. "Okay, that does it. Does anyone else want to tell a cute joke about my personal life? Since it's open season on Leandra, let's hear it. C'mon, don't be shy." She moved her head from side to side, waiting.

The room was suddenly quiet.

Then Mark spoke up. "I'm glad it's you and not me, Sis. When you were away, I was the one who got all the teasing remarks. Seems if you're single and a Flanagan, you don't stand a chance of getting any peace around here."

"Amen to that," Leandra said, Mark's words calming her down a bit. "How did you deal with it, Mark?" she asked him, ignoring Jack's smirk and Richard's grin.

Mark winked, then said, "I just kept right on eating my dinner, and as you know, I always carry some ready reading material. It tends to drown out the superficial small talk."

Michael spoke up then. "We gave up on you long ago, Mark. You're a lost cause. But we're still holding out for little Lea here. *If* she can learn to cook."

"Now, boys," Howard said, his tone soft but firm. "There's no law that says a woman has to know how to cook to get a man. There's more to love than fried chicken and turnip greens."

"Maybe," Richard replied as he stabbed another slice of brisket, "but it sure doesn't hurt."

"What are you worried about, little brother?" Jack asked Richard, laughing. "You can outcook any woman around here—except Mom, of course."

"You saved yourself there, Jack," Colleen replied, one hand on the high chair to hold Philip in and the other on the windup swing right by her chair, where baby Carissa snoozed away to a soft lullaby. Little Corey was in another high chair beside his parents. "And Richard, you're engaged, so you don't count."

Richard chewed his meat, then nodded. "Yeah, and I miss Sheila. I'll be glad when she's done with medical school in Dallas. I'll see her during Christmas, at least."

Leandra groaned. "So *I'm* the center of speculation these days. How did y'all find out about my dumplings, anyway?"

Everyone spoke at once, each blaming the other.

"Richard told me."

"Well, Michael told me."

"Kim called me."

"Jack told Margaret and—"

"That explains it," Mark shouted over the fray. "Margaret can't keep a secret."

Kim spoke up then. "She kept her pregnancy a secret for four whole weeks."

Margaret glared around the room, her tiny hands on the table. "I didn't want to spoil *your* being the one with the new baby," she said to Kim. "Even though you're ahead of me in the girl department."

"Sorry." Kim stuck out her tongue, then smiled over at her baby daughter. "There's enough joy for both of us, though—boy or girl."

Margaret nodded to that. "And—I can keep a secret. It wasn't me," she told the group. "Richard got the whole thing started about Leandra cooking for the Welbys. It was just so funny, picturing Leandra stringing lights and cooking dumplings. Dumplings, of all things? Lea, why didn't you start with something simple like canned soup?"

Leandra slapped a hand on the table, her patience growing thin. "Okay, okay. I'm trying not to lose my temper, since you are all family and some of you are in a delicate way. But that's enough. Can we change the subject, please?"

Sensing that her daughter was about to cause a scene, Colleen nodded. "Leandra's right. This is none of our business."

"Good," Leandra replied, taking a piece of Texas Toast to sop up barbecue sauce. "I'm glad someone in this room can be tactful."

"Let's change the subject then," Richard replied. "Let's talk about…oh…say…birdhouses. I was expecting to have at least half a dozen to sell before Christmas."

"Birdhouses?" Margaret perked up again. "You mean, like the one on the table in the front hallway. Didn't Nate—"

Leandra stood up then. "Yes, Nate made the birdhouse, for Mama, as a means of repaying *her* for Thanksgiving."

"That was nice," Mark said, a hand on his sister's arm. "Sit down and tell us about it, Lea."

Leandra saw the warning look in Mark's eyes. Ever the calm, detached professor, he was telling her to let it go. If she lost her cool, they would just suspect that she really did have feelings for Nate. But Mark looked as if he already knew that, too.

She sank back down in her chair, defeated. "Yes, Nate makes birdhouses in a little workshop out in his barn. I was impressed with the craftsmanship, so I told Richard about them, hoping that he would display some of them in the store."

"Which I agreed to do," Richard said, his tone serious at last. "Only I have yet to receive any. Did you talk to Nate about bringing them by?"

"Not really," Leandra admitted. "We didn't get around to discussing it."

"Better things to do," Michael said, giving his wife a knowing look.

Leandra gritted her teeth, then asked God for patience. "I was getting the children to bed and cleaning up the kitchen."

"Dumplings everywhere—" Jack began, but his mother's hand on his arm stopped him. "Oh, back to the birdhouses—do you think Richard could actually sell some of them? I mean, are they that good?"

Richard pointed toward the front hallway. "Have you looked at the one up front? It's truly the work of an artist. I think Nate has real talent."

"So do I," Leandra said, glad to be focusing on something besides her personal feelings for Nate. "I had hoped to convince him to turn it into a business. He could market them and sell them on a regular basis. The money would make a nice nest egg for his children's education."

"He'd need start-up funding, honey," Howard reminded her. "Did you talk to him about that?"

"No," she said. "But I'm glad you're willing to consider lending him the money."

"I told you, we'd already agreed to that years ago," Howard said. "Just too bad he never came back in to secure the loan."

Jack spoke up then. "Lea, I had doubts about Nate, but if Dad thinks it's worth a shot, then I'm behind it. I wish him luck." He smiled over at her then. "And you, too."

"Thank you," Leandra said, feeling better. "Nate would appreciate that. He told me he grew up in an orphanage—he's not used to accepting help from others. He'd want to do this on his own, his way, I'm sure."

Which is why she'd been hesitant about approaching him. He'd probably just turn her down flat. Especially now, when she'd already interfered in his personal life.

Howard gave her a reassuring look. "Nate has a good credit record and he pays his bills. He could get the loan on his own merit, so don't worry about that." Then he pointed a finger around the room. "And of course, this information shouldn't leave this room."

"Of course." Jack nodded, then gave his wife a meaningful look.

"I know the rules," Margaret said, rolling her eyes. "We don't discuss bank customers' finances."

"Even if we are a talkative, informative bunch," Mark teased.

"So when are you going to talk to him, get this thing rolling?" Richard looked at Leandra across the table.

"I don't know," she said, aware that everyone was staring at her. "We've both been so busy."

"Well, don't waste too much time," Richard replied. "We've only got a few days before Christmas and this Saturday will be my busiest day. We could use a good, quality product—people love unique handmade things to give for Christmas. Then after the rush, he can see about turning this into a full-fledged business venture."

"I'll try to talk to him soon," Leandra said.

Finally, the conversation drifted to other things. An hour later, dinner was over, leaving Leandra to do the dishes and wonder just when she'd find a chance to talk to Nate. They'd managed to be civil to each other over the last couple of rehearsals, in spite of being thrown together as the lion and the lamb. But it was easy to stand quietly like a demure lamb when you were actually wearing fleece. And she had to admit, Nate made a formidable lion, tall and golden, and almost savage-looking in spite of the cute costume.

The hard part was trying to avoid Nate when they weren't in costume. The man seemed to be everywhere at once. Whereas before, she could usually find him away from the crowd, now he was right in the center of things.

Was it all an act for her benefit, or was Nate beginning to see that he needed to spend more time with his children? Was he actually enjoying himself?

He'd helped with the set, just as he'd promised. He'd nailed his lion's roar on the first try, causing everyone to clap and laugh. He even seemed more comfortable around the members of the troupe, most of whom belonged to Leandra's church. And she'd seen him talking quietly to Reverend Powell on several occasions. He'd even donated his check back to the church, as a means of thanking the Reverend for being so kind to his family.

She'd had to find this out from Margaret of all people!

Because Nate didn't speak to Leandra unless it was absolutely necessary. That made having to stand by him, knowing he was right behind her onstage, even harder to bear. She could sense his presence as surely as she could smell his clean, woodsy soap. She could hear him breathing when the music ended and everything grew quiet.

She could easily reach out and touch him, given how Mr. Crawford had positioned them at the right side of the manger scene, set apart from the donkeys and camels, since they represented peace on earth.

Peace on earth. But no peace in her heart. Not as long as Nate was around.

And not as long as her well-meaning family continued to tease her and question her about her relationship with Nate and his children. She still needed to ask him about those beautiful birdhouses, but Leandra couldn't find the nerve to approach him.

As she climbed in to bed that night, snuggled underneath her mother's old quilt, birdhouses were the last thing on Leandra's mind. That little idea would have to be put on the back burner. Nate wouldn't listen to her idea, not now. Maybe not ever.

And she wouldn't interfere again, no matter how much she longed to be snuggled with him on the couch in front of the fire.

Two days later, Leandra was working at city hall, doing the final paperwork on expenses for the Christmas pageant, when the phone rang.

The receptionist told her, "It's Layla Welby. She sounds really upset."

Wondering what was wrong, Leandra remembered the children had left today's early rehearsal with Mr. Tuttle. Since Nate hadn't been able to get away from work, the kindly old man had promised to see them home safely.

"I'll talk to her," Leandra said, a million worries flowing through her head. While the fourteen-year-old was more than capable of taking care of her younger siblings, Leandra still worried about the children when they were home alone after school, and now all day because of the winter break. Taking a deep breath, she waited for the connection. After getting the go-ahead from the receptionist, she said, "Layla, it's Leandra. Is everything all right?"

"Miss Lea, you've got to come quick. Daddy's at work, but I called his cell phone and I can't reach him. I left a message with the dispatcher, but Daddy hasn't called back. I didn't know who else to call."

Leandra's heart stopped in her chest, then took up a fast-paced beat. "What is it, honey? Are you hurt? Are Brittney and Matt okay?"

"We're fine, but there's a strange woman knocking at the door. She wants us to let her in but I don't know if I should let her come in the house. She says she's our Aunt Helen."

"Then what's the matter?" Leandra asked, confused. "Surely if she's your aunt—"

Layla gulped, then raised her voice for emphasis. "Miss Lea, you don't get it. We don't have an Aunt Helen."

Chapter Twelve

Leandra tried not to break the speed limit on the way out of town, but the need to get to the Welby place made her push her car to the limit. Trying to think back, she remembered that Nate didn't know his parents or any family, so this woman couldn't be any relation to him.

But what about Alicia's parents? Her mother was dead, but what about her father?

Nate never mentioned his father-in-law. He'd said Alicia's folks were just starting to come around, had just reconciled things with Alicia when she'd been killed. And then her mother had died. Had they tried to made amends with her husband and their grandchildren before that death? Nate hadn't shared much about that with her. And she'd never heard him mention an Aunt Helen.

There was a lot Nate hadn't shared. The man was locked up as tight as a jar of pickled peaches. Sealed. Not to be opened until he was good and ready. And Leandra was beginning to think Nate might not ever be ready to open himself to the world, or God, ever again.

*Lord, we need You right now. I need You to help me.
I promised I wouldn't interfere again but I have to help
Layla. I can't ignore the plea of a child.*

She wouldn't ignore Layla's call for help. No matter
how mad it might make Nate later. But how could he
be mad at her for this? If his children were in danger,
he'd want someone to come. Even Leandra.

Bearing that in mind, she pulled the car up to the
house, noticing the rented sedan parked in the driveway.

Leandra stopped her own car behind the big sedan.
And that's when she noticed the woman pacing back
and forth on the front porch.

No wonder Layla refused to let the woman in the
house.

Aunt Helen, or whoever she was, was wearing a
bright-red Christmas sweater. Rudolph the Red-Nosed
Reindeer was plastered across the front in vivid brown
and white sequins, and each time the woman moved,
Rudolph's shiny red nose blinked brightly. Underneath
the thick sweater, she wore black wool pants, impec-
cably cut, over three-inch-heeled black patent pumps.
She had a ring on every finger, in every color of jewel
imaginable. Each time she moved her hands, her long
red fingernails warred for attention along with her dia-
monds, emeralds and rubies. Her hair was a silvery-gray
and her lips were the same striking red as her sweater.
When she heard Leandra's car pull up, she picked up an
expensive-looking black patent leather purse that looked
more like a suitcase and whirled around, one hand on
her tiny hip, to stare down at Leandra.

"And who are you?" the woman asked, looking through her dark sunglasses at Leandra.

Leandra took another calming breath. Up close, the woman was really beautiful. And well preserved. Her makeup was minimal, except for the bright lipstick, and her dark eyebrows arched out over her big eyes in perfect symmetry. She had an air of wealth about her in spite of the fluffy, big hair and the ridiculous sweater. She also held an air of intimidation, as if she were used to giving orders and expecting them to be followed precisely.

"I'm Leandra Flanagan, a friend of the Welbys," Leandra told the woman as she walked slowly up the steps. "And I don't think we've met."

Inside the house, Mutt barked loudly at this intrusion. At least the children had a capable watchdog.

The woman took off her dark shades and shoved them into the bottomless purse, then put out a hand to Leandra. "Well, I'll be. You're a tiny little thing, ain't you? I'm Helen Montgomery."

Leandra took her hand, noted the firm handshake, then gave the woman a slight smile. "Can I help you, Mrs. Montgomery?"

"It's Miss, honey. Never married, never wanted to. But I would like to see my nieces and my nephew in there before I die. If that's all right with *everybody* here." She glared toward the front door, where all three Welby children were peeking out from behind the glass panes, and Mutt's shaggy face could be seen peering over the window seal. "Stubborn lot, ain't they? Got that naturally, I reckon."

Leandra immediately liked Aunt Helen, even if she wasn't quite sure if she could trust her. "I'm sorry. They're just following their father's orders. He's at work and they've been told never to open the door to strangers. That's why they called me."

"But I ain't no stranger," Aunt Helen said, clearly appalled. "I'm a Montgomery, honey." When Leandra could only stand there with a questioning look, the woman added, "Of the *Kentucky* Montgomerys. Land sakes, girl, I'm their grandfather's sister."

Realization dawned on Leandra. "Their grandfather—you mean, Alicia's father?"

"The very one," Helen Montgomery said, bobbing her head. To her hairdresser's credit, not one hair moved when she did it. "Davis Montgomery is my brother."

"I see," Leandra replied, clearly caught between a rock and a hard place. "Well, it's nice to meet you, but I don't know if Nate—"

Aunt Helen threw up her bejeweled hands, causing the gold coin bracelet looped around her tiny wrist to jingle against her aged skin. "Look, Leandra is it? I've been all the way around the world, been traveling for years, moving here and there. Well, I'm tired of traveling. When I got home to Kentucky and asked my brother about these three children—children I've haven't seen in years—I knew I had to come here. My brother is a stubborn old cuss, but I'm even more stubborn than him. And I want to get to know my kinfolk hiding behind that door."

Leandra could feel for the woman. And for the children behind the door, too. Why on earth hadn't Nate and Mr. Montgomery tried to work things out between the two of them, for the sake of those three precious children?

She looked heavenward, thinking, *What should I do, Lord?*

Helen watched Leandra, her intense blue eyes moving over Leandra's face with all the bearing of a hawk. "Look, honey, I don't blame you for worrying. I guess I am a sight, standing here stomping my feet in the cold." Then she reached over to take Leandra's hand in hers. "I'm a churchgoing, God-fearing woman, believe it or not. And I have to do right by those children in there, since my brother hasn't bothered to make amends." She held tight to Leandra's hand, then leaned close. "I don't have any younguns of my own, and my brother is like a brick wall, hard as stone. I'm hoping I can bridge the gap between him and Nate."

When Leandra saw the genuine concern, coupled with real tears, in the woman's eyes, she knew she couldn't turn her away. "Nate won't like this," she said, thinking he'd blame her for interfering again. But what choice did she have?

"Suga', you let me handle Nathan Welby," Helen Montgomery told her, patting her hand. "Now, can we please go inside out of this cold? I'm gonna take a chill, standing here without my coat on."

Leandra finally motioned to the children. "You can open the door, Layla. It's all right."

The teenager unlocked the big door, then opened it slightly, her gaze traveling over Aunt Helen in a mixture of awe and fear while Mutt tried to claw his way through the crack. "Are you sure, Miss Lea?"

"Positive," Leandra told her, hoping she'd made the right decision. "Hold Mutt off her, okay?"

Layla opened the door, then told Mutt to get. The dog sniffed Helen a couple of times, but when she growled at him with arching eyebrows and an amused expression on her porcelain face, he took off running out into the yard.

Leandra guided Helen inside, then turned to the three wide-eyed children standing in a circle in the hallway. "This is Helen Montgomery—your mother's aunt, which makes her your great-aunt."

"So you really are our Aunt Helen?" Brittney asked shyly, her little hands covering her face.

"That I am, suga'," Aunt Helen said as she dropped down on her knees right there on the floor. "Can Aunt Helen have a big ol' hug?"

Brittney glanced up at Leandra for direction. Leandra smiled and nodded. "It's okay, honey."

Brittney rushed into the woman's open arms then, hugging her as if she'd known her all her life. "I never had an aunt before."

"Yes, you did," Aunt Helen replied, looking up at Leandra. "You had me all the time. You just didn't know it. And bless your hearts, you don't remember me, do you?"

The children stood there with blank expressions on their faces.

"My hair's gone more gray since they last saw me," she explained to Leandra with a hand over her mouth.

"No, we don't remember." Layla stood back, still wary, but when Helen rose to give her an unnerving head-to-toe appraisal, she shrugged. "I'm sorry I wouldn't let you in."

"That's all right by me," Helen told her. "You were just doing what your daddy taught you. And you did a mighty good job of it, too."

Leandra noticed she didn't push for a hug from Layla. Instead, she just reached out and touched a gnarled hand to the girl's cheek. "So like your mother."

Then she turned to Matt. "And you, young man. From what I can tell—and if my memory serves me correctly—you look a whole lot like your papa—handsome fellow."

"How'd you know that?" Matt questioned.

Helen gave him a bittersweet smile. "I was at your mama's—" She stopped, then quickly changed her story. "Your lovely mama, bless her, sent me a picture of the two of them on their wedding day. They sure looked happy." She brightened, then touched a finger to his nose. "And you sure look like Nathan."

"Everybody tells me that," Matt said, his blue eyes big with wonder. "Where'd you get all those rings and bracelets?"

Aunt Helen hooted with laughter, then grabbed Matt to hug him close, the rings and bracelets sparkling and clanking as she did so. "I got them here and there, all over the place. Italy, Morocco, Greece, Japan. I been everywhere and then some. 'Course you'd never know that from this Southern drawl, would you now?" She stood back then, her gaze moving over the three awestruck children. "But let me tell you something right now—there is no place like home. And there is nothing like having family."

"Is that why you came to see us, 'cause we're family?" Brittney asked, her finger reaching out to touch a dangling bracelet.

"Certainly," Aunt Helen replied, taking the colorful beaded bracelet off to drape it around Brittney's tiny arm. "Hold on to that for me, will you? And don't lose it. It was handmade by my Native American friend in Oklahoma—a full-blooded Caddo."

"You know Indians?" Matt asked, fascinated.

"I know *Native Americans,*" Aunt Helen gently corrected. "In fact, I'm a walking history lesson. Betcha didn't know you had such a smart ol' aunt, did you?"

"We didn't know we had you at all," Brittney said by way of an apology. "Or we woulda let you in."

"That's okay," Helen said. "I'm in now, darlin'. And I ain't going anywhere for a good long while."

Leandra felt tears pricking at her eyes. That might be good news to the children and good for Aunt Helen's sense of family obligation. But she knew one person who might not like having a long-lost relative coming for a holiday visit.

Nate Welby did not like surprises.

And he especially wouldn't like *her* being involved in this one.

Not one little bit.

A little bit further and he'd be home.

Nate pushed the old truck up the highway, looking forward to a hot meal and maybe a warm fire in the fireplace. His pledge to be a better father was actually turning into a real commitment. Maybe prayer really did work.

Except that today, he hadn't been able to take a break from work to attend the rehearsals, and to top things off, the batteries on his cell phone needed recharging. He'd forgotten to charge the thing last night. Too many distractions. Well, he'd make up for those slipups by spending the evening with his children.

He had dinner in the take-out bag next to him in the truck—good food—fresh cooked vegetables and baked chicken from one of his favorite diners out on the highway. He'd make a fire—that had been the ritual since Leandra had started that first one the other night—then he'd read Brittney the Christmas story she'd been begging him to read to her for weeks now. And while the children were out of school for the Christmas holidays, he also planned to help Matt with his math, put in some overtime so his son would be up to speed once school started back up. Adding and subtracting sure had changed since Nate's school days.

But a father could change and adjust with the times, too, he guessed.

It was amazing how he *had managed* to change his schedule, change his whole mind-set, so he could spend more time with his children. It hadn't been as hard as he'd envisioned.

He just had to take it one step at a time, the same way he'd been doing everything since Alicia had died. The dread of coming home each night was slowly being replaced with the need to see his children, to know they were safe and happy, something he'd only monitored from a distance until now.

And he had to admit, it was good to find the house all aglow with holiday lights each night. The bright lights and Christmas decorations chased away the gloom, the bad memories. And maybe this spring, he'd start on that remodeling project he and Alicia had always talked about. He could handle that, if he just took things slow.

Start off slow, work your way up to it.

That's how he viewed everything in life and now his own philosophy was working fine. Except when it came to his feelings about Leandra.

One whole week and he missed her already.

One whole week of being in that huge auditorium with her, with other people all around. And yet, sometimes it felt as if he and Leandra were the only two people in the room. He'd get a whiff of her perfume before she rounded the corner. He'd see her in that funny lamb's costume, white fleece from head to toe, and remember the way she felt in his arms. Then he'd remember the pain in her eyes when he'd accused her of not knowing anything about being a mother.

Lord, I wish I could take that back, he thought now.

But it was too late. Too late for him to admit that Leandra had been a kind, considerate friend to his children, even if she'd never been a mother to anyone before.

"She has the right instincts," he said out loud, the country tune on the radio echoing in his head. "And I shouldn't have been so cruel to her."

If only he could have another chance. He wouldn't rush headlong into it this time around. He wouldn't give her a birdhouse and a kiss. He'd just take things slow, nice and easy, to be sure he knew what he was doing.

Nate turned the truck into the yard, then stopped at the mailbox. Leandra's car was parked at his front door, beside another car he didn't recognize.

Nate shook his head, then slapped a hand on the steering wheel. "I hear You talking, Lord. And I guess You're answering my prayer." A little hesitant, he had to wonder what Leandra was up to now.

And maybe now was his chance to make amends with Leandra, to take things slow and win her over with a steady, sure heart. If only he could be so sure.

One way to find out.

He grinned then. "Please, Lord, all I ask is no more dumplings. A man's stomach can only take so much."

Chapter Thirteen

Standing back to admire the set dinner table, Leandra laughed at how Helen Montgomery had performed her culinary wizardry and kept the children entertained all at the same time. She had produced an exotic pasta dish from a few noodles and some butter, milk and cheese, complete with steamed vegetables and colorful chopped peppers. And she'd let the children help with each step, guiding them, coaxing them, telling them stories every bit as colorful as the food. She also taught them words in several foreign languages as she went along from the main course to some sort of poached dessert involving apples and cinnamon.

For someone who'd never had children of her own, Aunt Helen sure knew a lot about how to control and entertain them.

Much more than I'll ever know.

That thought made Leandra wince, but she tried to keep her own smile intact while she glanced at the clock. Nate was late and she was worried. Dreading the moment he arrived, she was still concerned that he hadn't called to check on the children. Maybe his promise to do better had all been an act, after all.

"And maybe I should have gone home for dinner," she mumbled to herself as she poured milk for the children and iced tea—Aunt Helen's own spiced recipe—for the adults.

She'd planned to do just that—go on home. But Layla had seemed shy and nervous around bubbly Helen. When Leandra had announced she was about to leave, the child had stopped her with an imploring look.

"Can't you stay with us, Miss Lea? You don't have to cook this time."

Aunt Helen immediately picked up on that little tidbit. "Oh, you *are* a close friend, then? Do you cook for Nathan and the children often?"

"I've only know the Welbys a short time," Leandra explained. "They're all involved in the Christmas pageant—"

"And Miss Lea is in charge of everything," Brittney added, grinning. "She says this is going to be the best Christmas pageant the town of Marshall has ever seen."

"Really?" Aunt Helen's perfectly arched brows shot up at that declaration. "I'm thinking I'd better stick around and find out for myself." Her sharp gaze centered on Leandra. "And what about you and Nate?"

Brittney looked up, mouth opened to reply to that particular question, but Leandra shook her head at the little girl and gave her a mock-stern look. Which caused Brittney's bottom lip to jut out in a pout.

"We're friends," Leandra hurriedly explained, then before the children could give their own definitions of what that meant, she shooed them into the kitchen to finish their chores—with Brittney glaring at her the whole time.

But she hadn't fooled Aunt Helen. "Friends, huh? I'm sure Nathan could use a *friend.* The poor man's been out here on his own for too long, from everything I've seen and heard—which hasn't been much since I've been out of the country for months on end. I should have kept in touch more."

Curious, Leandra asked, "What *do* you know about Nathan? Does Mr. Montgomery ever mention Nate and the children at all?"

"Stay for dinner and we'll talk," Helen had replied, her gaze both knowing and understanding.

So now here Leandra stood two hours later, waiting and watching, hoping for answers to all her burning questions, hoping to find some way of understanding Nate and his pain and his anger. She and Helen hadn't had that talk yet. The older woman had somehow managed to keep too busy with cooking and cuddling the children to answer Leandra's earlier question.

Of course, Helen had been more willing to answer all the questions the kids asked—mostly about their beautiful mother. After hearing the tidbits of information and anecdotes Helen dispensed so clearly and lovingly, Leandra felt as if she'd never live up to the image of Alicia Montgomery Welby.

And yet she had so many questions.

Why am I here, Lord? What am I searching for? Why does this family seem to draw me? Why does Nate seem to be the one?

That thought stopped her. The one? *The one for me? The one I could so easily love? Am I crazy?*

"No," Leandra said to herself. "No. I'm just concerned for this family, for these children and their plight." And she did care about Nate. But she wouldn't let her feelings develop into anything other than those of a concerned friend.

She only wanted to help, not hinder.

But would Nate see that, understand when he came home to find a strange woman in his kitchen and Leandra supervising the whole thing?

She heard the front door opening, then whirled to face him. "Nate, hello."

He filled the doorway in his battered leather jacket and worn jeans, a big man with a wavy tawny-colored mane and eyes that seemed to see right through her denials as their depths changed from golden to bronze.

"Hello, yourself," he replied, a bemused smile on his face. Then he sniffed. "That sure smells good, but I brought dinner." He held up the two white take-out bags he balanced in one hand. "If I'd known—"

Leandra didn't miss the implication. She should have called him. "The children couldn't reach you," she tried to explain. "So Layla called me at work."

Nate's expression shifted from a smile to a frown. "The batteries went out on my cell phone and I was away from the site office. I didn't get any messages." Then he continued, "Is everything all right?"

"Yes—no." Seeing the fear and concern in his eyes, Leandra held up a hand. "Everything's fine, Nate. It's just that...the children had a visitor—"

"Who?" At the sound of voices in the kitchen, Nate slammed the door shut with his booted foot, then headed down the hall, past where Leandra stood in the formal dining room. Taking a deep breath, she hurried around the long table to head him off in the kitchen.

But she was too late. By the time she got around the corner, Nate was standing there on the other side of the big kitchen, the take-out bags still in his hand, a look of utter shock and confusion coloring his face. "Helen?"

Helen Montgomery turned around from the stove, the Rudolph nose on her sweater blinking at Nate just over the ruffles of the white apron she'd donned early. "Hello there, Nathan. How are you?"

Nate stood there, his mouth dropping open as memories assaulted his senses. Alicia had loved her Aunt Helen.

"She's like Mary Poppins," Alicia had told him. "She drops in with all her tales of traveling the world, brings me all sorts of fun gifts and treasures, makes life so much fun, then she leaves again. And I always miss her so much. She'll understand, Nate. She'll understand about us and how much we love each other. She'll come to our wedding. I know she will."

And she had.

Nate closed his eyes to the pain and the memory of Alicia's words. Helen Montgomery had understood almost too well just exactly how much he had loved her niece. Which meant she now knew exactly how much he was hurting. And he didn't want or need the pity he thought he saw in her crystal-blue eyes.

"Well, don't just stand there with your chin on the floor, boy. C'mere and give me a hug."

"She likes to hug," Matt warned his daddy as Nate somehow managed to set the bags on the counter. In two strides, he was across the room, enveloped in Helen's arms.

"Ah, it sure is good to see you again," Helen told him. "It's been too long."

He remembered a big car pulling up to the gravesite. He remembered a petite woman swathed in fur and jewels getting out of the car. She had stood apart from the rest, watching and listening as the minister said one more prayer over Alicia's grave. And she had stayed at the gravesite long after everyone else had left. Nate knew this because he'd found Helen there when he'd gone back later that day. She'd given him a calm pep talk—something about remembering all the good in life—then after a brief, silent hug, she'd climbed in the big car and...left.

And now, here she stood in his kitchen.

"Over three years since the...funeral," Nate said now, conscious of the children watching him. They probably expected him to rant and rave, to throw one of his fits. Truth told, that's exactly what he wanted to do. Then he looked over at Leandra and saw that same expectation in her dark eyes, too.

Well, he'd just have to show them, all of them, that he was trying to change. So he pushed back the dark memories swirling like a wintry fog around his head and mustered up a smile that felt like plastic pulling at his skin.

"What brings you to Marshall, anyway?" he asked Helen as he stood back to look down at her. Even in her high heels, she was still a petite woman. But what she lacked in size Helen made up for in integrity and determination.

Nate *was* glad to see her.

"I came to see my nieces and that handsome nephew," she said, waving a hand at Matt. Then she looked back up at Nathan. "I had no idea things weren't good between you and Davis... I wish I'd known."

"He doesn't discuss us," Nate said, pulling away.

And *he* never talked about Davis Montgomery. What was the point? They'd both made a feeble attempt, while Mrs. Montgomery was still alive, but once she'd passed on things had changed and Davis had stopped calling. The man had long ago washed his hands of Nate and his own grandchildren.

"Davis is a bitter, self-centered old man," Helen replied, nodding her understanding as she untied her apron.

"Who's Davis?" Matt asked, curiosity widening his blue eyes.

Helen's gaze flew to Nate's face. "You mean to tell

me these children don't even *know* about their grandfather?"

Layla glared at Nate then. "We're not allowed to talk about him, or our mother, either."

Nate ran a hand over the five o'clock shadow of his beard, figuring it was payback time and Layla had a lot of resentment stacked against him. "Now, Layla, that's not entirely true—"

"Yes, it is," she replied, capitalizing on having someone's attention at last. "Every time I ask you something about Mama, or our grandfather in Kentucky, you change the subject or tell me you don't want to talk about that right now." Then she lowered her head, breaking Nate's heart with her soft-spoken plea. "We need to know, Daddy. Can we ask Aunt Helen…let her tell us some more stories about Mama and…and our granddaddy?"

"We have a granddaddy?" Brittney asked, her eyes wide, her little hands on her hips. "Nobody *never* tells me anything."

And nobody tried to correct her grammar this time, either.

Nate glanced around to find every eye in the room centered on him. Waves of guilt and remorse washed over him, beating him back even as they cleansed him. How could he have been so blind, so stupid? Why had he denied his children this one thing—the legacy of their mother's memory?

Because he was bitter and unforgiving, pure and simple.

Looking toward Layla for understanding, he nodded. "Honey, you can ask Aunt Helen anything you'd like, okay?"

Surprisingly, the room stayed quiet. Where Nate had expected the three children to bombard their great-aunt with questions, instead they all just stood there, staring at him as if he'd actually changed into the lion they'd forced him to play in the pageant.

Then Layla walked over to him and put her arms around his midsection to give him a hug. "Thank you, Daddy," she said before backing up, her head down. "Supper's ready."

He watched as Helen gave him a quiet, questioning look before she herded the kids through the wide doorway leading to the dining room. Then he turned to Leandra. "I've still got a long way to go, don't I?"

She glanced up at him, pride evident in her eyes. "That was a first step, Nate."

Nate pulled her close then, fighting the need to hug her tight. "I am trying, you know. And I—I need to apologize for the things I said the other night—"

"You don't have to do that," Leandra replied. "I'm just glad you're not angry with me for being here tonight. I didn't want you to think I was interfering again."

He brushed a wayward curl off her cheek. "How could I think that? You came when my children needed you. I'm grateful for that."

She relaxed then, her smile reminding him of how pretty she really was. She was wearing a long, cream-colored sweater over a floral skirt in shades of rich brown and stark gold with a little red mixed in. His autumn woman.

When had he decided she was *his?* he wondered. He couldn't lay claim to her. It wouldn't be fair to either of them. But he sure liked having her in his arms.

Oblivious to Nate's inner turmoil, Leandra laid her head against his chest then looked up with a little chuckle.

"Aunt Helen gave us quite a scare," she said with a shrug and a shake of her head, making her hair fall back across her face. "She is…a very interesting woman."

"She doesn't suffer fools," Nate replied, grinning. "It was just such a surprise."

"I hope you don't mind that I let her in—after giving her the third degree, of course."

"No, I don't mind. It's kinda nice, having her here again." *And having you to come home to,* he thought. Maybe he *could* ease into being with Leandra. He'd been thinking about her all day and now here she was. Just like everything else, if he took things slow…

Leandra laughed then. "And…guess what?"

Nate quirked a brow, enjoying this intimacy, this brief stolen time with her, and wanting badly to kiss that laugh on her beautiful lips. But that wouldn't be taking it slow. That would be another hasty mistake. So instead, he said, "What?"

"I didn't cook dinner."

"Well, amen to that."

When she playfully hit him on the arm, he grabbed

her hand. "May I escort you to the table, Miss Flan-again?"

"I'd be delighted, Mr. Welby."

Nate guided her into the dining room, a sense of peace settling over his shoulders. But when he glanced down the table to find Helen's cool blue gaze on him, he instantly regretted that sense of peace.

Alicia's aunt was here for a rare visit, and he'd just been standing in the next room, longing to kiss another woman. What had he been thinking?

And what was Helen Montgomery thinking about him right now?

"I'm thinking our Nate likes you," Helen told Leandra later as they cleared the kitchen. Nate was in the den playing a video game with Matt. Every now and then, they could hear a groan of frustration from the father as his child scored yet another baseball victory.

Leandra glanced over at Helen, trying to decide if the woman was for her or against her. All through dinner, Helen had laughed and chattered away in her rich drawl, mostly talking to the children. But Leandra hadn't missed the keen, interested looks or the knowing expressions Helen had sent toward her and Nate.

Deciding she had nothing to hide or be ashamed of, Leandra nodded, then faced the other woman. "He does like me. We're good friends."

"So, you feel the same about him?"

Leandra focused on the constantly blinking Rudolph

nose centered on Helen's left shoulder. "Yes, I do. I like Nate a lot and I adore the children."

Helen stood there, staring, those perfectly sculptured brows lifted in two highly feminine arches. "I see."

"Does that bother you?" Leandra asked, her hands on the counter.

"Should that bother me, honey?" Helen retorted, the keen stare intact.

Leandra knew she was being studied and dissected. "Alicia was a special person," she said, groping for the right words. "Anyone who enters this house can see that. I'm not trying to take her place."

"And anyone who comes here can also see that Nate's let time come to a standstill," Helen replied. "Alicia had such high hopes for this old house. She woulda fixed it up into a showplace."

"But now—"

Helen turned to face Leandra, interrupting her with a hand on her arm. "But now, it's time for Nathan to get on with his life. Is that what you were going to say?"

Leandra faced her squarely, with a clear determination. "No, actually I was going to say that I hope Nate can pour the love he felt for Alicia into raising their children. That should be his top priority. They need their father, to guide them in life and in their faith."

Helen dropped her hand away from Leandra's arm. "And they need their grandfather, too."

Surprised, Leandra lifted her own brows. "Do you think Nate and Mr. Montgomery will ever be able to get past their resentment and anger?"

"Only one way to find out," Helen replied in a low voice. "Get them together."

"Is that why you came here?" Leandra asked, dread in her heart.

"Yes, it is," Helen told her. "And now, I'm even more sure I'm doing the right thing."

"Oh, and why is that?"

"Because of you, young lady. I had my doubts at first, but now I know. I was hoping someone around here would help me bring Nate and my stubborn brother together, and I do believe you're perfect for the job."

Chapter Fourteen

Leandra opened her mouth to speak, then stood there staring across the kitchen counter at Helen Montgomery. "You can't be serious?"

"As serious as cactus thorns," Helen replied, her gaze steady and level. "Now don't tell me you ain't up to the challenge. I thought I had you pegged for a fighter."

Leandra didn't know whether to be flattered or on full alert. "I fight for what I believe in—"

"And don't you believe those children need some attention and love from their grandfather?"

"Of course I'd like to see that happen, but—"

"But what? Afraid Nate will pout and fume? I don't doubt he'll throw a good and mighty fit. But we can't let Davis and him keep us from doing what's right." Helen let out a deep breath. "The good Lord knows those two are as stubborn as the day is long. When I last talked to Davis, he told me he was going to try hard to reconcile things with Nate—"

"How long ago was that?" Leandra interrupted, wondering if Nate had turned the man away.

"About two years," Helen admitted. "I'm as guilty of neglecting them as anyone," she added, shaking her head. "But I had some wanderlust left in my soul. Didn't think I had to worry, since Davis promised me." She stopped, banged a hand against the counter. "I could just shake both of 'em."

Leandra understood completely, but she had to make Helen see that she wasn't the one to help bridge this gap. "I don't think Nate would appreciate me being involved in this. He's already made it clear that I should let him raise his children the way he sees fit."

"He can't see past his grief and his love for Alicia, honey," Helen returned. Then the fire in her crystal-blue eyes softened at the expression of pain and discomfort Leandra couldn't hide. "'Course, you know all about that, don't you?"

"Yes, I do," Leandra said. "I care about Nate, but I've accepted that we can't be anything more than just friends. And I have to tell you, I'll be leaving Marshall right after Christmas."

Helen's pout was pure disapproval. "And why's that?"

"I have to go back to Houston. I've got to find another job or I'll have to give up my apartment, my life back there."

"Are you so sure you want to go back?" Helen asked, her brows arching in that disconcerting way again. "Honey, we just met and I don't know all the details, but the way you look at Nathan Welby—well, I get the impression you'd like things around here to change in a positive way, with you being part of the positive. Am I wrong?"

Leandra couldn't answer that. If she spoke the words out loud, she'd melt into a helpless puddle of defeat. Instead, she said, "As I told you, Nate and I have agreed to be friends. And… I have to make some decisions regarding my future. I've held off long enough."

Helen lifted her chin, then gave Leandra a sideways glance. "Sometimes, we just have to trust in the Lord and let things take place in a natural kind of way."

"You sound like my mother."

"We're older, wiser, and we've got the blessed assurance of God's wisdom," Helen replied. "Now, can I count on you?"

"Count on her for what?" Nate asked from the hallway. He strolled into the kitchen, a slight smile on his face. "The munchkins and the Mutt are all in bed at last, but what are you two up to?"

Helen gave Leandra a warning look. "I want to get to know Leandra a little better and I'm counting on her to come around more while I'm visiting," Helen said. "To help me adjust."

"Just how long are you planning on staying?" Nate asked, a teasing light in his eyes.

"Oh, you know what they say," Helen countered. "After three days…"

Nate grinned, then put an arm around her shoulders. "You can stay as long as you want, you know that."

"Mighty generous of you," Helen said, hugging

him close. "How about through next week—at least till Christmas?"

Nate glanced over at Leandra. "That'll be just fine. We could use some cheerful company around here for the holidays."

"Then it's settled," Helen said, lifting her arm away. "And on that note, I'm going to bed. Layla said I could bunk with her."

"She's up there getting your spot ready right now," Nate told her. "Sleep tight."

"Don't let the bedbugs bite," Helen finished. Then to Leandra, "It was good to meet you, suga'. Hope to see you soon." She leaned close. "And don't worry about that other. I'll take care of it."

"What other?" Nate asked, a mock frown on his face.

Helen handled him with a wave of the hand. "Just Christmas surprises—nothing for you to be concerned about just yet."

"Thanks," Leandra told the other woman, relief flooding her senses. "I'm sure we'll see each other again."

After Helen went upstairs, Nate turned to Leandra. "Wanna walk out to the barn with me? I need to check on Honeyboy, make sure he's all warm and toasty in his stall."

Surprised at the invitation, Leandra told her heart to slow down. It took off so fast, she was sure it skipped a few beats. "Sure," she said, a little breathless. "Let me get my coat."

The night was clear and cold, with a full glowing

moon and a million silver-blue stars hanging against a velvet-soft sky.

Nate took her hand to help her down the steps. "Watch that rotten board," he said, grinning up at her.

"I remember it well," she replied, her hand in his. His fingers felt so strong, so sure wrapped around hers.

Together, they slowly made their way down the sloping yard toward the big barn.

"I'm glad you stayed for supper," Nate said. "I didn't like how we left things the other night."

"I shouldn't have been so pushy," she replied. Hoping to make him understand, she added, "You're a very good father—I didn't mean to imply otherwise."

They reached the barn door and Nate turned to face her. "But you were right about a lot of things. I just didn't want to hear the truth."

Longing to ask him what really *was* the truth, Leandra kept her mouth shut. It was enough that they'd formed a tentative bond for now. She didn't want to ruin another evening with Nate. And she reminded herself, now might be the perfect time to bring up the possibility of showcasing some of his birdhouses at Richard's general store. That was a safe, businesslike topic, at least.

She waited as Nate turned on the dim overhead light then tugged her toward Honeyboy's stall in the back.

The big horse snorted hello then pushed his nose over the stall to get a closer look at them.

"He's a beautiful animal, Nate," Leandra said, coming close to let the horse nuzzle her hand. "I think he wants a late-night snack."

Nate obliged by giving Honeyboy a handful of grain. "Not too much now, fellow."

After making sure the horse was comfortable and warm, Nate started back toward the front of the barn.

But Leandra held back. "Nate, could I see some of your work? Maybe some of the birdhouses?"

Giving her a sly grin, he teased. "Want to see my etchings, huh?"

Leandra's blush of warmth sent the chill in the old barn right out the door with her good sense. Ignoring the tingling sensations racing down her spine, she tried to remain serious. "I want to see what you do out here every night. What you've created."

He glanced around, hesitant. "Oh, I don't know about that. There isn't much to see, really."

Leandra pushed ever so gently, determined to show him that his talent shouldn't be hidden away. "C'mon, if all of your designs look like the one you gave my mother, then I'd say there's a lot to see."

"It's just a hobby," he told her. But he took her by the hand even as he said the words. "I don't expect to make anything out of it."

Sensing an opportunity, Leandra said, "Richard was really impressed with our birdhouse. He said he could probably sell dozens of them in his store—what with the Christmas rush and everything."

"Is that a fact?" He grinned, then took her over to the workshop area. He stood silent for a minute, as if remembering, then said, "I don't know if that's possible."

"But wouldn't you like to see?"

Nate turned to face her again. "What's cooking in that pretty head of yours, Leandra?"

She smiled, her eyes widening, her tone hopeful. "I really think you have talent and I also think you should try to promote that talent. I should know. This is what I did for a living back in Houston."

Nate put his hands in the pockets of his leather jacket. "Now *there's* something *I'm* curious about. Tell me about Houston. What happened back there?"

So Nate had found an opportunity to seize the moment, too, Leandra mused. Well, maybe it *was* time she told him the truth. Maybe if he could see that she trusted him enough to let him in on her own failings, he'd learn to trust her in return.

"It's not a pretty story," she said in a low voice.

He reached out to touch her cheek, the warmth of his fingers gliding over her skin making her feel all flush inside. "I want to know."

Deciding to push one more time, she said, "If I tell you all about it, will you show me the rest of your birdhouses?"

"You drive a hard bargain," he replied. Then he nodded and lifted her chin with the pad of his thumb. "Start talking."

Leandra swallowed, suddenly aware that the old barn had become silent and still, waiting. An occasional creak and Honeyboy's contented snort now and then finally broke the silence, but Nate's warm gaze on her kept Leandra from hearing anything over the beating of her pulse.

"I worked for a large advertising firm," she began, her hands in the pockets of her black wool topper. "I did a good job and soon I was promoted to senior account executive."

"What does a senior account executive do exactly?" he asked in that teasing drawl.

She smiled, tried to relax. "I solicited major companies to advertise through us. We designed their ad campaigns and took care of all their public relations and marketing, working with their in-house departments, of course."

He stepped closer. "Of course."

Trying hard not to be distracted by his ever-changing eyes or his intense expression, Leandra continued. "As I said, I was very good at my job and soon, I was making more money than I ever dreamed possible."

"And you became that city woman you always wanted to be."

She didn't miss his frown.

"Yes, that was me." She shook her head, turned to lean against a large support post. "And I made so many mistakes." She let out a sigh, wishing she could just go back and change things. But it was too late for that. And she needed to get this out in the open. "My boss—the president and owner of the company—was an older man named William Myers—" She stopped, remembering that just a few days ago, she'd let it slip to Nate that she'd been involved with her boss. Now she was mortified that he wanted to hear the whole story.

"Go on," Nate said, his gaze level, his expression neither condemning nor questioning.

"We worked together on one of the major campaigns and after that…we started dating." She shrugged, tossed her hair off her face. "At first, it was just platonic—someone to be seen around town with—companionship. He'd never been married and he was content to remain a bachelor. I was convenient, since I didn't make demands on him. And I wasn't ready for marriage or children either, so our relationship worked for both of us."

"What a perfect setup."

She gave him a wry smile. "Or so it seemed." Pushing hair off her face, she began again. "We went along like that for a while. Then something changed in William. He started wanting more and I thought I might be ready to give it, but I wasn't sure if I loved him enough to make such a commitment. I thought he wanted to get married."

Shaking her head, she added, "I got this silly notion that I'd be the wife of a successful executive. I'd live in the big mansion on the hill, have fancy cars, eat at the finest restaurants—all the things I'd dreamed about growing up. But suddenly, having a family *did* seem important. And yet, part of me kept saying, 'But you don't want to get married. You don't want children. You want to enjoy life, stay single.'"

He stopped her there. "Why was that so important, staying single, not having children?"

Letting out a sigh, she replied, "Because I grew up in this large, loud family. I watched my mother always cooking and cleaning, and doing the car pool thing, the volunteer work with the PTA and the church. I guess I just needed some space, away from all the commotion, away from my overbearing, lovable brothers." Shaking her head, she laughed. "I don't know how my mother does it. I only knew I didn't want to find out."

She paused, took another breath. "So what you said the other night—"

"I was wrong to assume that about you," Nate interrupted, anger clouding his face in the moonlight from the partially open door. "You'd make a great mother."

Leandra almost bolted then. The soft, husky catch in his voice only made her want to give in and fall into his arms. She wanted *him* to give her that chance to prove she could be a good mother.

Holding on to the pole behind her, she pushed back the need to be consoled and reassured. "It doesn't matter. You were right. At one time, I only wanted wealth and success. I thought those things would fulfill me, make me complete, give me the world I'd always thought I was missing living here in this small town." She let go of the pole, dropping her hands at her sides. "But I was so wrong. And soon, all my big, shallow dreams were thrown right back in my face."

"What happened?" Nate asked, frustration playing across his face. "I can't stand this—just spit it out."

She had to smile at his impatience, but she dreaded telling him the truth. Finally, after a long deafening silence and the intensity of his unwavering gaze, she blurted the truth. "William didn't ask me to marry him,

Nate. He asked me to move in with him, to live with him."

She watched Nate's face for his reaction. Would he turn away from her, disgusted with her superficial whinings?

"Let me get this straight," he said, his voice quiet. "The man didn't want to marry you, yet he wanted to…to…"

"As my mother would say, he wanted me to live in sin with him."

"And you turned him down flat."

Yet again, he'd somehow managed to make her smile in spite of her misgivings. It had been a statement, not a question. Nate somehow knew exactly what she'd done, which meant he thought she had *some* good qualities, at least.

"Yes, I did. Because I realized that contrary to all my sophisticated pretentious thinking, I was really a country girl at heart. And a Christian. I couldn't do something that went against my moral fiber."

"So you quit."

Another statement. Another sweet assumption.

"No." She actually managed a chuckle. "I broke things off and concentrated on my work. But William couldn't take rejection, especially from someone he considered an underling. So…he started harassing me at work, making demands on me, criticizing everything I did. I was still the same—still hardworking, dedicated. I handled several exclusive accounts but one by one, they were snatched from me and handed over to someone else."

Nate groaned. "What did you see in this weasel, anyway?"

"I started asking myself that same question," she replied. "I had been so blinded by ambition, by success, that I'd almost thrown away everything I believed in, just to say I'd made it in the world. I actually might have married William without loving him, if only he'd asked me."

"You can do much better than that kind of creep," he said, anger justifying his words.

Nate's self-righteous defense of her only endeared him to Leandra even more. "Yes, I know that now," she admitted. "And each time he punished me, I saw more and more that I didn't really belong in that kind of world. A world where money and power are put ahead of people and integrity. The final straw came when he gave me my annual evaluation. I didn't get a promised raise, and two of my best accounts were handed to another woman in the office—a woman he'd just started dating a few weeks before that."

"Scum," Nate mumbled under his breath.

"Exactly," Leandra replied. "I saw the pattern, realized I'd been a complete idiot, and understood that he'd only wanted me as a decoration. He never really cared about me." She dropped her head then. "I felt so used, so dirty.

"But the worst of it was—I'd been using him too, for my own purposes. When I stopped to analyze my own motives, I felt empty, sick at heart. I'd been so selfish, trying to control my life, fighting against the very instincts that make me who I am inside. I'd turned away from God, turned away from the love and support of my family, neglected my own soul's nurturing, and I came very close to making a big mistake. William and I had treated what should have been a deep and abiding love and respect between a man and a woman with little more than a casual passing. When I thought of the love my parents feel for each other, even after all these years, well… I knew I'd been so wrong.

"I went home one night, stood in the middle of my upscale, ritzy apartment, and saw the emptiness all around me. I realized I was just as bad as William. So I did some heavy praying and after pacing the floor all night, I reached a decision."

Drained and exhausted, tears misting her eyes, she looked up at Nate. "The next morning, I turned in my resignation and… I came home."

Nate pulled her into his arms, hugging her with such a fierce warmth and strength, Leandra knew at that moment that she had indeed come home. At last.

Nate stroked her hair gently. "No matter what you think you did, the man had no reason to ruin your career or treat you that way. You should sue him."

"Sure I could sue him for harassment, and bring out the fact that I had been dating him." Leandra stood back and shook her head. "He'd make mincemeat of me, convince people that I'm just a woman scorned. I won't put my family through that kind of pain. I just want to forget the whole thing, get on with my life."

Nate stepped close again, his hands still caught in her hair. "So what are you going to do now?"

Leandra's heart knew the answer, but she couldn't voice what her heart was shouting at her. "I don't know. I only know that... I've changed in the last few months. I *do* want the simple, basic things—a home to come to whether I'm hurting or happy, and a family that loves me, no matter what, and no matter the size of that family."

"Anything else?" he asked, so close now she could see the tiny flecks of brown and green in his cat eyes. And a gentle yearning.

Did she dare tell him her sweet dream? Her fragile hope?

"I'd like to have a family of my own someday," she said, thinking that would cover everything without revealing anything.

But Nate had a determined, awe-filled look on his face, a look that matched her own hope even while it scared her. "What made you change your mind, city woman?"

Hesitant, she said, "I told you—I realized that William and I had been—"

"All wrong," he interrupted, his face lined and shadowed from the muted overhead light, his big hands pushing through her hair so she couldn't look away. "I understand that, but I think there's more. So I'll ask you again. What made you change your mind, Lea?"

He'd called her Lea. The intimacy of that, the gentle way he'd said it, brought her a kind of joy she'd never experienced before with any man.

"I think you know the answer to that," she whispered as she reached her arms around his shoulders.

He tugged at her hair, urging her to him. "I want to hear you say it."

Leandra looked up at him, a thousand wishes merging into a silkened thread of need in her heart. "You," she said at last, breathless. "*You* changed my mind, Nate."

His expression shifted from determined to doubtful, and yet he held her there. For a long time, Nate just stared down at her, his gaze traveling like a whisper over her face, finally touching on her lips.

And Leandra held her breath, waiting for the war inside him to end. Waiting for him to find some sort of peace.

"*I'm* no good for you," he said even as he pulled her close. "Maybe you *do* belong in that big mansion on the hill."

Leandra could almost read his mind. He was afraid, because Alicia had given up everything to be with him, and to his way of thinking, she'd paid dearly for that choice. Could he risk that again with Leandra? Could he ask her to do the very same?

Yes, she would risk a lot by falling in love with Nathan Welby. This wasn't safe or shallow. This was very real, more deep and abiding than any form of friendship. And Nate knew that better than anyone. Was he testing her? Giving her one last chance to walk away?

She didn't want to walk away. She wanted... *Oh, Lord,* she prayed, *give me the strength to be worthy of this man. And please, give him some peace, some comfort.*

"I belong right here," she told him, a hand touching his cheek. "If only you'd let me in."

Nate closed his eyes, kissed her hand, then moved close to kiss her lips, testing her, demanding proof and draining her of all willpower. Leandra pushed a hand through his thick, wavy hair, savoring the coarse feel of it, savoring the sweet taste of his lips. This couldn't be wrong, not when it felt ten times more right than anything she'd had with William.

And yet, she could still sense the hesitancy in Nate. As much as he needed her, he didn't want to let go completely.

Leandra pulled away to give him a beseeching look. "What can I do to convince you?"

He looked down at her, the tenderness and doubt in his eyes only adding to her own fears and needs. She wanted so much to wipe away all his pain.

"Just keep kissing me," he finally said, his mouth capturing hers again.

The kiss was long and sweet, filled with a thousand sensations and a thousand hopes. Leandra could feel the shift in Nate as he slowly gave in to what they both felt so strongly. With a deep longing, she returned his kiss, hoping this tender thread that had somehow bonded them wouldn't be broken again.

When he finally lifted his head, Nate took a breath and grinned, sighing as he managed to regain control. "I think I'd better show you those birdhouses."

Leandra's heart glowed with a warm fire and a burst of white-hot joy. Nate trusted her, at last.

Chapter Fifteen

"This is amazing," Leandra told him much later as she stood admiring the rows and rows of birdhouses Nate had made. He'd hidden them away on a high shelf underneath a canvas tarp. But they needed to be out in the world. Quickly, she counted at least twenty tiny houses of various shapes and sizes, some made out of pine, some made out of oak. A cypress one here, complete with Spanish moss, a pirogue—a boat draped in fishing net—and a tiny Cajun sign that read *laissez les bons temps rouler*—let the good times roll—hanging over the door. A cedar one over there, rustic and fresh smelling, the tiny trees surrounding it a miniature of the tree from which he'd built the house. Each house had its own distinctive character. Each looked like a home. The careful details, the ornamentation, all spoke of a gifted hand.

She whirled around, dancing toward him. "Nate, we have to show these to someone. You—you have such talent."

He shook his head. "I told you, it's just a hobby. Something to pass the time away."

Something to keep the memories away, too, Leandra thought. This man, this gentle, sweet, sad man, built miniature houses for God's small creatures, to replace the real home he thought he'd lost when his wife died.

And yet, his own house sat crumbling around him.

She had to make him see the connection, the correlation between the two. She had to make him let this go, give this gift to others, so that he could find the gift of forgiveness and grace that God readily offered to him.

"Nate, please," she began, asking God to help her do this the right way, "let me display some of these in Richard's store, just to see."

He shook his head again. "I don't think I'm ready for that."

She watched his face, saw the pain centered there in the lines of fatigue around his eyes. His smile didn't reach into those golden eyes. And he refused to look at her.

"And why not?" she finally asked, needing to hear what was in his heart. "Why would you want to keep making these wonderful houses and not show them off to the world?"

He stalked around the workbench, a dark frown marring his face. "I don't think people would be interested. They're just birdhouses, Leandra."

"They're art," she replied, determined to make him open up, one way or another. It would be the only way he'd ever come to her, and back home to God, completely.

"I don't know about art," he said, lowering his head to gaze at her, a stubborn, proud expression giving him the lionlike quality she'd seen in him when they'd first met. "I just know I like to stay busy, work with my hands. It's doodling, playacting, something to do."

"Playacting," she repeated. "Building little homes, beautiful little objects with such exquisite detailing. Why wouldn't you want to share that gift with others?" Then she tossed him the one question he wasn't ready to answer. "You gave *my* family one. Why did you do that, if you don't want anyone to see them?"

Nate stared at the woman across from him, his heart near bursting with the need to pull her back into his arms. But his whole body was stiff with resistance. So he told her a lie. "I was just returning a kindness, nothing more."

Why *had* he given Leandra and her mother the birdhouse? He'd wanted her to have something beautiful from him, something that was a part of his heart, his past, his dreams. He hadn't been able to give that gift to anyone, until now. And he still wasn't sure why he'd done it for Leandra, except that it had seemed important at the time.

Oh, Lord, what's happening to me? Is this Your answer, Your way of telling me to snap out of it?

Well, he didn't want to snap out of it. He'd taken this too far, way too far with his gifts and his kisses. But earlier, Leandra had felt so good, so right, in his arms.

Earlier, he'd told himself it was okay to hold her, to kiss her, to listen to her innermost secrets. He'd asked her to tell him everything. He'd needed to know.

He'd given in to this—this opening up of his own wounds, his own festering regrets and secret yearnings. He had no one to blame but himself.

And yet, he wanted to lay blame at God's door, just as he'd done for so long. That was so easy, so simple. It took all the responsibility away from Nate's own shoulders.

And he wanted to be angry again, to hide the hurting need inside his heart. To hide the truth.

"What are you trying to say, Leandra?" he asked now, a cold shield of frustration making the question edgy and sharp. *Please, God, give me something to be angry about.*

She looked as frustrated as Nate felt. "I'm trying to make you see that you have a gift, a talent. Why are you letting it go to waste? Why are you hiding it away underneath a dirty canvas? Why don't you open it up and let it out in the world? Is it because Alicia's not here to share it with you?"

His head came up then, but he couldn't begin to speak. But Leandra had a lot more to say.

She stopped long enough to take a breath, then said, "I know about the loan, Nate. You and Alicia came to my father—I know this was your dream. It can still happen. My father will help you in any way he can—"

"No."

Okay, he had something to be angry about now. It

should feel good, but instead he felt miserable, alone, suffering. At least *that* was familiar.

"How dare you?" he said, halting her with a shaking hand up in the air between them.

With each question she'd hurled across the workbench at him, Nate's anger had grown until all he could see was the red pain of grief—his old friend—there in the muted light of the barn. But now, oh now, blessed, welcome rage replaced the grief. This time, she'd gone too far.

"What do you mean?" Leandra asked, going quiet. "I was just trying to explain, to help—"

"I don't want your help," he told her, shouting so loudly the rafters shook and Honeyboy let out a whinny of protest. Pointing toward the birdhouses, he said, "That was *our* dream—Alicia's and mine. How dare you—you discussed it with your father? He had no right to tell you anything about what Alicia and I wanted, no right."

"He only told me when I insisted—about the birdhouses," she tried to explain. "He…we want to help you, Nate."

The anger flared like a torch in the night, burning at the emotions he'd tried to deny. "I don't need your help. Can't you understand that? Can't you see that I loved my wife and no woman can ever replace her?"

No matter how that woman makes me feel!

And then he knew, he'd succeeded once and for all. He'd hurt Leandra beyond repair. Yet, he felt no victory. The anger, the grief, felt as dry and bitter as dust and dead leaves in his mouth. It cut to his very core as he watched her face, saw the pain there, saw the hurt, the shock, the realization.

"Yes, I can see that," she said, her voice so quiet, so raw he had to strain to hear her. "I see everything, Nate. It's all very clear to me." She waved her hands toward the tarp, then turned and yanked it down, away from the clutter of the birdhouses. "I can see that you want to hide away here in this old barn, away from your pain, your regrets, away from the knowing faces of your own children. And I feel so sorry for you, so sorry."

"I don't need your pity—"

Leandra pivoted, her eyes all fire and flash now. "Oh, it's not pity. It's…a sad kind of acceptance. You don't want to be happy, really happy, ever again. You want to stay hidden away, covered up, like your precious designs, because if you come out into the light, if you ask me, or my family, or God Himself, for help, then you'll be betraying Alicia. But worse, you'll be tearing down that big wall of grief you're hiding behind."

She came around the table then, her hands at her side, her expression calm and rigid. "If you let go of that grief, you'll have to come clean. You'll have to let go of Alicia's memory and actually forgive yourself. But you can't do that. You can't accept that you're really worthy of forgiveness."

The silence encrusted them in a cold, brisk snap, like a branch caught in a frozen wind.

Then finally Leandra spoke again. "But you're so wrong, Nate. Your children think you're worth forgiving. They just don't know if you can ever forgive *them* for being a part of their mother. Do you know that Layla thinks you hate her? Do you?"

His heart caught in his chest, weighing him down so he had to catch his breath. "Stop it—"

"No," she shouted. "I won't stop it. I won't let you continue to punish yourself this way. Forget the artwork, this goes deeper. You need help, Nate. But then, I've tried to help you, haven't I?"

When he didn't answer, she said, "Well, it's your turn. Now it's all up to you. *You* have to find the strength to help yourself. And…*you* have to ask God, really ask Him from your heart, to give you grace. You have to learn to love yourself again, before you can love your children…or…me."

"I don't love you," he shouted, wagging a finger at her, denial his last true weapon. "I don't…love you."

"I know that," Leandra said, simply, quietly. Then she turned away and headed for the door.

Nate watched her go, his heart calling for her to come back, come back.

A still, silent emptiness penetrated the old barn. The building was full of clutter, full of colorful, decorative little houses.

Empty houses.

Just like his soul.

Was this how Leandra had felt that night, standing all alone in her apartment? He remembered what she had told him, and then he remembered how she'd handled her failings. She'd come home to her family and her Heavenly Father, seeking solace, seeking grace.

But Leandra had much more courage than he could ever possess. He stood there, paralyzed, afraid of his own emotions, and wondered what to do next. He wanted Leandra, but he couldn't have her.

"I don't deserve to be happy again," he said into the stillness.

Then a piercing shard of moonlight from the partially opened door shot through the night, coloring Nate's creations in a glow of pure translucent beauty. He looked up, his gaze never wavering from that one bright spot. Standing there, he remembered Leandra's words earlier about coming out into the light. But he was so afraid, so afraid.

Then suddenly, he understood. He'd been praying, but not with his whole heart. He hadn't let go; he'd wanted to control the blessings God gave out to him. Nate had been in charge, so sure he didn't need anyone, so sure he could never love another woman again. So sure he didn't need God's help or guidance in raising his children. And he'd failed miserably.

"God, dear Lord, help me, help me," he said at last. Then he fell to his knees and cried the tears of the weary.

"I do love you," he finally said, the confession cutting through his throat like bramble as he fought against both it and his tears. "I do love you." He was not only talking to God, but he was telling Leandra the truth at last.

Realization and acceptance poured over Nate like baptism water, drenching him, cleansing him, purging him of all the hostility, all the blame and guilt, all the self-hatred and self-denial.

He wiped his face and got up, then rushed to the door. "Leandra, come back—I do love you."

But she was already gone.

Christmas Eve. Leandra glanced out the kitchen window, wondering if the predictions of snow the weatherman had hinted at would come true. It rarely snowed in East Texas, but the weather had been bitterly cold and icy all week and a huge winter storm was bearing down on them from the northwest. Would they have a white Christmas?

"Honey, do you want some hot chocolate?" Colleen asked as she walked into the kitchen. "Before you head out for the pageant?"

Leandra turned to face her mother, hoping the drained, tired expression she'd seen in the mirror just minutes before was well hidden behind the smile she tried to muster. "Sure, Mom. That sounds great."

"The last performance," Colleen said as she automatically measured milk, cocoa, cinnamon, sugar and vanilla into a big pot on the stove. "Sit down while I stir. I'll be done soon."

Like a sleepwalker, Leandra obeyed her mother. One more night, and then it would all be over. The strain of the last few days was catching up with her. Only through sheer determination and constant prayer had she made it through the first couple of performances.

But her heart wasn't in the program. She kept remembering how angry Nate had been, how he'd declared he only loved Alicia. Leandra had rushed out of that old barn, determined to never set foot on the Welby property again. But when she'd reached her car, she'd fallen against the cold steel and metal, her head in her hands, and cried tears of frustration and anger.

The night had been so cold. And she'd felt so alone. She'd actually thought she'd heard Nate calling to her just as she opened the car door. But it had only been the wind, moaning a forlorn, lonely whine.

Now, she was sleepwalking. Was this how Nate felt each day as he pined away for Alicia? Only half alive, only going through the duties and motions of each day, his soul lost in the past, lost in what might have been?

The production had been a success, with each actor playing his part, each song right on key, each drama clear and deeply moving. Everyone had complimented Leandra on doing a good job.

But she had to wonder, could they all see the pain, the heartbreak in her eyes, in her gestures, in her movements? Did they know that each night as she stood there beside Nate, both of them in their costumes, that he had broken her heart beyond repair? Had anyone noticed how she avoided Nate's gaze, how she managed to ignore him when he called her name, how she managed to stay on the other side of the stage until it was time for them to play their parts?

Did anyone notice that she was so in love with him she could barely breathe?

Someone had noticed.

"Lea, we need to talk," Colleen said in a quiet firm tone. "Here's your cocoa."

Leandra glanced up, completely unaware that her mother had even finished making the hot drink. "What is it, Mom?"

"Sweetie, I'm worried about you. You haven't been yourself over the last few days. Are you worried about going back to Houston?"

Leandra shook her head, the effort of moving almost too much to bear. "No. I'm ready to go back. I need to get back to my life." *Except that I don't have a life anymore.*

Colleen settled on a stool across from her daughter. "I had so hoped you'd decide to stay here. Chet could use your help down at city hall—said he'd ask the city council to give you a raise and make you marketing and public relations director for the city. Have you thought about that?"

Leandra nodded, tried to muster up a smile. "Chet's mentioned it a few times. He wants an answer, but I don't think—"

"It's Nate, isn't it?" Colleen asked, her hand falling across Leandra's. "Honey, tell me what happened."

Leandra knew she could pour her heart out to her mother, just as she'd done when she'd first come home from Houston, and Colleen would listen and try to advise her, without condemnation, without judgment, but always with a mother's strong, fierce love. But where to begin?

"Mom, how do you know when it's real?"

Colleen looked confused for a minute, then said, "You mean love?"

Leandra nodded, unable to say more.

Colleen smiled, patted her hand, then let out a long sigh. "Love is hard to explain, honey. It's a kind of magic, but not like that in a fairy tale or like a magician pulling flowers out of a hat. Love, true love, involves the magic of faith, in knowing that this was part of God's plan. It comes from the heart, and it's more powerful than anything on earth."

Leandra looked up then, tears streaming down her face. "More powerful than a man's love for his dead wife?"

"Oh, honey." Colleen came around the counter to take Leandra in her arms. "I thought as much. You're in love with Nate, aren't you?"

Leandra nodded against the sweet warmth of her mother's old wool cardigan. "But he says he doesn't love me."

"Do you believe him?"

Leandra pulled away, wiped her eyes. "No. I think he does love me, but he's too afraid to admit it. He thinks he'll mess things up, the way he believes he did with Alicia. He feels so much guilt."

Colleen pushed a strand of damp hair off Leandra's face. "You know, honey, it's Christmas. A time of miracles and love. Give Nate some time to settle things with

God. If he cares about you, he won't let you go back to Houston." She stood back then, her smile reassuring. "And something tells me he does love you, very much. I had that figured the day you brought that beautiful little birdhouse home."

"I wish I felt as sure as you do," Leandra said.

Because time was running out.

Chapter Sixteen

He didn't have much time left. Nate pushed the old pickup up the highway, headed for town. It was Christmas Eve and he wanted to spend it with his children and the woman he loved.

Leandra.

Would she ever be able to forgive him?

He'd sent Layla and the young ones on with Mr. Tuttle and Aunt Helen—those two had sure become fast friends—so they could get ready for the last performance of the pageant. But not before Helen had come out to the barn to give him a good talking-to.

"How come you stay cooped up out here so much?"

Not wanting to go into detail, Nate grunted. "I work out here."

"Yeah, so I hear. Every night, it seems." When he didn't respond, she asked, "So what are you doing out here on Christmas Eve?"

"I'm working on something—a Christmas gift for a friend."

"And would that friend happen to be named Leandra Flanagan?"

Nate had given up trying to hide his feelings. If he'd learned one thing since falling for Leandra, it was that the truth would come out, one way or another. "Yes, it's for Leandra. And Helen, I'm sorry if you don't approve, but—"

"But what? Who said I didn't approve? I like that girl. She's pretty, honest, and…she loves your children. What more could I ask?"

Surprised, Nate smiled for the first time since he and Leandra had parted. "You never cease to amaze me, Helen."

"Are you in love again, Nathan?"

"Yes," he told Helen. Then he showed her what he was making.

Helen nodded her approval, a smile gentling the frown that had her eyebrows standing straight up on her face. "Well, she hasn't been around since the other night, and she sure keeps her distance at the Christmas pageant. You two been fighting?"

"Something like that."

"You're a stubborn one, Nate Welby."

"Too stubborn for my own good." He looked up then, the honesty making him feel edgy, almost dizzy. "I don't want to lose her."

Helen punched the sleeve of his denim jacket. "Well, when are you gonna give this to her, and for land sakes, when are you gonna tell her you love her?"

"Tonight," he replied. "Tonight, after the Christmas pageant."

Helen had given him a secretive, knowing smile. "I think tonight is gonna be chock-full of surprises. I love Christmas."

"It's the Christmas Eve performance and Heather Samuels comes down with bronchitis," Chet said, one hand on his head and the other on his stomach. "What are we gonna do, Leandra? We gotta have a solo of 'Silent Night.' It's a tradition."

They were at the civic center, getting ready for tonight's sold-out performance. Leandra didn't think she could take much more.

"I know, I know," she replied, looking down at her watch. Thirty minutes until production and now this. Heather Samuels had the voice of a pop diva and was every bit as pretty. "Is there anyone else who could possibly do it?"

"I can," a small voice said from behind her.

Leandra whirled to find Layla standing there, her big blue eyes filled with hope. "I can sing the solo, if that's okay with y'all."

"Are you sure, honey?" Chet asked, shrugging as he glanced over at Leandra. "Heather's hard to beat, what with her winning all them contests and titles and such."

"I can do it," Layla said, her voice gaining strength. "Mrs. Flanagan—Colleen—says I have a natural talent for singing. Not that anybody at my house would notice."

Leandra knew the girl was referring to her father. She'd already heard Layla complaining that he'd stayed out in the barn most of last night. And now he was late again. Had he just gone back into his self-imposed exile rather than face the truth?

"Okay, Layla," she said, instinct telling her to give Layla a chance. "You will sing the final solo—'Silent Night.' Do you need a warm-up practice?"

Layla's smile was sheepish and shy. "I've been practicing in the bathroom already." Then she looked up at Leandra.

Leandra saw the doubt and sadness in the girl's eyes. "What's wrong?"

Instead of answering her, Layla rushed to hug Leandra close. "We all wanted you to be our new mother. I'm sorry it didn't work out."

Leandra told herself she wouldn't cry. Yet tears pricked her eyes. "Me, too, honey."

Nate reached the auditorium a few minutes before the time for the production to start. After hurrying to get into the lion costume, he saw Leandra backstage. The look she cast toward him told him she wasn't too pleased with his being late.

And maybe he was too late. Too late to make amends with his children. Too late to heal the rift with their grandfather, something Helen had been urging him to do. And way too late to make Leandra see that he'd been the biggest kind of fool.

He just wanted to get through this, so he could make Leandra see reason. So he could tell her that he loved her.

But right now, all he could do was wait for his cue.

An hour later, Nate came back out on the stage along with all the other players. Taking his position as lion, he watched Leandra's face underneath the white fleece of her own costume. The lamb didn't look peaceful: And the lion felt like roaring his own discontent. It was time for the last solo, and Nate couldn't wait for it to be over.

"Silent Night."

As the choir off to the right hummed and swayed, the audience members each lit their own thin white candles, passing the flame until the darkness flared brightly with hundreds of tiny beacons. Those beacons seemed to be calling to Nate.

Then with the candlelight to guide them, the angels came to watch over baby Jesus. Little Brittney sure made a beautiful angel. Even rambunctious little Philip looked angelic as he strolled onto the stage. And his own Matthew stood straight and tall, a true shepherd.

Unlike during the other performances, tonight, Nate's impatient, bruised heart seemed to fill with a joy he'd never experienced before. Alicia would be so proud of their children. And he was proud of them, too. Yet it had been a long time since he'd told them that.

Just one more thing he needed to do, to set things right again. If he could just get through this night.

Where was Heather, anyway? It was time for the solo.

And then the entire building seemed to hold its

breath as one beautiful angel walked out onto the stage. Nate waited, expecting the local beauty queen to sing as she had during the other productions. But when he instead saw a beautiful blond-haired girl, dressed in flowing pink, his heart stopped.

Layla.

He must have gasped, because Leandra turned to look up at him. Nate didn't even realize he'd reached up to grasp both of Leandra's arms until he looked down and saw he was clinging to her as she stood in front of him. But he couldn't let go.

And then he heard Layla's soft sweet voice and wondered if the angels were indeed singing tonight.

As his oldest daughter sang this most holy of songs, Nate's heart let go of the last of its bitterness. All was calm, all was bright. He had a future filled with hope, and…his heart was filled with a heavenly peace.

He could almost hear Alicia's sweet words echoing in his daughter's beautiful voice.

Nate, be happy. Be strong. Be at peace. It's all right now, darling. Everything is as it should be.

When Layla finished the song, Nate fought against the tears falling down his face. He leaned toward Leandra then, his hands still gripping her arms.

"I didn't know," he said, the whisper full of an urgent tenderness. "I didn't know."

To his great relief, Leandra didn't pull away—they were onstage after all. Instead, she turned to glance up at him, her own eyes misty and brimming with tears. Then she placed a hand on his arm. "Now you do."

* * *

"That was the most beautiful—" Helen stopped, dabbing at her eyes with a tissue, her expensive white wool suit smeared with tear streaks. "Layla, darling, you are blessed with an incredible voice. What a songbird!"

Nate, still in costume, stood with his family in the hallway just beyond the stage. Pulling Layla close, he said, "Honey, I am so proud of you. Why didn't you tell me you could sing like that?"

"I tried," Layla replied, hugging him tightly.

"But I never listened, did I?"

At her muffled "No," he lifted her chin with a thumb. "Well, from now on, things are gonna be different. I'm going to be a better father, to all of you."

"That's a start," a gruff voice said from behind him. "And I'm going to join in that promise by being a better grandfather."

Nate turned to find Davis Montgomery standing there in an expensive wool overcoat and tailored business suit.

"Hello, Nate."

Nate glanced over at Helen. "You called him."

"I surely did. Merry Christmas, Nathan."

Davis came closer, then smiled down at the three wide-eyed children standing with Nate and Helen. "Layla, I'm your grandfather Montgomery. And I just have to say that you have the voice of an angel."

"You heard me?" Layla asked, a smile brightening her face.

"I heard you." Davis extended his hand to Nate. "And

if your father doesn't mind, I'd love to follow y'all home for a Christmas Eve visit."

Nate looked down at the hopeful, expectant faces of his children, then reached out to shake the other man's hand. He had to start living up to his promises and tonight was as good a time as any. "I don't mind at all. We'd be glad to have you."

"Then we'll just go on home and get the coffee started and the pecan pie cut," Helen said, grabbing Nate by his lion's mane to turn him around. "While you take care of that…unfinished business."

Nate followed the direction of her gaze.

Leandra was watching them from the other door.

Leandra told herself to just go. Get out of this silly costume and go on home. But her family was waiting for her at the church across the street. She couldn't skip the Christmas Eve service. She needed to be with her family, now more than ever.

But Nate was waiting for her at the end of the hall.

At least, he looked like he wanted to tell her something. But then, he'd had plenty of time, all week, to talk to her.

You avoided him, remember?

She watched as he kissed his children and sent them off with Helen and their grandfather. She'd figured out the tall, distinguished-looking man must be Davis Montgomery. Would Nate turn him away, too?

It didn't look that way. Davis was laughing and talking, with Brittney up in his arms and Matt right at his heels asking questions as they left the building with Helen.

The now quiet, deserted building.

Leandra stood at one door, and Nate stood at the other.

Then he motioned for her.

And she went to him.

"Can you come out to the prayer garden with me?" he asked.

Her heart tapped at her chest like a bare branch hitting a window. "Nate, I—"

"Please?" he asked, his gaze never wavering.

In spite of the agony she felt deep inside, Leandra saw something there in his eyes. Something firm and sure. And complete.

"Let me go change," she replied, not willing to have a serious conversation in a lamb's suit.

He looked down at his own outfit. "Yeah, I guess I'd better do that myself. I'll meet you there in about five minutes."

A short time later, Leandra was dressed in her best burgundy wool Christmas dress, her black wool topper keeping the chill of the icy wind off her as she made her way over to the prayer garden. It was nearly dusk, and the church service would be starting soon, *but Nate wanted to see her.*

She kept telling herself not to get excited. *Don't let your heart do this.* He just wants to say goodbye.

That's all.

But when she looked up and saw him coming toward

her in his jeans and worn leather jacket, her heart got the better of her. He was carrying a large, gift-wrapped box. And he was smiling.

"What's this?" she asked when he handed her the box. The shiny Christmas paper felt cool against her hands as she took the package.

And then it started to snow, the shimmering flakes falling like crystallized teardrops all around them.

She held a hand up to catch a delicate snowflake. "Maybe we'd better—"

"Open it, Leandra. Before I lose my nerve."

She looked up at him, watching the tiny perfectly formed snowflakes as they hit his thick, wavy hair and settled on his bronze face. Nate ignored the snow, his gaze locked with hers, and in the silence of the white cadence, Leandra saw hope there in his eyes.

She sat down on the bench—the same bench where he'd first kissed her. With shaking hands, she tugged at the colorful holiday paper, then tried to get the box open.

"Let me help," Nate said. Bending down on one knee, he kneeled in front of her to hold the square box while she reached inside to claim her prize.

And then she saw it. A small, Victorian house. Another birdhouse. Though the churchyard lights were muted because of the falling snow, Leandra could tell this was an exact replica of his own house.

Except this one wasn't rundown or forlorn looking.

And over the doorway, there was a small gold-etched sign that read Lea's House.

"Nate," she said as she held the dainty white-and-blue house on her lap, "it's so...perfect."

"It can be," he said, still on bent knee. "If you'll still have me."

"What do you mean?"

"I mean," he said, reaching up a hand to crush her hair against her face, "that I was wrong. And I'm asking you to forgive me. I didn't tell you the truth the other night."

She leaned her head into his open hand, pressing her cheek against the warmth of his palm. Then she closed her eyes. "What is the truth, Nate?"

He urged her head up. "Look at me."

She opened her eyes then, to find him so close, his gaze holding her there.

"I love you," he said. "And... I want you to be my wife." When she tried to speak, he quieted her with a finger to her lips. "And I want you to live in a house just like this one. My house. Our house. I'm going to remodel it from basement to turret, rebuild it like I built this little house, just for you, Lea. Only you."

Leandra couldn't stop the tears from falling. Nor could she stop her next words. "But...it was Alicia's—"

"Was," he said, the one word filled with so much pain and despair, she wondered if he still had doubts himself. *"Was,"* he repeated, stronger now, his finger still brushing her lips. "But I'm okay with that—I've made my peace with the Lord. And I'm willing to show off those birdhouses, if you still have a hankering to be my marketing manager." He moved his fingers over her face, touching on teardrops and snowflakes alike, then leaned close to give her a quick kiss. "I'm a changed man, thanks to you."

"Nate, I didn't mean to change you."

"Ah, but you did. You did. And I thank God for it. And… I want you in my life now and forever." Taking the little house from her, he placed it back in the box. "Now, what do you say? I can't offer you fancy cars and city lights, but I can offer you this love I feel with all my heart. Will you marry me?"

Before she could answer, they heard running feet moving across the parking lot. Leandra looked up to see three children barreling down on them. Three happy, grinning, blond-haired children.

"Did she say yes? Did she?" Brittney asked as she slammed into her father and sent him sprawling in the newly formed snow. "Aunt Helen told us you were gonna ask her. Can we watch?"

Matt and Layla reached them then, their faces cherry-red from the cold and their own excitement.

Layla, as usual, stood back, waiting. And behind her, Helen and Davis huddled together, brother and sister alike as their wing-tipped brows shot up in a questioning expression.

"They insisted on finding you," Helen explained with a shrug.

"Well?" Matt asked, his hands on his hips, his head slanted at a sideways angle. "Are y'all really getting married?"

Nate, on the ground with Brittney glued to his neck,

lifted his face toward Leandra. "That all depends on Leandra. Will you marry us, Miss Flan-again?"

Leandra looked down at the man at her feet, her breath catching in her throat. He sat there in the snow, with a child on his lap, looking so lovable, so honest, that she knew she couldn't ever leave his side again.

"Yes, I will marry you—y'all," she said, tears streaming down her face. "Yes."

Nate lifted himself up, holding Brittney tightly in one arm as he placed the other around Leandra and kissed her firmly.

"Thank you."

"For what?" she asked, her lips inches from his.

"For believing in me, for agreeing to be my wife. For forgiving me."

"I love you," she said.

Brittney giggled as Nate stood and held her high in the air, swinging her around in the soft, silent snowfall. "She loves us, sunshine. What do you say about that?"

Brittney smiled her delight as her father whirled her around and around. "I'm glad," she called out, enjoying the echo of her words as she flew through the air. "But I told you she was perfect, didn't I?"

"You sure did," Nate said, lifting her out over his head.

"I'm a snow angel," Brittney said, squealing in delight as she held her arms out, the snowfall hitting her face. "And I've finally got a new mommy."

"That's good enough for me," Helen said, grabbing children in both hands. "Now, Nate put that child down before you both throw up. Why don't we head back to the house for a real celebration?"

Nate dropped Brittney to her feet, caught his breath, then pulled Leandra up off the bench. He took Leandra's hand on one side and Layla's on the other. Looking back at Matt, Helen and Davis, he said, "I've got a better idea. Let's go to church."

And that's exactly what they did. As a family.

Epilogue

The next Thanksgiving...

"Leandra, thank you so much for inviting us to your home for Thanksgiving." Colleen looked down the long table at her daughter, her words lifting over the drone of many voices talking all at once.

Leandra smiled at her mother, then glanced at her husband. "Thank Nate, Mom. He's the one who insisted it was our turn to play host. I think he just wanted to show off the house."

Jack held up his tea glass. "Well, the house *is* beautiful, but I'd like to especially thank him for keeping *you* out of the kitchen. Nate, the smoked turkey and baked ham sure do look good."

Nate laughed while Leandra wagged a finger at her brother then said, "I made the fruit salad, thank you."

Margaret bobbed her head. "I watched her. She knew exactly what she was doing."

"Just so she didn't make any of her famous dumplings," Richard said, grinning from ear to ear.

Davis Montgomery, sitting by Aunt Helen, lifted a brow. "I don't think I've ever had your dumplings, Leandra. Maybe you can whip up a batch while I'm here."

Helen, resplendent in a dark-brown sweater with a happy, grinning gold-and-orange turkey embroidered across the front, winked at Leandra, then slapped her brother on the back. "I'm sure she'd be glad to do just that, right, Lea?"

Nate smiled, then leaned over to kiss his frowning wife. "Everyone should experience your dumplings at least once, honey."

When her brothers all started snickering and hiding their grins behind their white linen napkins, Leandra couldn't resist her own smile. "Okay, enough," she replied, slamming a hand down on the Battenburg lace tablecloth. "Everyone contributed to *this* meal, and I'm just thankful that we're all here together."

"Me, too," Nate said, taking his wife's hand. "And I'd like to say grace now."

While everyone held hands around the table, and the children—Cameron and Philip, Corey, Brittney and Matt sitting at the smaller children's table, and his all-grown-up Layla sitting quietly by Mark—all closed their eyes to give thanks, Nate took a moment to reflect on the past year.

He still couldn't believe how good his life was now. He had three wonderful, healthy children and he'd inherited a large, loud, pushy, nosy, loving family when he'd married Leandra back in the spring. As he looked around at the people gathered at his dining table, Nate once again thanked God for giving him a second chance to be happy.

His children now had their Aunt Helen and their grandfather Montgomery in their lives on a regular basis. He was glad they'd come to be here today, too.

Jack and Margaret sat together by Leandra's parents. Those two had taken some time to get used to, but they'd turned out to be his closest friends. And now they had a brand-new baby daughter, Emily. Michael and Kim had accepted Nate right away. He watched as they fussed over their toddler, Carissa. Mark was still the quiet, observant one, but he'd been the best man at their wedding, and he was a good listener—and still very much single.

And Richard—Richard had helped Nate to launch Welby Woodworks by pushing Nate's designs in his store and setting up a Web site on the Internet. Now, it seemed everybody wanted a Welby birdhouse in their own home. He had orders well into next year.

Nate also owed a big thanks to Howard and Colleen Flanagan. They'd accepted his children as their own grandchildren by offering advice, baby-sitting and car-pooling whenever he and Leandra were busy.

And they stayed very busy these days, what with his regular job as construction foreman and his business on the side, and her work at city hall. But they were never too busy for family. Now, Nate's after-hours work was scheduled with family in mind—the children and Leandra pitched in and helped, and kept him company while he worked. The barn was now a place for all of them to be together, not just a retreat for a man with a broken heart.

And Leandra.

Thanks to Leandra, his heart was full and happy again. And his house was built on a strong foundation of faith. Leandra had made this place a home by working tirelessly to redecorate and refurbish each and every room. Today, the whole house shined and glistened with all the colors of fall—pumpkins on the porch, gold, orange, and burgundy colored mums growing in the many flower beds and sitting in clay pots and brightly painted containers all over every available surface of the house. The Welby home was full of so much bounty—more than he ever dreamed possible.

Nate finished the prayer, then smiled at the people, the family, that filled his home on this special day. But he had one more thing to be grateful for on this Thanksgiving. Giving Leandra a questioning look, he whispered, "Can I tell them?"

"Tell us what, Daddy?" Brittney said from her spot at the children's table.

Philip grinned and swiped her roll while she wasn't looking, but a frown from his grandfather made him put it right back down.

"You've sure got big ears," Nate told his youngest daughter. "But your mom and I do have a surprise." He sent Layla a special, secret look. She already knew— they'd had a long talk last night. Her smile told him she couldn't wait to share the news with the rest of the family.

"What? What?" Brittney asked, jumping up in her chair.

"Don't knock your milk over," Nate warned. Then he turned to Leandra. The tears in her eyes only added to the glow on her face. His wife had never looked more beautiful.

"Tell them," she said, her eyes bright.

Taking her hand in his, Nate looked out over the table, took a deep breath, then said, "We're going to have a baby."

Everyone started talking at once. Margaret and Kim both got up to hug Leandra, while Howard and Colleen hugged each other and grinned. Davis and Helen gave each other a long, meaningful look, then shook hands with Leandra's parents. Brittney danced around the table, clapping her hands and squealing her delight.

"I hope it's a boy," Matt said, rolling his eyes at his sister's embarrassing display of pride.

Leandra's four brothers gave each other high fives and hooted with laughter. "She finally did it," Richard said.

"That's great," Mark added, his gaze centered on Leandra. "I'm happy for you, Sis."

Leandra wiped the tears from her eyes, then glanced out the window to the big, sunny side porch just off the dining room. "Look, Nate. The cardinals are in their house. Maybe they'll have babies soon, too."

Nate watched as the birds fussed and played on the

tiny porch of the Victorian birdhouse he'd built for Leandra last Christmas. Like a beam straight from heaven, rays of noonday sunshine poured a bright golden light over the dainty little house.

Lea's house.

He'd never seen a more beautiful sight.

* * * * *

SUGAR PLUM SEASON

Mia Ross

For Grandma and Grandpa

Acknowledgments

To the very talented folks
who help me make my books everything
they can be: Elaine Spencer, Melissa Endlich
and the dedicated staff at Love Inspired.

More thanks to the gang at Seekerville
(www.seekerville.blogpot.com). It's a great place
to hang out with readers—and writers!

I've been blessed with a wonderful network
of supportive, encouraging family and friends.
You inspire me every day!

There is no fear in love, but perfect love casts out fear.
—*1 John* 4:18

Chapter One

Carpenter Needed.

Standing outside Arabesque, Amy Morgan studied the sign from the sidewalk in front of her dance studio, wondering if she should've added some details. Unfortunately, she admitted with a sigh, she really didn't have any. She'd spent most of her life at the front of the stage, so she was well versed in choreography, costumes and toe shoes. The more practical elements of set design and construction, not so much. Now that her performing days were behind her, she'd have to learn the mundane aspects of the business, she supposed. She wasn't exactly looking forward to it.

"So, you're looking for a carpenter?"

Startled by the deep voice that came from behind—and far above—her, she spun into a wall of plaid flannel. Looking up, she saw that it led to windblown brown hair, tanned features and a pair of hazel eyes shot through with gold. When their owner smiled, they sparkled with honest male admiration, and her polite response flew straight out of her head.

Once she regained some of her usual composure, she carefully straightened to her full height, which was still a foot shorter than his. "Yes, I am."

The smile warmed, and he offered her the biggest hand she'd ever seen. Covered in scars, some old and others more recent, it clasped hers with a surprisingly gentle touch. "Jason Barrett. My day job's building custom pieces out at the sawmill, if you'd like some references for my work."

"Amy Morgan." When she registered his name more clearly, she asked, "Are you related to the Barretts who founded the town and run Barrett's Mill Furniture?"

"Yeah, I am." He pointed across the street to the trolley facade of the town's famous diner. "I made the new planter benches for the Whistlestop and replaced the park benches and seats around the old gazebo in the square."

Amy had admired the handmade pieces many times and was impressed with his obvious skill. "They're very nice. You did them by yourself?"

"Start to finish." Cocking his head, he grinned. "I take it that means you're looking for someone who's good at working alone."

"And quickly," she clarified with a sigh. "My uncle Fred was building sets for our production of *The Nutcracker,* but he hurt his back during our family football game on Thanksgiving Day. I've only got three weeks until the show, so I need someone who can pick up where he left off and get everything done in time."

"Sounds doable. Mind if I check things out before I promise something I can't deliver?"

Unlike my ex-fiancé, she grumbled silently. He'd promised her the moon and then bolted when she needed him most. Still, her schoolgirl reaction to this towering stranger bothered her. The last time she'd followed her foolish heart, it hadn't ended well. Who was she kidding? she chided herself. It turned out to be a complete disaster, and she still wasn't over it. But she was a dancer, not a contractor, which meant she needed someone's help. If she waited even a day or two longer to give other people time to respond, there was a good chance the charming sets she'd planned would have to be trimmed back to something less elaborate that could be completed in time.

Being a perfectionist by nature, that simply wasn't acceptable to her. "Sure. Come on in."

"This is real nice, by the way," he said, motioning toward the huge display window. It was decked out with a rendering of Tchaikovsky's famous ballet in miniature, and she'd just finished framing the scene with twinkle lights. "Makes me wanna come see the show."

"I hope lots of people feel the same," she confided. "The studio hasn't been doing all that well in this economy, so Aunt Helen turned it over to me, hoping some new ideas will bring in more business. I'm doing everything I can to make sure she doesn't regret it."

Pulling open the entry door for her, he said, "Helen

gave classes here when I was a kid. My mom used to drag my four brothers and me here to get us some culture to go along with the hunting and fishing we did with my dad."

The way he phrased it made her laugh. "Did it work?"

Spreading his arms out, he looked down at his clothes and battered work boots, then grinned at her. "Whattaya think?"

"I don't know," she hedged, tapping her chin while pretending to study him carefully. "Looks can be deceiving."

"Not with me," he assured her in his mellow Virginia drawl. "What you see is what you get."

How refreshing, she thought as she led him into the studio. In her world, you never knew what was truly going on behind the performer's mask. Here in Barrett's Mill, it was a relief to find people who were content being who they were, rather than acting like something else altogether. Knowing that didn't totally make up for the glittering life she'd left behind, but it helped ease some of the sting that had a way of sneaking up on her when she wasn't prepared for it.

Putting past regrets aside, she surveyed her studio with a sense of pride for what she'd accomplished since Aunt Helen handed over the reins to her. After plenty of scrubbing, painting and refinishing, the original plaster walls and wide-plank floors had a fresh, timeless quality to them. The wide-open space was dominated by the stage, bracketed by faded burgundy velvet curtains she'd replace as soon as she had the money. Structurally, the platform was as sound as the days when she'd starred in her aunt's dance recitals.

So long ago, she thought wistfully. If she'd known her ballet career would end before she was twenty-five, she'd have valued those productions more.

"This music is nice," her visitor commented in a courteous tone that made it clear he'd rather be listening to something else. "What is it?"

"One of Mozart's violin concertos. Number four, I think."

"Pretty," he went on with a grin. "It suits you."

She wasn't sure how to respond to that, so she didn't say anything. As they made their way to the stage, she found herself appreciating the self-assured nature of Jason's long strides. He was well over six feet tall, with wide shoulders and a powerful build to go with the outdoorsy history he'd mentioned earlier. He had a strong, solid look to him; it made her think of an oak tree that could stand up against any storm nature chose to throw at it. And yet he moved with a confident grace she envied. She'd give anything to walk that freely again.

When he stopped to look at the framed pictures displayed on the wall at stage left, she knew what had drawn his attention and braced herself for the inevitable question. He turned to her with an amazed expression. "This is you?"

"They're all me," she replied politely, the way she always did when someone asked. "Back in my performing days." Sometimes, they struck her as being from another lifetime. Other days, she felt as if she'd just stepped off the stage after taking her bows. When she allowed herself to think about them, she missed those days with an intensity that made her wonder if teaching was really the right decision for her. The problem was, dance was all she'd ever known, which didn't leave her with any other options. She'd simply have to find a way to make the best of things.

"I'm not an artsy kinda guy, but these are incredible. What's this move called?"

Going to join him, she saw where he was pointing and did her best to smile. "An arabesque jump. It was my favorite to perform, so I renamed the studio Arabesque."

His eyes roamed over the rest of the grouping and stopped on one of her dancing Clara in a youth production of the holiday ballet she'd chosen for this year. The photographer had caught her in midair, making her look as if she was flying. It was by far her favorite shot and the one she would have most liked to shred into a million pieces.

Staring at it for a few moments, he looked down at her with a remarkably gentle smile. It was as if he'd sensed her reaction and was making an attempt to ease her discomfort. "Incredible. How old were you?"

"Twelve. I'd been taking classes at a ballet school in D.C. for four years, and that was my first Christmas production."

"Not really," he teased, tapping his finger on a

framed print of her as a six-year-old Rosebud. "I was here for this one, and I remember you."

"You do not," she huffed. "I barely remember it myself."

"You came onstage after the other flowers," he corrected her with a grin. "The older ones all stayed in line, doing their thing, while you floated around like a butterfly. They were good dancers, but there was something different about you. Not to mention, I thought you looked like the pretty ballerina in my cousin's jewelry box."

Amy felt a blush creeping over her cheeks, and she blinked up at him in total bewilderment. She'd always assumed boys that age were more interested in bugs and snakes than classical dance, and that he still remembered her all these years later was astounding.

Realizing she'd been staring up at him like a brainless twit in some old-time romance movie, she gave herself a mental shake. "I'm flattered."

A slow, maddening grin stretched across his features, transforming them into something she was certain most women couldn't resist. Fortunately for her, she'd been burned by a master, and she'd learned to be very cautious around the male species. Since you couldn't accurately predict when they might turn on you, she'd learned it was best to avoid close contact with them whenever possible.

"So, let's see what Fred left you with."

Jason easily leaped onto the low stage, then reached back to offer her a hand up. More than a little jealous of his athletic maneuver, she shook her head. "I'll just take the stairs."

That was all she said, but compassion flooded his eyes, and he jumped down as easily as he'd gone up. "You're hurt, aren't you? That's why you came back here, because something happened and you can't dance anymore."

His quick assessment came in a sympathetic tone that made her want to scream in frustration and weep at the same time. Getting a firm grip on the emotions he'd unleashed, she straightened her back as far as it would go and gazed defiantly up at him. She might have lost a lot of things, but she still had her pride.

"I've changed my mind about the sets," she said curtly. "Thank you for coming in."

He didn't even flinch. Small as she was, most people backed off when she glared at them the way she was doing now. Apparently, Jason was made of sterner stuff, and she grudgingly admitted he had some grit to go with those rugged looks and killer smile. "You're not getting rid o' me that easy, Miss Amy Morgan."

"I don't need your pity."

"Wasn't giving you any," he reasoned, folding his arms as if daring her to argue with him. When she didn't, he went on. "I admire anyone who can take a hit, then pick themselves up and keep on going. You're tougher than you look."

No one had ever spoken to her that way, so directly and with such obvious sincerity. Accustomed to people who fawned or blustered depending on the circumstances, she wasn't sure how to take it. "Thank you?"

"You're welcome. Mind if I ask what happened?"

She winced, but decided that since he seemed determined to work with her, it was easier to get the explanations out of the way sooner rather than later. "In a nutshell, two years ago I was driving back to D.C. and took a shortcut that turned into a patch of ice. Next thing I knew, I woke up strapped into a hospital bed, completely immobilized. They told me I had a fifty-fifty chance of ever walking again."

"Guess you proved them wrong."

"That was the plan."

The response came out more tersely than she'd intended, but Jason didn't seem the least bit fazed. "Good for you."

Flashing her an encouraging smile, he offered his arm, and for some insane reason she took it. The old-fashioned gesture seemed appropriate for him while standing in this old building, dressed like someone who spent his days working hard. Now that she thought about it, he reminded her of the guy on the wrapper of her paper towels.

Only this lumberjack had a real twinkle in his eyes, and he'd managed to get past her usual defenses without any effort at all. That could only mean one thing: he was trouble. And she'd had enough trouble lately to last her the rest of her life.

Amy Morgan was still the prettiest girl he'd ever seen, Jason thought while he inspected the progress

Fred had made on the set pieces. Some were partially assembled, but others lay in a heap backstage with hand-drawn schematics thumbtacked to them. Everything was still in raw form, with no paint or details at all.

It was a big job to complete in only three weeks, and with the holiday shopping season in full swing, it was all hands on deck filling custom orders at the mill in time for Christmas delivery. While he'd much rather be back in Oregon logging, his first obligation was to the family business. It wasn't only Jason and his brother relying on it now. A dozen other people worked there, too, and closing the doors wasn't an option for any of them.

But if he didn't take on Amy's project, who would? Everyone was busy this time of year, and being single, he had more spare hours than most. Each day she spent trying to find a handyman was another day of lost build time. If he didn't step up, when someone finally did it might be too late, and she might have to cancel the show. Some of those kids were probably the same way she'd been, working hard and eager to get their turn in the spotlight. He'd feel awful if they lost out and he could've done something to prevent it.

"I know there's a lot to do," she lamented with a worried look. "Uncle Fred's collision shop just lost a good mechanic to that new chain over in Cambridge, and he's been working extra hours to keep up. He fit this in whenever he could."

"Yeah, it's tough."

She seemed to think he was framing a no, and she stepped forward with desperation clouding her china-doll features. "I can pay you for your time. It wouldn't be much, but you could use it to buy some nice Christmas presents for...whoever."

For some crazy reason, Jason got the feeling she was trying to determine if he was unattached. He couldn't imagine why she cared, but women were funny that way. A guy just asked you straight out if you were seeing someone, while a woman skirted the direct route and snuck in sideways. One of the many reasons he avoided getting tangled up with anyone in particular. He liked his nice, uncomplicated life just the way it was. Drama—especially female drama—he could do without.

Recognizing she was in a tight spot, in the spirit of the season he decided to give her a break and not yank her chain. "My shopping's done, so I don't need the money."

Her dainty mouth fell open in a shocked O. "Are you serious? Everyone needs money."

"I've got a little more than enough." Grinning, he added, "And I don't have a...whoever, so I'm good."

That got her attention, and he watched curiosity flare in those stunning eyes of hers. Crystal-blue, with a lighter burst in the center, they made him think of stars. Wisps of light brown hair had escaped her loose bun, framing her face in a halo of curls. Dressed in pale gray trousers and a white sweater, she brought to mind the angel on top of his parents' Christmas tree.

Dangerous, he cautioned himself. It was okay to admire a woman in a general way, but when he started comparing her to heavenly beings, it was time to take a giant step back and get a grip. Then again, the adorable ballerina she'd once been had stayed in his memory for twenty years. Gazing down at her now, he saw none of the joy on display in the framed photos on the wall. In its place was a lingering sadness that tugged at his heart, making him want to come up with a way to make her smile like that again.

And so, against his better judgment, he held out his hand. "I'm your guy, Amy. I promise not to let you down."

She looked at his hand warily, then said, "The last time a man said that to me, it didn't end so well."

Laced with wry humor, her comment made him laugh. "He was a moron, and if I knew his name, I'd go tell him so."

She studied him for a long moment, then her somber expression lightened just a little. It was such a subtle change, he couldn't help wondering if she'd actually forgotten how to smile. "You know, I believe you. I'm not sure why, but I do."

"About the talking-to or about not letting you down?"

"Both."

Taking his hand, she sealed their deal with a shake that was surprisingly firm for someone so petite. Jason got the distinct impression that something important had just happened to him, but he wasn't exactly sure what it was. One thing was certain: he wouldn't be bored this Christmas.

The thought had just floated through his head when

the sound of jingling bells announced another visitor at the front door. When he glanced over, he had to look twice. From where he stood, it looked like a larger-than-life nutcracker in a flashy soldier's uniform was bobbing through the large front room on its way toward the stage. When it got closer, he was relieved to see that underneath it were very human feet, clad in tie-dyed sneakers that were a dead giveaway about who'd come in.

"Hey, you," he greeted Jenna Reed, the town's resident artist, with a chuckle. "Who's your friend?"

When she set it down, he noticed it was almost as tall as Amy. "The nutcracker prince, of course. He's not as big as the signs I made for the sawmill, but he's got a lot more personality." Turning to Amy, she said, "I know he's not up to the standards you're used to in the Big Apple, but what do you think?"

"It's perfect for this show," Amy replied with an approving smile. "And you shouldn't sell yourself short. This guy is just what I had in mind."

"Awesome." Jenna eyed Jason with curiosity. "No offense, JB, but I'm used to seeing you out at the mill. You look a little outta place in here."

"Finishing up Fred's sets."

"I forgot he hurt himself tackling your nephew," she said to Amy. "How's he doing?"

"Aunt Helen has all she can manage just keeping him off his feet," Amy explained with a sigh. "The doctor said he needs to take it easy for at least a couple of weeks. It's only been two days, and he's already driving her crazy."

Jason knew how he'd feel if he was laid up for that long, and inspiration struck. "Maybe I can knock down some of the pieces for him to assemble and paint at home. That'll give him something to do, and your aunt can keep her sanity."

Amy stared up at him with an expression he couldn't quite peg, and he worried that he might've overstepped his bounds. Then she gave him a grateful smile, as if he'd come up with the answer to every problem she'd ever faced. Knowing he'd been the one to coax a smile from this troubled woman made him feel like a hero.

"That's brilliant," she said, "but are you sure you want to do that? I mean, you'd be making more work for yourself."

He shrugged. "No big deal. If he's happy, maybe he'll heal up quicker and get back to the garage where he belongs."

"And out of Aunt Helen's hair," she added with a nod. "I like the way you think."

They were still staring at each other when Jenna interrupted with a not-so-subtle cough. When she had their attention, she shook her head. "Are you sure you guys just met?"

"More or less," Jason hedged, figuring Amy wouldn't appreciate him relating their first-meet story from twenty years ago.

"That's funny, 'cause from where I'm standing, you've got that 'known each other awhile' vibe."

"That's crazy," Amy huffed. "Not to mention impossible."

The artist laughed. "I call 'em like I see 'em. Anyway, at least this time you stumbled across one of the good guys."

"I thought they went extinct years ago." There was more than a hint of bitterness in Amy's tone, and he couldn't help wondering what had really happened with her ex. Not that it impacted him in any way, of course. He was just curious.

"Not around here," Jenna corrected her. "I think this is where they all landed."

"I'll have to take your word on that one," Amy retorted as she passed by on her way to somewhere behind the stage that dominated the studio. "I've got your check in the office. I'll be right back."

Once she was out of earshot, Jenna stepped in closer to Jason. "I've gotten to know Amy since she landed here in town this summer, so I'm gonna do you a favor."

Every trace of humor had left her expression, and he returned the somber look. "What kinda favor?"

"Leave the poor girl alone. You're not interested in anything serious, and she's had a really rough time the last couple years. She's not up to any more heartache."

"The accident, you mean."

Jenna's eyes widened in surprise. "She told you?"

When he repeated the gist of his earlier conversation with Amy, Jenna slowly shook her head. "I knew her a month before she told me any of that stuff. How did you get her to open up so fast?"

"It's a knack," he replied with a grin. "People like me."

"Uh-huh. Well, watch yourself, big guy. Amy's been through a lot of twists and turns, and her head's still spinning. The last thing she needs is more trouble."

"Trouble?" he echoed in mock surprise. "From me?"

"Don't get me started," she grumbled, as Amy reappeared at the back of the stage with her check. Jenna took it and without even glancing at it shoved it into the back pocket of her paint-spattered overalls. "Well, kids, it's been fun, but I left my kiln going. The thermostat's busted, so if I don't keep an eye on it, it'll burn my whole studio down. Later."

After the door jingled shut behind her, Amy gave him a knowing feminine look. "She likes you."

"She likes everybody. When you're a freelance artist, it's good for business."

"Are you seriously telling me you're not the least bit interested in her? She's gorgeous and perky, and more fun than any three people I know."

"You're right about all that," he agreed, "which is why Jenna and I are friends. But she treats me like an annoying little brother, and that's fine with me."

"Why? I mean, most guys I know would fall all over themselves to get her attention."

In the cynical comment, he got a glimpse of who Amy had become while she'd been working so hard to establish her career. To his mind, it seemed as if she hadn't enjoyed herself all that much since her early dancing days, at least not on a personal level.

Obviously, she'd spent way too much time with losers

who didn't know a remarkable woman when one was standing right in front of them. Sensing an opportunity to distinguish himself from them, he grinned down at her. "Well, I'm not like those guys. Before this show opens, I'm gonna do everything I can to make you believe that."

Her eyes narrowed with suspicion, and she frowned. "You met me an hour ago. Why do you even care?"

"I just do," he replied easily, because he honestly meant it. "But if you need more of a reason, call it Christmas spirit."

With that, he began strolling toward the rear of the stage, stopping when she called out his name. Turning, he said, "Yeah?"

"You're starting now?"

"Molly filled Paul and me up with one of her farmer's breakfasts, so I'm ready to go. Thought I'd start by knocking down some of those bigger pieces that are already put together. Then I'll haul 'em over to Fred's so he can get started painting. Then I'll come back and we can go over whatever plans you've got for getting all this done. Is that okay with you?"

Clearly bewildered by his quick pace, she slowly nodded. "Thank you."

"No problem."

She rewarded him with a timid smile, the kind that could sneak into a man's head and make him forget all kinds of things. Like how he needed to be careful around this woman, because she was fragile and needed time to heal.

The problem was, something about Amy Morgan tugged at the edges of his restless heart in a way no woman ever had. And in spite of his misgivings, he wasn't convinced he should even try to keep her out.

Chapter Two

"She does good work," Amy commented, moving to the side to study the brightly painted nutcracker sign from another angle. "When Jenna and I first got to know each other, I was surprised there was such a talented artist here in Barrett's Mill."

"Must've been nice to find another creative type to hang with out here in the boonies."

He'd nailed her feelings so exactly, she gaped at him in amazement. With his rugged appearance and carefree attitude, she'd never have guessed he'd be so perceptive. It made her wonder what other qualities might be hiding behind that wide-open grin.

Pushing those very personal observations from her mind, she dragged herself back to the task at hand. "I have to start advertising the show right away, so I'd like to get this guy set up out front. Would you mind helping with that?"

"'Course not." Picking up the sign, he tucked it under his arm and motioned her past. "After you."

The rough-and-tumble streets of Washington and New York had left her accustomed to fending for herself. Men didn't typically defer to her this way, and she found his gentlemanly gesture charming. *Southern boys,* she mused as she walked through the studio. She could get used to this.

Out front, she stopped to the left of the door. "I thought he'd look best here, next to the window. What do you think?"

That got her a bright, male laugh, the kind that sounded as if it got plenty of use. "I'm about as far from a decorator as you can get. Lumber, saws, hammers, that's me. You're better off following your own gut on this one."

His innocent comment landed on her bruised heart like a fist, reminding her of the last time she'd followed her gut—and the unmitigated disaster it had led her into. If only she'd kept to her original course instead of taking that shortcut, she'd still be on her way to becoming principal ballerina for an international company. Never again would she deviate from the plan, she promised herself for the hundredth time. Improvising had cost her everything.

Swallowing her exaggerated reaction to his advice, she focused on identifying the perfect location for her sign. Jason set it in place, and she considered it for a moment, then shook her head. "Jenna made him doublesided on purpose, and I want to make sure people get a good view of him from the sidewalk and the street. The idea is to draw them in so they'll look at the other decorations and the playbill in the window. Try angling him this way."

Demonstrating with her hands, she waited and then reassessed. "Now he's too much toward the studio."

After several more attempts, Jason plunked the sign on the paved walkway and rested an arm on top of his Cossack's helmet. "You're kidding, right? We've tipped this thing every way but upside down. You're seriously telling me we haven't hit the right spot yet?"

"There's no point in doing something imperfectly," she shot back in self-defense.

He gazed at her thoughtfully, and she got the eerie feeling he could see things she'd rather keep to herself. "That doesn't sound like something someone our age would say. Who taught you that?"

"My mother. And she's right, by the way. Perfection is the only goal for a balleri—ballet teachers."

In a heartbeat, his confused expression shifted to one of sympathy, and he frowned. "You were gonna say *ballerina,* weren't you?"

"I misspoke. Now, are you going to help me finish this, or should I do it myself?"

He opened his mouth, then closed it and shook his head. "You don't want folks feeling sorry for you, I get that. Your life's taken a nasty turn, and I respect what you're doing to get it back together." Moving a step closer, he added, "But you're here now, and you don't have to do everything on your own anymore. Folks in Barrett's Mill are real fond of your aunt and uncle, and they're gonna want to help you, whether you like it or not."

"Including you?"

Warmth spread through his features, burnishing the gold in his eyes to a color she'd never seen before. When he finally smiled, for the first time in her life, she actually felt her knees begin quivering. If he took it into his head to kiss her, she was fairly certain she wouldn't have the strength—or the will—to stop him.

"Including me," he said so quietly, she almost didn't hear him.

Struggling to keep her head clear, she pulled her dignity around her like a shield. "That's really not necessary. I'm very capable of taking care of myself, and I didn't get where I am by letting people poke their noses into my life and tell me what to do."

Mischief glinted in his eyes, and he chuckled. "Me, neither."

Because of her size, Amy was accustomed to being misjudged, underestimated and generally dismissed by others. Sometimes it actually worked to her advantage, lulling people into a harmless perception of her that masked her relentless determination until she was ready to bring it out into the open. By then, it was too late for whoever had dared to step in between her and whatever she wanted.

But Jason Barrett, with his country-boy looks and disarming personality, didn't seem inclined to follow along. Instead, he'd taken stock of her and had apparently come to the conclusion that she didn't scare him in the least. She'd given it her best shot, and it had sailed wide. So far wide, in fact, that the only sensible thing left to do was admit defeat.

"Okay, you win. This time," she added, pointing a stern finger at him in warning. "But Arabesque is my business, and things around here will be run my way. Got it?"

"Yes, ma'am." Tacking on yet another maddening grin, he went on. "But I've got an idea about how to balance this entrance display. If you're done scolding me, would you like to hear it?"

The concept of someone her size hassling the brawny carpenter was absurd, and she got the distinct impression he was trying to get her to lighten up. Since he was bending over backward to be entertaining, she decided the least she could do was smile. "Sure. Go ahead."

Propping the nutcracker in place against a shrub, he moved to the other side of the walkway that led to the studio's glass front door. Holding out his arms, he said, "Imagine a nicely decorated Christmas tree over here. Then you could do narrow pillars with an arch over the top strung with lights and a sign telling people when the show is."

"I don't think Jenna has time to do another sign for me."

"It's just lettering," he pointed out. "I'll get some stencils and knock it out in no time."

Squinting, she envisioned what he'd described. Since the sun went down so much earlier this time of year, people running errands on Main Street after work would be drawn to Arabesque, just the way she was hoping. They'd come over to check out the cheery display window and get a look inside the freshly redecorated studio. Not only would it boost attendance for *The Nutcracker,* it might gain her some new students. Profits were the name of the new game she was playing, and anything that had the potential to bring in customers was worth a try.

"I like it," she announced. "When do you think you can have it done?"

"How's Monday afternoon sound?"

She had no idea how much work was involved in what he'd described, but he sounded so confident, she didn't even consider questioning the quick turnaround. "Perfect. Thank you."

Plunging his hands into the front pockets of his well-worn jeans, he said, "I oughta warn you, it probably won't be perfect. But I can promise you it'll be good enough to do the job."

"Like you?"

"And you." Slinging the wooden soldier over his shoulder, he gazed down at her. "For most of us, that's enough."

"Not for me," she assured him. "I don't stop until whatever I'm doing can't possibly be any better."

"We've all got flaws, y'know. It's what we accomplish in spite of 'em that makes us who we are."

The last thing she'd have expected this morning was to find herself in a philosophical debate with a guy carrying a life-size nutcracker. "That's a nice thought, but some of us are more imperfect than others. It keeps us from being our best."

"Maybe that's 'cause you're meant to be something else."

Clearly, he meant for his calm, rational explanation to make her feel better about her lingering injuries. He didn't mention God by name, but the silver cross on the chain around his neck filled in the blanks nicely for her. While she respected his right to hold that faith, his comment sparked a flame of resentment she fought to control. "Maybe I wanted the chance to choose for myself."

All her life, she'd done everything her Sunday-school teacher had taught her to do. She went to church, said all the prayers, sang all the hymns. She'd worked relentlessly to polish the talent God gave her until it shone as brightly as any stage lights in the world.

And then He took it all away.

Lying in that lonely hospital bed, she begged Him to help her, to make everything the way it was before. And what happened? Nothing.

She didn't trust herself to speak calmly right now, but from the sympathy in Jason's eyes, she might as well have told him her whole tragic story.

"We don't always get what we ask for, Amy."

"Tell me about it."

More worked up than she'd been in a long, long time, she marched away from him and yanked open the door to escape into the only part of her world she still understood.

* * *

The rest of his day at Arabesque passed by in silence. Except when he was hammering or drilling, anyway. Other than that, Amy avoided him with a deftness that impressed and saddened him all at the same time. He'd been around enough wounded people in his life to recognize the regret that trailed after her, darkening her eyes with the kind of unrelenting sorrow he could only begin to imagine.

He'd just met her, but he instinctively wanted to do whatever he could to pound down the road ahead of her to make it easier for her to walk. The women who usually appealed to him were engaging, uncomplicated types who didn't eat much and laughed easily. Something told him Amy Morgan was complicated by nature, which should've been an enormous red flag for him.

Unfortunately, it only made him wonder what it would take to make her laugh. Then again, he thought as he packed Fred's tools into their cases, maybe he was getting ahead of himself. After all, he'd barely been able to tease a smile out of her, and they'd been together most of the day.

Stopping by her office, he knocked on the frame of the open door. "Everything's put away, so I'm gonna get outta here before your students show up. I'll be back Monday with those extra pieces we talked about."

"Thank you."

"No problem. Have a good rehearsal."

Since he was out of things to say, he waved and

began backing away. When she called out his name, he paused in the hallway. "Yeah?"

"Things were so hectic today, we never settled on your hourly rate."

"I thought we agreed on zero."

Narrowing her eyes, she tilted her head in a skeptical pose he suspected was fairly common for her. "I assumed you were joking about that."

"Nope. I'm sure Fred wasn't charging you, so since I'm filling in for him, it wouldn't be right for me to do it."

"Where I'm from, strangers don't do things for nothing."

"Huh," he said with his brightest grin. "And here I thought we were friends."

While he watched, the brittle cynicism fell away, and the corner of her mouth lifted in a wry grin. "I should warn you, I'm not the easiest person to be friends with."

"That's cool. I like a challenge."

Before she could warp their light exchange into something heavier, he turned and headed for the front door, whistling "Jingle Bell Rock" as he went. When the orchestral holiday medley coming over the studio speakers increased in volume, he knew she'd heard him and was registering her disapproving opinion of his taste in Christmas music. Didn't matter a bit to him, he thought as he stepped from the studio. So they didn't enjoy the same kind of tunes. It wasn't as if he was going to marry her or anything.

Outside, he paused to take in the view of his hometown at the holidays. While he'd been gone, he'd seen plenty of towns, big, small and everything in between. He recalled most of their names, but none had ever measured up to Barrett's Mill for him. At first glance, this Main Street resembled so many others, lined with buildings constructed in a time when skilled craftsmen took great pride in building things that would last forever.

The structures had a solid look to them, which gave the village a quaint, old-fashioned appeal for residents and visitors alike. Especially this time of year, when each business went all out to win the Chamber of Commerce award for best commercial decorations. The jewelry store's front window was dominated by a glacial scene that had sparkling rings and earrings pinned into the fake waterfall. Next to it, a shop that sold office supplies had set up a huge pile of brightly wrapped gifts, with a few open at the front to display the latest gadgets you could find inside. Every window was rimmed in lights, and on a cloudy day like today they gave off a cheerful glow that looked like something straight out of a holiday movie.

Across the width of the street, volunteers had strung the lighted garlands and wreaths the same way they'd done for generations. For as long as Jason could remember, when those festive greens went up, he knew Christmas was right around the corner. Even when he'd lived out West, he'd come back home every year, even if it was only for a few days. As he got older, reconnecting with those lifelong memories comforted him, no matter what might have gone wrong for him elsewhere.

He recognized a few of the people out window-shopping and lifted a hand in greeting before climbing into his truck. Actually, it was one of the mill trucks, older than dirt and held together by rust and a lot of prayers. Paul had gotten it running over the summer and offered it to Jason when he finally broke down and bought a pickup manufactured in this century. To start it, Jason usually needed a screwdriver and a boatload of patience. Since it hadn't been idle all that long, he took his chances and turned the key. Nothing happened at first, but when he gave it another shot, the engine whined a bit and caught. Pumping the gas pedal, he let the motor settle into the throaty rumble that told him it would keep running long enough for him to get where he was going. Usually.

As he made his way toward the edge of town, the pavement gave way to gravel, and he turned in by the sign Jenna had made to mark the very first business in town: Barrett's Sawmill, Est. 1866. He felt a quick jolt of pride, recalling how his older brother, Paul, had left his wandering ways behind and come back to re-open the bankrupt family business. Now a humming custom-furniture manufacturer, they made things by hand the old-fashioned way, in a mill powered by its original waterwheel.

It was a far cry from the lumber camps Jason had been working at the past couple of years. About half as exciting, he mused as he parked next to Chelsea's silver convertible, but way safer. Before he'd even closed the driver's door, baying echoed from behind the mill house, and a huge red bloodhound raced out to meet him.

"Hey there, Boyd." He laughed as the dog leaped up to give him the canine version of a high five. "What's shakin'?"

The dog barked in reply, letting him go and racing around him in circles all the way up to the front porch. Inside, Jason paused outside the office's half door and waved in at his newest sister-in-law. "Hey, Chelsea. How're the numbers looking this week?"

Beaming, she gave him an enthusiastic thumbs-up. "I love Christmas shoppers. They need things fast, and they're willing to pay extra for quick delivery."

Jason groaned, only half joking. "Sounds like we're gonna get real busy."

"I wouldn't take up any new hobbies," Paul advised from the open sliding door that led into the rear of the mill. Wiping grease from his hands on a rag, he went on. "This is supposed to be your last Saturday off till the end of the year. What're you doing here?"

"Making a Christmas tree."

Chelsea laughed. "Doesn't God already take care of that?"

While Jason explained what he was up to, he kept things vague to avoid creating the wrong impression about his situation with Amy. Despite his best efforts, though, Paul's expression grew increasingly suspicious.

"Uh-huh." Dragging it out longer than usual, he folded his arms in disapproval. "Now, how 'bout the truth?"

"That *is* the truth," Jason insisted, as much for himself as his nosy brother. "The lady wants a tree and a nice arch overtop, so I'm making them for her. And for the kids. They're working hard on their show, and they deserve a big audience. I figured it's a nice, Christmassy thing to do."

"It's very nice." With her kitten, Daisy, cradled in her arms, Chelsea came out to back him up. Sending a stern look at her husband, she smiled at Jason. "I'm sure she really appreciates your help."

"Don't encourage him," Paul cautioned her. "He's got a weakness for pretty faces and sad stories."

"I do not," Jason protested. Paul raised an eyebrow at him, and he decided it was pointless to argue. "Okay, you're right, but this time's different."

"How?"

He didn't want to lie, but it wasn't his place to air her personal history, so he hedged, "Amy was advertising for a carpenter to replace Fred, and the job's easy enough. Everyone else in the family does work for the church or charities this time of year, and I've been looking for a way to pitch in somewhere."

"You've been doing that ever since you moved in with Gram and Granddad." Paul rested a hand on his shoulder with a proud smile. "His cancer's getting worse every day, and she needs your help after Mom goes home for the night. We're all grateful to you for stepping up like that."

The praise settled well, and Jason smiled back. "That's why this project is so great. Working at Amy's,

I'll be five minutes away if they need me. The show's the week before Christmas, so my part'll be over soon enough."

"You realize you're doing an awful lot of work for a woman you met—" Pausing, he chuckled. "When did you meet her, anyway?"

"This morning, after you and I had breakfast at the Whistlestop. She was decorating out front of the dance place, and since she's new in town, I went over to say hi." When Paul leveled one of those big-brother looks at him, Jason let out a frustrated growl. "You're acting like I proposed or something."

"Well…"

"That was a long time ago," Jason reminded him, poking him in the chest for emphasis. "I learned my lesson with her, and I've got no plans for making that mistake again anytime soon."

"I have to ask," Chelsea interrupted. "Who on earth are you talking about?"

"Rachel McCarron," Jason replied with a wry grin. "It didn't work out."

"That little minx took off with your best friend and your truck," Paul reminded him, as if he'd lost his memory or something. "Oh, and the ring. Nice girl."

"Whatever."

Paul opened his mouth, then closed it almost immediately. Jason didn't understand why until he noticed the chilly stare Paul was getting from his wife. It reminded him of Amy's disapproving looks, and he smothered a grin. He'd never had the opportunity to compare one woman with another this way. If he could somehow figure out what was going on in their heads, it might actually be entertaining.

"Fine." With a look that was half smile and half grimace, Paul stepped back to let Jason into the working area of the mill. "Whattaya need?"

Chapter Three

Monday morning crept by at a pace that would have embarrassed the slowest turtle on earth. Banished to her office at the rear of the studio by her carpenter, Amy chafed impatiently and tried not to check the old schoolhouse clock on the wall every two seconds.

She was dying to see what he'd come up with for the entryway. Before she went completely bonkers, she decided it was better to distract herself until he was finished. She could use the free time to inventory her costume collection, assessing what Aunt Helen had on hand so she could determine what they needed to buy for the cast.

Because the studio had been built on her aunt's stellar reputation as a dance instructor, Amy had insisted Aunt Helen remain a silent partner in the business. So every decision was a "they" situation, which was new for someone who'd spent most of her life focused on her own career. It was one of many changes Amy had encountered since coming back to Barrett's Mill after so many years away.

Like Jason Barrett.

The man couldn't be any more different from her ex, and she couldn't help but compare the two. A dancer himself, Devon hadn't been able to cope with the somber prospect of being shackled to a wife who was so limited physically. He bolted shortly after her grim final diagnosis, taking his great-grandmother's engagement ring with him.

Since then, the men who'd crossed her path had been either medical professionals or old friends who viewed her as more of a younger sister than a romantic interest. Heartbroken by Devon's betrayal, her new hands-off status with the male species actually suited her just fine. She had no intention of letting another one close enough to hurt her by taking off just when she needed him most.

Not that Jason fell into that category, she reminded herself as she eased out of her chair. In a few short days, he'd proven himself not only respectful but dependable, two qualities she valued in anyone. On her way into the storeroom, she made several attempts to classify him based on other guys she'd known, but came up empty. Then she heard his teasing voice in her mind.

And here I thought we were friends.

Smiling to herself, she decided he was indeed her friend, one she might enjoy getting to know better. After all, she mused as she began pairing up satin slippers, you never knew when a big, strong carpenter might come in handy.

From the doorway, she heard a low whistle and turned to find him staring into the oversize closet. "It looks like a cotton-candy machine blew up in here."

The comment was so spot-on, she couldn't help laughing. "I guess it does. That's what happens when you cast too many sugar-plum fairies."

"How many extra do you have?"

Glancing up, she quickly did the math. "Ten, I think."

"Why didn't you just make them something else? Save yourself a little netting?"

"Because all the girls wanted to be Clara or a sugar-plum fairy. For this production, no one's en pointe, and only Heidi Peterson could manage the basics for Clara. That means I need lots of these," she added, fluffing the layers of pink tulle hanging on the rack.

Something in his expression shifted, and he took a step inside the cramped room. "You mean, you adjusted the traditional cast so they could play the roles they wanted?"

"Of course. They're kids, and it's Christmas." Baffled by his reaction to her scaled-down production, she frowned. "Why?"

"Because that's the last thing I'd expect from a perfectionist like you."

The gold in his eyes glittered with an emotion she couldn't begin to define, and she found herself caught up in the hypnotic warmth of his gaze. He didn't move toward her, but his imposing presence filled the room with something that was more than physical. In a jolt of understanding, she recognized that it came from a heart so generous, he'd volunteered his time and talents to a stranger simply because she needed his help. Instinctively, she knew he was someone who treated people well as a matter of principle, not as a means to an end.

The kind of man who'd treasure the woman fortunate enough to be the one he loved.

That realization struck her with a certainty so powerful, it actually knocked her back a step. Trying to regain her perspective, she dragged her eyes away and made a show of hunting for the slipper that matched the one still clutched in her hand. "Did you need something?"

"Your stamp of approval." Cocking his arm, he offered it to her with a bright grin. "Wanna come see?"

She did, very much, but she was hesitant to take his arm. Since she couldn't come up with a way to refuse it politely, she fell back on logic. "That's sweet, but we can't fit through that door side by side."

"Got me there. Ladies first, then."

The way he kept referring to her as a lady made Amy want to giggle, and she firmly tamped down the impulse. He was obviously trying to charm her, but it would work only if she let it. She'd handled many situations like this in the past, and she was well aware that keeping him at a safe distance was the best approach.

But it wasn't half as much fun as going along, she admitted with a muted sigh. Being sensible could be such a killjoy. Before they turned the corner to enter the front section of the studio, he abruptly stopped walking.

"Is something wrong?" she asked, standing on tiptoe to look past him. Big as he was, she couldn't see a thing, and she started to worry. "It all fell down, didn't it?"

"That's insulting," he informed her with a good-natured chuckle, "but since you don't know me very well, I'll let you get by with it. Close your eyes."

"Why?"

"So you'll be surprised."

He said that as if it should have been obvious to her, and she felt a twinge of regret for not sharing his enthusiasm for what he'd built. She was the one who'd asked him to do it, and she knew she should be more excited. Sadly, since her dream of dancing had ended up wrapped around a light pole outside D.C., it was all she could do to keep trudging forward.

"I'm not very fond of surprises," she said as evenly as she could manage. "I much prefer it when things go according to plan."

Most of the people she knew would bristle at that or chide her for being a control freak. But not this guy. Instead, he gave her an encouraging smile. "My sister-in-law, Chelsea, used to be like that before Paul showed her how much fun she was missing."

"I don't see what that has to do with me."

"Just that folks can change, is all. Now, close your eyes."

She couldn't understand why it meant so much to him, but he'd put in a lot of work and hadn't charged her a dime. The least she could do was humor him. "Okay, they're closed."

Unfortunately, that threw off her equilibrium, and she felt as if she was going to fall. The sensation was alarming, and she clutched his arm more tightly to maintain her balance. It reminded her of the torturous first steps after the surgery that had shored up her spine but ended her career, and she felt a cold sweat breaking out on her face.

"You're all right, Amy," Jason murmured in a gentle drawl near her ear. "I've got you."

Sure enough, he was bracing her with one strong arm, and she was stunned to find it wasn't scary at all. Not trusting herself to speak without a whimper, she nodded and let him lead her through the studio and out the front door.

Crisp, cool air greeted her, and she fought off a shiver that had nothing to do with the weather. That was the scent she'd noticed on Jason the first day they met, fresh and outdoorsy. Something told her that from now on whenever she was caught outside on a winter day, she'd think of him.

Deliberately pulling her mind back to practical things, she asked, "Can I look now?"

"Go ahead."

She opened her eyes, then blinked in total disbelief. He'd mentioned something about adding a tree and an archway, but this was way beyond anything she could have imagined even on her best day.

The simple arch she'd envisioned had become a full-fledged arbor, twined with greenery and twinkling white lights. The tree wasn't made of wood, but was a seven-foot-tall artificial spruce with more lights and a multipointed crystal star on top. Gifts wrapped in gold and silver paper were clustered around the base, and one box looked as if it had spilled open to show off a collection of wooden soldiers like the ones that would march onstage in a few short weeks.

On the left side was her nutcracker. Sort of. The static sign Jenna had made now swung from hooks that allowed it to move in the breeze. The new arrangement made him look as if he was dancing. Awestruck by the combined effect of all those Christmassy elements, she was convinced a professional designer couldn't have devised a better representation of the popular holiday ballet.

Apparently, there was more to the towering lumberjack than axes and hammers. Who would have guessed that? Astounded by the results, she stared up at Jason in disbelief. "You did this?"

"Yup." Folding his arms, he cocked his head with an eager expression. "You like it?"

"Are you kidding? I love it!" Forgetting her vow to remain detached, she laughed and gave him a quick hug. "It must've taken you forever. How did you manage to get so much done over the weekend?"

"The tree I made didn't turn out so well. Then I remembered your aunt used to put one up. I found it out back in your storage shed."

"You mean, the one that's locked and I can't find the key to?"

"That's the one."

"How did you get it open?" As soon as she finished her question, she had to laugh. "Let me guess. Sledge-hammer?"

"Bolt cutters, and I replaced the lock with a new one. The keys are in your office." Glancing around, he leaned in and murmured, "I made the arbor for my gram's garden. I'm gonna need that back before Christmas."

Impressed beyond words, she went up to examine it more closely. Flowers and vines were carved into every piece of wood, curling up to meet in the middle of the arch in a heart with a script *B* in the center. "Jason, this is absolutely beautiful. You're incredibly talented."

He gave her an aw-shucks grin that made him look like an overgrown little boy. "I'm sure you're used to fancier stuff, so it's nice of you to say that. The power box is down here." He pointed to an open-back square of wood. "The cord runs to your outside receptacle by the front door, and I marked the switch in the lobby that controls it. That way, you can turn everything on and off from inside."

She was amazed that he'd thought to set it up so she wouldn't have to go out in the cold to shut things down. They barely knew each other, and already he'd come up with a way to make her life easier—and warmer. After fending for herself for so long, she liked knowing he was looking out for her.

Despite her usual reserve, she could no longer deny she was warming up to this irresistible man. "Jason, I don't know what to say. This is way beyond what I was expecting. How can I ever repay you?"

"Another one of those hugs would be cool."

Laughing because she couldn't help herself, she obliged him, adding a peck on his cold cheek for good measure. Pulling away, she frowned. "You must be freezing, after working out here so long. Would you like some coffee or something to warm you up?"

"That'd be great, thanks."

"I don't have any made in the office right now, but there's some out back. Come on."

Again, he motioned for her to go in ahead of him. For years, she'd been living in big, bustling cities where everyone rushed past her as if she didn't exist. It might be old-fashioned of her, but she had to admit she liked Jason's way better.

Amy's apartment was...not what he'd expected.

Raised by his parents to be respectful above all else, Jason stood awkwardly in the middle of the narrow doorway, trying to come up with something nice to say. Built onto the rear of the studio, it was a single room with a tiny kitchenette and a small bathroom. The walls were raw drywall, and several buckets scattered around the floor alerted him there were leaks in the roof. Unfortunately, that wasn't the worst part. "There's something wrong with the furnace back here. I've been in freezers warmer than this."

"You have not," she scoffed.

"I worked for a butcher in Utah for six months, and trust me, his cooler temp wasn't far off this place. How do I get to your utilities?" She blinked up at him, then began casting around as if she had no clue. It shouldn't have been funny, but he couldn't help laughing. "There must be a way to get into the crawl space under the addition. Do you know where it is?"

"I'm sure Uncle Fred does."

Jason hated to bother the man for something that simple, and he shrugged. "No problem. I'll find it."

"That's not necessary. I'm hardly ever in here, so it doesn't bother me."

"Must get cold at night, though."

After a couple of moments, she relented with a sigh. "Okay, you got me. I sleep on the couch in the office."

"That can't be good for your back," he chided her as gently as he could. With an injury like hers, she should have the most supportive mattress she could get, not some lumpy old sofa. "You keep doing that, pretty soon you won't be able to get up in the morning."

"It's fine," she said curtly.

"It's not fine, and before I go, I'll make sure you've got heat. While we're at it, have you got any idea where your roof's leaking from?"

"Umm...above?"

A smart aleck, he groaned silently. Just what he needed. Then again, he'd had more fun with her than any other woman he'd met recently. He wasn't entirely sure what that meant, and fortunately, he didn't have time to ponder it now. "I'll climb up there, too, and find out what's going on. My hunch is you lost a few shingles in that bad storm we had last week, and now the water's getting in. There's some extra roofing stuff in the shed, so I'll do a patch that'll keep things dry in here."

Gratitude flooded her eyes, and she gave him a sweet but cautious smile. "Thank you."

Something in the way she said it got to him, and it took him a minute to figure out why. When he landed on an explanation, he couldn't keep back a grin. Troubled but unwilling to ask for help, her fierce sense of pride reminded him of himself. "I'm confused. Why're you living like this when your aunt and uncle are right here in town?"

"I prefer having my own place, even if it's not ideal."

Her suddenly cool tone warned him not to push, and he decided it would be wise to let her have this one. It was none of his business anyway, so he focused on something less personal. "So, we've got the furnace and the roof. What else is wrong?"

"I hate to impose on you," she hedged, handing him a bright red cup with a handle molded to resemble a candy cane. "You're already doing so much for me."

He didn't think this serious and very independent woman would respond well to a damsel-in-distress joke, so he sipped his coffee and saluted her with the festive mug. "'Tis the season and all."

Another hesitation, then she finally gave in and rattled off a list of problems, from leaky plumbing to some kind of vague fluttery sound above the drop ceiling.

"I'd imagine there's a bird stuck in there," he commented. "Or a bat."

Every bit of color drained from her face, and he

reached out to steady her in case she fainted on him. After a few moments, she seemed to collect herself and pulled back. "Bats?"

"Kidding." Sort of. But her reaction had been real enough, and he made a mental note that the pretty ballerina wasn't a big fan of the local wildlife.

"I do not want anything flying or crawling or scurrying around where I live," she announced very clearly.

"Don't worry. If I can't get rid of 'em myself, I'll call an exterminator."

"But don't hurt them," she amended, her soft heart reflected in those stunning blue eyes. "Just take them out to the country where they belong."

"Will do." While they chatted, he'd been eyeballing the old floorboards, searching for some kind of opening. When he located it in the kitchen, he popped the edge with the heel of his boot and set it aside. "Got a flashlight?"

That she had, and after she gave it to him, he swung it around in the darkness. The opening was a pretty tight fit for a guy his size, but he decided to give it a shot. Worst case, he'd get stuck and Paul would come rescue him. And never let him hear the end of it.

Thinking again, he handed his phone over to Amy. "There's gonna be some banging and grumbling down there, so don't worry. If I'm not back in ten minutes, call my dad and tell him to bring a reciprocating saw. His name is Tom, and he's speed-dial number 2."

"Reciprocating saw," she repeated with an efficient nod. "Got it."

"I don't suppose you've got a pair of pliers or a wrench or anything?"

To his amazement, she went to an upper cupboard and brought out a small toolbox. "Uncle Fred left me this in case I needed something. Will anything in there help you?"

"Maybe." Jason took what he thought would be most helpful and tucked the tools into the back pockets of his jeans. Then he sat on the edge of the opening and gave her a mock salute. "Here goes nothin'."

He wedged himself into the cramped space and pulled himself along on his back, hand over hand from one floor joist to the next. When light suddenly flooded the darkness, he yelped in surprise. "Whoa! What'd you do?"

"I wheeled in a portable spotlight from the studio," she replied in a voice muffled by the floor. "Is it helping at all, or should I change the angle?"

"It's awesome," he approved heartily. "Thanks."

"You're welcome."

Even from a distance, she sounded pretty proud of herself, and he chuckled. To his relief, the furnace malfunction was nothing more than an air duct that had wiggled loose and was dangling free. He nearly shouted out the problem, then thought better of it. From several comments she'd made, he gathered Amy was concerned about money. She probably wouldn't be thrilled to discover she'd been paying to heat the crawl space under her apartment.

Reaching into his pocket, he fished out a screwdriver

and tightened the screws on the collar that fastened the duct in place.

One extra turn for good measure, Jason. He heard Granddad's voice in his memory. That kind of thing happened more often lately, as Will Barrett's time on earth gradually ticked away. Swallowing the lump that had suddenly formed in his throat, Jason grimaced even as he followed his grandfather's advice.

When he was finished, he carefully shimmied back out the way he'd come in, settling on Amy's kitchen floor in a cloud of dust. "Sorry about that."

"Don't be silly," she scolded with a delighted expression. "Do you feel that? It's warm air!"

Grabbing his hand, she held it over a nearby register to prove it. When their eyes met, she seemed to realize what she'd done and abruptly let go. Feeling slightly awkward, he did his best not to read anything into the odd exchange. She'd been freezing, and he was the one who fixed her furnace. No biggie.

But another part of him saw things differently. Until now, she'd been polite but reserved with him, making him believe it would take a long time—and a truckload of patience—to gain her trust. That quick but impulsive gesture told him he was making progress, and she was beginning to warm up to him.

He didn't know what the lady had in mind, but he was looking forward to finding out.

Chapter Four

Rehearsals with her little troupe of dancers were always interesting.

Having been involved with professional dance companies for most of her life, Amy had to frequently remind herself these were kids in a small town whose first exposure to ballet was coming through her. Her purpose in starting with *The Nutcracker* was twofold: it had a nice story and it had an unlimited number of roles available. When they were finished, she hoped her students loved it as much as she did.

But for now, she'd give anything to get Brad Knowlton to pay attention long enough to absorb the set blocking she'd just explained for the umpteenth time. "This is your mark," she repeated as patiently as she could. "We taped it here last week, remember?"

His eight-year-old face wrinkled into a frown, and if he'd been a grown-up, she would've assumed he really was trying to cooperate, but his mind was elsewhere. Since this was her first formal experience with teaching, she wasn't sure what the problem was. So she took a stab at identifying whatever was troubling her nutcracker prince. Clapping her hands to get their attention, she announced, "Let's take a break, everyone. Get a snack, use the bathroom and meet me back onstage in ten minutes."

That was one trick she'd learned the first day with her raucous crew. They loved being on the big stage, with its many spotlights overhead, and its triple rows of elegant velvet draperies that could be opened and closed as needed. Giggling and chatting excitedly, they went off in a more or less orderly line to get cookies and juice from the small fridge she always kept stocked with treats. Teaching dance to kids under the age of twelve was kind of like being a lion tamer, she mused with a smile. It never hurt to keep some of their favorite foods close by.

She let them all go ahead of her, then helped herself to a bottle of water. The cookies looked yummy, but her lingering injuries limited her physical activity, and she had to keep an eagle eye on her weight. Slight as she was, if she gained too many pounds, her reconstructed back and spine would pay the price, and she'd be in major trouble. As with most things, she'd learned that the hard way.

Averting her eyes from the temptation, she took a seat next to Brad, who'd crammed a chocolate-chip cookie into his mouth and stacked three more on his napkin in the shape of a pyramid. While he chewed, she casually asked, "Having a good time tonight?"

Still munching, he swallowed and then nodded. His brown eyes looked unsure, though, and she edged a little closer. "You're not really, are you?"

After hesitating for a moment, he shook his head and sipped some juice. Since he didn't seem eager to confide in her, Amy debated whether to let it go. She hated it when people forced her to talk, but with the days to opening night ticking down like an Advent calendar, she didn't have much choice. If Brad didn't want to play the lead, she had to find another boy who did ASAP.

She tried to put herself in his place but discovered even her vivid imagination wasn't that good. She'd never been a young boy, after all. What did she know about how their brains worked?

Hoping she wouldn't come across to him as a disapproving adult, she began her inquisition. "You seemed to be having fun with this the last time we rehearsed. Did something happen between then and now to make you change your mind?"

While he considered her question, she fought the urge to step in and help him make the right choice. Patience wasn't exactly her strong point, but she tamped down her anxiety and summoned an understanding smile. She didn't want to lose him, but she only wanted him to remain in the cast if he was enjoying himself. This was supposed to be fun, and she didn't want any of the kids to feel pressured.

Finally, he said, "My mom took me to see *The Nutcracker* this weekend."

"What a great idea! How did you like it?"

"It was awesome," he replied, eyes wide with enthusiasm. "The soldiers and battle stuff were really cool. They shot off a cannon, and the prince got to kill the mouse king with his sword. How come we're not doing that?"

Boys and their toys, she thought, muting a grin that would only insult him. His mother probably wanted to expose him to some culture, and his takeaway was the battle scene. "First of all, I don't own a cannon, so that was out. Secondly, I wanted to keep our show short enough for little kids in the audience to enjoy. You have a two-year-old sister. How long can she sit still?"

"Not very long," he admitted. "But having a sword would be cool."

She could envision it now: the nutcracker prince chasing flowers and sugar-plum fairies all over her studio, waving a blade over his head like some marauding pirate captain. In an attempt to avoid being the bad guy on this issue, she asked, "How do you think your mother would like that?"

His hopeful expression deflated, and he stared down at the table with a sigh. "She'd hate it. She'd say I could poke someone's eye out or something stupid like that."

"I'm sure you wouldn't hurt anyone on purpose, but accidents can happen when there are so many people onstage together. Someone could stumble and poke themselves, and then we'd be in trouble."

"I guess."

He was one of a handful of boys she taught, and by far the most talented. With a wiry, athletic build, he seemed to genuinely enjoy learning the routines, and he had a natural stage presence rare in someone his age. Because of that, she hated seeing him so disheartened and searched for a way to ease his disappointment.

Inspiration struck, and she suggested, "Why don't we both think about it and come up with something else cool for your character to have? Maybe we could add something to your costume that would make you stand out more from the other soldiers, or give you a solo dance in the spotlight without Clara."

She could almost hear the very proper Russian choreographer she'd last worked with shrieking in horror, but Amy put aside her artistic sensibilities and focused on Brad. If adding a quick progression for him would make him happy, she'd gladly do it. The success of Arabesque hinged on keeping her students—and their parents—coming back for more lessons and recitals. While this wasn't the performing career she'd dreamed of, at least by teaching she was still involved in dancing.

She didn't know how to do anything else, so if the studio failed she'd have no other options. When she let herself think about it, she got so nervous she could hardly breathe. So for now, she blocked out the scary possibilities and waited for Brad's answer.

After what felt like forever, he met her eyes and gave her a little grin. "Can I jump like the prince I saw this weekend? It was like he was flying."

This boy was far from a full grand jeté, but she didn't bother pointing that out. Instead, she nodded. "It'll take some extra work, but I think you can do it. What do you say?"

"Sure. Thanks, Miss Morgan."

She was so relieved, she almost hugged him, then thought better of it. She'd learned that boys were funny about that kind of thing, and she didn't want to destroy the rapport she was building with him by overstepping her boundaries. Instead, she held up her fist for a bump like she'd seen him do with his buddies. "You're welcome. We're due back in a couple of minutes, so finish up."

"Yes, ma'am."

He chugged the rest of his drink, then bolted for the bathroom. Glancing around at the rest of her class, she noticed how cheerful they seemed to be. Here, with their friends, surrounded by the Christmas setting she'd painstakingly designed to invoke the spirit of the ballet they were learning. It was almost time to get back to work, so she picked up her water and slowly moved toward the stage. On her way, she passed the photo Jason had pointed out during his first visit, and while she normally ignored those old pictures, this time she felt compelled to stop and look.

And remember.

For most of her life, she'd spent the holidays onstage, in the background as part of the supporting cast and later as Clara, twirling with her nutcracker and later meeting up with her prince. During the curtain call, she'd look out to find her mother in the audience, proudly leading the standing ovations, a huge bouquet of pink roses and baby's breath in her arms. From her first production to her last, Mom had always been there, dancing every step with her, tears of joy shining in her eyes.

What would she think of this one? Amy wondered. With her daughter in the wings, adjusting costumes and fetching props instead of twirling her way through the footlights? They hadn't been able to get together for Thanksgiving this year, so she hadn't mentioned the show to her mother yet. Still, anyone with half a brain would be able to figure out Amy would be staging this, her favorite ballet, to open her new studio.

And Connie Morgan had much more than half a brain, Amy thought as she speed-dialed Mom's number.

"Hello!" Mom answered, a little out of breath. "How's my girl today?"

"Fine. Are you on the treadmill?"

"Oh, you know how it is," she answered with a laugh. "If I keep running, maybe old age won't be able to catch up with me."

Amy laughed in response, wishing for the umpteenth time that she'd inherited her mother's breezy attitude toward things in general. "I won't keep you, then. I just wanted to let you know we're putting on *The Nutcracker* on the eighteenth, here in Barrett's Mill."

She would have loved for Mom to attend, but not wanting to pressure her, she stopped short of putting that desire into words. The delighted gasp she got put her worries to rest.

"Your directing debut—of course I'll be there! I

wouldn't miss it for the world. Then we can have a nice family Christmas with Helen and that big brother of mine."

More relieved than she'd anticipated, Amy relaxed enough to tease, "It's been a while. Do you remember how to get here?"

She humphed at that. "My new car has one of those fancy navigation systems."

"Sure, but do you know how to use it?"

"Such a comedian. Are you doing stand-up in your spare time now?"

"There's not much call for that down here." Amy chuckled. "Besides, that's the extent of my material. You gave me an opening the size of an 18-wheeler, and I took it."

"That's my girl, making the most of her opportunities," Mom praised her warmly. "It's so good to hear the old spunk back in your voice. It's been a long time coming."

That was a colossal understatement, but fortunately her break was over, so she didn't have time to brood about it. "I'm sorry to cut this short, but I have to get back to the kids now. See you soon."

"I'm looking forward to it. Love you, sweetie."

"Love you, too, Mom."

Ending the call, Amy sipped her water while studying the photos that chronicled her promising ballet career, which had been her only goal for as long as she could remember. When the kids started thundering back up the wooden steps and took their places onstage, her eyes drifted away from her past to focus on them.

Chattering to each other in hushed voices, they giggled while practicing the new steps she'd shown them earlier. With his soldiers trailing behind, Brad bounded up to take his spot, fresh enthusiasm glowing on his freckled face.

Apparently, the solution she'd come up with worked for him, she mused with a smile of her own as she went up the stairs to join her dancers for the second act. Maybe she was starting to get the hang of this teaching gig, after all.

"These look great, Fred," Jason commented while he assessed the older man's carpentry skills on some of the smaller set pieces. Not only had he finished cutting all of them out in detail, he'd painted them, too. His efforts would save Jason a ton of time. "I only dropped them off a couple days ago. How'd you get 'em done so fast?"

"Bored outta my mind," Fred grumped, but the smile on his face said he appreciated Jason's praise. "You can only watch so much of the History Channel."

"I hear that. I'd rather be doing something than watching TV any day. Has the doctor said when you can get back to work?"

The town's most talented mechanic groaned. "Another week, if I follow orders. 'Course, Helen won't let me do otherwise," he added with a mock glare over at his wife.

"You don't want to miss out on Christmas, do you?"

she challenged with a glare of her own. "Especially with Amy here now and Connie coming in for a visit. We haven't all been together in years, and I'm not about to let you spoil it by being stubborn."

"Besides," Jason added with a grin, "with all the work you're putting in, you're gonna want to see *The Nutcracker*. It'd be a shame to have to make do with a recording when you could see it in person."

"Yeah, yeah. I get it. Just bring me some more to do," he pleaded. "I'm going bonkers cooped up here at the house."

"It's no picnic from where I'm sitting, either," his wife informed him testily.

They'd been married for longer than Jason had been alive, and he'd always been amused by their good-natured bickering. Done with fond smiles and a light touch, their back-and-forth was evidence of a solid relationship that had probably started before the two Barrett's Mill natives entered junior high.

They reminded him of his parents, who shared the kind of close, loving bond Jason longed for in his own life. Not long ago, he thought he'd found that with Rachel. He pictured himself settled in a home with a wife and kids, and when he'd asked her to be part of that, she'd quickly agreed. When she took off with another lumberjack and no explanation, Jason realized she'd told him only what she'd thought he wanted to hear.

Water under the bridge, he reminded himself, and better left behind. They wanted different things, and now that he'd recovered from the sting of her rejection, he hoped she was happy.

"...not busy tomorrow night," Helen was saying, "I'd like to have you over for dinner, to thank you for all your help with the studio. I'll be making fried chicken."

Jason was pretty swamped these days, but he wasn't one to turn down a home-cooked meal. "I do like your fried chicken."

"That's settled, then. Just come by when you finish at the mill, and I'll have a place ready for you at the table."

"Sounds great. And I'll bring some more work for you," he promised Fred as he gathered up the pieces on his way to the door. "It sure is nice to have someone helping out who actually knows what they're doing."

"Connie's not all that mechanical, either," her uncle agreed with a chuckle. "Amy got that from her, I guess."

Jason had been wondering about Amy's father, and with that casual family comment it seemed the man was completely out of the picture. He knew how that went. He nearly mentioned that he'd also been pitching in to make repairs at the studio, then thought better of it. Hearing how much had slipped through the cracks while he was laid up wouldn't help Fred's recuperation at all, especially since the apartment in question was his niece's. Instead, Jason simply said good-night.

When he got to Arabesque, the parking spots in front of the studio were empty, so he took the one right in front of the door. The lobby was dark, but he noticed the lights over the stage were still on. Framed by the window, the elegant curtains drew his eyes to a single figure silhouetted in a spotlight.

It was Amy, clearly unaware that anyone was watching her. With her arms in a graceful pose, she seemed to glide over the floor, spinning slowly here and there, then pausing to write something on a piece of paper. When she tried a certain movement, even from a distance he saw her wince and grab her back with her hands.

His heart shot into his throat, and before he knew what he was doing, he was standing beside her. "Are you okay?"

"I'm fine," she all but snarled. "What are you doing out there spying on me?"

"Not spying," he corrected with a smile. "Admiring. Until you hurt your back, anyway. Before that, it was like watching a cloud move across the sky."

"It's nice of you to say that."

From her tone, he could tell she didn't share his opinion. He hadn't known her long, but she fascinated him, this delicate woman who had a vein of pure steel running through her. With a tough outer shell guarding a tender heart, she spoke to him in a way he'd never experienced before. In turn, he found himself wanting to protect her from harm and applaud her determination to take on the world single-handedly.

He didn't understand why, but there was definitely something special about Amy Morgan. Rather than argue with her, though, he opted to change the subject. "What're you doing?"

"Blocking steps for the kids." She showed him her

notes, which featured a diagram labeled with things he couldn't begin to comprehend. "The original choreography is way too complicated for beginners, so I'm simplifying it for them. I'm designing a new dance for the prince and was trying it out when you came in."

"And interrupted you," he guessed with a sheepish grin. "Sorry. It looked good to me, though."

"I wish I could see for myself," she said wistfully. "I can't dance and watch at the same time."

"That fancy phone of yours must have a video function on it. You could record yourself."

Before he finished speaking, her face twisted with the kind of pain no one should have to endure. "I hate watching myself move," she ground out through clenched teeth. "It's ugly."

"Nothing about you is ugly," he assured her in his gentlest tone. "You're still the prettiest girl I've ever seen."

"That's sweet, but you don't have to lie to make me feel better."

Her eyes filled with equal parts gratitude and tears, and Jason scrambled to come up with some comforting words. "I'd never lie to a lady. My mom'd kill me."

"You're a grown man. How could she possibly find out?"

"Trust me, she'd know."

After a moment, Amy's wary look mellowed into a more friendly one, and she gave him a tentative smile. "In that case, you could help me with this. If you don't mind," she added hastily. "I know it's late."

Five a.m. would come pretty early, and he should have been in bed an hour ago, but her shy request drove any thoughts of sleep right out of his head. "I've got some time. Whattaya need me to do?"

Grasping his arms, Amy moved him into place and rattled off a series of moves. A dancer would be able to follow along, but a lumberjack? Not so much.

"Right," he responded with a laugh. "How 'bout in English?"

"Was I unclear?"

"Oh, I heard you fine. It's just I don't have a clue what you meant." Inspiration struck, and he suggested, "Maybe you could show me."

That got him a decidedly suspicious look. "Are you trying to get me to dance with you?" When he grinned, she rolled those beautiful eyes at him. "You're pathetically easy to read."

"I figure there's no sense in making a big mishmash of things." Opening his arms in his version of a ballet-style pose, he said, "Are we dancing or what?"

After a few seconds, she apparently decided he was harmless and ventured closer. He listened carefully to her instructions, and they slowly moved through the steps. Involved in one sport or another all his life, he'd managed not to embarrass himself at proms or his brothers' weddings. But next to Amy, he felt like a serious clod, and he reminded himself to be especially careful not to stomp on her toes.

Glancing down, he noticed how ridiculous their feet looked opposite each other. His shoes were not only huge, they were scuffed and stained—the opposite of her black patent flats with their classy velvet bows. The contrast was so complete, he couldn't help chuckling.

"What?" she asked, glancing around to see what was so funny.

"Our feet. They don't really go together, do they?"

She peeked at their shoes, then met his eyes with a laugh. "Not any more than the rest of us does. You're like a big redwood, and I'm a little twig."

"A beautiful twig," he amended with a warm smile. "One with gorgeous flowers that smell incredible."

She blushed, but to his surprise, she didn't look away. Instead, she held his gaze, searching his eyes for something. In that moment, he no longer cared that what he was feeling for her didn't make any sense. Whatever she was looking for, he wanted her to find it in him.

"It's jasmine," she said quietly, the corner of her mouth lifting invitingly. "Do you like it?"

"Very much." Sensing that he was approaching a line with her, he veered away before he crossed over it. Amy had been through an emotional wringer, and their growing friendship was fragile, at best. He wasn't about to destroy it by pushing things too fast. "'Course, I spend most of my time at the mill with machines that leak oil and guys that smell like… Well, you get the drift."

She laughed, a bright, carefree sound very much at odds with the serious woman he'd been getting acquainted with. It made him think of the young ballerina in the pictures on the wall, and he was pleased to discover that joyful girl still existed. Then and there, he decided he'd have to come up with some more ways to draw her out into the light. She deserved that, and odd as it was, it seemed he had a knack for doing it.

After a few minutes, she stopped directing his steps, shadowing him as he moved across the stage. They drifted from spotlight to spotlight, through the half-decorated ballroom to the huge tree with its flickering electric candles and old-fashioned ornaments. Since they weren't touching, it wasn't as if they were actually dancing together, but he felt a connection to her that went beyond the physical. He couldn't have explained it if he tried, but he liked the way it felt.

Pausing in front of the incomplete marble fireplace, he said, "I forgot to show you this."

Flipping a switch hidden behind the wall, he set the electric flames in motion. They reflected off the tinsel and sparkling balls, giving the set a warm, cozy glow.

"It's perfect," Amy breathed. She stared up at him, the Christmas lights twinkling in her eyes.

The urge to drop in for a kiss was nearly overpowering, and he sternly tamped it down. Amy trusted him, and he wanted to retain his good-guy status. "It's what you asked me for."

As sadness drifted through her expressive eyes, she frowned. "I don't always get what I ask for."

Laced with anguish, her comment drove through him like a knife. That this sweet, talented woman had been denied her life's dream struck him as the worst kind of tragedy. He pictured her alone in some hospital, begging for divine help that had never come. She'd picked herself up and moved on, but he could see part of her was stranded in the past, wishing for things that could never be. While he could imagine God redirecting her onto a different path for some reason, Jason knew that explanation would not only anger her, it might make her pull away from him. Whatever it took, he was determined not to let that happen.

"That's true for all of us. But you've made a new start here, and from where I'm standing, it looks like it's going really well."

"This isn't what I want," she confided in a desperate whisper. "I want to dance."

Suddenly, nothing meant more to him than to see her happy before he left. With that in mind, he said, "Then let's dance. Show me the routine you worked out for Clara and her prince."

As he took her hands in his, she stared at him as if she was seeing him for the first time. "Are you for real?"

"Yup. And I'm all yours." As soon as those words popped out, he realized how they sounded, and he cringed. "Sorry about that. I meant—"

"I know what you meant," she assured him, rewarding him with a grateful smile. "Thank you."

Being there felt so right, he'd have gladly stayed on that stage with her all night long. But he didn't think he should tell her that, so he went with an old standard. "You're welcome."

Chapter Five

"Is that what you're wearing?"

Jason stopped at the head of the stairs and turned to face the music. Olivia Barrett, his grandmother and authority on all things etiquette related, stood in the middle of the hallway, hands on her hips and a look of horror on her face.

"Yeah," he responded, trying not to laugh at what she clearly thought was a major fashion error. "Why?"

She let out an exasperated breath that spoke of decades of fighting with the Barrett men. "You look like you're going to a barn raising instead of dinner with the Morgans."

"It's Fred and Helen." Her odd expression set off alarm bells in his head, and he gave her a hard stare. "Right?"

She hesitated a few seconds, then said, "And Amy."

Groaning, he muttered, "What're you trying to do to me?"

Obviously embarrassed, she made a show of dusting something off the hand-carved newel post. Which of course was spotless. "Helen and I just want you kids to be happy."

Why did it not surprise him that Amy's aunt was in on this? Come to think of it, he should've figured out something was up when she asked him to dinner in the first place. Luring him in with fried chicken, no less.

Recognizing she and her friend meant well, he reassured Gram with a smile. "I'm very happy, being home and working at the mill. What makes you think I need more than that?"

From the glimmer in her eyes, Jason guessed the town gossip mill had ratted him out. "Brenda Lattimore saw you two at the studio last night. Dancing," she added in a triumphant voice.

"So? Amy's a dance teacher, and I was helping her put together some moves for her students." Even to his own ears, that sounded lame, and he couldn't help chuckling. "All right, you got me. I like her, okay?"

"We like her, too," Gram told him as they headed downstairs together. "She's a sweet girl who's taken a terrible blow. She needs all the understanding she can get."

"And you think I'm the one to give it to her, is that it?"

They'd reached the bottom of the stairs, and she turned to him with a look so full of love, he silently thanked God for making him part of her family. "Yes, I do. You've got a wonderful heart, just looking for the right woman to make a life with. Amy didn't land back in Barrett's Mill by accident, you know. God brought her here."

"For me," he said, filling in the blank for her. When she nodded, he shook his head. "I appreciate that, but before you and Helen start picking out wedding music, maybe we should find out what Amy thinks first."

"She'll love you, of course. All the girls do."

Which was the problem, complicated by the fact that Paul's assessment was dead-on: Jason was a sucker for a pretty face and a sad story. He fell too hard, too fast, and as he edged closer to twenty-five, he knew he couldn't keep on going that way. A guy could take only so much rejection, after all, and he'd promised himself the next time he proposed would be the last.

Since he hated to burst Gram's romantic bubble, he shook off his brooding with a chuckle. "How 'bout I go have dinner and then we'll see what happens after that?"

"But—"

"Let him go, Olivia," Granddad called out from the hospital bed that occupied their dining room. "You look fine, by the way. No matter what a woman says, a man looks better in his own plain clothes than someone else's fancy suit."

Jason had been living with them since returning to help out at the mill, but he still wasn't quite used to seeing the frail patient that had taken Granddad's place. At first, he could hardly stand to look at him, connected to an IV that fed him medicine to ease the pain of the cancer destroying his body. Gradually, the man's upbeat attitude, driven by a belief that his life had gone according to divine plan, eased some of Jason's sadness.

But this Christmas would be his last. The whole family knew it, and Will and Olivia refused to avoid the topic, instead choosing to keep it in the open and treasure every day they had together. Jason and Paul had come back from Oregon to fulfill Granddad's wish for reopening the mill to produce furniture again. That he'd lived long enough to enjoy their success was something Jason thanked God for every night before he went to sleep.

When Jason realized his grandparents were staring at him, he put aside his dark thoughts and summoned a smile. "Well, I'm off. I've got my cell phone if you need me."

"I don't suppose you'd bring me some of Helen's fried chicken?" Granddad asked hopefully. "Hers is almost as good as Olivia's."

"You got it." Jason waved as he opened the door. Kissing his grandmother's cheek, he said, "'Night, Gram."

"Good night, little bear," she replied, using the nickname she'd given him as a child. "Mind your manners, now."

Knowing she'd hear all about his behavior from Helen long before he made it home, he couldn't help laughing. "Yes, ma'am."

"Everyone will be here Sunday after church to decorate the house," she reminded him through the screen door. "Amy's got quite the eye for Christmas decorations, from what I hear. Maybe you can get some suggestions from her."

A blind man could see where she was headed with that one, and he teased, "It'd be easier to just invite her over to help."

"If you want," she said, as if the possibility hadn't even crossed her mind. Her expression mirrored the one Helen had given him yesterday, and he trotted down the steps shaking his head.

If she got her way, he and Amy would be hitched by Valentine's Day. Given his less-than-stellar track record, the mere thought of that should've chilled the blood in his veins. But it didn't. That meant one of two things, he mused as he went down the driveway and turned onto the sidewalk. Either the idea was so ridiculous he'd already dismissed it, or he liked it. Whichever one was correct, he had the feeling his nice, quiet life was about to get a lot more complicated.

As he strolled toward the Morgan place, it occurred to him that the stick-to-the-plan ballet teacher probably wasn't the type who'd be thrilled about having a surprise guest for dinner. Taking his phone from the pocket of his good jeans, he thumbed through his contacts list to the number she'd given him when he signed on to tackle the sets for her show.

"Jason? Is something wrong?"

"Nah, just calling to warn you I'm coming for dinner tonight. Your aunt made it sound like payback for helping at the studio, but Gram let it slip that they're trying to get us together."

She'd called herself a perfectionist, and he assumed she'd be irritated by the unexpected change in plans. Instead, she laughed. "That explains the good china and five-layer chocolate cake in the kitchen."

"Aw, man. You mean the one with her secret raspberry sauce and fresh raspberries?"

"That's the one."

"No one can resist that cake," he said. "It tied for first place at the county fair last year."

"With what?"

"My gram's cranberry cobbler," he replied proudly. "You should try it sometime."

After a moment, she asked, "Are you asking me over for dessert some night?"

Was he? He hadn't intended to, but now that he replayed his comment in his head, he could see how she'd get that impression. He was normally much smoother than that around women, and this one was on the other end of the phone, so he had no excuse for the slipup. What was wrong with him, anyway?

Then he recalled Gram's invitation, and as he entered the Morgans' driveway, he decided to go for it. "Sure. How 'bout Sunday?"

She was standing on the front porch, and she waved to him as she said, "That would be nice. What time?"

Closing his phone, Jason took the steps two at a time and greeted her with a smile. "Does lunchtime work for you?"

"Sure."

"I should warn you, we'll be decorating the house

that day, so the whole family will be there. It might get a little zooey, but the upside is there'll be lots of good food and Christmas music."

"I like both those things," she commented with a shy smile that made his heart roll over in his chest. "Thanks for inviting me."

"No problem."

He opened the door for her to go inside, and she turned to him with a frown. "Aunt Helen told me your grandfather's not doing well. I'm so sorry."

"We all are."

With eyes full of sympathy, she touched his arm in a comforting gesture. "If there's anything I can do to help, please let me know."

Pushing aside a sudden wave of sadness, he forced a grin. "Coming over and pretending you don't mind being set up with me will do fine."

"I can manage that."

Smiling, she moved past him and went inside. The scent of fried chicken and fresh corn reached him where he was standing in the living room, and he poked his head through the doorway. "Helen, that smells amazing."

"You haven't seen anything yet."

"I heard something about chocolate and raspberries."

"You heard right," she assured him. "For now, could you run out and tell Fred dinner's ready? He's tinkering out in the shop and can't hear me over that saw."

"I heard you," Fred grumbled from the back door. "I

was waiting for Jason 'cause I knew you wouldn't be putting anything on the table till he got here."

Southern hospitality, Jason thought with a grin. He sure had missed it during the five years he'd been wandering around the country. Once they were all seated at the table, Helen brought in a platter heaped with crisp, golden-fried chicken that made his stomach rumble in anticipation. "Sorry about that. I worked through lunch today."

"So, things are busy out at the mill?" Fred asked as he passed dishes along.

"Crazy busy, but we're all glad for the work."

"Carpentry isn't as exciting as lumberjacking, I'd imagine."

"True," Jason responded, "but I'm not liable to break my neck doing it, either. Besides, I like being home, especially during the holidays. I used to race back for Christmas and leave right after. This year, I won't be doing that."

"That means you'll be around for the Starlight Festival," Helen said while she spooned fluffy mashed potatoes onto his plate. "When's the last time you went to that?"

"It's been a while," he admitted.

"I vaguely remember that," Amy said, punctuating the comment with her fork. "There's all kinds of goodies, and white lights strung all over the place like stars. Then they light up the tree in the square."

Her eyes shimmered with excitement, and he was pleased to get a glimpse of the joy he kept hoping to see in her. It made him wonder if the little girl she'd once been was still in there somewhere, waiting for a chance to come out and play again.

"The whole town turns out for it," Fred told her. "Local business owners donate the food, and it gives us all a chance to get together to celebrate the holidays."

The conversation died down while they worked their way through Helen's excellent meal. When she brought the promised cake and coffee to the table, she said, "Amy, I was just thinking the festival might be a nice way to let more people know about Arabesque. I could help you put something together, if you want."

Amy's expression dimmed, and she sighed. "I'd love to, Auntie, but we're just scraping by as it is. If enrollment doesn't pick up, I'm not sure we're going to make it until spring."

Jason was well acquainted with the tough business climate around Barrett's Mill these days. Reopening the mill had been a godsend for the local craftsmen they'd been able to bring on. He just wished they could afford to hire more of them. Expanding the crew would not only make less work for each pair of hands, it would give some talented people a welcome influx of cash.

While the delicious cake fell apart in his mouth, an idea popped into his head, and he quickly swallowed. "How 'bout if you advertise the show at the Starlight Festival?"

"There's no marketing allowed," Helen reminded him. "It's supposed to be a fun, free event."

"Sure, but if you offered a treat free of charge, you

could wrap it in something *Nutcracker*-ish with the studio's logo on it, right?"

Amy's eyes lit up, and she leaned forward with sudden interest. "What did you have in mind?"

Turning to Helen, he grinned. "Your pralines. They're made with nuts, so they tie in with the show. And they're delicious, besides. It's a win-win."

"That's a great idea, Jason." Amy turned hopeful eyes on her aunt. "If you make them, I'll take care of the wrapping and handing out."

"Count me in," Jason added. "It'll be fun."

Faced with the two of them, Helen tipped her head with an indulgent smile. "I suppose I could whip up a batch or two. But where will you find *Nutcracker* wrappers?"

"Online," Amy answered immediately. "I'll get them overnighted so we have them in time. We'll wrap them up Saturday morning right before the tree lighting. It'll be perfect," she added, beaming across the table at Jason.

"Yeah, it will." Returning that smile was the easiest thing he'd ever done, and he ignored the annoying voice in the back of his mind cautioning him that he was headed onto very thin ice. Even if that ended up being true, his gut was telling him trouble with Amy would be well worth it.

The Barrett's Mill Starlight Festival definitely lived up to its name.

The night was brisk, but nothing compared to the

winters she'd spent in New York City. The clear sky was filled with stars that rivaled the twinkle lights strung through the oaks and elms in the square. In the middle of it all, standing regally above the fray, towered a blue spruce comparable to any she'd seen outside of Rockefeller Center. Draped in strands of lights, it was dark, waiting for the lighting ceremony later in the evening.

"See the star up there?" Jason asked, pointing to it. "Granddad's father made that for the first time the town decorated the tree."

"What a nice tradition," Amy commented as her eyes traveled up to it. "They probably didn't need a cherry picker to put it up back then."

"Yeah, they conned some poor sap into scaling the trunk and wiring it in place." Chuckling, he shook his head. "Can you imagine how sticky he'd be with pine pitch all over him? Stuff must've stuck to him for a week."

Amy hadn't considered that, and she marveled at the practical way his mind worked. She was a creative person by nature, and her involvement pretty much ended at the concept stage. In the short time she'd known him, Jason had proven himself adept at making her fanciful designs work in three dimensions. Piece by piece, together they were bringing her vision for *The Nutcracker* to life. Theirs was an unusual collaboration, to be sure, but so far it seemed to be working.

Hefting the large basket of pralines, he scanned the crowd from his much higher vantage point. "Okay. Where did you wanna start?"

"You know, I'm perfectly capable of carrying that myself," she protested.

"Not as long as I'm here."

She bristled at that. "Excuse me?"

He seemed to realize he'd insulted her, and he deflected her temper with a soothing grin. "That didn't come out right. I meant I'm happy to help a lady out by hauling a basket around the square for her. Since these are your aunt's treats, I'm figuring it'll lighten up quick enough."

As if to prove his point, a middle-aged couple approached them with bright smiles. They looked vaguely familiar, but Amy couldn't quite place them until the man began talking.

"Good evening, you two." While his greeting was for them both, he added a fatherly nod for her. "It's wonderful to see you again, Amy. It's been a while, so I'm not sure you remember me."

"Pastor Griggs," she said, a sinking feeling in the pit of her stomach. It only worsened when she glanced at his wife, and she struggled to keep her composure. In her mind, they represented everything she'd turned her back on, and running into them tonight was awkward, at best. "Mrs. Griggs. How are you tonight?"

"Busy as always during the holiday season," the woman replied in the gentle voice that had taught her the Sunday-school lessons she'd adored. The ones where she'd learned that God loved and watched over all His children. She'd believed that for a long time, until harsh experience had taught her otherwise. The day He abandoned her was the beginning of the worst time in her life.

It was bad enough the rest of the year, but Christmas was especially hard for her. While everyone else was full of grace and good cheer, she mourned what she'd lost out on that dark, icy road, knowing it was gone forever.

Jason was calmly chatting with them as if nothing was amiss, even though he'd confided to her how sad he was about his grandfather. She found herself envying his levelheaded perspective, and she made an attempt to copy his behavior. Smiling and nodding, she did her best to participate in the lighthearted conversation, and to her surprise, her dark mood began to brighten.

Until the pastor said, "I'm sure you're very busy with the studio, Amy, but we'd love to have you back at the Crossroads Church. Our little family hasn't been quite the same without you."

Amy saw absolutely no reason to worship a God who'd turned His back on her, and she swallowed hard to keep from blurting out her true feelings. "Thank you for the invitation."

Apparently, Mrs. Griggs sensed her attitude and changed tracks with a laugh. "Don't be fooled, dear. What he's really after is another soprano for the choir. We've lost a few and are hunting for some to replace them."

"No one's sick, I hope," Amy said.

"One of the ladies has a baby due on Christmas Eve, and she won't be able to sing. Another moved unexpectedly when her husband got a new job out of state, and the others—" She shrugged. "You know how it is."

"You have such a lovely voice, though," her husband chimed in with an optimistic look. "I'm sure your singing would be wonderful."

He'd nailed her weakness, Amy groaned silently. Despite her ongoing battle with the Almighty, she loved Christmas music for its upbeat, joyful content. Peace on earth, goodwill toward everyone—even a lapsed Christian like her could appreciate such hopeful messages.

But agreeing to sing would make her the worst kind of hypocrite, and she wouldn't be able to live with herself. "I'm afraid I'm not active in the church anymore. Much as I'd like to help out, it wouldn't feel right to do that when I don't attend services."

The Griggses exchanged a look that told her they already knew what she'd just told them, and the pastor's wife patted her shoulder in a comforting gesture. "We completely understand, dear, and we're not trying to coerce you into doing something you're not comfortable with. If you'd like to join us, we'd be happy to have you."

Amy couldn't believe she'd heard the woman correctly. "You mean, I can join the choir but not come to church?"

"Yes," the pastor replied without hesitation. "No one will pressure you for more than you want to do. You have my word on that."

At first, his promise made no sense to her at all. Then it occurred to her he was probably thinking she'd change her mind once she got reacquainted with the people in the congregation. Maybe he was right, she acknowledged, maybe not. But she couldn't deny that celebrating Christmas in her hometown held a nostalgic appeal for her.

She glanced up at Jason, who met her questioning look with a grin. "Most of us can't sing a lick, but it's a lotta fun."

"You're in the church choir?" she asked, well and truly amazed.

"Sure. It's a great place to meet girls."

His wicked grin made her laugh, and she had to admit that knowing he'd be there was a plus for her. She'd been on her own for so long, wishing she could find a way to belong to a community somewhere. Here was a golden opportunity, staring her in the face. All she had to do was go into the church for rehearsals, she reasoned. How hard could it be?

"Your cousin Brenda has the music," the preacher nudged gently. "I'm sure she'd copy it for you, and then you could decide after that. If you're interested, we rehearse on Tuesday nights, from six to eight."

"I'll definitely think about it."

They each took a praline, agreeing to spread the word about her upcoming production. As they headed off to circulate, she wondered at the turn her evening had taken. If they'd asked her about the choir an hour ago, she'd have politely but firmly refused. Now, for some reason, she was more open to it. Could it be the town's undeniable Christmas spirit was rubbing off on her? Anything was possible, she supposed.

"Punch?" Jason asked, nodding toward the table loaded down with huge punch bowls and paper cups.

"Please."

She took the basket from him, fully intending to keep it. But when he returned with their drinks, he smoothly retrieved it from her. While they resumed their aimless course through the square, she said, "You're a very stubborn man."

That got her a bright grin. "Yeah."

"Jenna complains about your brother Paul being the same way. It must run in your family."

His expression dimmed, and in his eyes she noticed something she hadn't yet seen: anxiety. He'd been so kind to her, she felt awful for upsetting him, even though it was an accident. "I'm sorry, Jason. Did I say something wrong?"

"No, it's just—" Taking her elbow, he guided her to a quieter spot in a stand of trees away from the crowd. "There's something you need to know about me."

It sounded so ominous, she felt her pulse ratchet up several notches. Did she want to know? she wondered. She'd learned to keep people—especially men—at a safe distance to avoid being hurt. But now, she was touched that he valued their friendship enough to share an important secret with her. Because he trusted her, she felt more confident about trusting him in return. "Okay. Go ahead."

After a heavy sigh, he fixed her with an intense gaze she'd never seen from him. "Paul and I aren't related."

"I don't understand. You and everyone else in town told me you're brothers."

"We are, but not the usual way. His mom, Diane, works with kids at teen centers she runs here and in Cambridge, which is where she met my mother twenty-five years ago. She and Tom adopted me from her before I was born."

Amy's jaw fell open in shock, and she frantically searched for a logical reaction to his stunning news. "Who is she?"

"I have no idea. That was part of the deal they made, and my parents have stood by their word."

"But didn't you wonder about her while you were growing up?" Amy pressed in a whisper. "I mean, she was your mother."

"She wasn't ready for me when I came along," he explained in a tone much calmer than hers. "She gave me a chance to have a better life, and whoever she is, I'll always be grateful to her for that."

"I'd be furious," Amy hissed at the selfish woman she'd never meet. How could a mother surrender her newborn child? Unmarried and alone at what she assumed was a similar age, her own mother had never even considered such a thing.

Jason took her anger in stride, easing her temper with a smile. "Your mom took on the world for you and made it work. Not everyone is that strong."

Since he'd come to terms with the situation, Amy

concluded that it was ridiculous for her to debate a teenager's decision with him. Shaking off her lingering resentment, she did her best to return the smile. "I guess you're right about that. Dad left when I was a baby, but Mom never let him being gone affect me. She's pretty amazing."

"You must've gotten that from her." Holding up his cup, he tapped hers in a toast. "To Christmas in Barrett's Mill. Welcome home, Amy."

She'd heard grander speeches, but none had warmed her withered heart the way his simple toast did. There was something about this towering lumberjack with the kind eyes that made her want to start dreaming of better things to come. "Welcome home, Jason. Merry Christmas."

He polished off his punch in one swallow and tossed his cup into a nearby bin. Then he rubbed his hands together and picked up the basket again. "Enough serious talk. Let's give out the rest of these so we can enjoy ourselves."

"Sounds good."

With his height and outgoing personality, it didn't take long for them to empty the basket. Several people asked about the studio and what kinds of classes she'd be offering after the holidays. Fortunately, Amy had the foresight to bring along business cards, and by the time they'd finished their circuit of the square, all the cards and candies were gone.

"This is fabulous," she approved. "If even half those

folks bring their kids in after New Year's, I'll have enough students for another beginning ballet class."

Jason gave her an admiring look. "Y'know, I snuck in the other day while you were teaching that bunch of six-year-olds. You're great with them, and the way they stare up at you is really cute."

"I like kids in general, but that group is so great, I think I have even more fun than they do."

"It shows. You're gonna make a fantastic mom someday."

His comment plucked a sensitive chord deep inside her, and she tried to accept his compliment the way she knew she should. Swallowing hard, she managed to thank him in a more or less normal voice.

Unfortunately, he was more perceptive than she'd anticipated, and his face clouded with concern. "Did I say something wrong?"

"No, it's nothing. Sorry," she added lamely. "It's been a big day, and I'm a little tired, I guess."

"It's not nothing, but if you don't wanna talk about it, that's fine. I understand."

Meeting his eyes, she found nothing but compassion in them. As a rule, she kept her private issues to herself, not wanting to discuss painful things with people who couldn't possibly relate to them. Jason was different, though. He'd trusted her with something very personal about himself, and she knew if she confided in him, he'd be sympathetic.

So, after a deep breath, she nutshelled it for him. "I can't have children."

"Because of the accident?" When she nodded, his rugged face twisted with sympathy. "Amy, I'm so sorry. Are you sure there's no way around it?"

"The surgeries I went through made sure of that. It was the main reason my fiancé left," she heard herself add. She hadn't meant to share that detail, but since it was out in the open, she decided to clear it all out of her system. "Having a family was really important to him, and he refused to consider adoption."

"Love is what makes a family," Jason said tersely. "If he was too narrow-minded to see that, you're better off without him."

The utter conviction in his tone drove off some of her sadness, and she rewarded his thoughtfulness with her biggest, brightest smile. "Thank you for saying that. It was very sweet."

He gave her a slow, very male grin. "That's me."

"The girls around here must fall all over you." The grin widened mischievously, and she couldn't help laughing. "Just so you know, I won't be joining them."

"Really?" The gold in his eyes sparked with curiosity, and he moved a half step closer. "Why?"

It was a moronically simple question, but while his gaze seemed to warm the chilly evening air, her brain went completely blank. He was so down-to-earth, with his easygoing demeanor and generous nature. Here, in her tiny hometown of all places, she'd found someone who accepted her just as she was, flaws and all. Being female, she couldn't help being drawn to him and his bright optimism, but at the same time she resisted getting any closer. The question, as he'd so directly put it, was why.

While she hunted for a decent response, he flashed her a confident grin. "That's fine. But fair warning—I'm gonna change your mind."

His smug tone irked her, and she snorted derisively. "Not hardly."

"Better watch yourself," he teased. "That Blue Ridge accent's starting to come back."

Relieved to switch to a less volatile topic, she griped, "It's hard not to talk that way when everyone around you does."

"Don't get your back up. I like it."

With that, he sauntered on ahead of her, swinging the empty basket and whistling along with the rendition of "Rockin' Around the Christmas Tree" playing on the loudspeakers. As she hurried to catch up with his long strides, she wondered who he thought he was, speaking to her that way. The fact that he could potentially be right had nothing to do with her current frame of mind, of course. It was just one more reason to keep a safe distance between them.

The trouble was, the time she spent with Jason was the happiest she'd ever been away from the stage. She wasn't a face-fanning romantic, but even she recognized that her desire to be with him meant something. Something that could derail everything if she lost sight of her goal to reclaim her independence and take control of her life again.

She simply couldn't allow that to happen, she reminded herself sternly as she joined the crowd milling around the tree. Because her instincts were warning her that if she lost herself in Jason Barrett, she might never find her way out.

Chapter Six

Who on earth was knocking on her door?

Slitting her eyes open just enough to see the clock on her bedside table, Amy groaned. Eight o'clock on a Sunday morning was sleeping time, not answering-the-door time. But the noise persisted, and she dragged herself from her comfy nest and peeked out the window to see who had the gall to interrupt her only day off this way.

"Come on, Ames," Brenda said in a voice far too chipper for the hour. "I see you in there."

Stubbornly refusing to give in, she grumbled, "I'm sleeping. What do you want?"

"I've got your choir music."

Home delivery, she mused with a yawn. How convenient. "Fine. Shove it under the door."

She heard crinkling, then a quiet laugh. "I can't now that Jason installed that door sweep. Quit being difficult and open up."

Since she apparently had no choice, Amy reluctantly turned the dead bolt and let her cousin inside. Dressed in her churchgoing best, her makeup impeccable and not a hair out of place, Brenda swept her with a practiced glance. "You're a mess. You can't go to church looking like that."

"I wasn't planning to," Amy informed her through another yawn, "or anywhere else, until I go to the Barretts' decorating party at noon."

"Let me get this straight." Her unwanted visitor plopped down in one of the two kitchen chairs and fixed her with a puzzled look. "You're going to sing in the Crossroads choir but not go to services?"

"Of course not." When Brenda tilted her head in confusion, she amended her quick answer. "Well, probably not, even though Pastor Griggs said I could. It's just that he caught me off guard at the Starlight Festival when he asked me to help out. Have you ever tried to say no to that man?"

"I see your point." She smiled, but it faded almost right away. "You know, it might be good for you to come this morning. I know it's been a while, but I think—"

"It's been a while for a very good reason," Amy reminded her curtly.

Brenda pressed her glossy lips together, as if she was choosing her words carefully. It wasn't like her to be so cautious, so she must be winding up for a doozy. "I'm getting a crick in my neck. Could you sit down for a minute?"

Never a good sign, but Amy did as she asked. When they were eye to eye, her cousin went on. "I know we all agreed never to talk about your accident, but there's something I've been wanting to tell you, and you need to listen until I'm done."

Because she adored her bubbly cousin, Amy braced herself for an unpleasant conversation and nodded. "Go ahead."

"I saw the pictures of your car," she began in a hushed tone. Slowly shaking her head, she went on. "This is hard for me to say, but I couldn't believe they pulled you out of that wreck alive. The cops and firemen said as much when your mom met them at the hospital."

"Really? She never said anything to me."

"No one wanted to upset you," Brenda explained, patting her hand in a consoling gesture. "We were so grateful to still have you with us, nothing else mattered."

"That was two years ago. Why are you bringing this up now?"

Brenda took a deep breath and fixed her with a somber look. "God didn't abandon you, Amy. He saved you. Back then, you ate, slept and breathed ballet. You might have been successful, but you never seemed very happy to me."

"I was engaged, if you'll recall."

"Sure, to a man who bailed when things got tough. If you ask me, Devon's the one you should be punishing, not God."

"I didn't ask you." The words may have sounded tough, but even Amy heard the uncertainty in her voice. The truth was, Brenda had touched on a very sensitive spot, and to make matters worse, she was probably right.

"No, you didn't, but that's never stopped me before." Setting the sheet music on the table, she stood and pushed the chair back in. "I won't mention church again, but I'll be saving a seat for you if you change your mind. Unless you'd rather sit with Jason," she added with a knowing look.

"Oh, please!" Amy moaned. "Not you, too. Which reminds me—thanks so much for spreading it all around town that we were dancing at the studio the other night. Folks can't stop talking about it."

"Because it's so cute," Brenda cooed. "He's this hunky lumberjack, and you're this tiny dancer, and it was just precious seeing you together that way."

Even though he wasn't there, Amy could hear Jason laughing at the dreamy description of them, and she couldn't keep back a smile. "Was it?"

"Absolutely. If you have any sense at all, you'll hold on to that one. He's as solid as they come, and more loyal than an old hound."

"If he's so great, how come he's not serious with anyone?"

"I heard something about an ex-fiancée who stole his truck and broke his heart," Brenda answered with a smirk. "Sound familiar?"

"Yeah," Amy admitted slowly. "Except for the truck thing."

Laughing, Brenda gave her a quick hug. "I hope we'll see you later. If not, enjoy your day with the Barretts."

Once her chatty cousin had left, Amy tried to get

back to sleep. But something Brenda had said kept echoing in her mind.

If you ask me, Devon's the one you should be punishing, not God.

She had a point, Amy reluctantly acknowledged. While the accident had been the first blow, Devon's betrayal had been the one that truly took her feet out from under her. That realization cleared her perception of what had happened, and she sat up in bed as the epiphany took hold. It wasn't as if she was handicapped, confined to a wheelchair or a bed. Using her connections, she could easily have gotten an administrative job with any dance company, and they could have adopted children to create the family they'd both longed for.

That was what Jason would have done. She believed that with a certainty that was more than a little frightening. They'd just met, and already she had more faith in him than she'd ever had in her fiancé. Was it Jason, with his grounded upbringing and generous heart? Or was it her, someone who'd made it through the fire and come out the other side with a fresh perspective? Instinct told her it was a combination of the two, and for the first time since her accident, she listened to that small voice in the back of her mind.

Feeling more energetic than she did most mornings, she flung back the covers and quickly got ready to leave. She chose a simple dress and shoes appropriate for church in a small town. Poking her nose outside, she decided a sweater would be smart, and she backtracked to get one from her closet.

The Crossroads Church stood at the head of Main Street, so she decided to walk. As she made her way toward the quaint country chapel, she noticed several families doing the same. They were all ahead of her on the sidewalk, chatting and laughing together. The town's two other churches were nearby, and people veered off to enter one or the other, waving to their neighbors as they parted ways. It was a familiar scene from her childhood that made her smile.

When she was alone on the sidewalk, though, doubt started creeping in. Logic told her she was headed to a building, nothing more. But the little girl who still lived inside her knew better. God was well aware that she'd shunned Him, and while she was convinced she was doing the right thing, she dreaded going into His house to ask His forgiveness.

Her feet began dragging, and as she approached the walkway leading to the front steps, she'd all but stopped moving. There was a small crowd out front, greeting each other before heading inside for the service. The sight of them stopped her cold, and she silently berated her cousin for talking her into coming. This was the last time she'd listen to Brenda, Amy vowed as she started to walk away.

"Amy?"

When she turned back, she was surprised to find Jason trotting down the steps to meet her halfway.

"Hey there," he said easily. "How're you this morning?"

"Fine. What are you doing out here?"

"Looking for you."

She rolled her eyes. "Did Brenda tell you to do that?"

"Nope. Thought of it all on my own." The sunlight warmed the gold in his eyes, and they crinkled as he smiled. "After what the pastor said last night, I was hoping you'd come."

"I wasn't going to, but Brenda came by this morning and got me thinking."

"About?"

How could she explain it to him when she didn't quite understand it herself? Sifting through her thoughts, she came up with something he might be able to grasp. "I've been punishing God for what happened to me, but what hurt the most was Devon leaving. He could have stuck it out, but he didn't. Looking back, there were other times he gave up when things got difficult. I just didn't see it that way at the time."

"So, if the accident hadn't ruined things between you, it would've been something else later on."

His clear view of her failed relationship nudged her that last step to admitting the truth she hadn't been able to put into words until now. "Exactly. With his wimpy attitude, sooner or later our marriage probably would've failed anyway."

He didn't touch her, but his admiring look felt like a gentle caress. "Not everyone is as strong as you."

No one had ever referred to her that way, and she blinked in astonishment. "You think I'm strong?"

"Very. Look at what you've overcome to get to where you are. Strength isn't always like this." To demonstrate, he made a fist. "Sometimes it's like this." Opening his hand, he went on. "When we put aside our own problems and reach out to help someone else. We all have that kind of power. We just have to make the choice to use it to make the world around us better."

"I guess I can leave now," Amy told him with a grin. "Even Pastor Griggs couldn't come up with anything better than that."

"You never know. He might surprise you."

The church bells started ringing, calling people in to worship, and he began walking toward the steps that had intimidated her into stopping. Confused that he apparently meant to go inside without her, she asked, "You're leaving?"

Half turning, he said, "If you're interested, I'll be sitting in the back pew on the left."

"Aren't you going to try to talk me into going with you?"

"Granddad taught me you can't convince someone to do something they're dead set against," he replied with a smile. "But if you change your mind, you're welcome to join me."

His faith was obviously very important to him, and the fact that he'd never attempted to coerce her into following his example told her just how open-minded he was. Since her accident, well-meaning people all around her had told her what to do, when and how much. She'd lost control of her own life, and that had made her resistant to advice in general.

Jason respected her wishes, even if they conflicted

with his own. As he disappeared into the vestibule, she waited a few seconds, debating with herself. Finally, she decided she was being ridiculous and trailed after him.

The service was about to begin, and the small sanctuary was filled to capacity. Tall stained-glass windows lined both walls, throwing prisms of light onto the old floorboards. Judy Griggs noticed her from the choir risers and sent her a delighted smile. Returning the gesture, Amy recalled a Christmas pageant when the pastor's wife had graciously allowed her to lead the angels down the aisle, twirling and leaping her way toward the manger set up in front of the altar.

When she was a budding dancer, it had been a dream come true for her. Thinking of it now reminded her that no matter what had gone on in her life since then, she'd once belonged here. God had houses all over the world, but she suspected that if she'd gone into any of them, she wouldn't have felt the same as she did this morning. But in this place, filled with such wonderful memories, she felt at home. That wasn't a coincidence, she knew, and it made her feel more confident about her decision to venture inside.

Just like he'd promised, she found Jason sitting on the far left side, with an empty space beside him on the pew. When she approached, he gave her an encouraging smile and patted the seat he'd saved for her. She sat, and then noticed that Paul and Chelsea were sitting much farther up with a large group of people she recognized as the Barrett clan.

"Don't you want to sit with your family?" she whispered to Jason.

"Maybe next time. Today, I thought it'd be better if you could make a quiet exit."

He'd chosen this spot to make her more comfortable, she realized. His thoughtfulness amazed her, and she rewarded him with a grateful smile. "I should be fine, but I appreciate you thinking of it. Thank you."

"You're welcome." As the organist began playing, he offered Amy a hymnal. "Mostly, I'm dying to hear how well you sing."

"Not that well," she confessed as they stood. "I'm hoping the choir is big enough no one will notice."

While the congregation started singing "Rock of Ages," his face lit up with enthusiasm. "You're gonna join the Christmas choir?"

Actually, she hadn't made up her mind until just now, but his reaction was all the proof she needed that it was the right choice. Nodding, she picked up the verse in midphrase to avoid annoying the people around them. Jason didn't seem worried about that, though, and he leaned in to murmur, "I have to tell you, I'm real glad you're here."

Taking her eyes from the page, she looked up at him and smiled. Because that was precisely how she felt about it herself, and she recognized that was mostly because of him. He hadn't allowed her to turn tail and run, but he hadn't dragged her into the chapel, either.

In his calm, steady way, he'd encouraged her to take

this step while allowing her to choose for herself. Because that was the kind of person he was.

Finding him at this point in her life was just what she needed. Singing words that had been written generations ago, she silently thanked God for bringing her back to where she belonged.

"Gram, Granddad," Jason said proudly, "this is Amy Morgan. Amy, these are my grandparents, Olivia and Will."

"Come in, come in!" Gram exclaimed, embracing Amy with enthusiasm. "We've known your aunt and uncle forever, and Jason's told us wonderful things about you. We're thrilled to finally meet you."

"Thanks so much for inviting me today," she said quietly. "I know this is a family gathering, and it was nice of you to include me."

"Always room for more," Granddad assured her. "It's a big house."

So far, so good, Jason thought. Amy was a little tense, but he hoped she'd relax once she met everyone and figured out how to keep them all straight. "It smells great in here."

"Roast beef and gingerbread," his grandfather announced eagerly. "I've been smelling it all morning, and I'm starving. Maybe you and Amy can go in and hurry them along."

"Gotcha."

Ushering Amy through the archway, he paused to let her get her bearings before wading into the bustling crew in his grandmother's kitchen. Mom was just taking a batch of gingerbread men out of the oven to add to the ones already cooling on a large rack. When she caught sight of him with their guest, she set the hot tray down and hurried over.

"There's my bear," she cooed, beaming up at him before turning her attention to the petite woman who seemed to be doing her best to hide behind him. Laughing, Mom grasped her hand and drew her forward. "And you must be Amy. I'm Diane Barrett. Welcome to chaos."

"Thank you for having me," she replied so quietly Jason could barely hear her. It struck him as odd that she'd be so timid around new people after all those years performing. Then again, in those days she'd been elevated on a stage, a good distance from the audience. Close-up contact was a whole different ball game. While he was mulling that over, she surprised him again.

"Is there anything I can do to help?" she asked, a bit more loudly this time.

"We're covered in here, but I think Paul and Chelsea could use a hand in the living room. We've got a ten-foot tree and a dozen totes filled with ornaments that need new hooks. Last year, somebody—" she glared across the kitchen at Jason's father "—tossed out all the old ones."

"They were rusty or bent, or both," he said defensively while he sharpened a carving knife.

Sensing an ongoing argument, Jason laughed. "Let me guess. You forgot to buy new ones."

"No, I bought a bunch after Christmas last year. I just forgot where I put them."

"Paul stopped to pick some up after church, and now he and Chelsea are stuck in the living room stringing ornaments," Mom said. "I'm sure they'd appreciate your help."

"It beats checking the lights," Jason commented, giving Amy a questioning look. "Wanna help?"

"Okay." Staying glued to his side, she murmured, "How many people are here, anyway?"

After a quick calculation, he came up with sixteen. Her eyes nearly bugged out of her head, and he chuckled. "Is that a lot?"

"For your immediate family, yes. Then again, it's usually just my mom and me, so I'm not the best judge." Outside the living room, she tugged him to a stop. "I've met Paul and Chelsea, but before we go in, can you point out the others for me so I can keep everyone straight?"

"Sure."

As he went through the gathering of brothers, wives and children, she watched carefully, and he assumed she was committing their faces to memory. When he took her around the room for introductions, she seemed more confident than she had earlier, and he marveled at the change in her demeanor when she was prepared. Since he was a by-the-seat-of-his-pants kind of guy, it hadn't occurred to him she might need a briefing on his large family before being tossed into the fray.

Obviously, this was one lady who preferred to test the

water before she jumped in. Lesson learned, he mused with a grin.

"Amy, I'm so glad to see you," Chelsea gushed from her seat on a hassock in front of a decorations bin. "Paul is no help at all."

"It's not my fault," he protested. "Those hooks are too small."

"They're normal-size hooks," his wife informed him curtly. "It's your hands that are too big."

"My hands are pretty small, so I'll help with these," Amy offered. "That way the guys can do the lights."

When Jason caught sight of the knotted balls of cords and bulbs, he groaned. "I thought we coiled 'em up nice and neat last year."

"We did," Paul confirmed, "but they didn't stay that way. We've gotta come up with something else for next time."

"We should wrap them around some of those empty wire spools we've got at the mill," Jason suggested. "They're just taking up space in the storage room."

"Great idea," Chelsea said approvingly. "You're elected to take care of that."

"Huh. That'll teach me to keep my big mouth shut."

Amy laughed at that, and he congratulated himself on making her feel more at ease in what was clearly a difficult situation for her. As he trailed after his big brother, he glanced back to find her chatting easily with Chelsea. Considering how the afternoon had started, he was relieved to see it was going to end up just fine.

"Okay, folks!" Mom called from the doorway. "Come and get it."

Everyone made a beeline for the dining room, and Jason positioned himself so Amy wouldn't get trampled in the crush. The sideboard was stocked with the average Barrett family spread, but when she got a good look at it, she laughed. "You're kidding, right?"

Following her openmouthed stare, he shrugged. "We Barretts go big, or we don't bother. The bonus is there's lots of leftovers to go around."

"That's not a problem for you," she commented as she took a plate from the stack. "Your grandmother obviously feeds you well."

"That she does."

They chatted lightly while they filled their plates with everything from mac and cheese to a tender roast, but he couldn't miss the way she kept glancing over at Granddad. His frail condition prevented him from moving around on his own, and even though he had a perfectly good wheelchair, he despised using it. So they all took their seats around the huge dining table, with his hospital bed in its place at the head.

Gram made sure he had what he wanted, then pulled her chair up beside him. Ever since Jason could remember, they'd been that way, together through everything life had thrown at them. Even now, with his days slipping away, their touching devotion to each other was plain to see.

While his father said grace, a wave of sadness swept over Jason. This was a bittersweet Christmas for the

Barretts, doubly so for him. If things had worked out the way he'd planned, he'd be sitting here with his wife. But the past was done and gone, and it was time to let it go. Making a vow to do just that, he added a heartfelt "Amen" at the end of Dad's prayer.

"Everything tastes even better than it smells," Amy announced with a smile for the cooks and another for their hosts. "Thank you so much for making me feel at home."

Gram returned the smile with a warm one of her own. "Jason's friends are always welcome here."

"Especially the single ones, right?" Amy teased.

"I have no idea what you're referring to, dear."

Grinning, Amy sipped her sweet tea but didn't say anything more. Jason hadn't seen this part of her yet, and he had to admit it intrigued him. Up till now, she'd come across as an intense, creative type obsessed with perfection in everything she did. Discovering she had a playful side was like getting an early Christmas present.

Once they'd plowed through their meal, the family split into groups for various decorating assignments. With Christmas music playing from four sets of speakers located around the main floor, the work went by quickly. Outside, inside, everything was done up the way it had been for more years than Jason had been alive.

On the porches, pine garlands twined with lights swagged from the railings, and each window held a wreath tied with a burgundy velvet ribbon. Poinsettias sat on the tables, while red-and-green-plaid cushions had replaced the everyday ones on the wicker chairs and porch swing. Around it all, the three rooflines were rimmed in white lights that made the house look as if it was glowing with Christmas spirit.

When they were done, everyone took a few minutes to admire their handiwork and exchange high fives for getting it done without anyone falling off the roof. Then they all congregated around the tree Paul had trucked in from the woods surrounding the mill. Lots of people had fake ones these days, but to Jason, nothing said Christmas like the scents of a fresh-cut pine and gingerbread.

Jason and Amy stood near the fireplace, and she glanced at the collection of framed photos displayed there. A picture of the five teenage Barrett boys on a camping trip caught her eye, and she tapped one of the faces. "I haven't met him yet. Where does he live?"

His jaw tightened, but Jason reminded himself she couldn't possibly know she'd hit a nerve and did his best to sound casual. "That's my older brother, Scott. He's been in Texas the last five years."

She gave him an odd look but didn't press him for details. That was a good thing, because Scott was a very sore subject for all of them, and Jason didn't want anything to spoil this evening for his family.

Before they got started, Dad and Paul muscled Granddad's bed through the wide archway, parking it in front of the fireplace so he could supervise. The tree had always been his responsibility, and this year was no exception. Dad might have been the one on the ladder, but Granddad was in charge of telling him where the long strings of lights needed to be adjusted.

When they finally met his approval, Dad handed him the remote. "You do the honors, Pop."

"You checked all those bulbs?" he demanded.

"Every last one," Dad assured him with a chuckle. "Just like you taught me."

"All right, then."

He flipped the switch, and the massive tree shone with every color in the spectrum. It had gotten darker outside, so the lights were reflected in the angled glass of the bay window, enhancing the effect.

"Oh, kids," Gram breathed, "it's beautiful just like this."

They stood and admired it for about two seconds before his nieces and nephews dived into the ornament bins, snatching up their favorites and clamoring for Chelsea to put a hook on each one.

"I'd better go help her," Amy said, edging toward a small chair.

"Not trying to get away from me, are you?" Jason teased.

"Not a bit. In fact, I was hoping you might walk me home later."

"Hoping?" he echoed in mock disgust. Thickening his usual Virginia accent, he went on. "I'm a Southern gentleman, Miss Morgan. I've got no intention of letting you go off alone in the dark."

Picking up on his tone, she batted her eyes up at him. "I have always depended on the kindness of strangers."

"Blanche DuBois, *Streetcar Named Desire*." Judging by her delighted reaction, she hadn't expected him to know the reference. Grinning, he added, "Except I'm not a stranger."

Suddenly, her demeanor shifted, and her eyes darkened somberly. "But you're very kind, even to a demanding woman who drives most people crazy. That means more to me than you can possibly know."

Standing on tiptoe, she kissed his cheek and left him with a dazzling smile that drove deep into his heart, leaving behind a warm trail he suspected wouldn't be fading anytime soon.

Chapter Seven

By the time they were finished decorating the Barrett homestead, Amy knew each family member by name and was actually starting to feel like one of them. It wasn't hard to envision these generous, caring people giving an adopted child not only a home but a boisterous extended family. To her surprise, no one asked a single awkward question about what might be going on between Jason and her. She wasn't sure if that was because they were too polite to pry or if they already knew everything from the gossip flying around town.

Probably the second, she mused with a smile while she and Jason said their goodbyes. Aunt Helen stood proudly at the center of the local news chain, and while she'd never embarrass Amy, the chatty woman wasn't one to hold back anything juicy, either. And in a small, close-knit town like this, nothing was juicier than the prospect of a blossoming Christmas romance.

"Headed out?" Paul asked, holding up Chelsea's sweater for her to slip into.

"Yeah." Jason's grumbling was totally spoiled by his troublemaker grin. "The boss wants me in extra early tomorrow."

Paul held up his hands in defense. "Hey, don't hassle me. If you weren't so good on the lathe, you'd get more time off."

Their good-natured argument continued while the four of them made the short walk through town to Arabesque. On the way, Jason asked Chelsea, "How're things going at your new place?"

"You mean, our old place," Chelsea corrected him, then explained to Amy, "We bought the old Garrison house on Ingram Street."

Amy searched her memory for the location. "You mean the one on the other side of the square?"

"That's the one," the newest Mrs. Barrett confirmed with a sigh. "It's a mess, but the price was right."

"Now we know why," Paul added grimly. "I thought the home inspector was kidding when he said the only good things were the foundation and the roof."

"Underneath all the ugly, it's still a lovely house," Chelsea assured them. "We just have to get it there."

Busy as they were at the mill, Amy admired their willingness to put so much effort into reclaiming the stately old Colonial. She was about to tell them that when she noticed Paul had stopped in the middle of the sidewalk and was staring at a pickup parked outside the Whistlestop. Because all the streetlights were on for holiday shoppers, it was easy to make out that it was dark green, with Idaho license plates. On the back bumper was a faded sticker that read "Ladies love country boys."

"Hey, Jason," he commented in a curious tone. "Isn't that your truck?"

Looking over, Jason scowled. "Sure is. They must've changed out the Oregon plates so the cops couldn't find it."

"So either Billy's here—"

"—or Rachel," Jason finished for him as the driver's door swung open and a petite—and very pregnant—woman stepped out.

Flipping long auburn hair over her shoulders, she arched her back in obvious discomfort and scanned the tiny business district with a helpless look. When her eyes landed on their group, they lit up with what Amy could only describe as joy.

For someone as front-heavy as she was, she moved pretty fast, and before anyone could react, she'd thrown herself at a flabbergasted Jason.

"Oh, Jason!" she choked out in a half sob. "I'm so glad to see you."

Moving like a man in a trance, he peeled her arms from around his neck and gently pushed her back. "How'd you find me?"

"I stopped in one of those internet cafés out on the highway and looked you up online. There's a bio of you on the Barrett's Mill Furniture website, and it was updated a couple weeks ago, so I was hoping you'd still be here."

The wonders of modern communication, Amy

groused, wondering how Jason was going to handle this bizarre—and delicate—situation.

Giving his ex a disapproving once-over, he asked, "How's Billy?"

"Gone, months ago," she replied, her face twisting in anguish. "As soon as he found out about the baby, he was done with me. Hey, Paul," she added, as if she'd only just realized they weren't alone.

She didn't even glance at Chelsea or Amy, and Chelsea raised a disapproving brow. Paul settled an arm around her shoulders in an obvious attempt at keeping the peace. "Rachel McCarron, this is my wife, Chelsea."

She giggled at that, then seemed to register his somber expression. "Oh, you're serious. Sorry about that," she told Chelsea. "Back when I knew him, Paul wasn't exactly the marrying type."

Her thoughtless comment hung in the night air, which was growing chillier by the second.

Finally, Chelsea broke the tension. "We're on our way home, so we'll see you two later." She hugged both Jason and Amy, pointedly leaving out their unwelcome visitor. Wrapping Paul's arm around her shoulders, she angled him away and headed cross-lots to their house.

Sighing dramatically, Rachel watched them go. "She doesn't like me."

Chelsea adored Jason, and knowing what this woman had done to him couldn't sit well with her. Amy would be amazed if Chelsea's opinion of Rachel McCarron ever came close to thawing.

In truth, she hadn't been all that crazy about Jason's

former fiancée even when Rachel was a distant memory for him. It had never occurred to Amy that they might actually meet someday. Or that she'd be pregnant and evidently in need of help. Then it hit her: Jason hadn't introduced them. After asking about Billy, he'd gone completely silent, as if he couldn't come up with anything more to say. Sadly, Rachel didn't share his affliction, but chattered along about this old friend and that one in a desperate attempt to fill the awkward silence.

When she finally stopped for breath, Amy seized what might be her only opportunity to air what she was thinking. Tapping his shoulder, she gave him a cool look. "Could I talk to you a minute?"

"Sure. Excuse me, Rachel."

Now he remembered his manners, Amy seethed while they moved a few yards away. She didn't know why she was so upset about his unexpected reunion with his ex, but her temper was simmering just beneath the surface, threatening to flare into an blistering tirade. Determined to avoid embarrassing them both, she took a deep breath to regain her composure.

Gazing down at her, he frowned. "What's wrong?"

"What's wrong?" she echoed furiously. "Are you serious?"

Patient as he usually was, she was stunned by the flash of anger in his eyes. "Look, this is a shock to me, too. You'll have to cut me some slack."

Most of the time, she gave in when people spoke to her that way. Then later, when she had a chance to think it over, she regretted allowing them to wipe their feet on her like some kind of doormat. Not this time, she vowed, pulling herself up to her full height and glaring at him for all she was worth. "By all means, take as much slack as you need. Good night."

Pivoting on her heel, she started across the street to where the cheery windows of Arabesque beckoned her inside where things still made sense to her. It was a fantasy, of course, but it was hers, and it was calling to her like the beacon marking a safe harbor.

Before she could reach it, Jason caught up with her and gently grasped her arm. When she yanked it free, he put up his hands in deference to her temper. "I shouldn't have done that, and I'm sorry. Please don't go off this way."

"What way?" she spat defiantly.

"Mad."

Stepping into an empty parking space, she folded her arms and scowled up at him. "Mad doesn't begin to cut it, mister."

"I'm confused. It's not my fault Rachel's here, y'know. I didn't ask her to come."

Clueless, she ranted silently, shaking her head. "Then I'll explain it to you. Paul introduced Chelsea to Rachel, but you left me standing there like the invisible woman."

By the startled look on his face, her complaint was news to him, and he hung his head like a woebegone hound. "I'm sorry. She caught me off guard, and my brain just shut off."

He looked so ashamed, she didn't have the heart to go on being angry at him. She understood his reaction, because she'd felt the same when she'd run into Devon shopping in Manhattan with his new girlfriend. *Uncomfortable* didn't even begin to describe the scene, and she recalled her tangled emotions vividly enough that she opted to give Jason a break.

"I guess I understand," she said, ducking to look at him. "And I apologize for overreacting."

His features brightened immediately.

"It's over between us, I promise. And that baby's not mine."

She'd figured that out for herself from their exchange about the absent Billy, but she appreciated him having the courage to meet the sensitive issue head-on. "What are you going to do?"

"I'm not sure," he confided with a glance over to where Rachel stood waiting for him. "I'm guessing she needs somewhere to go, or she wouldn't have come all this way."

"What about her family?"

He grimaced. "She's from Iowa, and her parents are the conservative, buttoned-up type. They're probably not real thrilled with her right now."

Despite her initial reaction to Rachel's surprise visit, Amy couldn't help feeling sorry for her. Alone and pregnant, she'd driven across the country to the one person she thought she could count on. That it was Jason didn't surprise Amy in the least. That was the kind of guy he was, after all, and she'd certainly benefited from it herself.

Taking her hand, he fixed her with a pleading gaze.

"It's a lot to take in, but I hope you can get your head around this. My no-good father left my mother to deal with her pregnancy and a baby when she was sixteen years old. If it hadn't been for the Barretts, who knows what would've happened to me? If Rachel needs my help, I'm gonna give it to her. It's the right thing to do."

While she still didn't like the situation one bit, Amy sensed he was appealing to her as a friend. Determined not to let Rachel get to her, she tamped down her irrational objections and did her best to appear calm. "I'm going home now. I'll be in my office doing the books, if you want to talk later."

He flashed her a little-boy grin. "Thanks."

With a quick "You're welcome," Amy gladly finished her walk to Arabesque. Fighting the urge to glance back at them, she unlocked the door to her apartment just as the vintage rotary phone on the counter began ringing. "Hello?"

"Who's that pregnant girl out there with Jason?" Aunt Helen demanded breathlessly.

"Are you using Uncle Fred's high-powered binoculars again?" she chided. "You know they're meant for bird-watching and spotting deer, right?"

"He's sound asleep, so he won't be missing them. Are you going to answer my question or not?"

Knowing she'd get the information one way or another, Amy decided to be helpful. "Rachel McCarron, his ex-fiancée from Oregon. And before you ask, the baby's not his."

She gave a very unladylike snort. "Of course it's

not. He'd never leave the mother of his child to fend for herself like that."

While her aunt launched into a melodramatic assessment of other local couples in dicey situations, Amy was astonished to discover she didn't doubt his claim for even a single moment. As a performer, she'd learned to be wary of people's intentions, never taking anyone at face value because most of the characters around her were superb actors. Because of that, she had a hard time believing anyone until she'd known them for a long time.

Somehow, Jason had earned her trust very quickly, and she took it on faith that he was being straight with her.

An interesting change, she thought while she *mmm-hmm*ed and *uh-huh*ed at the right spots in their one-way conversation. She didn't know the dictionary definition of *faith,* but she understood it basically meant believing in something you couldn't see or touch.

She believed Jason, but did she also believe *in* him? She hadn't considered that before, but she had to admit she probably did. She certainly felt he'd been honest with her, right from their first meeting through tonight. He was funny and sweet, and he had a way of making her feel special without saying a word.

"Don't you think so?" Aunt Helen asked, finally dragging Amy back into the discussion.

"Absolutely." Since she hadn't heard the question, she hoped her response made sense.

"A good boy, through and through. And from what Olivia tells me, he really likes you. You could do worse."

I have, Amy thought grimly. But over the past few days, Jason had convinced her she deserved better, and at some point she'd started to agree with him. "Aunt Helen, I hate to cut you off, but I really should get going on the books."

"Oh, listen to me, rattling along when you've got work to do. You go on, and I'll see you soon."

Adding a noisy air kiss, she hung up. Amy disconnected with a relieved sigh. She adored the woman, but an extended chat with her could be exhausting. Normally, she detested opening her bookkeeping program and logging everything in, but after the hectic day she'd had, she was actually looking forward to sitting down at her desk for some Mozart and number crunching.

After watching Amy to make sure she'd gotten inside all right, Jason cast a hesitant look over at Rachel. For the life of him, he didn't know what to say. Jamming his hands into the pockets of his jeans, he trudged back to where she was waiting, searching his uncooperative brain for a way to start a conversation he'd never anticipated having. When she took off nearly a year ago, it had taken him a while to accept she was really gone. Once he did, though, he'd assumed he'd never see her again.

But here she was, and he had to come up with a way to deal with it. Inspiration struck, and he asked, "Are you hungry?"

"Starving," she replied in a voice tinged with desperation. "I put the last of my money in the gas tank this morning."

Jason had a hard time accepting that someone in her family wouldn't at least send her some cash. "Do your parents know about the baby?"

"Sure they do. They offered to help me 'take care of it.'" She spat the words with disdain. "When I refused, they told me never to call them again."

The bitterness in her voice wavered, and her dark eyes filled with tears. Jason wondered if his mother had faced the same heartlessness from her own family and gave him up to make sure he'd be raised by people who would always love him, no matter how badly he messed up.

His instinct was to gather Rachel into his arms and comfort her, but he didn't want to create the wrong impression for her or the curious eyes he assumed were watching this little drama unfold. Instead, he took her hands and gave them a reassuring squeeze.

"Rachel, look at me." When he had her attention, he steeled himself against her tears and tried to think practically. "First, we're gonna go inside and get you something to eat. Next, I'll find you a place to stay the night, and tomorrow we'll figure out what to do."

Sniffling, she blinked up at him in obvious confusion. "You mean, you're going to help me?"

"Did you come all this way thinking I wouldn't?"

"I was hoping." He opened the door of the Whistlestop for her, and the scent of good Southern cooking spilled out into the night air. Taking a deep breath, she sighed. "That smells incredible."

The place was about half-full, and he led her to a booth near the back where they could talk in relative privacy. After the waitress took her order, Rachel reached across the table to take one of his hands. "Thank you, Jason. I know this must be really hard for you, after the way things ended with us."

Glancing down, he noticed the fingers on both her hands were bare. It hadn't been much of a diamond, but it had been the most expensive thing he'd ever bought that didn't have tires and a steering wheel. "Sold the ring, huh?"

Nodding, she frowned. "I'm sorry."

By the misery clouding her features, he believed she meant it. Once he'd taken that in, he realized that if she kept apologizing to him, they'd both have to relive their failed engagement over and over. He saw no point in doing that, so he forced a smile. "You can quit saying you're sorry. I forgave you a long time ago."

"You did?" When he nodded, she gave him a forlorn look. "How could you, when I haven't forgiven myself?"

The Rachel McCarron he'd known had never regretted anything. A free spirit in every sense of the word, she'd appealed to him for just that reason. Beautiful and untamed, she'd been driven by the wind to wherever she was headed next. At the time, the fact that she'd chosen to settle with him made him so proud, he'd ignored Paul's warnings about her, along with the ones in the back of his own mind.

At first, Jason had often pictured seeing her again, imagining what they might say to each other. As the months went by, those images had faded, and now all he felt for her was sympathy.

Once she had her food, he smiled to ease the sorrow clouding her face. "That was a long time ago, and it's best to leave it in the past. Now, eat up."

Digging into her meat loaf, she hummed in appreciation. "This is awesome! It reminds me of that great little diner in Oregon you and Paul used to take me to. Who does the cooking here?"

"Molly Harkness. She and her husband, Bruce, have been keeping the town well fed since before I was born."

"Do you think they need any kitchen help?" Rachel asked after wolfing down another bite. "I could wash dishes or something."

Jason eyed her pregnant frame doubtfully. Slender as she usually was, he thought, all that extra weight must be murder for her to carry around. The last thing she needed was to be on her feet all day. "When're you due?"

"January twentieth." Swallowing some milk, she added a wry grin. "Great way to start the new year, right?"

"Could be." Chewing on that for a few seconds, he had a brainstorm. "Lemme check around town, explain your situation. Maybe someone's got some light work you could manage."

"Do you really think anyone here will hire me? I

mean, this is your hometown. They must all know how badly I treated you."

More remorse, he thought. Maybe impending motherhood had forced her to mature a little and own up to her failings. Whatever the reason, it was definitely a step in the right direction. "These are good folks, and they've all made mistakes, too. I can't promise anything, but I'll try."

"That's more than I could ask for," she said with a grateful smile. "Thank you."

"The Donaldsons here on Main Street have an apartment out back in an old carriage house. Paul and Chelsea moved out when they bought their house, and it's still empty. It's small, but the rent's cheap, and it'd be all yours. Plus, Hank and Lila would be nearby if you needed something."

"When I said I have no money, I meant none at all," she protested meekly. "If I can't get a job, that's not going to change anytime soon."

"Let's just ask and see what they say." Pulling out his cell phone, he made the call and got the response he'd expected.

"Oh, that poor thing, and at Christmastime, too. Bring her over, Jason," Lila said without hesitation. "I'll send Hank out to raise the heat and turn on the lights. We'll work out the details later."

"Thanks, Lila. We'll be there in a few minutes."

While he paid the check, his gut was warning him to put some distance between himself and this particular damsel in distress. Amy's baffling reaction to Rachel's sudden appearance kept popping into his mind, and he resolved to smooth things over with her once he got Rachel settled. Women were complex, and it was best never to lose sight of that. If that meant a longer night than usual, Jason suspected in the long run it would be easier than trying to mend fences with one woman over helping another.

In the space of an evening, his life had gotten very complicated. He only prayed he could deal with the molehills before they became mountains.

Jason helped Rachel into the cab of the truck he'd thought he'd never see again and climbed in beside her. The interior was a disaster, and on the rear jump seat sat a single duffel bag.

"Have you been living in here?" he asked. When she nodded, he bit back a curse. "If I ever get my hands on Billy…"

"Please don't," she whimpered, closing her eyes and leaning her head against the window. "I don't even want to think about that nasty piece of work. I just want to curl up in a ball on a real bed and go to sleep."

In response, he started the truck and saw the low-fuel light was on. Fortunately, they didn't have far to go, so he made the short drive up the street to the Donaldson place. Just as Lila had promised, the carriage house was bright and inviting when he grabbed Rachel's bag and carefully walked her down the pathway to the front door.

Standing in front of it, she stared at the simple cottage with large, tear-filled eyes. Then she lowered her head and folded her hands in prayer. When she was finished, she looked up at him with an awed expression. "It doesn't seem like enough, but thank you."

"You're welcome." Opening the door for her, he followed her inside. "Where do you want your stuff?"

"Anywhere," she answered, sinking onto the bed with a weary sigh.

Realizing she needed someone to take care of things for her, he left the bag on the floor of the single closet.

"So, the bathroom's through there—" he pointed "—and this is the kitchen." When he opened the fridge, it was empty, and he frowned. "That's not good."

"The story of my life."

This defeated young woman was nothing like the vibrant, fearless Rachel he'd once known. Hopelessness did that to people, he knew, and he searched for a way to bring back even a sliver of her old optimism. Sliding his wallet from his back pocket, he thumbed through the cash he'd taken out of his account to buy Christmas presents. Removing half of it, he set it on the tiny kitchen table.

"I can't take your money," she objected instantly. "After what I did to you, I couldn't live with myself."

"It's not for you," he reasoned in a stern tone very unlike him. Because of his own sketchy history, there was no way he'd be backing down on this one. "It's for your baby. You've got a month to go, and if it's gonna be born healthy, you have to eat right and take care of yourself. That little one's counting on you, and you're in no position to choose your pride over food."

She gave him a wan smile. "You're right, but I'll pay you back. I promise."

She'd made promises to him before that hadn't worked out, so he tucked this one away with a nod. If she ended up repaying him, he'd be happy. If not, he'd take it in stride. That was how things worked with Rachel; he'd learned that the hard way. She wasn't a bad person, but she wasn't all that reliable when it came to following through. He prayed motherhood would change that, but only time would tell.

"The bathroom's stocked, and the bed's made," he said as he edged toward the door. "Need anything else?"

"Just a solid night's sleep." Peeling back the covers, she slid beneath them and closed her eyes.

"Then I'll say good-night. I've gotta work in the morning, but I'll make some calls during my breaks and see if anyone's looking for help during the holidays. Sound good?"

"Mmm-hmm."

Since she was clearly too exhausted to take care of the lights, he flipped the switches, leaving the nightlight in the bathroom on for her. There was a set of keys on the table, which he left for her. Setting the lock, he pulled the door shut behind him and headed back up the walkway. Inside the house, he noticed Lila standing in the kitchen window and held up his hand in thanks. She acknowledged him with a nod and turned off the light.

Keeping an eye on him, he mused with a grin. While he hadn't doubted their reaction to Rachel's plight, he appreciated Hank and Lila proving his claim that the residents of Barrett's Mill were good, helpful folks. As a single, expectant mother, Rachel needed all the grace she could get.

After a quick debate, he decided to leave his filthy truck where it was until he could give it a thorough cleaning inside and out. When he got to Arabesque, he noticed the lights were still on and knocked at the front door.

Stepping aside to let him in, Amy asked, "How did it go?"

"Which part?" He grinned, hoping to ease some of the tension he heard in her voice.

"Whichever part you want to tell me about," she hedged, leading him back to her cozy office.

Decorated in classical theater and ballet posters, it reminded him of old movies where a character's luggage was plastered with stickers from other countries. As foreign to him as those faraway places, the designs were Amy's style, wrapping up her eventful life like colorful paper on a gift.

"I just heated water for tea," she said as he settled into one of the threadbare velvet chairs. "Would you like some decaf coffee?"

"That'd be great." In less than a minute, he had a steaming mug in his hands and took a long, appreciative sip. "Delicious."

"I'm glad you like it."

They traded a few more overly polite comments, and he stifled a groan. He'd gotten accustomed to the warm back-and-forth he enjoyed with Amy, and this was as far from it as he could get. It hadn't occurred to him that his encounter with Rachel would affect Amy so much, and he resolved to set things to rights as quickly as humanly possible.

"So," he began, setting down his half-empty cup. "Should I start with Rachel past or Rachel present?"

Amy shrugged, but those gorgeous blue eyes darkened ominously. He didn't know what the color shift meant, but he instinctively didn't like it. So he spilled the whole crazy story, from the day he first met Rachel singing at a Renaissance fair in Seattle, to their months living in Oregon, to her pulling into Barrett's Mill in his stolen truck. When he was finished, he forced himself to smile. "So, that's everything."

Without saying anything, she drank some of her tea and deliberately put her dainty china cup on its saucer next to the hefty mug she'd offered him. Pinning him with a direct stare, she asked, "How do you feel about seeing her again?"

He suspected she was fishing for something, but he had no idea what she was after. "I'm not sure what you mean."

"She took off with a man you considered a friend, stole your truck and the ring you gave her." To emphasize, she ticked Rachel's sins off on her slender fingers. "Now she's come crawling into town, asking you to help her? She's either completely destitute or she's got an awful lot of nerve."

"Actually, it's both."

"Oh, Jason," she lamented with a pained expression. "Tell me you didn't give her any money."

"She's got nothing but a duffel bag and a baby who needs to be fed somehow. What was I supposed to do?"

"You left the truck at the Donaldsons', didn't you?" When he nodded, she sighed. "What's to keep her from taking off again?"

Feeling quite proud of himself, he reached into his pocket and dangled the keys for her to see. "Unless she's learned how to hot-wire an ignition, she's not going anywhere."

Amy's frown gave way to a smile, and she clapped quietly. "Very well played."

"Thank you, thank you. I'll be here all month." They both laughed, and he was relieved to have gotten through the tough part. "So are we okay?"

Tilting her head, she studied him through narrowed eyes. He knew her wariness was driven by Devon's betrayal and not anything Jason had done, but it still bugged him. Someday, he hoped he'd see nothing but joy in those stunning blue eyes of hers. "I'll be honest— I'm not crazy about this whole scenario. But I admire you for stepping up to give a hand to someone who seems to have no one else to turn to."

She didn't trust Rachel, he realized. For some reason, the fact that Amy was so protective of him made him feel incredible. People assumed a big, strong guy like him could take care of himself, and aside from his family, no one worried about him all that much. Tiny as she was, he'd gained a sincere respect for how formidable an opponent Amy could be when she put her mind to it.

"There's nothing to admire in this," he corrected her. "It's the right thing to do."

"Just don't let her take advantage of you like she did before," Amy warned him with a stern look. "I might have to hurt her."

Her threat made him chuckle. "I'll keep that in mind."

"I'm serious, you big oaf. Women like Rachel sail through life wrapping men around their little fingers and gouging them for everything they've got. Then, when the mood strikes, poof!" She illustrated her point with an intricate waving of fingers that was easy to interpret.

"I'll keep that in mind, too," Jason assured her as they both stood. "It sure is comforting to know you've got my back."

"Someone needs to watch out for you." She gave him an indulgent smile. "You're too nice for your own good."

"Guess I wouldn't last long in the big city, huh?"

"Half an hour, tops."

Gazing down at her, he took in the intelligence sparkling in her eyes, the set of her delicate jaw. She might look as if she was made of porcelain, but under all that polish ran a streak of steely determination that appealed to him just as much. "Then it's a good thing you ended up here. Otherwise we never would've met."

Smiling, he reached out to smooth a stray lock of hair back into her loose ponytail. The motion took his fingers across her soft skin, and he cradled her cheek in his hand. Because he couldn't help himself, he leaned in and brushed a kiss over her lips. That brief connection to her did something strange to his heart, which suddenly felt as if it meant to pound its way out of his chest.

Startled by the intensity of his reaction to her, he pulled back and watched her eyes blink open with the same bewildered look he must be wearing. Assuming he'd pushed too far too fast, he stammered, "Amy, I'm s—"

She cut off his apology by pulling him in for another, much longer kiss. For a few moments, he rode that wave of emotions, gathering her in, savoring the way her slender frame fit against him. Then, because he was a gentleman, he drew away and held her at arm's length.

Figuring humor would give him the best exit, he said, "Thanks for the coffee."

That got him the laugh he'd been hoping for, and she waved him off. "You're welcome. And if anyone asks, it was the mistletoe."

She pointed at the kissing ball dangling from the ceiling, but he still didn't know what she was referring to. Then he noticed the bare window that looked into her office. It didn't take a genius to know some busybody had seen that kiss and was quickly spreading the word. "Gotcha. 'Night, Amy."

He was on his way out the door when she said, "Sweet dreams, Sir Galahad."

Flattening his palm on the doorjamb, he poked his head back in. "What? I'm not Lancelot?"

"His affair with Guinevere destroyed Arthur and then Camelot," she explained. "Galahad was known for pure gallantry, expecting nothing in return. That's you."

He'd gotten his share of compliments from women over the years, but none had the impact of this one. "I had no idea you saw me that way."

"I know." Shaking her head, she gave him an approving smile. "That's what makes you so special."

Amy thought he was special, Jason mused as he let himself out the studio door. Replaying the kiss that had nearly knocked him over, he couldn't help grinning as he strolled toward his grandparents' house. He'd never really considered himself anything out of the ordinary, but Amy had seen a lot more of the world than he had. Not to mention, she'd come into contact with more people, not all of them nice. That was where her cynicism came from, he realized. The fact that a small-town boy like him had captured her interest was incredibly flattering.

Then again, Devon had been one of those worldly guys she'd known, and he'd let her down in the worst way imaginable. Abandoning someone who needed you was something Jason simply couldn't understand. As he arrived home, he made a silent vow.

Whatever happened between Amy and him, he'd always put her wishes before his own. No matter how much it might hurt.

Chapter Eight

"Tell me everything," Brenda insisted before Amy had even sat down for their pre-Christmas shopping breakfast. "Don't leave anything out."

"There's really not much to tell," Amy hedged, opening the menu hoping to appear nonchalant. "Rachel Mc-Carron drove into town last night on fumes."

"And bursting at the seams," Brenda supplied helpfully.

As she stacked her hands and rested her chin on them, Amy's eyes were drawn to the rings on her left hand. They weren't flashy, but the gold and modest diamond setting caught the overhead lights in a pretty display. Amy had only gotten half a set herself, and she'd felt compelled to return the diamond when her engagement ended. Rachel hadn't, though, she groused silently. According to Jason, she'd sold it at a pawnshop somewhere in Colorado.

"Hello? Earth to Amy."

"Sorry. What were you saying?"

As if on cue, Molly Harkness stopped at their table. The best cook within a hundred miles, she had five kids, fourteen grandkids and the sharpest ears in town. "She was saying she doesn't know what you're thinking, leaving Jason alone with his ex that way."

"What was I supposed to do?" Amy demanded in exasperation. "It's not like we're a couple or anything. And even if we were, I'd never step in where I'm not wanted."

"I would," Brenda declared without hesitation. "I'd protect what's mine before Bambi got any bright ideas. Rare as that might be," she added with a giggle.

"Honey, she's right." Molly patted her shoulder in a gesture that was obviously meant to be supportive but just ended up making Amy feel as if they were ganging up on her.

"Rachel's pregnant," she reminded them both more curtly than she'd intended. "If I make a fuss over her, he'll think I'm awful."

The other two women traded a grim look, and Molly sighed. "You've hit the nail on that one. A good breakfast oughta help the thinking along. What would you girls like?"

Brenda ordered her usual platter with everything but the kitchen sink, but the idea of food made Amy's stomach roll over in protest. "I'll just have the fruit plate."

"Farmer's breakfast it is," Molly vetoed her, hustling off while Amy was still sputtering her objections.

"Just go with it, Ames," Brenda advised while she sugared her coffee and handed the dispenser across the table. "Molly's seen everything at least once, and she's always right."

"I guess." Feeling dejected, Amy stirred her coffee, watching the creamer and sugar swirl around in the cup. The music playing on the diner's speakers changed tracks, and the opening of "I'll Be Home for Christmas" made her smile. "I love this song. This year, it really fits me, doesn't it?"

"I'm so glad you're back home again," Brenda gushed, reaching over to pat her hand. "You always were my favorite cousin. I remember when Mom and I used to drive to Washington to see you dance in those productions. I'd sit in the audience and hold my breath the whole time you were onstage, praying you wouldn't mess up."

"I did a few times," Amy confided.

"I never noticed. To me, you were flawless."

"Not so much anymore." The words slipped out before she could stop them, and she fiddled with her napkin to avoid meeting her cousin's gaze.

"It's okay, you know," Brenda said gently. "Being imperfect is what makes us human. It helps us sympathize with other people's weaknesses."

"Such as?"

"Such as Jason Barrett's heart is bigger than it needs to be. Which is probably why he's bringing that car thief in here for breakfast." When Amy angled to look, Brenda ordered, "Don't you dare. If he wants to see you, he'll come over on his own. Don't for one second let her think she bothers you. He's interested in you now, not her."

"Do you really think so?" Amy asked.

"Did he kiss you last night or not?"

Amy narrowed her eyes in annoyance. "I didn't tell you that."

"Don't be dense," she scolded with a laugh. "If you don't want folks knowing your business, put a curtain on that window in your office."

A server dropped off their plates, giving Amy time to regain her perspective. Before diving into her eggs, she grinned. "It was the mistletoe."

"Good excuse," Brenda approved through a mouthful of home fries. "Seeing as it's Christmas and all."

"Speaking of which, what do your kids want to find under the tree on the big day?"

In response, Brenda reached into her purse and pulled out a sheaf of lined notebook paper, which she handed to Amy. At the top of each was one of her kids' names, followed by a long list of wishes.

Flipping through them, Amy laughed. "It's a good thing we get along so well. Looks like it's gonna be a long day."

Even from a distance, Amy Morgan was still the prettiest thing Jason had ever seen.

Fortunately for him, Rachel was too hungry to talk much, so he just let her eat while he tried to watch Amy without letting on that he was staring at her. She and Brenda were chatting and laughing, apparently oblivious to the other folks in the dining room. Considering the unpleasant tasks he had ahead of him this morning, he'd much rather have been starting his day out with their lively company.

But he wasn't, so he'd just have to make the best of it. His restless night had left him tired and cranky, which wasn't helpful when what he needed was to be patient and understanding.

Summoning his usual optimism, he started what could only be an awkward conversation. "So, when's the last time you saw a doctor?"

Chewing on some toast, she considered that for long enough to make him very nervous. "San Antonio."

He bit back a sarcastic comment and tried again. "When was that?"

"A couple weeks ago. It was a clinic, and the nurse said everything looked fine to her."

"I'd feel better if Doc Peterson checked you over. Y'know, make sure everything's okay."

"Doctors are expensive," she reminded him, as if he'd forgotten.

"He and my dad go way back, so I'm sure he'll do us a favor."

"Okay."

She shrugged as if it didn't matter to her, and alarm bells went off in Jason's head. "Are you all right?"

"It's just…"

Her voice trailed off into some minor waterworks, and she dropped her face in her hands. Worst-case scenario, he groaned inwardly as people at the tables nearby politely turned their heads away from the heart-wrenching scene near the window. Completely out of his depth, Jason searched for a way to comfort her. Or at the very least make her quit crying.

Then, as suddenly as they'd appeared, the tears stopped. With a shaky breath, she gave him a wan smile. "Sorry about that. Sometimes it catches up with me, how alone we are."

She rested a protective hand over her stomach, and he marveled at how much she'd changed since he'd known her in Oregon. While he hated to consider what she'd gone through before reaching Barrett's Mill, he was glad to know her restlessness was a thing of the past. "Once you feel settled, things'll get better."

"You think?"

"I know."

"You were always so sweet."

When tears started welling up again, he stopped her with a hand in the air. "If you're fixing to apologize again, save your breath."

"Okay." Her eyes drifted over to the booth where Amy and Brenda had their heads together over a pile of notebook paper. "She's really pretty."

"Yeah, she is. She's also a great teacher, and her students love her."

Rachel's gaze swung back to him with sudden interest. "What about you? Do you love her, too?"

Did he? He hadn't known Amy that long, and they were so different. But he couldn't deny that they'd clicked that first day, and he had a very hard time getting her out of his thoughts long enough to concentrate on anything else. He loved the graceful way she moved, the light, flowery scent of her perfume, even the way she went toe-to-toe with him over necessary mechanical changes to her set design.

She definitely intrigued him, and it wouldn't take much for him to fall hard for her. But love? As he considered the woman sitting across from him, he realized he hadn't moved as far on as he'd assumed. Rachel had broken more than his heart. She'd shattered his trust in himself, in his ability to let go and simply let himself feel.

Because he wasn't willing to explore that any further on a couple of hours' sleep, he dug into his cooling omelet and changed the subject. "So, you said your last job was singing at a bar in Phoenix. I'm thinking that's not such a good option for you now."

That got him a rueful grin, which was a big step up. "Ladies and gentlemen, Jason Barrett, the master of understatement."

He laughed, but abruptly stopped when he noticed Amy and Brenda headed their way. Any guy with a brain could guess how this was going to go, and he wasn't looking forward to the collision.

Standing, he dredged up his best smile. "'Morning, ladies."

"Jason." Brenda sniffed, giving Rachel a suspicious look before offering her hand. "I'm Brenda Lattimore. Welcome to Barrett's Mill."

Her chilly greeting had the ring of a cobra inviting a

mouse into range, and Amy rolled her eyes with a sigh. "How are you doing this morning, Rachel? I hope you slept well."

"It's much better than sleeping in the truck."

Brenda's flinty look dissolved, and her mother's instincts took over. "Oh, you poor thing! How awful."

"I'm just grateful to be here with nice people around who care about what happens to me and my baby."

"So are we," Amy assured her with a warmth that couldn't be faked. "Every child should come into the world knowing they're loved."

Jason sensed she was including him in that gracious comment, and he silently thanked her for it. Overcome by gratitude for her understanding, it was all he could do not to kiss her right there in front of everyone. "What are you ladies up to today?"

"Christmas shopping." Those soft lips curved flirtatiously, and she added, "Would you like me to add in anything for you?"

Returning that smile was the most natural thing he'd ever done. "Nope. I got everything I want."

"All right, you two," Brenda jumped in, pulling her cousin away. "Save it for under the mistletoe. Bye, now."

Still standing, Jason watched them stroll down the sidewalk toward the shops so lavishly decorated for the holidays. He kept them in sight until they turned a corner, then stifled a sigh as he sat back down.

"I don't care what you say," Rachel told him with the authority of an expert. "You're in love with her. The good news is, she feels the same way about you."

"You're nuts. We just met."

"Oh, that doesn't matter even the teeniest little bit," she informed him while she salted her eggs. "When two people go together, that's it. Logic has nothing to do with it."

"I thought *we* went together."

"No, you didn't," she corrected him quietly. "You tried to make it happen, because more than anything you want a family of your own to love and take care of. Your mistake was trying to fit me into that box."

"And what makes you think Amy's open to being in the box with me?"

"I'm a woman," she reminded him with a coy smile. "We always know."

Jason chewed on that for a minute, then decided she might be right. But even if Amy already knew how she felt about him, he wouldn't be surprised if it took her a while to own up to it. They'd both gotten burned in the past, and that would make it tougher for them to take that step again.

But anything was possible. After all, it was Christmastime.

Amy was getting ready for choir practice when someone started honking out front. Grabbing a light jacket, she went through the studio and saw a minivan waiting outside the large bay window.

Brenda.

I should have known, she thought as she let herself out the front door and locked it behind her.

Pausing on the sidewalk, she glanced back to admire the festive look she and Jason had created to draw people into Arabesque. Even if she'd worked at it for months, she couldn't have designed a better representation of both the studio and the show. Odd as it seemed, they made a great team, her with the ideas and him with the practical experience to bring them to life.

When she climbed in beside her cousin, she chided, "You really didn't have to do this. I would've met you there."

"It's no big deal. You're on my way."

Right. Any other day, she might have continued the debate just for fun, but thinking about Jason had left her feeling generous, so she let it drop. "I wrapped the kids' gifts last night. Do you want to stop and get them after rehearsal so you can put them under your tree?"

"Not a chance," Brenda replied as she parked in the church's lot. "They'll shake and nudge and peek until they end up opening them 'by mistake.'" She punctuated this with air quotes and laughed. "It's safer to hang on to them and bring them Christmas morning."

"Will do." They got out of the van, and Amy said, "I can't believe how many people are here. The lot's almost as full as it was on Sunday."

"The difference is, most of us are here alone," Brenda pointed out as they went up the steps. "On Sunday, those same cars are full of people."

"Is that why you do this? To get some time to yourself?"

"Pretty much. I love my kids to pieces, but I have to get some me time once in a while or I'll go bonkers."

In her wistful tone, Amy heard a desperate plea for a break. She'd been trying to come up with a gift for her vivacious cousin, and the lightbulb went off: spa day. There had to be one around here somewhere, she reasoned. It occurred to her that Chelsea Barrett would be the kind of woman who'd know something like that, and she made a mental note to call and ask her.

The buzz of voices inside the chapel dragged her back to the present, and she braced herself to go through the open double doors. Sunday had gone well, but for some reason she was nervous about tonight. She'd never suffered from stage fright when she was dancing, but singing in front of so many people was a different thing altogether.

"You'll be fine," Brenda whispered encouragingly, giving her a quick squeeze around the shoulders. "It's Christmas music, so just hit as many notes as you can. That's what most of us will be doing, anyway."

Amy laughed, and behind her a familiar voice drawled, "I like the way this is goin' already."

She spun to find Jason standing there, wearing a grin that made her glad there was no mistletoe around. If there was, even though they were in church she might not have been able to resist stealing a kiss. "How are you tonight?"

The grin deepened, and for the first time she noticed a dimple in his tanned cheek. "Better now."

"I think someone's looking for me," Brenda announced, winking at Amy before flouncing away.

"She never was subtle, your cousin."

"Cheerleaders usually aren't," Amy pointed out. She debated asking about Rachel, then decided if she didn't, he'd think she was avoiding the subject. Beyond that, remaining in the dark would make her crazy. "How's Rachel doing?"

"As well as you could expect. Turns out Doc Peterson's receptionist quit, and he needed someone to fill in through the holidays till he can hire someone permanently. It's easy, sitting-down work, which is good. Rachel's not all that organized, but she's decent with the computer and on the phone, so it's a good solution for now."

And then what? Amy was dying to ask, but Mrs. Griggs was calling everyone into the sanctuary, so her answer would have to wait.

Amy eyed the risers hesitantly. There were no handrails, and because of her limited mobility, the vertical distance was a little high for her. She didn't want to make a fool of herself by falling in front of everyone.

In his usual way, Jason came to her rescue, offering his arm. When she was safely standing in the soprano section, she thanked him.

"Anytime."

Once he'd moved on, Brenda popped up next to her and said, "I forgot my music. Can I share with you?"

"Sure." Amy opened her folder of music and held it so they could both see.

As the pianist began playing the opening chords of "Hark the Herald Angels Sing," Brenda murmured, "Just for future reference, I make an excellent matron of honor."

Out of respect for the pastor's wife, Amy simply shook her head. Despite the overly sentimental rumors flying around town, she and Jason were a long way from choosing a wedding party. In fact, after the disastrous way his last engagement had ended, she wouldn't be at all surprised to learn that he wasn't keen to get serious with anyone. That should have been a huge relief to her, since she wasn't interested in a relationship, either.

But for some strange reason it just made her sad.

Jason was totally focused on turning a spindle for the back of the rocking chair he was working on, so he didn't realize he had company until his ear protectors disappeared. "What the—"

The rest of his protest trailed off as Jenna Reed dragged him through the workshop and out the back door of the mill house. By his ear.

When she decided they were far enough from the rest of the crew, she let him go, giving him a firm shove for good measure. "What's wrong with you?"

"Well, my ear kinda hurts." Rubbing it, he glared back at her. "What's your problem?"

Today, her faded denim overalls were covered in stone dust, which told him something of major importance had interrupted her chiseling time. "Are you a complete idiot?"

"Sometimes." He added a grin, but she merely planted her hands on her hips while the glare hardened into an unforgiving scowl. Sensing humor wasn't the right approach, he spread his hands in a calming gesture. "I give. What's up?"

"What'd I tell you about Amy?"

"That she's been hurt enough, and I should be careful. Which I'm doing."

"Then how come a customer just told me you've been cozying up with Amy at her place?"

"You hate gossip," Jason reminded her. "Since when do you listen to anything like that?"

"Since it involves a very good friend—" she narrowed her eyes "—and you."

He laughed. "Gimme a break. You make me sound like the Big Bad Wolf going after Little Red Riding Hood."

"Are you?"

The insult stung, and he bit back some pretty harsh words. Something was going on here, and while he didn't understand it, he decided it was best not to further provoke her by retaliating. "You know me better than that."

"Do I? I've been here six months, and in all that time, I've never seen you with the same girl for more than a couple weeks."

She had him there, Jason had to admit, but Amy wasn't like those other women. The more time he spent with her, the more she fascinated him. Usually, a few dates were enough to convince him it was time to move on. Between the show and other holiday goings-on around town, he and Amy saw each other every day, and he eagerly looked forward to connecting with her. In fact, he wouldn't have minded if they spent even more time together.

He wasn't ready to share those feelings with anyone else, so he shrugged. "Amy's different."

"How?" Leaning against a nearby tree, Jenna folded her arms with a curious expression. It beat the looks she'd been giving him, and he relaxed a little.

"She's smart and funny," he began, then couldn't keep back a smile. "And she's still the prettiest thing I've ever seen."

"Prettier than Rachel?"

"To me, she is."

"Spare me," Jenna scoffed. "Even eight months pregnant, Rachel's gorgeous. I can't imagine how she is on a normal day."

Being male, he couldn't deny she held the more obvious appeal. But Amy's appearance was more refined, and she had an elegant style no woman he'd ever met could match. More reserved by nature, she kept a lot to herself, and that only made her more captivating to him. While he considered how to explain his preference, something clicked into place for him, and he smiled. "Guess I outgrew Barbie dolls. Now I want something else."

"Meaning Amy?"

"Maybe," he allowed, still unwilling to discuss this with Jenna when he hadn't brought it up with the lady in question. "But only if that's what she wants. We're about as different as two people can get, and I've got no plans to change. I'm figuring she doesn't, either. Which is fine with me, 'cause I think she's perfect the way she is."

"I'm not big on compromise myself, so I get that." Apparently satisfied with the result of her interrogation, she pushed off from the tree. "Okay, I'm going. But you watch your step, JB. I've got my eye on you."

"Good to know," he tossed back, getting a smack on the shoulder in reply. While he watched her get into her van, his cell phone vibrated in his pocket. Pulling it out, he saw the caller ID and answered. "Hey, Mom. What's up?"

"I'm with your grandparents, and we need you here right now."

The line went dead before he could ask for details, and his pulse shot into the stratosphere. Going back inside to explain would only waste time, so he ran for his truck, dialing as he went. "Chelsea, I'm headed to Gram and Granddad's. Tell Paul."

He ground the engine into gear and flew down the pitted lane, ducking reflexively from the stones pelting his windows. It couldn't be Granddad, logic told him, or Mom would've called in Paul and Chelsea, too. That meant something had happened to Gram, and Jason pulled in long, deep breaths to combat the dread seizing his heart. He took one curve a little too fast and frantically steered the truck back onto the dirt road. Easing back on the gas, he reminded himself he couldn't help anyone if he crashed into a tree on the way into town.

The drive felt twice as long as on a normal day, but he finally made it home. Leaving his door open and the cranky engine running, he ran up the front steps and into the dining room. Granddad was even paler than usual, and he pointed toward the kitchen. "They're in there."

"Is Gram okay?"

"More or less. I tried to get up and help them, but they won't let me."

Jason realized his panic was the last thing anyone needed to see right now, so he forced calm into his voice. "Can I get you anything?"

"I'm fine. See to your grandmother."

He didn't look fine, but Jason obeyed him out of habit. In the kitchen, he found the two women who'd raised him sitting on the floor. Gram's arm was at an odd angle, resting on an overturned pot padded with towels.

Hunkering down, he summoned a little humor. "I've heard those things work better upright on the stove."

"Oh, you," Gram chided him in a shaky voice that scared him down to his boots. Resolute and strong, she inspired the Barrett family with her faith and unrelenting optimism. Seeing her this way was a stark warning that in a heartbeat, things he'd relied on his entire life could change.

Firmly shutting the negative thought away, he glanced around and noticed a three-step stool on its side. Obviously, she'd wanted something from one of the high cupboards and needed the stool to reach it. Even though he knew it was pointless, he felt awful for not being there. "You couldn't wait for me?"

"Don't you be giving me those guilty eyes, young man. You were at work, and I'm perfectly capable of fetching things on my own."

There was no sense in debating that, so he asked, "Is it broken?"

"I'm not sure," Mom replied with a frown. "X-rays are the only way to know, but she refuses to go to the hospital."

"I'm not leaving Will," Gram insisted stubbornly.

This brought to mind why he hated playing chess. He always got into some kind of standoff with his opponent, and he couldn't come up with a way to get out of it. But this was real life, and he couldn't throw in the towel just because things had gotten dicey. Then he had a brainstorm, and he prayed it would work. "Then we'll bring him with us. Where's that wheelchair?"

Gram sent a worried look into the dining room, and Jason took advantage of her distraction to wink at his mother. Her raised eyebrow told him she understood, and he kept his expression neutral when his grandmother's eyes settled back on him. When they narrowed, he knew she was onto him, but at least she nodded.

"All right, you win," she finally agreed. "Who's taking me to the hospital?"

"My truck's already running," he answered, standing to get her a sweater from its hook near the back door.

Holding it up so she could slide her uninjured arm into one sleeve, he looped the rest around her and did up the top two buttons to hold it closed. Hoping to lighten the mood a little, he chuckled. "I remember when you used to do this for me, Gram."

"Now I'd need a ladder," she responded with a fond smile. "Hand me my purse, would you?"

"No, but I'll carry it for you." Dangling the strap over his forearm, he held the other one out for her. "Ready?"

"I suppose. The sooner we leave, the sooner we'll be back."

"That's my girl," he approved heartily. Her ability to cope with bad situations never failed to amaze him.

"I'll keep an eye on Will and have lunch ready when you get back," Mom promised, patting his shoulder while they passed by. "If you need me for anything, just call."

After very carefully helping his grandmother into his truck, Jason got in beside her and drove the ten miles to the hospital in nearby Cambridge as smoothly as possible. The emergency-room nurse was a plump woman with dark, sparkling eyes and a Christmas tree pin on her smock that blinked with multicolored lights.

Tsking with sympathy, she gently guided Gram toward an exam room. "You come with me, honey, and we'll get you fixed up in a blink."

Since she was already in their computer system, all Jason had to do was confirm nothing had changed since they'd treated Gram for pneumonia earlier in the year. After that, he slumped in a waiting-room chair and finally released the iron grip he'd kept on his emotions. It was how he handled a crisis, and it worked well until things settled down and he had a chance to come to terms with what had happened.

As a family, the Barretts had all learned to live with the constant threat of a health issue with Granddad. When you loved someone who had terminal cancer, that kind of acceptance came with the territory. But a problem with Gram was something else entirely.

Their family orbited around her like the sun, and if anything happened to her, Jason feared Granddad wouldn't be physically strong enough to survive her loss.

She's fine, he told himself sternly. *It's only her wrist.* His next thought flipped to Rachel, who'd surely call him in a panic when she went into labor. She had no one else to turn to, and while she and her baby weren't technically his responsibility, he'd already decided that when the time came, he'd be there for them. That trip would be a hundred times more stressful than this one, he knew. Was he ready for it?

Suddenly, he was exhausted, and he bent over, dangling his arms over his knees while he stared at the speckled tiles on the floor. Footsteps hurried toward him, and he lifted his head to find himself gazing into Amy's worried eyes.

"Is your grandmother okay?"

"They're doing X-rays soon, so we'll know more then. How'd you know I was here?"

"Your mom called me," she explained as she took

the seat beside him. "She didn't want you here by your-self, pacing and hounding the nurses for information they don't have."

He'd been about five minutes from doing just that, he realized, and he marveled at how well Mom knew him. "That was nice of her, but I hate to drag you over here. Don't you have your Ballet Tots class at noon?"

"I canceled it. We'll make it up later in the week, or they can get a refund for the day. This is much more important." Reaching over, she rested one of her deli-cate hands over his much larger one. "On the way here, I said a prayer for Olivia to be okay."

Knowing how she'd felt about God not long ago, her revelation astounded him, and he turned to face her. "You did?"

"I'm not sure it will help," she confided, "but it felt like the right thing to do."

"It was," he agreed with heartfelt gratitude. "Thank you."

Suddenly, she seemed uncomfortable, as if her ges-ture had surprised her as much as it did him. "Can I get you anything?"

Settling his arm across the back of the couch, he gave her shoulders a light bump. "This works for me."

"Well, you'll be hungry soon. There's a deli down the street, so let me know what you want, and I'll get it for you."

"That'd be great. We ate here a lot when Granddad was a patient, and the cafeteria's not the best."

"They never are," she agreed with a grimace. "The

hospital I was in after my accident would make a good weight-loss camp. Mom smuggled real food in to me, or I would have starved."

"Sounds pretty awful."

"Don't get me wrong—everyone on the staff was fantastic. I still hated every second of it, not being able to sleep, having people tell me what to do all the time. I wasn't crazy about having to move back in with Mom while I rehabbed, but at least she didn't expect me to be a cheerful patient."

"After what you went through, it must be tough for you to be here," he said gently. "I really appreciate you coming to keep me company, but if you want to go, I'll understand."

"You've done so much for me, and I thought this would be a good way to start repaying you. I'll hang around until Olivia's ready to leave."

"I didn't sign on to the show to make you feel like you owe me something," he argued. "I wanted to help."

She rewarded him with a brilliant smile. "I know that, Galahad. That's why I'm staying."

With that, she snuggled a little closer and rested her head against his shoulder. He wasn't in the mood to talk, and he appreciated her allowing him to sit there in silence. Most women he knew felt compelled to fill every silence longer than three seconds, but not Amy. She seemed to understand that he needed to focus all his energy on absorbing what had happened during what should have been a busy but ordinary day.

Instead, he felt as if it had gone on forever, and it

wasn't even lunchtime. Considering what could have happened, Gram had gotten off lightly, and he thanked God for watching over her. Just having Amy there made things look brighter, he realized. Accustomed to fending for himself since leaving home, he hadn't had anyone to lean on. Even when he and Rachel were together, he'd been the one to take care of everything.

Despite the rocky start he'd gotten, he'd been raised by a family of strong, loyal people who supported each other through every conceivable peak and valley life could throw at them. Paul and Chelsea were the next generation in the Barrett chain, and he'd watched them with growing respect while they built their future with hard work and love.

Rachel's betrayal had soured him on making that same commitment himself, but now he was beginning to think that with the right woman, he could have the kind of relationship he longed for. The kind where two people took on life together and made the best of what God handed them. Over time, he'd realized his mistake with Rachel had been to treat her like a doll, keeping her on a pedestal while he handled everything himself.

He'd never even consider doing that with Amy, and if he went astray, he had no doubt she'd jerk him back into line. And very clearly warn him never to do it again. The thought of it amused him, and in the middle of that sterile waiting room, he couldn't keep back a smile.

He and Amy might look like two mismatched socks,

but in his gut he knew that no matter what happened down the road, pairing up with her would be a decision he'd never regret.

Chapter Nine

Amy left Jason and his grandmother in the hospital parking lot with hugs and a promise to check in with them later. As she drove back to Arabesque, she mulled over what had gone on and what it meant.

Mostly, she tried to analyze what had compelled her to appeal to the God she'd been so angry with. Jason had clearly been stunned by it, and she could relate to how he felt. Maybe attending services with him and singing all those uplifting Christmas hymns had mellowed her attitude, chipping away at the grudge she'd carried for so long. Whatever the explanation, she couldn't deny feeling liberated, as if a huge weight had been taken from her.

Even more surprising, throughout the afternoon, that light feeling stayed with her. To her, that meant it wasn't a fluke or some lingering effect from an emergency situation that had turned out well. It was sticking because it was real. Understanding settled in, and as she cued up her favorite section of *The Nutcracker* score on the studio's sound system, she glanced up with a smile. "Thank you."

A warm softness brushed her cheek, as if someone had reached down to reassure her. Tears sprang into her eyes, and she resolutely blinked them away but held on to the emotion they evoked in her heart. It was comforting to know someone was watching over her, even when she thought she was alone.

Jason and Brenda were right, she finally admitted to herself. God had never deserted her, but had seen her on the wrong path and manipulated her circumstances to correct her direction. That fateful course shift had brought her to Barrett's Mill and a man who could see beyond her imperfections to who she truly was.

Suddenly anxious to hear Jason's voice, she thumbed through her contacts list and chose his number. While she waited for him to answer, she impulsively added him to her very short speed-dial list. It was only for people she spoke to frequently, and since they talked at least twice a day, she figured he belonged there.

After a few rings, he picked up. "Hey there. What's up?"

From the background noise, she knew he was at the mill. She didn't think now was the right time to share her epiphany, so she kept things light. "Checking in, as promised. How's Olivia doing?"

"Home with Mom and Granddad. Gram's supposed to be resting, but I hear she's trying to come up with a way to make dinner one-handed."

"Can't your mother take care of that?"

He let out a tired-sounding laugh. "Sure, but that's not how it works in Gram's kitchen. She's in charge, and everyone else assists. I think that's where Paul got his bossy gene from."

"I heard that," his brother chimed in from a distance. "Are you assembling that rocking chair or flirting?"

"Both."

Paul groaned, and Amy interpreted the sound of a slamming door as her cue to finish up. "You're busy, so I'll let you go."

"I've got three more of these rockers to do, but I'll be in after rehearsal to paint that marble detail on the fireplace."

"Why don't you just go home after work?" she suggested. "The painting can wait another day."

"Are you sure? That'll put us off your schedule."

Her schedule, she echoed ruefully. After the long, trying day he'd had, he was willing to stretch it even further to keep her happy. She hated the idea that her inflexibility was putting more pressure on this kind, compassionate man. After all, what was the worst that could happen? Certainly not anything that warranted him wearing himself out during the holidays. "We'll get it done. If we really get in a jam, I'll ask Jenna to come help us out."

"Oh, man," he groaned. "Don't do that. She'd never let me hear the end of it."

"Everyone needs a hand now and then. Even big, strong lumberjacks like you."

"I'll finish those sets myself if it kills me," he assured her. "I made a commitment to you, and I never go back on my word."

Amy was more than a little impressed. She'd given him an out, but he stubbornly refused to take it. Most people she knew were quick to choose the path of least resistance, but not this one. Even though he had a perfectly viable excuse, she trusted him to deliver exactly what he'd promised her, in time for their show. That was the kind of guy every girl needed in her life, she mused with a smile. The kind who stood up and took his responsibilities seriously instead of dodging them at the first sign of trouble.

"All right, but I'm willing to help if you tell me what you need." The line went quiet, and after a few seconds she said, "Jason?"

"Yeah, I'm here."

"Is something wrong?"

"No, it's just—" Heaving a sigh, he went on. "I guess I'm more tired than I thought is all. I'll see you tomorrow."

Something in his voice sounded off, but she couldn't quite peg it, so she accepted his explanation. After all, he'd been through a lot today. She'd experienced enough of that herself to understand how draining it could be. "Have a good night."

"You, too."

She'd no sooner hung up than her phone rang again. Checking the caller ID, she was surprised to see it was the doctor who'd led the surgical team that operated on her after her accident. They hadn't been in touch recently, and she couldn't imagine what he wanted. "Hello, Dr. Fitzgerald. How are you?"

"Excited," he replied in his usual brisk way. "I think you will be, too, when you hear what I have to say."

Amy felt her pulse spike, then cautioned herself to remain calm. Her hopes had been raised many times in the past, only to be dashed later on. Steadying her voice, she said, "Go ahead."

In a tone laced with more of the same enthusiasm, he described an experimental procedure he and some colleagues had developed for treating injuries like hers. Their initial trials had gone well, and they were looking for volunteers to undergo the treatment for real.

"Based on your age and general health," he continued, "I think you'd be an excellent candidate."

"Why haven't I heard about this on the news?" she asked warily.

"It's experimental, and we don't want to publicize it until we have some solid results to report. I have to warn you, there is a potential downside."

Of course there was, she groused silently. There was always a downside. "I'm listening."

"If it's successful, this surgery should restore your full range of motion through your back and legs."

"And if it fails?"

"You could be paralyzed."

Could be, she echoed silently. Two tantalizing words she'd heard so often, clinging to the slender hope that somehow her body would find a way to heal itself and function the way it was supposed to. But that hadn't happened, and she wasn't certain she could muster the emotional energy to risk suffering through that kind of disappointment again.

Still, the idea of walking freely—maybe even dancing again—was incredibly tempting. She wasn't foolish enough to think she'd ever be a prima ballerina. That dream had died long ago, but she might be able to take on secondary roles in a small company somewhere. It wasn't her ideal, but at least that way she'd be doing what she loved.

"I'll have to think about it," she finally said. "When do you need my answer?"

"Tomorrow, at the latest. One of our original volunteers opted out, and we have to fill the spot quickly to keep everything on track. We've reserved a section of the hospital for our patients, and we need to do quite a bit of prep work beforehand. You'd need to be here in New York right after Christmas, and the actual procedure would be done in early January. If you decide you're not interested, I have to start going down my list and find someone else."

Oh, she was interested, all right. The timing would allow her to finish up *The Nutcracker* and spend time with her family before leaving for New York. Since her mother was coming for the show, she'd catch a ride back with her and be able to stay at her Manhattan apartment following her surgery.

Was she really considering this? While her mind clicked through the things she'd have to do to make this work, it became obvious that part of her was already on board.

Another part, the one she'd only recently begun to discover, whispered a single—but very important—objection.

What about Jason?

Putting aside a question she couldn't easily answer, she wrapped up her call. "I'll definitely get back to you, one way or the other. Whatever I decide, I'm so grateful you thought of me. This is a wonderful opportunity for someone like me."

"We'll talk tomorrow, then. Goodbye, Amy."

She hung up, watching as the wallpaper on her phone's screen faded back into place. It was a picture of Jason and her at the Starlight Festival, gazing upward as the star on top of the town tree was being lit. Chelsea had taken the photo and texted it to her, and it had immediately become Amy's favorite. He stood behind her in the protective way she'd come to associate with him. Although he wasn't touching her, she could almost feel those strong arms wrapped around her, shielding her from the press of the crowd.

It was a comforting sensation she'd come to rely on as their unexpected friendship continued to grow. If she agreed to the surgical trial and it went well, what then? In her heart, she knew that if there was even a sliver of a chance for her to perform again, she wouldn't be content teaching no matter how adorable her students were.

But if it turned out to be another failure, she might never walk again. Then what would she do to support herself? Beyond that, if she was confined to a wheel-chair for the rest of her life, her flickering hopes of marriage and adopting a child might be gone forever.

Completely overwhelmed by the choice she was faced with, she did something that not long ago would never have occurred to her. Looking up, she said, "I trust that You brought me to this point for a reason. Please help me do the right thing."

Nothing.

While she hadn't expected an immediate response, some kind of sign would have been nice.

The alert on her phone chimed, reminding her it was almost time for rehearsal. As if on cue, the front door jingled and high-pitched voices blended with the classical Christmas music she'd left playing in the studio.

Her answer would have to wait, she supposed as she stood to meet her early arrivals. Because if this turned out to be her final *Nutcracker* production, she was determined to give it everything she had.

"It's me!" Jason hollered on his way into Arabesque the following day. "Don't shoot!"

Amy was onstage adjusting the long drapes that hung around the fake bay window in the ballroom. When she turned to look at him, his heart rolled over in his chest like a lovesick hound. Even though he'd been engaged before, this sensation was like nothing he'd ever felt, and he wasn't sure what to make of it. He'd just seen Amy yesterday, but it felt as if it had been much longer.

Oh, man, he thought with a mental groan. Somehow,

when he wasn't paying attention, he'd stumbled into some dangerous territory. It was one thing to admire a pretty girl, but for a guy like him who'd been dropped hard, doing emotional cartwheels wasn't smart. If only he knew how to stop.

"Hi there," Amy said when she met him in the wings. "How's Olivia today?"

"Better, I think. She never complains about anything, so it's hard to tell."

"I wish more people were like that," Amy commented wryly.

"Tell me about it." Setting down his toolbox, he mentally reviewed where they were on her list. "So tonight, it's the bookcases and fireplace, right?"

"Jason, we need to talk."

Not what he wanted to hear. Those were trouble-maker words every man dreaded, and he braced himself for the worst. "Okay."

"I'm sorry," she began, twisting her hands in obvious distress. "I didn't mean to jump into it like that. Would you like a snack or something?"

"No, I'm good." She looked so upset, he wanted nothing more than to chase away whatever was bothering her. Even if it turned out to be him. Taking a seat on the steps leading down from the stage, he patted the one above him. She hesitated, but finally sat down, and he gave her an encouraging nod. "Go ahead."

Another pause, then she plunged right in. "One of the surgeons who operated on me after my accident called me. He and some of his colleagues have developed a new procedure that could restore my full range of motion."

"Amy, that's awesome!" When she frowned, he felt his expression fall to mirror hers. "It's not awesome?"

"It could be," she allowed, avoiding his gaze while she picked at a stray piece of tape on the stage. "But if it doesn't work, I could end up being paralyzed."

For a few seconds, Jason was so stunned he couldn't think of a single thing to say. When his brain began functioning on all cylinders again, he understood why she was so skittish about sharing her news with him. "You're seriously thinking about doing this, aren't you?"

"Yes."

She didn't say anything more, but when her eyes met his, the defiance glittering in them spoke for her. She wasn't asking for his opinion, he realized, or his permission. But he couldn't stand by and watch her risk her health this way. "I think it's a bad idea."

"I didn't ask you."

"That doesn't mean I don't have a few thoughts on the subject."

Jumping up, he began pacing in front of the huge Christmas tree they and the kids had decorated for the show. He'd lifted Clara up to place the star on top, and like a moron he'd envisioned doing that with his own little girl someday. The memory surfaced from nowhere, and he firmly pushed it back down to wherever it had come from.

Staring up at the pulleys and cables that operated the stage curtains, he closed his eyes and sent up a fervent prayer for patience. When he felt calmer, he turned to face Amy. "Please explain to me why you're considering this."

"Because it could be my last chance to fix what's wrong with me."

That was the root of the problem, he understood. Her obsession with perfection had bothered him in the past, but never more than in this moment. Because he'd always been aware of his own failings, he couldn't comprehend her perspective on what it meant to be flawless. But he did understand that in the past she'd been just that, and she longed to reclaim as much of it as she could.

That didn't mean he couldn't try to change her mind, though.

"There's nothing wrong with you," he insisted, crossing the stage to hunker down in front of her. "You're perfect just the way you are."

Her wistful gaze communicated more than any words could possibly say. "That's sweet of you, but we both know it isn't true."

Taking her hand, he met those sorrow-filled blue eyes with every ounce of compassion he had in him. "I believe it is, with all my heart."

"Please don't take this the wrong way," she begged in a tearful voice. "But that doesn't really matter. What matters is what *I* believe."

Since he shared that particular conviction with her, he had no choice but to give her that one. Thankfully, another argument floated into his mind. "Okay, so what'll you do if the surgery goes wrong and you're paralyzed? It's hard to teach dance when you can't show the kids the steps."

"I'll find another job somewhere."

He could tell she was trying desperately to appear confident, but the shadow of doubt in her expressive eyes gave her away. The only thing she'd ever wanted to do was dance, or teach dance, so he was fairly certain she'd never learned how to do anything else. It was mean of him, but he forged ahead in what he suspected would be a last-ditch attempt to make her see reason. "Doing what?"

"I don't know, something," she retorted defiantly. "Rachel's not exactly a rocket scientist. If she can find a job, so can I."

The uncalled-for attack on his ex made Jason's temper flare, and he wrestled it under control to keep this from getting personal. He couldn't accomplish anything if he lost his cool and started yelling. "We're not talking about her right now. We're talking about you. What's really bothering you?"

At first, Amy just glowered at him, which worked in his favor because it gave him a chance to rein his own emotions back into line. She meant a lot to him, and he wanted nothing more than for her to be happy. This just didn't seem to him like the smartest way to go about it, but Granddad had taught him that the best way to resolve a disagreement was to listen to the other side all the way through. And since this was such a huge decision for Amy, Jason figured he owed her that much.

"This is very important to me," she finally said, her voice trembling with a mixture of anger and disappointment. "I thought you'd be more supportive than—"

She cut off abruptly, but it didn't take a genius to fill in that blank.

"Devon?" This time, he didn't bother hiding his frustration and stood to his full height. As he folded his arms in his most intimidating pose, it was his turn to scowl. "You're seriously gonna compare me to that snake?"

"He always told me what I should do," she argued, "how I should handle my career. You're doing the same thing now, trying to talk me out of having this surgery."

"Because it could ruin your life!"

"It's my life, and I have no intention of letting someone else talk me into anything."

She tilted her chin rebelliously, and he recognized that he was treading on extremely thin ice with her. She was a grown woman, and ordinarily he'd honor her right to choose the option she felt was best for her. But what she was contemplating made absolutely no sense to him. Beyond that, she'd come so far in making a new career here in Barrett's Mill. Whatever the outcome of her surgery, he feared she'd eventually regret leaving the studio for the slim possibility of reviving her performing career.

"What about your students?" he demanded. "I thought you liked working with them."

"I love it," she affirmed in a wistful tone. "But there's no way for me to have that and my own career besides."

Sensing that she was wavering, he took a single step forward into the space he normally kept between them. The urge to hold her was so overwhelming, it took some serious willpower to keep his hands at his sides. Very quietly, he said, "That's a tough choice to make."

"I know."

She looked up at him with such longing, he almost couldn't stand it. Part of him wanted to jump in and offer to go with her, even if only until her surgery was complete and she knew the outcome. Once the holidays were over, things would slow down at the mill enough to allow him to take some time off. Then logic reasserted itself to remind him he was a country boy who'd be completely lost in the big city.

It killed him to admit that, but he couldn't deceive her. Or himself. He might give that life a shot to please her, but he'd visited enough busy places to know that in the long run he'd never last. They were too crowded, and the hectic lifestyle made him long for wide-open spaces where he could breathe. Amy fit nicely into Barrett's Mill, but he couldn't envision himself doing the same in a bustling place like New York.

Because of that, if they were going to remain together, she was the one who had to compromise. Which meant he had to come up with a way to convince her to stay. "What happens to the studio if you leave?"

"Aunt Helen will finish out this block of classes and then close it down. That was her plan before I came here, anyway."

"It's a shame to disappoint all those kids," he ventured, hoping to appeal to her affection for the children she'd come to like so much.

"There's a good teacher over in Cambridge. I'm sure she'll be happy to take them on."

"She's not you." *In so many ways,* he added silently.

"I don't expect you to understand," she said, backing away from him in an unmistakable effort to put some distance between them. "But this could be my last chance at being the way I used to be. I have to take it."

He'd tried every trick in his book, knowing all the while how it would end. When Amy set her mind on something, there was simply no budging her. Grudgingly, he gave in. "Like you said, it's your life."

"Yes, it is." Glancing around, she came back to him with the same detached look in her eyes he'd seen the first day he met her. "I think the sets are far enough along that Uncle Fred and I can finish them up. Thank you so much for all your help, Jason."

Offering her hand, she stared at him with an unreadable expression. Now that he'd voiced an opinion that differed from hers, apparently he'd slid down the list from good friend to hired hand. Must be some kind of record, he groused as he politely shook her hand. There were so many things he wanted to tell her, but he knew they'd sound either lame or pathetic or both, so he kept them to himself. "You're welcome."

Since there was really nothing more to say, he picked up his toolbox and headed for the door. The bells jingled, a cheerful sound at odds with the heaviness weighing him down as he left. He knew he should just keep going, but he couldn't help looking back. What he saw just about broke his heart.

Standing alone in the middle of the ballroom, framed in the halo of a spotlight, Amy was staring up at the star on top of the lighted tree. The scene brought to mind their evening at the Starlight Festival, when they'd confided in each other and started building something that had become much more than friendship for him. The little ballerina he'd admired as a child had grown into an exquisite, aggravating woman who had an uncanny ability to challenge him one moment and charm him the next. Watching her now, he wished there was something more he could do to persuade her to rethink her decision and stay. Since there wasn't, he turned and headed for home.

On his way, he passed by the Morgan house. The lights were on in Fred's garage workshop, and Jason impulsively switched direction. As he approached, he could hear smooth jazz music, and he grinned when he heard Fred mimicking a soulful high-range trumpet solo with considerable gusto.

Outside the partially open door, he knocked to get the mechanic's attention. Fred appeared surprised to see him, but waved him in. When his eyes locked on Jason's toolbox, he scowled. "Those sets aren't near done yet. What happened?"

"Amy fired me."

Heaving a long-suffering male sigh, Fred pulled up a couple of apple crates and motioned for Jason to take one. Once they were seated, he fixed Jason with a woebegone look. "The women in this family can drive a man right off a cliff."

"Got that right," Jason growled back.

Amy's uncle listened patiently to the entire sad story, nodding and frowning in all the right places.

"I've never been booted in the middle of a job before," Jason said. "She'd rather have you help her finish things up before the show next week."

"No can do." Holding his lower back, Fred winked. "I think I tweaked my lumbar again."

They both laughed, and Jason appreciated the conniving support. "Whattaya think I should do?"

"Ignore her and finish what you started." Taking out his key ring, he slid one off and handed it to Jason. "This way, she doesn't have to let you in."

"Thanks." Pocketing the key, he added, "Now, about the other thing."

Scratching a thumb over his stubbly chin, the older man chewed on that one for a few seconds. "Well, now, that depends on what you're really after."

"I'm not following you."

"Women are complicated."

Jason snorted his agreement. "Tell me about it."

"What I mean is it's best to pick one thing and go full bore instead of spreading yourself too thin." Jason didn't respond, and he continued, "Do you want her to stay here so you can see where things go with her, or pass on the surgery 'cause you think it's a mistake?"

"Both."

Chuckling, Fred shook his head. "You're not listening, son. To you and me, those two things are one and the same. To Amy, they're completely different."

At first, that made no sense to him. Then he reconsidered it from her perspective, and the pieces clicked into place. "Because one's professional and the other's personal. If you don't mind me asking, where do you and Helen stand on this experimental procedure?"

"Against, one thousand percent. But Amy and that headstrong baby sister of mine have got other ideas. I guess Connie sees it different than we do, 'cause when she was younger, she was planning to be a big-time ballerina herself."

"Then she had Amy," Jason guessed, getting a nod in reply. "That explains why Amy's dead set on getting back to it. Her mom missed out, so Amy's trying to make up for what she lost."

"Don't get me wrong. From the time she could walk, Amy danced the way most of us breathe, and that car crash was a tragedy in more ways than one. It wasn't easy for her to dust herself off the way she's done, but she's making the most of the gifts God gave her."

"I thought she felt that way, too," Jason confided glumly. "Now I'm not so sure. She seems to love teaching those kids, but now she's ready to give all that up for something even the doctors are warning her might not work."

"You're not seeing it from her angle. If you'd fallen out of a tree in Oregon a couple years ago and were done with logging, what would you have done?"

"Come back here and make furniture at the mill."

That got him a wise look, but he didn't understand the significance of his answer. Eventually, it dawned on him. "I get it. I chose that even when I didn't have to. Amy took over the studio because that was the only way she could still be involved in dancing."

"Now you've got it." With a suddenly somber look, Fred asked, "And what about the other thing?"

Jason blanked, then caught on and grinned. "Are you asking about my intentions toward your niece?"

"Yes, I am."

Since there were all manner of tools only an arm's length away, Jason straightened up and looked him directly in the eye the way he'd been taught. "She's the most incredible woman I've ever met, and I'd love to get to know her better."

Fred seemed to appreciate that, and he nodded his approval. "From what I see, you're a good influence on our girl. She's a mite serious for someone her age, and you lighten her up. She smiles a lot more these days, and I like that."

"That's good to hear."

"But." Brandishing a heavy wrench that looked as if it had seen plenty of action, he warned, "If that ever changes, you and I are gonna have a problem. Understand?"

Jason nodded soberly. "Yes, sir."

"Good boy. Now, get outta here so I can finish up before Helen starts yelling for me to come inside already."

Figuring it was best to get while the getting was good, Jason retrieved his toolbox and made a quick exit.

While he mulled over Fred's advice, he had to admit he was having a tough time letting Amy go the way she wanted him to. He'd never had trouble doing that before, so his newfound reluctance puzzled him. Even with Rachel, once he'd gotten over the initial shock of her bolting like that, he'd counted his blessings that she'd skated before they'd walked down the aisle. Afterward would've been a lot tougher for him to recover from.

Amy was a different story.

She always had been, he realized with a start. As a boy, he'd been awed by her, and when they reconnected as adults, he just picked up where he'd left off. He didn't recall many things from that time in his life, but he'd never forgotten the spritely ballerina with the sparkling eyes and dazzling smile.

Had she remained in his memory all these years for a reason? He'd always believed that God created a match for everyone, and he couldn't deny it was possible Amy was meant to be his. The kicker was, if a relationship between them was ever going to work, one of them would have to do some pretzel-style bending of a fairly strong will.

He wasn't prepared to make that kind of life-altering concession, and Amy had made it clear she wasn't, either. So where did that leave them? His thoughts spiraled downward from there, and by the time he reached his grandparents' house, he was as discouraged as he'd ever been in his life.

As if Granddad's worsening illness wasn't enough, now Jason could add losing Amy to the list. Hands down, this was going to be the worst Christmas ever.

Chapter Ten

After stewing for a while, Amy came to the conclusion that she'd unfairly pummeled Jason with months' worth of frustration and resentment. And God bless him, he'd stood there and taken every blow without either retaliating or backing down. He'd held his ground, making it abundantly clear he was doing it for her own good. She wasn't accustomed to fighting so vigorously with someone and not coming out the winner.

Unfortunately, this time she might have won the argument, but she'd lost the respect of someone who'd come to mean more to her than she'd fully realized until now. Truth be told, Jason had pinpointed some of her reservations so accurately, it had frightened her. And when she was scared, she puffed herself up like a threatened kitten and lashed out with her claws. It wasn't pretty, and she wasn't proud of it, but there it was. He'd treated her with nothing other than kindness and care, and she'd rewarded him with venom.

At the very least, she owed him an apology. The

humble-pie kind best delivered in person. A quick glance at the clock showed her it was still relatively early, and she had plenty of time to go to choir rehearsal, stammer her regret and slink into her usual place in the soprano section.

She knew it was best to get things like this over with, so she pushed away from her desk and reluctantly headed for the front door. The night air was cool but pleasant, and it felt good on her face. The view of Christmas lights and decorations up and down Main Street lifted her spirits considerably, and by the time she reached the Crossroads Church, she felt slightly better about talking with Jason.

He was the most patient, tolerant man she'd ever met, she reassured herself as she climbed the steps. Now that the dust had settled, he must understand how important this opportunity was to her. She only hoped he'd be able to forgive her cold behavior and they could remain friends. Because she had to admit, the shy little girl who still lived inside her adored the burly lumberjack with the generous heart. Perhaps, if they stayed in touch, their paths would intersect again and...

What? Pausing in the vestibule, she took a moment to let that thought play out. Unfortunately, it dead-ended right there, leaving her with a big, unanswered question echoing in her mind. Did she want more than friendship with Jason? Even if she did, he might not feel the same. And if he shared her feelings, how on earth would they make a serious relationship work? Soon, it would be more than distance separating them. She was as driven as he was easygoing, and she'd probably make him nuts within a month.

Then again, she reasoned as she went into the chapel, they'd been working together at the studio all this time and after getting accustomed to each other's vastly different styles, they'd proven to be an excellent team. Then there were those promising kisses under the mistletoe. She wouldn't mind some more of those. The trouble was, she'd learned the hard way that things didn't always go the way she wanted them to. If a romance with Jason went awry, she'd lose him altogether. She didn't even want to consider that.

Left with a thorny problem and no concrete solution, she took her spot next to Brenda and greeted the other singers around her. Jason wasn't there yet, so she distracted herself by admiring the decorations the Ladies' Aid had brought in.

Evergreen ropes were swagged all around the little church, and each windowsill held a rich burgundy poinsettia and an electric candle. On either side of the altar stood a tall tree, decorated in tasteful white lights and velvet ribbons. Each had a crystal star at the top that caught the light, tossing prisms onto the old wooden floorboards. Simple elegance, she thought with a smile. She couldn't imagine a more fitting way to deck out this charming country chapel nestled in the Blue Ridge valley.

Mrs. Griggs called for their attention, and everyone quieted down. A quick glance over at the tenors showed Amy that Jason still hadn't arrived, and she frowned.

As he'd so emphatically told her, he didn't duck his responsibilities, and she worried that something might have happened.

Leaning in, she asked Brenda, "Is everything all right with the Barretts?"

"As far as I know," she whispered back. "If it wasn't, Mom would've heard about it and told us."

Amy didn't doubt that for a second, and as the soprano line picked up their part in "O Holy Night," she decided Jason must be working late to finish one of his many projects at the mill. Christmas was coming up fast, and furniture orders had to be shipped soon to arrive on time. Reassured, she put him out of her mind and focused on accurately hitting as many of the notes as she could.

As a dancer, she'd spent most of her holidays onstage, so the prospect of a Christmas Eve performance was nothing new for her. But back then, she'd been one of the stars, not part of a large group like this. The camaraderie was a novel experience, and she found herself enjoying it more than she'd anticipated.

Much of the time she'd spent back in her hometown had been like that, she realized with a smile. She couldn't recall being this content anywhere else, and she knew Jason had a lot to do with that. With his thoughtful, attentive nature, he'd helped to heal old wounds she hadn't been aware she was still carrying. She only hoped the rest of her stay here would be just as happy.

Before she knew it, rehearsal was over. Mrs. Griggs reminded them all that next week would be their last practice, and they should plan on arriving early Christmas Eve to warm up their voices and do a few runthroughs before the service began.

Eager to put her apology behind her, Amy stopped outside and brought up Jason's number from her list. When he didn't answer, she assumed he was in the noisy workshop and couldn't hear his phone. She wanted to speak to him in person, so she opted not to leave a message. That way, he'd see he missed a call from her and could return it if he wanted to talk to her.

If he didn't...well, at least then she'd know where she stood with him. After the way she'd behaved, she didn't deserve his forgiveness, but she prayed he'd give it to her anyway.

Strolling up the sidewalk toward Arabesque, she noticed a subdued glow in the front window. She'd deliberately left the outside display on, but the studio itself had been dark when she left. Then it occurred to her that Jason must have told Uncle Fred he was going to have to finish the sets for the show. She felt horrible for imposing on a man still nursing an injured back, but she really had no choice.

Hoping to make things easier on him, she picked up her pace and mentally prepared herself to be as helpful as her meager carpentry skills would allow. She unlocked the front door, quieting the bells while she closed it and turned the dead bolt behind her. When she caught the sound of classic rock coming from the stage, she looked over in surprise.

There was Jason, a paintbrush in either hand, applying the faux marble finish she'd chosen for the fireplace. Normally, he looked happy while he was working, but tonight he wore a grim expression, as if he was putting in his time and couldn't wait to leave. That was her fault, but the upside was that since she'd done it, she was the one person who could undo it.

Before she had a chance to reconsider, she walked through the wings and paused behind him. He didn't acknowledge her presence in any way, and she swallowed hard before saying, "That looks really nice."

"It's what you said you wanted," he said, not looking at her as he continued painting. "I'm just following orders."

Flat and emotionless, somehow his words still had a bite to them. At first, she didn't understand why, but she quickly figured it out. Jason always spoke to her with warmth in his voice and a twinkle in his eyes. While she knew the cold shoulder was well deserved, she couldn't bear communicating with him this way. "Could you stop for a minute?"

"I have to keep blending or the paint'll dry the wrong color."

"I don't care."

Pausing midstroke, he angled a look back at her. "Seriously? I thought everything had to be perfect for the show."

"It will be." Hearing the confidence in her tone, she realized she truly meant what she'd said. "You'll make it perfect, because that's what you do."

Setting the brushes across the top of an open can, he stood and faced her. "I try."

"I know you do," she assured him quickly. "Jason, please forgive me for the way I acted yesterday. I was feeling overwhelmed, and I took it out on you. That wasn't fair, and neither was comparing you to Devon. You're nothing like him, and it was wrong of me to accuse you of being otherwise."

Gazing down at her, his eyes shone with compassion. "You're scared about the surgery, aren't you?"

"Terrified," she confirmed on a shaky breath. "But I'm more scared of not giving it a chance. I mean, what if it works?"

"What if it doesn't?"

"That's the problem," she agreed solemnly. "I've never had to make a huge decision like this that could mess up the rest of my life. One minute, I'm sure going ahead with the procedure is the right thing for me, and the next I want to call Dr. Fitzgerald and back out. I'm so confused, it's like I'm spinning in circles."

Grasping one of her hands, he reeled her into his arms and held her tightly against his chest. With his heart beating a steady cadence under her cheek, Amy felt as if nothing in the world could possibly harm her. Part of her wanted nothing more than to stay right where she was, but the tug of a dream left unfulfilled was pulling her in another direction.

Tipping her head back, she gazed up at the man who'd done so much for her. He'd brought the very best part of her back to life, and the thought of leaving him behind was almost more than she could stand.

Cupping her cheek in his callused hand, he leaned in to brush a gentle kiss over her lips. Then he rested his forehead against hers and sighed. "This surgery is really what you want?"

The acceptance in his tone, despite the misgivings he'd so loudly stated, touched her deeply. "Yes, but I'm still petrified."

"That's 'cause you're a smart cookie." He ticked the tip of her nose with his finger. "But if it doesn't work, I hope you know there's always a place for you here in Barrett's Mill."

"With you?" The words slipped out on their own, and she felt her face reddening in embarrassment. When would she learn to think first and blurt later?

Thankfully, Jason met her slipup with a chuckle. "Well, I'm not going anywhere."

It wasn't a yes, but it wasn't a no, either. Normally, she detested getting a wishy-washy maybe, but considering the circumstances, she'd have to take what he was willing to offer her. For now, it was enough to know he didn't hate her and would support her decision, even though he didn't understand it.

Some days, that was the best a girl could hope for.

"There's my girl!" Stepping out of a rented convertible, Connie Morgan all but smothered Amy in an enthusiastic hug. Eyeing her critically, she smiled. "You look wonderful. I wasn't sure you'd like it here after so many years away, but it seems to agree with you."

"Aunt Helen and Uncle Fred have been taking good care of me," Amy replied with a smile of her own. "And it's fun getting to hang out with Brenda again. She always was my favorite cousin."

"Oh, I remember you two when you were little. Always whispering and giggling about one thing or another."

"It's pretty much the same now," Amy told her. "It's just now we talk about her kids instead of all the cool new clothes we want for our Barbies."

"How fun." With an arm still around her shoulders, Mom turned to look at the front of the studio. Amy had left all the decorative lights on, and in the cloudy morning the effect was pretty much the same as at night. "Just beautiful. I especially like the arbor and the tree with all those twinkling lights. They really capture the whimsy of *The Nutcracker.*"

"Have you been reading Broadway reviews again?" Amy teased, hugging her mother back. "I'm glad you like it, but I had a lot of help."

"Jason," Mom said with a knowing look. "I've heard a lot about him, but not from you. I wonder why that is."

A blush crept over Amy's cheeks, and she hedged, "I figured Aunt Helen would tell you everything you needed to know."

"Hometown boy, back from the wilds of Oregon to help save his family's business and yours, besides. He sounds like a hero straight out of a romantic movie."

Amy couldn't agree more, but she hesitated to voice her opinion of him and give her mother the wrong idea. Her relationship with Jason was tentative, at best, and she wasn't at all certain how it would end. Her family had been through so much since her accident, she didn't want to drag them through any more drama.

Then she noticed a familiar green pickup coming up Main Street, and she realized her plan was about to be blown apart. Once her mother saw her with Jason, she'd have to fess up and admit she felt more than friendship for the tall lumberjack. A lot more.

"Is that him?" Mom asked.

"Yes. Please behave yourself."

"Why would you—" He stepped from the cab, and Mom let out a sigh of approval. "Oh, my."

Amy couldn't help grinning, because she felt the same way as he strode toward them. Strong and solid, he moved with an innate confidence that made other men look small by comparison. "Mother, try to remember he's my age."

"Oh, sweetie, I'm just looking," she said airily, then giggled. "And admiring."

"All the girls around here do."

"Do what?" Jason asked as he joined them.

"Think you're a hunk," Amy replied, laughing when he made a face. Resting a hand on her mother's shoulder, she went on. "Jason Barrett, this is my mom, Connie Morgan."

"Pleased to meet you, ma'am," he said, shaking her

hand gently. "I have to say, this is quite the daughter you've raised. You must be real proud of her."

"Every day." Giving him a chiding look, she warned, "But if you call me 'ma'am' again, we're going to have a serious problem."

"Yes, m—Ms. Morgan," he amended with a quick grin.

"Connie."

"All right, then. If you ladies can swing the door for me, I've got the last of the set pieces in my truck. I painted them last night, so they're dry and ready to put in place."

"Last night?" Amy echoed in disbelief. "You mean, after you worked till eleven at the mill?"

"You needed 'em today."

His casual response made his effort sound like it was nothing, but to her it was a very big deal. No one outside her family had ever gone to such lengths for her. Not to mention, he'd kept on working when she'd specifically—and quite rudely—ordered him to stop. She couldn't envision anyone else doing the same, and that he'd persevered in spite of her was remarkable, to say the least.

Mom had discreetly moved away and was making a good show of checking out Arabesque's charming window display. Amy took advantage of the relative privacy to reward her Galahad with her very best smile.

"Yes, I did." Since they were in full view of anyone on Main Street, she stood on tiptoe to kiss his cheek. "Thank you."

Leaning in, Jason murmured, "If I go in and set 'em up right now, can I get another one of those afterward?"

"I think that could be arranged."

That got him moving, and in no time the *Nutcracker* ballroom was complete. Amy went through the wings to the control panel and hollered, "Stand in the audience area and tell me how everything looks from there."

She dimmed the houselights and flipped all the switches connected to the stage. At first, she didn't hear anything from out front, and she feared something had gone wrong.

Then her mother called out, "Amy, it's absolutely perfect! Come see."

Amy hurried out to join them and was thrilled to see Mom was right. Sneaking an arm around Jason's back, she gave him a quick hug. Smiling up at him, she said, "It *is* perfect, and it's all because of you."

"Well, you gave me a book full of detailed instructions," he teased with a grin. "It's pretty hard to miss when someone lays it all out for you."

"I hope the show goes as well," she confided.

"It will," he commented with a reassuring squeeze. "Just have a little faith."

Not long ago, she'd have tightened up if someone had said that to her. Now that she'd found her way back to her Christian roots, his advice settled warmly over her and made her feel more confident about tomorrow's performance. God had brought her back to her tiny hometown for this, she realized. He knew all along this was where she'd find the man who could accept her as she was and help her overcome the crushing disappointment that had stripped her of her dream.

Barrett's Mill had come to mean more to her than she could have expected when she reluctantly returned to take over the struggling studio. Jason in particular had shown her there were selfless people in the world who did what they thought was best for those they cared about, even when it hurt.

While Jason and Mom chatted about the upcoming show, it struck Amy that she'd become quite attached to this alternate life of hers. While it hadn't been her first choice, she now considered it a good option for her. Teaching came with none of the stress of performing, not to mention she could pretty much eat whatever she wanted. With an aunt whose scrumptious family recipes consistently won blue ribbons, that was an important consideration.

With Jason's arm lightly around her shoulders, she recognized that she had two good lives to pick from. One included him and this close-knit community populated by down-to-earth folks who looked out for each other and pitched in without a second thought. The other was filled with bright lights and excitement, both onstage and off.

Which was better for her? A few weeks ago, the answer would have been obvious to her, but now she wasn't so sure. Professional success had always taken precedence over her personal life, and she'd been content that way. That was before she met Jason, though, and learned what it meant to step out of the spotlight and just be herself.

Her thoughts were so jumbled, she felt as if she was standing at the juncture of two vastly different paths. Unaccustomed to being confused about the direction she should take, she sent up a quick prayer for guidance. After all, God had gone to a lot of trouble to lead her back here. Certainly, He knew which course was best for her to follow.

Although she knew better than to expect an immediate response, she couldn't deny being a little disappointed not to get some kind of sign. Apparently, as He'd done before, He believed she could handle this one on her own.

If only she could agree with Him.

Jason had never been so nervous.

Peeking around the side of a velvet curtain, he noticed the seating area in front of the stage was even fuller than it had been the last time he checked. At her post near the door, Brenda Lattimore greeted each person brightly, taking their money and handing them one of the parchment tickets Amy had designed and printed herself. Elegant but understated, just like the woman moving through the crowd, welcoming her guests and wishing them a fun afternoon.

As if they could help it, he thought with a grin. The ballroom behind him glowed with the subtle lighting he'd installed, ready to be cranked up to full wattage once the kids were in their places onstage. For now, classical Christmas music was playing quietly over the speakers, and he checked the notes Amy had given him—again—with his cues for switching tracks to Tchaikovsky and when to open and close the curtains.

If he messed this up for her, he'd kick himself until the Fourth of July. Assuming her surgery went the way she hoped, this would be Arabesque's one and only production. While he was usually laid-back about things, this time he wanted everything to be perfect.

He was starting to sound like Amy, he chided himself, taking a deep breath to calm his nerves. After one last glance, he folded the paper and slid it into the inside pocket of his only suit jacket. Then he closed his eyes and pictured the kids taking their bows after a stellar performance, the audience standing and clapping in appreciation.

It was a visualization trick Granddad had taught him when he was a young pitcher about to face a particularly tough batter, and it had always worked. That reminded him to check that the tripod and video camera were still centered behind the rows of chairs. Since his grandparents weren't able to attend the show, he'd promised to record it and watch the video with them later. While it was a good solution, it only highlighted how frail his grandfather's health was, and that each day they had with him was precious.

Because it just might be the last.

Pushing those negative thoughts aside, Jason focused on Amy. She'd finished her rounds and caught his eye with an elegant nod. Giving her a thumbs-up, he went into the wings and dimmed the houselights, then brought them back up the way she'd requested. Folding his hands to keep them from shaking, he stood ready while she made her way onto the stage and waited for folks to find their seats and quiet down.

Extending her arms in a graceful dancer's pose, she said, "Welcome, everyone, to Arabesque. For those of you who don't know me, I'm Amy Morgan. My mother, Connie, and my aunt Helen—" she smiled at the beaming women seated front and center with Fred "—nourished my love of dance from the time I was a child. I'm honored to have had the opportunity to do the same with the group of very talented children you'll be seeing today."

A ripple of giggles passed behind the curtain, and Jason smothered a grin as he stepped in and made the cut sign across his throat. Kids. What could you do?

"And so, it's with great pride that the Arabesque dance company presents to you our version of Tchaikovsky's beloved holiday ballet, *The Nutcracker.*"

That was his first cue, and Jason pulled the ropes that lifted the velvet drapes to bracket the dimly lit stage. After counting three Mississippis, he gradually increased the ballroom lights with one hand and brightened the tree decorations with the other. Somehow, he managed to accomplish that at the same rate so they all came up together the way they were supposed to.

Glancing across to the other wing area, he got a brilliant smile and the okay sign from Amy. Apparently, the producer was a little edgy, too, he mused. It was nice to know he wasn't the only one.

Since there were no adults in the production, willowy Heidi Peterson took her brightly colored wooden nutcracker from under the tree, floating around the stage with a delighted look on her face. As she went, she tossed in some exuberant jumps that reminded Jason of the pictures of Amy in her younger days. Judging by the nostalgic smile on her face, she was thinking the same thing.

Someday, he hoped to see that kind of joy in her again.

That thought caught him completely by surprise, and he did his best to shake it off and concentrate. Once Amy left for New York, the chances of him seeing her again were remote, at best. She'd be there for a while, rehabbing and then doing whatever it took to rejoin the world she'd so unwillingly left behind.

And he'd be in Barrett's Mill, a million miles from the glitz and glamour she seemed to thrive on. He'd come to the conclusion that they wanted completely different things, and even if he could figure out what she needed to be truly happy, he had no clue how to make it happen.

The best he could do was hit all his marks today and do his part to make the show a success. After that, they'd celebrate the holiday with their families, and too soon it would be time to say goodbye. He'd been through many farewells in his life, and normally he accepted them as being for the best.

But this one would be different. Because hard as he'd tried not to let it happen, when Amy left, she'd be taking a piece of his heart with her.

The kids were doing a fabulous job. The trouble was, it was only intermission, and there were plenty of things that could still go wrong. First on the list: Brad's solo dance. He attacked it with the aggressiveness of an eight-year-old boy, and his delivery was still more pirate than prince, but Amy had finally decided to let him do it his own way. After all, the audience was made up of friends and family members. They'd love it no matter what he did.

While the show would be a nice end to the studio's fiscal year, to Amy the most important thing was for her students to get a taste of classical dance and discover they enjoyed it. Hopefully enough to continue taking classes and someday expose their own children to what Amy had adored ever since she could remember. Glancing over at the framed pictures on the wall brought to mind the excitement of the lights and being onstage, the fun of exploring a different world for a little while. Those were the elements she recalled most fondly from her own childhood as a performer.

Oddly enough, the photos that used to make her sad now filled her with pride. Was it because she believed the new surgery could bring her back to that place? Or—

"They're doing great," Jason said as he hurried out from backstage. "How're you holding up?"

Only Jason would think to ask how she was faring, when she technically wasn't even a part of the show. His unerring thoughtfulness had touched her so many times, she'd lost track of the number. "I'm fine, thanks to you. Have you ever worked in a theater before?"

"Nah, I just catch on fast."

His hazel eyes twinkled at her with a little boy's enthusiasm, and she couldn't help laughing. "Lumberjack, carpenter, stage manager. Is there anything you can't do?"

"Actually, there is. I never learned how to waltz."

She laughed again and patted his arm. "I think I can help you with that before I go."

"I'm good at scaling trees, but music and counting steps aren't really my thing." Moving closer, he murmured, "I might need more attention than most of your students."

That sounded promising, she mused with a smile. But they were surrounded by people who were listening in while trying to appear engaged in their own conversations. Not to mention Brenda was at the snack table, and she'd been keeping an eye on them since Jason appeared. "I'm sure we can work something out. After tonight, the studio will be closing for the holidays, and I'll have time for a private lesson."

"How 'bout two?"

Oh, he was hard to resist, this towering man with the gentle heart. Endearing and determined all at once, with seemingly no effort at all, he'd reached the part of her that had shut down after her accident. The part that still looked eagerly into the future and believed that anything was possible if she wanted it badly enough.

Staring up at this incredibly generous man who'd drawn her out of herself and back into the world, she felt the tug of a new dream. One that had stubbornly wrapped itself around him and refused to let go. In the past, she never could have imagined something being more important to her than dancing. But now, here he was, standing in front of her with undisguised hope shining in his eyes. And in a flash of understanding, it hit her.

Jason wanted her to stay. He couldn't say that in front of all these people, of course, but his silent message was unmistakable. Shaken by that realization, she blurted, "Intermission is almost over. We should round up the kids for the dream scene."

"You got it, boss."

Flashing her a confident grin, he trotted up the steps and disappeared backstage. His cavalier behavior puzzled her, but she didn't have time to dissect it right now. Heading to the opposite wing, she gathered her troupe of flowers and sugar-plum fairies together, tweaking their costumes and making sure everyone had their slippers on the right feet.

When she met up with Brad, she stood in front of him and smiled. "You look awesome."

In his jaunty costume, with its plumed hat and rows of shiny gold buttons, he was a hybrid of toy soldier and swashbuckler. She congratulated herself on allowing him to wear his own black boots rather than dance shoes. After getting a fresh coat of polish, they topped off his outfit with jaunty style.

"Now, remember," she whispered while they waited for his entrance. "Clara's made of glass. Spin her gently."

"Okay," he squeaked, clearly anxious about his big solo.

Whenever someone told her not to be nervous, it only intensified her fear, so Amy gave his shoulders an encouraging shake. "Go on out there and show them what you've got."

Nodding, he entered the scene, tentatively at first, but growing more confident with each stride. By the time he reached the spotlight for his dance, his motions were fluid and right on the mark. She mentally took each step with him, willing him to remember them all. When he finished with a triumphant flourish, it looked more like a touchdown sign than ballet, but she couldn't possibly have cared less.

The audience broke into thunderous applause, and she motioned for the rest of the cast to hold their positions while Brad took a couple of impromptu bows. This was what it was all about, she thought as she traded thumbs-ups with Jason across the stage. As much as she loved performing, there was a unique satisfaction in teaching others those skills and watching them fly.

From that point on, the show flowed through the rest of Clara's dream, ending when she woke up back in the ballroom, asleep under the Christmas tree, clutching her beloved nutcracker. The curtains were still closing when the audience jumped to their feet, cheering and clapping, more than a few loudly whistling their appreciation.

Amy quickly assembled the cast behind the curtain, so overcome with joy, she had to steady her voice before speaking. "You guys are amazing," she praised them with a huge smile. "Now it's curtain-call time, but forget about what we practiced. Just go out there and have fun."

They all cheered at her suggestion, and she motioned for Jason to pull the curtains. To her surprise, though, the kids didn't run forward to ham it up in front of their adoring fans. Instead, they surrounded her in a group hug, moving her forward with them. Caught off guard, she had no choice but to follow along, fighting back a flood of tears that threatened to spill over.

She'd thought the crowd had been raucous enough before, but apparently they'd been holding back. People stood on their chairs, whooping and whistling, cheering for her along with the children. In all her years of performing, she'd never experienced anything like it. She chanced a look into the wings and saw Jason wearing a huge grin, clapping for all he was worth. When she motioned for him to come out, he shook his head and stayed put.

Despite all the work he'd done to make the show a success, he was refusing to share in the credit. He understood how much it meant to her, and he was willingly staying in the shadows to give her this moment in the spotlight. Jason was the first man she'd ever met who was secure enough to step back and allow some-one else to shine.

Something told her it would be a long time before she met another one.

"Well, that about does it," Jason announced when he returned from packing up his truck. "All I have to do is hide that arbor from Gram for a few more days."

"What do you think she'll say when she finds out her Christmas present has been in full view of everyone in town all this time?" Amy asked.

"She'll laugh and tell me how clever I am, of course."

"Of course," Amy echoed, taking stock of their dismantling project. Without its holiday finery, Arabesque's facade had regained its classy, understated appearance. The effect should have pleased her, but for some reason it made her sad.

Jason must have noticed her expression, because he strolled over to stand beside her. "It looks nice."

"I guess," she allowed with a sigh. "I miss my nut-cracker, though."

"You could take him to New York with you, like a souvenir."

Frowning, Amy shook her head. "Mom's apartment is pretty tiny, and I'll be staying with her for a while. He really belongs here, anyway."

The words rattled around in her head after she'd spo-ken them, making her wonder if the same sentiment ap-plied to her. As the days passed and she faced the reality of leaving Barrett's Mill—and Jason—the temptation to stay grew stronger. Was it fear of the unknown? she wondered. Or was it something deeper than that?

"Hey, I've got an idea," Jason said, breaking the silence. When she looked at him, he grinned. "You don't have any more classes to teach, right?"

"No, we're done until after New Year's."

"Maybe now's a good time for that waltzing lesson we talked about."

Clearly, he was trying to distract her, to make her feel better about her questionable future. While she would have loved to spend some more time with him, she hesitated to torture them both with it. "Are you sure? I mean, you must have things to do out at the mill."

"Nothing that can't wait. Even my slave driver of a brother is letting up a little, now that all the holiday orders have gone out. Today, he and Chelsea are finishing up their Christmas shopping."

"Two days before?" Amy asked. "Are they crazy?"

"Tell me about it," he agreed with a laugh. "I wouldn't go near a mall right now."

The lighthearted exchange eased some of her concern, and she smiled. "Then it sounds like the ideal time for a dance lesson. As long as you have some other shoes to wear," she added with a glance down at the battered work boots on his feet.

"My church shoes are in my truck."

Church shoes, she thought with a little grin. He was so adorable sometimes. Then she caught on and narrowed her eyes with suspicion. "You planned on doing this now, didn't you?"

"Um…yeah."

He gave her a shameless grin, and she had to laugh. "Why on earth would you go to so much trouble? You've done so much for me, all you had to do was ask me for a lesson and I'd have gone along."

The grin widened, joined by the twinkling eyes that had captivated her more times than she could count. "It's more fun this way."

There was no point arguing with that, and she shook her head. "Okay, go get your shoes. I'll meet you inside."

By the time he joined her, she'd cued up several waltz tracks on the stereo system. She'd already changed into dance shoes, so she took the opportunity to watch him do the same. For someone his size, he moved with an easy grace that had always impressed her. She'd seen those hands swing a hammer and tie a child's sneakers with equal skill, bringing a large measure of care to whatever task he chose.

He was such a remarkable man, she thought wistfully. Was she making a huge mistake walking away from him for some vague chance at normalcy?

When he stood to face her, his eager expression dimmed considerably. "What's wrong?"

"Nothing," she hedged, forcing optimism into her voice. "Just thinking about the traffic in New York."

"Busy, huh?" When she nodded, he said, "I'm sure you'll get used to it again in no time."

It was the perfect thing for him to say, of course, upbeat and positive. That was his nature, she'd come to realize, the way God had wired him so he could have a good life despite his rocky start. For the first time, she envied someone else's temperament, because being more easygoing would make things so much easier for her.

But maybe that wasn't the point, she mused while she fiddled with the music. Maybe God was giving her what she needed, too, but she was missing the big picture. Hopefully, when she was back in the environment she was more accustomed to, it would all make sense.

For now, she had a lesson to give, and she turned to her eager student with a reassuring smile. "This won't hurt a bit."

"Not me, anyway," he commented with a chuckle. "I'll do my best not to squash those pretty little feet of yours."

When the music came on the speakers, he said, "Hey, I know this. It's from my niece's favorite Disney movie."

"*Sleeping Beauty* is another ballet by Tchaikovsky," she told him. "It's one of my favorites, too."

"Nice. Okay, what's first?"

She instructed him on how to stand, guiding his arm around her back while she put her hand in his. It looked like a child's hand nestled there, and the gentle way he held it made her heart sigh in contentment. Gazing up at him, she saw the same emotion playing over his face, lighting his eyes with the look she'd come to adore.

This was dangerous territory for two friends gamely trying to avoid getting entangled in something deeper that would end in a few days. The trouble was, being this close to him had fogged her mind so thoroughly, she was having a hard time remembering how the very simple dance began.

Once they got started, her training took over and she talked him through the rhythmic progression until he'd grasped it well enough to lead. "Don't count. Let the music flow through you and move your feet for you."

"Is that how it feels when you dance?" he asked with a curious look. When she nodded, he said, "I never really understood until just now. What's it like to just let go and follow where the music goes?"

"Amazing," she responded without even thinking. "It feels like you're part of something beautiful that takes you in and makes you special, too."

"Now I see why you miss it so much, why you want to get back to what you love. For you, it's like going home."

Astounded by his insight, she confided, "I'm happiest when I'm onstage. I always have been."

"It's where you belong. I noticed that during the show, when you were in the spotlight with the kids. You looked right out there."

"Is that why you stopped asking me to stay?" She'd resisted bringing up a sore subject, but since they were being so truthful with each other, it seemed like a good time.

"Yeah," he admitted with a heavy sigh. "That night after everything was over, it hit me that if I managed to convince you to forget about the surgery, you'd always wonder how your life would've been if you'd gone ahead with it. Sooner or later, you would've resented me for standing in your way and you'd hate me."

"I could never, ever hate you." Shaking his arms, she made sure she had his full attention before going on. "You weren't trying to stop me out of selfishness, but out of concern for me. I know that, and I appreciate it more than I can ever say."

"Yeah, I'm a real prince," he muttered.

"To me, you are." Part of her longed to ease his frown with a kiss, but she didn't want to muddy the friendship waters with such an intimate gesture. Instead, she reset her frame and smiled. "Would you like to try it one more time?"

He didn't respond at first, standing in front of her with his hands at his sides while he thought it over. She was keenly aware of how he must feel, wanting more time with her even though he knew it would only hurt more later when they had to say goodbye to each other. She felt the same way, and it was all she could do to put on a brave face while she waited for him to figure out what he wanted to do.

"Sure," he finally agreed, stepping into the position she'd shown him. "It's not every day a guy like me gets a private dance lesson with such a pretty teacher."

"Flattery will get you everywhere, Mr. Barrett," she simpered, batting her eyelashes for effect. "But my hourly rate is still the same."

Grinning, he retorted, "Seeing as I'm not paying you, does that mean I'm getting my money's worth?"

"I guess that's for you to decide."

The tense moment had passed, and she was relieved that their usual camaraderie had kicked back in. Although she enjoyed the next hour with him very much, the entire time a voice in the back of her mind was whispering to her:

Can you really leave all this behind?

Chapter Eleven

"I'm not sure about this," Rachel fretted when she and Jason arrived at the Crossroads Church on Christmas Eve. Standing in the entryway, she peered anxiously into the sanctuary dressed in its holiday finery and filled with people. "I mean, look at me."

She held out her arms, and Jason obliged by giving her a quick once-over. Since she'd been able to get more rest and eat properly, she looked much healthier than when she'd first arrived in town. *Plumper* was the description that came into his mind, but he figured that was the last thing a lady who was eight months pregnant wanted to hear. "I think you look nice. Is that dress new?"

Judging by her quick grin, she'd picked up on the fact that he'd sidestepped the obvious source of her concern. "When she was in town the other day, your sister-in-law Anne brought me a couple bags of maternity clothes. It was really generous of her to do that, considering."

"No one in my family considers all that except you.

You're here now, and you've got a little person on the way. That's what matters to those folks in there," he chided her with a nod toward the open doors.

"I guess I'll have to take your word on that one."

"I've never lied to you, and I never will."

After a few more seconds, she let out a deep breath. "Okay. I'm ready."

"No one's perfect, Rachel," he reminded her gently. "What we do after our mistakes is what's most important."

"You're such a good guy," she said as they walked inside together. "I hope Amy knows that."

She did, but it wasn't enough. He was a straightforward country boy, and apparently he didn't have what it took to compete with her lifelong love of dancing. Hopefully, before too long he'd come to terms with that and be able to think of her fondly. Right now, though, knowing he didn't measure up made him wish he had more to offer her. Since he didn't, he was going to have to swallow his objections and let her go.

He escorted Rachel to the section where his family was sitting in a group across two pews. Like the gentleman he'd raised them all to be, Dad stood and moved into the aisle. "Would you like to join us, Rachel? We've got a seat right here for you."

Eyes wide with gratitude, she nodded in reply and slid in next to Jason's mother. Putting an arm around their guest the way she did with everyone she met, Mom said, "Merry Christmas Eve, honey. How are you and the baby doing these days?"

"Dr. Peterson says we're both fine," Rachel answered politely. "Thank you for asking."

"We always have a gathering back at the house after church," Mom continued. "If you're not too tired, we'd love to have you come by for a while."

Rachel cast a hesitant look at Jason, and he said, "No one should be alone at Christmas, Rachel. It's up to you, though."

Clearly overwhelmed by the gesture, she looked from one of his parents to the other with a faint smile. "That sounds wonderful. Thank you again."

Satisfied, Jason left Rachel chatting with his family, trusting them to make sure she wouldn't feel like an outsider in the congregation full of strangers. Then he yanked his nicely knotted tie off to the side and trotted up the risers. Moving carefully through the rapidly filling row, he landed at the opposite end of the tenor section from where he normally stood. That put him next to the sopranos. And Amy.

She gave him a curious look, and he grinned back. "Hey there."

"Hey yourself." The beautiful smile she gave him drove the last of his sadness away, at least for now. "Did you come over here for a reason?"

"To tell you how incredible you look in that dress. Green's my favorite color, y'know." She didn't respond, and he shook his head with a chuckle. "Let me guess. Chelsea filled you in."

"Maybe, but I bought the dress. Was that all you needed?"

His strategy for getting a few moments with her had slipped his mind, but he quickly recovered. "Mom's busy, and my tie's gone all wonky. Think you can help me out?"

"You mean, the tie you yanked out of place on your way up here?" she teased as she went up a step so she could reach to pull it loose and start over.

"Busted," he admitted with a laugh, pleased to hear her join in.

She quickly got serious, though. "I see Rachel's here."

Here we go again, he thought with a sigh. "I know you won't be crazy about this, but I invited her to come tonight, and Mom asked her over to the house afterward. She's got no one else to spend Christmas with."

"So she's celebrating it with you," Amy sniped in a tone that made it clear she liked the idea even less than he'd anticipated.

"Not really."

"How do you figure that?"

"I'm spending mine with you," he told her with a smile. "Rachel's just gonna be one of the hundred or so guests at my grandparents' party tonight."

After taking a moment to absorb that, her expression softened and she continued in a less combative tone, "It was nice of you to seat her with your family. I mean, if anyone can understand what she's going through, it'll be your mom."

Considering how she felt about Rachel, Amy's generosity amazed him. "I thought so, too. But I'm glad you get it."

"Oh, I do," she assured him with a quick laugh. "I'm still not wild about the whole thing, but I get it."

In his mind, he heard Fred Morgan grousing about the women in his family being able to drive a man straight over the edge. Now that Jason had firsthand knowledge of it, he marveled at how the mechanic had remained his easygoing self all these years. With a grin, he said, "Guess I'll just have to take what I can get."

"Hold it right there," Brenda ordered, lining up a shot with her camera phone. Checking the result, she sighed. "You two are just too adorable."

Ignoring her cousin, Amy finished shoring up his tie and tapped his nose with her finger. "All set."

"Thanks." They'd never been level with each other this way, and judging by the smirk on her face, she found it as amusing as he did. "You like being as tall as me, don't you?"

Glancing around the church, she said, "It's quite the view from up here, isn't it?"

"Yeah, it is."

Those incredible eyes came back to him, glimmering with something he'd never seen in them until tonight. Not tears, he realized, but emotion. A mixture of joy and sorrow, the same as he was feeling. Fortunately, the pastor walked through the door behind the altar into the chapel, and Mrs. Griggs motioned for the choir to take their places.

Jason offered Amy a hand down, keeping her hand in

his until she was standing beside him again. And then, reluctantly, he released her. The wistful look she gave him must have mirrored his own, and he dredged up a grin, hoping to make her feel better. She responded with a flicker of her usual smile, and then it was time for them to sing.

Normally, the Christmas Eve service was his favorite one of the entire year. Filled with warmth and hope for a better future, it encompassed all the things his family had taught him to value. But this time, even Pastor Griggs's touching sermon on God's never-ending love for His children wasn't enough to lift Jason's spirits.

All he could think of was Amy leaving. And how empty his life was going to feel without her in it.

Following the service, Amy and Jason began a leisurely stroll toward his grandparents' house. Diane had flown from the church with Rachel and everyone else in tow, hurrying back to make certain everything would be ready for the Christmas Eve party that was apparently an annual Barrett tradition.

"I wish they would've let me help," Amy ventured to break the silence.

"Someone must've told them you can't cook."

The sarcastic edge on his voice clued her in that he'd been the one to warn them off, but she really couldn't blame him. He didn't want her poisoning his family during the holidays. Totally understandable. "I could carry dishes in to stock the buffet or wrangle kids or something."

Smiling down at her, he took her hand gently in his much larger one. "You're coming as my guest. Guests are supposed to relax and enjoy themselves."

Returning that smile came so naturally to her now, she could barely recall feeling self-conscious around him. But she had, and he'd patiently drawn her out, encouraging her, cheering her on, until she'd learned to trust him without question. When they reached the square, she paused to admire the town's tree one last time.

"Do you remember the Starlight Festival?" she asked.

Chuckling, he wrapped an arm loosely around her shoulders. "Sure. It was the best one ever 'cause you were there."

Blushing at the compliment, she nearly swallowed what she wanted to say next. But she forged ahead because there was something very important she wanted him to know. Turning, she met his eyes, saw the honest affection he felt for her twinkling warmly in them.

"That night, I told you things I haven't shared with anyone, not even my mother. You didn't even blink, just accepted everything about me the way it was. Your attitude made me believe other people could do the same, and I'll always be grateful to you for doing that."

"Since we're here—" he reached into the pocket of his suit jacket "—I have something for you. I was planning to give it to you later, but this seems like the right place for it."

Amy took the small box wrapped in shiny gold paper, then fished in her purse for the one she'd brought for him. They looked similar, and he laughed. "I hope they're not the same thing."

"Me, too."

They tore their gifts open at the same time, and Amy opened her box with a little creak. Inside, on a cushion of burgundy velvet, she found a pair of crystal earrings fashioned into multifaceted stars. They looked remarkably like the sterling-silver tie tack she'd gotten for him, and she couldn't help laughing. "We seem to have similar taste in jewelry."

"Does that mean you like 'em?" In answer, she reached up and drew his face to hers for a grateful kiss. She felt his lips quirk into one of those grins, and he murmured, "I really like the way you say thank-you."

Gathering her into his arms, he gave her a longer, deeper kiss. Savoring the warmth of being surrounded by him, she had a hunch the effect of those stolen kisses would linger far past Christmas Eve. Footsteps approached them, and she knew without looking who'd stopped to say hello.

"Nice tree, isn't it?" Uncle Fred asked in a casual tone that did little to mask his true purpose for pausing here at that exact moment.

Eyes still locked on her, Jason replied, "Very nice."

"So we'll see you at the Barretts' party, then," Aunt Helen chimed in.

"Oh, leave them be," Mom scolded, shooing them away. To Amy, she whispered, "It's a beautiful night for stargazing. You two just take your time."

She continued on with her brother and sister-in-law

in tow, and Jason commented, "I guess they've got us pegged."

"I'm so glad we got some time together before I have to go." Resting her hand on his jaw, she frowned as the impact of her choice hit her full force. "I'm really going to miss you."

"You could stay," he suggested in a voice tinged with hope. He hadn't done that recently, and the temptation to say yes was so strong, she didn't trust herself to speak. When she didn't respond, he sighed. "But that would mean you'd have to give up on ever dancing again."

"I pray someday you'll understand why I'm doing this."

"I already do," he muttered as he stepped away from her. "That's what makes it so hard for me. I want you here, but I want you to be happy even more. If that means you have to go somewhere else, I'll just have to learn to live with it."

He took her hand again, and they walked the rest of the way in silence. Blinking back tears, Amy wished she was one of those people who could be satisfied with second best. She'd always considered her unrelenting drive to be an asset. Accompanied by years of hard work, it had propelled her to heights most people could only imagine, and she was tremendously proud of what she'd accomplished as a performer.

But tonight, seeing how much her ambition was hurting someone she cared about, she was beginning to have her doubts.

Even before they reached Will and Olivia's house,

she could see it was lit up like one of Macy's famous holiday window displays. Cars lined both sides of the street, and the sounds of laughing conversation mixed with Christmas music floated out on the night air.

People were standing on the front porch with food and drinks, and through the open front door she saw dozens more in the dining room. "Half the town must be here!"

"It's Christmas Eve," he said, as if that explained everything.

"Are you sure this isn't too much for your grandparents?"

"It's just what they need," he assured her as they went up the front steps. "Too much quiet drives 'em bonkers, and besides, we always do the party here. After the kids open their gifts at home in the morning, everyone comes back here for lunch and presents."

Since moving away, she and Mom had quietly celebrated the holidays together, so Amy wasn't used to large family gatherings like this one. What Jason described struck her as something out of a classic Christmas movie, and she smiled. "It sounds perfect."

"Not really. Something goes wrong at one point or another, but we have a lotta fun."

Bulldozing ahead of her, he made a path for her to follow to a buffet table loaded down with roast beef, all manner of veggies, three varieties of homemade rolls and three of the biggest hams she'd ever seen. It took a while for them to get through the line, but every morsel smelled as if it would be totally worth the wait. Once they had their food, Jason angled his way into the living room, where they found Will and Olivia in the place of honor near the tree.

"Here they are," Olivia announced, as if they'd been waiting all night just to see the two of them. "I told you they'd be along soon."

"I hope you took this lovely girl for a stroll," Will said with a wink at his youngest grandson.

"Yes, sir. Just like you taught me."

While they chatted back and forth, the fondness that rippled between Jason and the grandparents who'd taken him into their hearts was touching to see. Raised with so much love around him, it took very little effort to picture him with a family of his own someday. Enjoying the holidays, honoring the faith that was such an important part of who he was.

The woman he chose to share that life with him would be blessed beyond measure. Surrounded by the warmth of the Barrett family's traditional Christmas, Amy only wished there was some way that woman could be her.

"I look like death warmed over," Amy complained as she scowled into the hallway mirror in her mother's chic Manhattan apartment. "When I go to the hospital for my physical tomorrow, they're going to think I'm sick or something."

Mom, who was whipping up some dinner for them, stepped out of her galley kitchen for a look. When she frowned, Amy knew her concerns were on the mark. "I hate to say this, sweetie, but you look like you haven't slept since we left Barrett's Mill."

She hadn't, at least not very well. She spent most of her nights tossing and turning, her mind going over and over all the things that could go wrong with her surgery. As if that wasn't enough, when she tried to conjure up something more pleasant so she could rest, the space behind her eyes filled with Jason's face.

Jason grinning at her, laughing with her at something one of the kids had done, gazing down at her with that adoring look she'd give anything to see one more time. She'd expected that longing to gradually fade, but instead it was getting stronger. She missed his strong presence and the comforting knack he had for showing up just when she needed him.

Quite honestly, she was having second thoughts about her decision to reclaim some of her past. Because that part of her life had nothing to do with him, as the days dragged by she was beginning to think that might not be what she wanted anymore.

Wiping her hands on a towel, Mom settled on one of the stools at the stylish breakfast bar that separated her kitchen from the small living area overlooking the city. Amy had always loved that view, but over the past few months she'd grown accustomed to trees and sprawling, old-fashioned houses, with plenty of open space to roam around in.

"Come talk to me," her mother nudged, patting the other stool. "Tell me what's wrong."

"Everything." Suddenly, she felt as if she was ten

again, trudging home from a rough day at school or rehearsal. Climbing onto the stool, she fought the impulse to drop her head onto the counter and weep. "Mostly, I'm confused."

"About?"

"Everything," Amy repeated ruefully. Realizing she wasn't being very helpful, she searched for words to explain how she was feeling. "I'm not sure what I want anymore."

"Because of Jason?" When Amy nodded, Mom gave her a wise smile. "He's a wonderful young man. I wasn't in town that long, but I could see how much he cares for you. Do you feel the same way about him?"

Amy nodded, tears welling in her eyes. "At first, he was completely against me trying this procedure because it's so risky. But after a while, he realized how important it was to me and said he just wanted me to be happy."

"What a generous thing to do. It's not everyone who can put their own feelings aside and do what's best for someone else."

"I know," Amy responded, more miserable than ever. "What do you think I should do?"

Standing, Mom went over the coatrack and grabbed their jackets. "I think we should take a walk. Let's get some lattes and go to Rockefeller Center."

"I don't think—"

"Don't argue with your mother," she scolded with a wink. "Just put your coat on and let's go."

By the time they'd stopped for coffees and made

their way to the holiday hub of New York, the knots in Amy's thoughts had begun to loosen up a bit. They strolled along, admiring the decorations and watching the skaters on the ice rink below. They chatted about the after-Christmas sales and whether the forecast for a dusting of snow would prove accurate or not. Basically, they discussed any topic that had absolutely nothing to do with Amy's dilemma, and she welcomed the distraction.

When they reached the walkway near the famous tree, they paused for a few moments. This time last year, Amy had been deep into her rehab and couldn't make the trek here, so it had been a while since she'd last seen it. The tree itself was enormous, strung with thousands of lights and topped with a custom-made star spun from the finest crystal in the world.

But to her surprise, it had lost some of the appeal it once held for her. Instead, she was recalling a more modest version, tucked into a square in a Blue Ridge town so small, most outsiders had no idea it even existed. Her memory flashed to Christmas Eve with Jason, and she fingered one of the earrings he'd given her. Thinking back over their time together, she found herself wishing she could rewind to that heartwarming evening and make it last just a little longer. And that was when she knew.

She was in love with Jason Barrett.

Despite the fact that they had almost nothing in common, somehow they'd forged a bond that still connected them across hundreds of miles. She longed to hear his mellow drawl, see the twinkle in his eyes when he looked at her. Mostly, she wanted to be circled in his arms, the place where she felt treasured and safe.

"I'm going back," she blurted, hesitantly eyeing her mother to gauge her reaction. When she got a knowing smile, she let out a relieved breath. "You knew that, didn't you?"

"I was hoping you'd come to that. What changed your mind?"

"My heart," she answered simply. "I love Jason, and I want to be with him."

"Life doesn't always go the way we want it to. What will you do if things don't work out between you two?"

"They will. I'll make sure of it."

"That's my girl." Laughing, Mom hugged her around her shoulders. "Let's go make some reservations."

Amy stared at her in disbelief. "Does that mean you're coming with me?"

"Are you kidding? I wouldn't miss this for the world."

"Jason," Chelsea said from the open doorway that led to the front of the mill house. "It's New Year's Eve. What are you doing here?"

Keeping his eyes on the gears he was oiling, he asked, "What are *you* doing here? Shouldn't you and Paul be doing the dressing-up thing for Mom's shindig tonight?"

"Olivia sent me to find you." Coming into the production area, she sat down on a nearby stool and waited for him to look up at her. "She's worried about you, and frankly, so am I. You haven't been yourself since Amy left."

The sound of her name set off a twisting sensation in his chest, and he winced. "I thought I'd skip this one. I'm not really in a celebrating mood."

"I sympathize with you, but this party is important to the family. You know that."

That knot tightened even more, and he swallowed hard around the lump in his throat. He'd never known his birth parents, and his adoptive grandfather was dying. Add to that the sense of loss he felt over Amy, and it was almost more than he could bear. Even his natural optimism wasn't enough to overcome the clouds hanging over him these days.

Looking over at Chelsea, seeing the compassion in her eyes, he relented with a sigh. "Okay, I'll be there."

She gave him an encouraging smile, then stood and folded her hands, waiting. When he realized what she was up to, he had to chuckle. "You're gonna follow me into town, aren't you?"

"Yes, I am."

"Does that work with my big brother when you want him to do something?" Jason asked as he flipped off lights on their way out the front door.

She gave him a proud, feminine smile. "Yes, it does. But don't tell him I said so. He likes thinking all those things are his idea."

They both laughed, and Jason was in a slightly better frame of mind by the time they reached his grandparents' house. They went in through the kitchen, and after greeting his mom, he took the back stairs three at a time to go up to his room and change into something more presentable for company.

Dressed and ready for the evening ahead, he took the front stairs and pulled up short halfway down.

"Amy?"

Like a vision straight out of his dreams, she balanced a dainty hand on the old newel post and bathed him in the most incredible smile he'd ever seen. She didn't say anything, but the emotions shining in her eyes were enough to make him nearly trip over his own feet as he hurried down the rest of the steps.

Although he knew people were watching them, he took her in his arms for a long, grateful hug. Holding her away, he looked her over to make sure he was really awake. "What are you doing here?"

"It's New Year's Eve," she replied, as if that should've been obvious to him. She placed a hand on his cheek, and this smile had a melancholy quality to it. "I missed you."

No one outside his family had ever gone to so much trouble to do something for him, and it touched him in a way he'd never expected. It was far from midnight, but he didn't care. Reeling her back in, he gave her a long-overdue kiss. Resting his forehead on hers, he murmured, "I missed you, too."

"Why didn't you call and tell me?"

"I didn't want you to think I was going back on my word, trying to convince you to live here and run the studio."

Tilting her head with a curious expression, she asked, "And now?"

"I love you," he answered instinctively, not stopping to consider how crazy it would sound to her. "I know it hasn't been that long, and you probably want to get to know me better—"

She interrupted him with a finger over his lips. "You, Jason Barrett, are the sweetest, kindest man I've ever met. I think I fell in love with you that first day, when you stepped in to rescue my show and fix all the things that were wrong in my apartment. It just took me a while to realize it."

Jason was so stunned by her revelation, he hardly dared to believe it. "You mean, all those arguments we had were for nothing?"

"They were fun," she corrected him with a playful grin. "Most folks back down when I get stubborn, but you roll up your sleeves and keep on fighting. I like that about you."

"Go figure."

It sounded to him as if she'd made some kind of decision, that this was more than a quick visit for a kiss at midnight. Trying to curb his excitement, he asked, "When do you head back for your surgery?"

"I gave it a lot of thought while I was gone," she confided. "But dancing isn't the right thing for me anymore. Being here is what I want."

Something more was sparkling in her eyes, and he took a shot. "With me?"

"With you."

As they stood there smiling at each other, a flash went off, and he saw Amy's mom checking the screen on her camera phone. Beaming, she gave them a quick wave and sauntered into the kitchen. Judging by his mother's delighted reaction, she liked the result, too.

"You'll have to excuse her," Amy said with a sigh. "Her picture's next to the definition of *hopeless romantic* in the dictionary."

They both laughed, and it occurred to him that he was the only one there who was surprised to see her. Now Gram sending someone to fetch him from the mill made total sense. "Gram knew you were here, didn't she?"

"Yes. I wanted to make sure she and Will were okay with me crashing the party."

"So you just assumed I'd be cool with it?"

In reply, she gave him that cute little smirk of hers, and he shook his head in defeat. Sliding an arm around her shoulders, he proudly escorted her into the living room, where the party was getting started. As midnight approached, Gram turned on the TV and they all gathered around for the big countdown.

"Don't you miss being there in person?" he asked Amy, nodding at the insane crowd gathered in Times Square.

"You're kidding, right? I wouldn't go anywhere near Times Square tonight. If I went into that mess, someone would squish me like a bug. Mom and I always watch it on TV, too."

"How 'bout that? Guess you learn something every day."

Standing behind Amy with his arms wrapped around the woman he loved more than anything, Jason had never been happier in his life. When the ball finally reached the bottom of its pole and burst into an array of sparkling lights, Amy spun around for a long kiss filled with unspoken promises for their future together.

Best New Year's ever.

Epilogue

"I told you I make a fabulous matron of honor," Brenda gloated, handing Amy the bouquet she was going to toss for the single women clustered in Will and Olivia's large dining room.

"Yes, you did. With all the practice you've had, you should go pro."

"What a spectacular job that would be." Her romantic cousin sighed.

Laughing, Amy spun around and heaved the flowers backward. Then she glanced over her shoulder to see who got them. Jenna looked as stunned to find them in her hands as the other girls did when they realized they'd missed.

Waving them over her head, she called out, "Who wants 'em?"

A dozen squealing women clamored for another chance, and she covered her eyes before throwing the bouquet into the fray. Turning away before they were caught, she grinned over at Amy and wiped pretend sweat from her forehead.

"You make it sound like getting married is some kind of torture," Amy chided her as Jason joined them.

"For you, no. Me, absolutely," her friend replied with a shudder.

"Jenna's a free spirit," Jason agreed. "I feel sorry for any guy who thinks he can't live without her."

"By the way, you two," she needled with her usual sarcasm. "Getting married on Valentine's Day? How cliché is that?"

Amy laughed at the sour face she made. "I always thought it would be fun to have a Valentine's wedding. This way Jason will never forget our anniversary."

"Like you'd let me," he scoffed.

Pinning him with a flinty glare, Jenna warned, "Just make sure you remember what I said, JB. If you don't treat Amy right, we're gonna have a serious problem, you and me."

With that, she sailed toward the buffet and started messing with Paul.

Jason let out a relieved whistle. "I'm not too proud to admit that woman scares me."

"She scares everyone," Amy assured him, fluffing the baby's breath on his boutonniere. Seeing it reminded her to ask, "How are Rachel and her little girl doing?"

"Doc said they're fit as a couple of fiddles. Those extra couple weeks almost drove Rachel bonkers, but in the end, everything turned out fine. They might stop by later, if that's okay."

Just a few weeks ago, Amy would have bitten her

tongue and gone along to please him. Now that she was his wife, she was feeling much more gracious. "Of course. I'd love to meet the baby. Eva, right?"

"Yeah. It's some kind of family name, I guess."

"Eva McCarron." Amy tested it out loud. "Very pretty. If she looks anything like her mother, that girl is going to be absolutely stunning when she grows up."

"You're being really great about Rachel deciding to stay here in town," he commented in a wary voice. "Is there a reason for that?"

In answer, she held out her left hand and wiggled her fingers so the gold rings he'd given her sparkled in the overhead lights.

"It all makes sense now," he replied with a grin. "In case you're interested, I was just talking to Joe Stegall from the hardware store, and he said those roofing joists I ordered came in this morning. With the mill cranking out everything else, we should be able to break ground on the addition behind Arabesque anytime now."

"When we were getting ready upstairs, Chelsea was telling me the orders for spring are finally ramping up. That means they're going to need more of your time soon," Amy argued. "The furniture business means a lot to the whole town, so the expansion can wait until your workload there dies down a little."

"Are you sure you want to put it off? You're used to living in that apartment by yourself, so it's probably gonna feel pretty cramped in there with the two of us."

Being anywhere by herself was the furthest thing from her mind these days, Amy thought with a smile. "We'll figure it out, the same way we've done with everything else. I don't want you taking on too much and not having any time for your wife," she added, snaking her arms around his waist for a squeeze.

"My wife," he echoed with a quick kiss. "I kinda like the sound of that."

"Me, too."

"Especially since that means we get to go on a honeymoon."

"Which is where?" she asked. When he grinned and shook his head, she grabbed his lapels for a thorough shake. "I know you're Mr. Spontaneous, but you can't spring something like that on me. I'm a girl, and I need to know what sort of clothes to bring."

"Just bring a little of everything."

"Are you trying to get us into our first married fight?" she demanded in mock anger. "Because if you don't quit yanking my chain, that's where we're headed, mister."

"Well, I'd hate for you to cause a scene in front of all these people. It's warm, with lots of water but no sand." She motioned for more, and he relented with a chuckle. "Okay, you win. You said you've never been on a cruise, so we're taking one of those big, fancy ships to the Bahamas. Only a few days, like we agreed, in case something happens and the family needs us here."

A constant for all the Barretts, the ongoing concern for Will had deepened since the holidays. Unable to sit upright on his own, he maintained his customarily positive attitude even while his condition was worsening. Amy didn't know how he managed it with the pain he must be in, but his acceptance of the inevitable boosted the spirits of those around him.

None of them knew when the end would come, but they could all see it advancing a little every day. Everyone had made a determined effort to celebrate Jason and Amy's engagement and wedding, but they'd missed out on some of the joy having a new couple in the circle should have brought them. Still, families stood together through good times and bad, rejoicing over some things and mourning others.

That was what made the Barretts so strong, Amy had come to understand. You weren't born with that kind of perspective. You acquired it by accepting what God handed you and doing the best you could with it.

Seeking to change the subject, she summoned a positive tone. "I have to tell you, it's very handy being married to a guy who knows how to build things. Without you, *The Nutcracker* might never have happened, and all those kids would've been so disappointed. That would've been such a shame, don't you think?"

Jason eyed her suspiciously. "I know that look. What've you got in mind?"

"Our Christmas show was such a roaring success, I was toying with the idea of doing another children's ballet in the spring. I thought back through the ones I danced in when I was younger, and a few of them could easily be scaled down to their level. Since so many of them already know the story of Sleeping Beauty and her prince, I think they'd really enjoy that one."

"Not to mention it's one of the director's favorites. What kind of scenery are we talking about?"

Reaching back into her memory, she began describing the forest scene and lavish castle where the heroic prince finds Sleeping Beauty in a tower, still under the witch's spell. "They won't want to do the kiss, of course, but I'll come up with another way for him to wake her up. We'll need a spinning wheel, and I'm sure Aunt Helen and I will be able to remake some of the sugar-plum costumes for the cast. To make the castle walls look like stone, we can use the same faux painting technique on them that you did on the fireplace for the *Nutcracker* ballroom, and—"

Laughing, Jason held up his hands in a T. "Time-out, sweetheart. We've been married for all of ten minutes, and I haven't had anything to eat since breakfast. Could we put off sketching out the set designs until after we have some food?"

"Sure," she told him with a light kiss. "Whenever you want."

He grinned down at her. "Are you seriously giving up control to let me pick when we start on this?"

"You sound surprised."

"Well—"

"Are you seriously trying to start a fight with me on our wedding day?" she teased, echoing his earlier question.

"Umm, no?"

Sliding her arms around him, she gave him a quick hug. "Good answer."

* * * * *

"Get back!"

Definitely a female voice, from the other side of the barn. He walked around the barn. If someone had asked him to guess what he might find there, he wouldn't in a hundred years have guessed correctly.

A young Amish woman—Plain dress, apron, *kapp*—was holding a feed bucket in one hand and a rake in the other, attempting to fend off a rooster. At the moment, the bird was trying to peck the woman's feet.

"What did you do to him?" Daniel asked.

Her eyes widened. The rooster made a swipe at her left foot. The woman once again thrust the feed bucket toward the rooster. "Don't just stand there. This beast won't let me pass."

Daniel knew better than to laugh. He'd been raised with four sisters and a strong-willed mother. So he snatched the rooster up from behind, pinning its wings down with his right arm.

"Where do you want him?"

"His name is Carl, and I want him in the oven if you must know the truth." She dropped the feed bucket and swiped at the golden-blond hair that was spilling out of her *kapp*. "Over there. In the pen."

Daniel dropped the rooster inside and turned to face the woman. She was probably five and a half feet tall, and looked to be around twenty years old. Blue eyes the color of forget-me-nots assessed him.

She was also beautiful in the way of Plain women, without adornment. The sight of her reminded him of yet another reason why he'd left Pennsylvania. Why couldn't his neighbors have been an old couple in their nineties?

"You must be the new neighbor. I'm Becca Schwartz—not Rebecca, just Becca, because my *mamm* decided to do things alphabetically. We thought you might introduce yourself, but I guess you've been busy. Mamm would want me to invite you to dinner, but I warn you, I have seven younger siblings, so it's usually a somewhat chaotic affair."

Becca not Rebecca stepped closer.

"Didn't catch your name."

"Daniel…Daniel Glick."

"We didn't even know the place had sold until last week. Most people are leery of farms where the fields are covered with rocks and the house is falling down. I see you haven't done anything to remedy either of those situations."

"I only moved in yesterday."

"Had time to get a horse, though. Get it from Old Tim?"

Before he could answer, a dinner bell rang. "Sounds like dinner's ready. Care to meet the folks?"

"Another time. I have some…um…unpacking to do."

Becca shrugged her shoulders. "Guess I'll be seeing you, then."

"Yeah, I guess."

He'd hoped for peace and solitude.

Instead, he had half a barn, a cantankerous rooster and a pretty neighbor who was a little nosy.

He'd come to Indiana to forget women and to lose himself in making something good from something that was broken.

He'd moved to Indiana because he wanted to be left alone.

Don't miss
The Amish Christmas Secret *by Vannetta Chapman,*
available October 2020 wherever
Love Inspired books and ebooks are sold.

LoveInspired.com

LIEXP0920

IF YOU ENJOYED THIS BOOK
WE THINK YOU WILL ALSO LOVE

Mikey's fingers contracted. "Suppose I told you that the hotel I own is actually a casino," he said slowly, "and it's in Las Vegas?"

Bernie's eyes widened. "You own a casino in Las Vegas?" she exclaimed. "Wow!"

He laughed, surprised at her easy acceptance. "I run it legit, too," he added. "No fixes, no hidden switches, no cheating. Drives the feds nuts, because they can't find anything to pin on me there."

"The feds?" she asked.

He drew in a breath. "I told you, I'm a bad man." He felt guilty about it, dirty. His fingers caressed hers as they neared Graylings, the huge mansion where his cousin lived with the heir to the Grayling racehorse stables.

Her fingers curled trustingly around his. "And I told you that the past doesn't matter," she said stubbornly. Her heart was running wild. "Not at all. I don't care how bad you've been."

His own heart stopped and then ran away. His teeth clenched. "I don't even think you're real, Bernie," he whispered. "I think I dreamed you."

She flushed and smiled. "Thanks."

He glanced in the rearview mirror. "What I'd give for just five minutes alone with you right now," he said tautly. "Fat chance," he added as he noticed the sedan tailing casually behind them.

She felt all aglow inside. She wanted that, too. Maybe they could find a quiet place to be alone, even for just a few minutes. She wanted to kiss him until her mouth hurt.

Don't miss
Texas Proud *by Diana Palmer,*
available October 2020 wherever
Harlequin Special Edition books and ebooks are sold.

Harlequin.com

Love Harlequin romance?

DISCOVER.

Be the first to find out about promotions, news and exclusive content!

Facebook.com/HarlequinBooks

Twitter.com/HarlequinBooks

Instagram.com/HarlequinBooks

Pinterest.com/HarlequinBooks

ReaderService.com

EXPLORE.

Sign up for the Harlequin e-newsletter and download a free book from any series at **TryHarlequin.com.**

CONNECT.

Join our Harlequin community to share your thoughts and connect with other romance readers!
Facebook.com/groups/HarlequinConnection

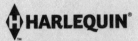

**ROMANCE WHEN
YOU NEED IT**

HSOCIAL2018